BORROW

Russell Dean

Bryn Coch Publishing

Borrowed Time by Russell Dean

Bryn Coch Publishing

Cover by RH Design.

First Edition

ISBN: 978-1-7396125-0-4

One

"I knew it would bloody rain."

I turned to my brother walking towards me, head crouched into his shoulders as if it would avoid him getting wet and his hand clasped to his mouth guarding a cigarette against the downpour. I shifted my umbrella to the side offering shelter and he squeezed alongside me underneath it, soaking the right side of my suit. He exhaled a plume of smoke that seemed to get stuck under the umbrella and spread like a fog, that familiar smell I'd always detested lingering long after the smoke had disappeared. I'd half expected him not to come.

"Miserable bastard's going out just like he lived," he said, taking a sharp inhale from the soggy cigarette. "Like a dark bloody cloud over us all."

I didn't respond. He wouldn't have expected me to. I tended to keep my opinions of our father to myself. It was easier that way. Instead, I kept my eyes forward, looking at nothing in particular but avoiding eye contact with everyone around me and willing the day over.

The rain hadn't stopped for hours. The hole in the ground in front of us had already begun to fill and form a puddle at the bottom, the water lashing down quicker than the ground could soak it away. That's what I focused on.

"There's more people here than I expected," he continued, prompting me to shift my gaze and look around.

He was right. Even without the bad weather, I hadn't expected to see so many faces. Old colleagues, I supposed. The few I did recognise were from the office and some relatives from my mother's side, but nobody that really represented him. Some may have been friends, but we'd met so few of them through the years that it would have been hard to be certain.

I returned my focus to my dishevelled-looking brother and looked him up and down. His eyes were dark and sunken, probably hungover, and he looked like he hadn't slept for days. Still, I was glad he'd at least managed to get himself into a suit, even if it did look a size too big and was creased from head to toe.

"You look like shit, Lee," I said, eliciting an unsurprised smile from him. He took another drag of his cigarette then leant back slightly to eye me up. He'd have been expecting me to say something about his appearance. I always do. The contrast between us was as evident as it ever was. Moreso, probably, given the formal wear. I'd always been the more organised twin and it would be a surprise to no one that I'd had my suit dry cleaned and pressed days ago, whilst his was likely screwed up in a ball at the bottom of a wardrobe until an hour before he arrived.

"You look uncomfortable enough for the both of us, brother," he replied dryly. "I'm sure Dad would be very proud of you for making so much effort."

I ignored him again and turned my gaze back to the hole in the ground. I couldn't see much of the bottom from where I was standing but I had no inclination to get any closer for a better look. Truthfully, All I wanted was to fill it so that we could all leave.

The service at the church had been short, thankfully, but the delay at the graveside had been long and not at all helped by the worsening weather. I'd even noticed two mourners leave and get into their car. I wanted to do the same.

Beside the open grave stood an easel with a canvas picture of my father printed upon it, its ink beginning to run and smudge from the downpour. I tried not to look at it. It didn't look like him. Not really. It was obviously my father, just not as I remembered him. The image my mother had chosen to represent her late husband looked warm and grandfatherly. Like someone you'd want to sit and talk to. His greying hair as immaculately styled as it always was, but with a grin so rarely seen on him in real life. I suppose you could say he looked happy, though he never seemed it. No, the picture was a lie. My mother's doing, obviously.

"Do you think he left specific instructions to make us wait in the rain?" Lee asked, taking a final drag of his cigarette then dropping it to the ground and stepping it out with a not-polished shoe. The idea made me smile, knowing it wouldn't be too surprising had it been true. Our father always made sure everything went his way and any negative effects that his actions may have had on us were of significantly less importance. 'A hard lesson makes for a hard man,' he would tell us, but mostly it made for resentful children.

As the owner of a publishing firm, he'd had a large number of employees to take charge of and he brought his authoritarian rule home with him at the end of every day. Lee and I were expected to do as we were told, to have the best grades, be the best at sport, and follow his lead as boys to grow up to be men who would be worthy of taking over his empire. When our sister Sophia died as a child he became even worse.

Lee did as teenage boys do and acted out. He got mixed up with a bad crowd and started drinking and smoking pot. Over ten years had passed and he'd barely stopped. I stayed home, of course, desperate for approval and respect as I played the dutiful son. Eventually, I took my place in the business while Lee partied his life away. I grew to resent the path my life had taken but with him gone I intended to finally forge a new one.

When dad's cancer diagnosis reduced his workload further, things eased up a little. He would stay squirrelled away in his study going over papers and documents, reading old dusty books and talking to himself and we'd only really hear from him when he wanted something brought to him. I'd long since moved out into a place of my own but he still insisted on daily reports and updates from the office so I used our meetings as an excuse to give my mum a break from his demands.

"Is it wrong that I feel such relief?" I asked, finally turning and looking at my brother properly. "Does it make me a bad person?"

He reached his arm around my waist and hugged me tightly into him.

"You're not a bad person, Tom," he countered. "We're all feeling it. Even mum."

"Has she said anything?" I asked.

"No. Not really. She just seems calm. It's been a lot to deal with and she's had to put up with him longer than any of us."

"She loved him."

"We all loved him, Tom. That doesn't mean he was always easy to love."

Lee's admission took me a little by surprise. It's not that I didn't think he felt it, I just couldn't remember the last time I'd heard him admit it.

"It's time," he said suddenly, pulling his arm from my waist. I turned towards the church and raised the umbrella to get a better view. The rain started hitting my face and making it hard to see but I could just make out my mother and the priest walking behind the coffin towards us.

They came to a stop beside the grave and the priest took his position beside it next to my mother. A man from the funeral home came to stand behind them holding an umbrella over their heads while the priest fought against the wind to keep the bible open to the correct page.

"That'll be ruined," I thought as he struggled. *"There's no saving that book."*

A clap of thunder roared overhead as the priest finally began to speak and a gust of wind blew the canvas from its easel, sending it face down onto the floor at the head of the grave. Lee let out a snigger and I gave him a gentle jab of my elbow to his ribs. I'd have laughed along with him but I didn't want the glares from my mother if she spotted us giggling like schoolboys. It was better to keep him in check.

The miserable October weather made it almost impossible to hear anything that the priest was saying. The rain was coming down harder than before and even my mother looked like she was ready to walk off for someplace drier.

After a few minutes of trying to pray through the rain, the priest slammed his bible closed sending droplets from its waterlogged pages spraying outwards. There's no saving that book. He made one final attempt to lead the group in the Lord's Prayer and I began to pray for a lightning strike to come and send either him or me down into the grave to put us out of our misery. I looked at Lee and even with his rain-soaked face I could see he was crying. Should I have been crying?

The pallbearers, who could obviously hear the proceedings better than the rest of us, suddenly moved in unison to the trolley upon which the coffin sat and hoisted it into the air and over to the hole in the ground. With a final few words from the priest, they began to lower it until it hit the bottom with a soggy thud. As if it were timed by my father himself, a chorus of thunder rolled through the clouds above us. That noise, like a clocking-off claxon in a factory, was all everybody needed to hear to make their hasty exits.

Just like in life, our father's funeral had ended with him surrounded by people who were uncomfortable and wanting to leave.

"Rest in peace John Jacob."

***

The day after the funeral had been set aside to begin the clear out of Dad's office. Mum had left to stay with her sister for a few days in Milton Keynes and had tasked us with the job of emptying it by the time she returned. Lee had stayed at mine for the night, too cheap to pay for a taxi to his flat on the other side of the city. I'd have offered to pay, but the truth was that I wanted the company.

I checked my watch for the umpteenth time and tapped my fingers impatiently on the banister waiting for him to come down the stairs. "Lee, come on," I shouted and I heard him start to shuffle across the landing from the bathroom.

"What's the rush?" he asked as he appeared at the top of the stairs, a cigarette hanging from his lips as he wrestled to get his arms into a denim jacket. I rubbed my forehead as he barrelled down the stairs with a grin on his face. He knew I hated being late.

"I'm sorry, brother," he said, and he scuffed up my hair as he pushed past me down the hallway to the door. "Come on then. What are you waiting for?"

I looked in the mirror that hung in the hall, smoothing out my hair as he grinned at me from the doorway, clouding the exit with a nicotine fog. When I was sure I looked presentable I grabbed my car keys and we left.

It wasn't a long drive to our parent's house but the morning traffic in town was holding us up. Lee pushed a cassette into the player on the dash and began miming a guitar solo, grinning at a girl in the car beside us as we crawled along the road. He'd learned to play when we were younger, and he was really quite good, but Dad put a stop to his lessons and got him a maths tutor instead.

The girl in the other car flashed him a smile and he turned excitedly to me. "How's my hair?" I gave him a cursory glance and a thumbs up and turned my attention back to the road. He reminded me of our father in the few pictures I'd seen of him when he was our age. The same brown hair, though Lee's was usually soaked with product and spiked up while our father's was side-parted and combed to a perfect point. They smiled the same, too. Just a little crooked but beaming and toothy. I suppose, by extension, that meant that I looked like him, too.

Lee and I weren't technically identical but we looked similar enough that people would often mistake us for the other. We shared the same hazel eyes and dark brown hair, and we were both just a little over six feet tall but he had a freckle under his left eye that I didn't have, and though I hated to admit it, his waist was a bit smaller too.

"Is there much to do today?" he asked as I took a right turn, pulling his attention away from the girl.

"I hope not. I need to get back early."

"Hot date?" he asked. "What's his name?" He tilted his chair back and kicked a foot up onto the dashboard waiting for the details.

"I should be so lucky," I laughed. Since our father had gotten sick and my workload had increased, I'd lost any semblance of a social life. My evenings consisted of spreadsheets, microwave meals and falling asleep on the sofa. Finding time to fit dating into the equation was an idea I rarely indulged in.

"It's just work stuff. Nothing to get excited about."

"You work too hard," he replied as though I chose it for myself.

Sometimes I envied him. Sure, he didn't have a job and he'd side-lined all of his ambitions in favour of his wayward lifestyle but he was at least content. He was never bored or boring. Everything was a joke or a tease and he was never bogged down by the stress of work or responsibilities. Truthfully, I wished I could be more like him. More carefree. We were days away from turning 27 but I was living my life like an old man.

"What do you think is in there?" I asked, changing the subject. "The study, I mean." Dad's office at home was like his fortress. Always locked, very private, and no entry was granted unless he invited you in. He'd hate the idea of us going through it.

"It's just full of boring files and paperwork. Unless there's anything of interest in the safe, I think you're going to be disappointed."

"What safe?" I asked, my curiosity piqued.

"What do you mean 'what safe'? The safe! The safe in his office." He waved his hands to emphasise the word 'safe' as though I should have had some idea of what he was talking about.

"I didn't know he had a safe," I replied

"I guess you'll see it soon enough," he said as I pulled onto the gravel driveway of our parent's home.

The house, though by no means a mansion, was fairly large, detached, and situated in one of the nicer parts of Cambridge near the river. I brought the car to a stop outside the front door, careful to avoid my mother's rose bushes, and parked in the spot usually reserved for our father's car.

An hour into emptying the cupboards of Dad's study and we'd found nothing of particular interest. The safe was where Lee said it would be, though it was smaller than I'd anticipated. Not much bigger than a shoebox.

"How are you getting on there, Lee?" I asked sarcastically, bringing another box down off a high shelf and exploring its contents. He'd spent the last half hour sitting in Dad's chair with his feet up reading through old newspaper clippings.

"Did you know Dad donated £10,000 towards the upkeep of a farm?" He asked, ignoring my question while waving a newspaper clipping toward me. The image at the top of the clipping was a grainy black and white picture of our father shaking hands with a man in overalls. The ink detailing the story underneath the picture had smudged with only a few words legible, but it was dated to 1968.

"Generous," I said, putting the clipping down on the desk. "I never had him down as a philanthropist."

"If he was doing it out of the goodness of his heart, he wouldn't have done it so publicly. It was free advertising."

"Free to the tune of ten grand," I replied, rolling my eyes at his cynicism. "Did you find a key to the safe?"

He put the papers down and started looking around the top of the desk as though it may have magically appeared there since I last asked. "Nope. Oh well. Coffee?"

I gave him a nod and he headed to the kitchen as I reached for another box to sort through. More old paperwork. Most of it needed to be burned. I'd organised a pile of files to take to the office but the majority of what we were finding was junk of no particular importance that he'd held onto for years. I slumped down at the desk needing a break, kicking the box that Lee was supposed to be sorting through out of the way as I did.

As it shifted, I noticed a pile of papers inside unlike any I'd seen so far and I spread them across the desk in front of me to examine them. Various maps sat before me, old, torn and faded with various scribbles on them. In the corner of one he'd written a name, '*Ellie*', with a map reference underneath it and the date '*1962*'. An old girlfriend, perhaps? It was dated three years before he married my mother so I was at least able to rule out an affair. It didn't matter now, anyway, I supposed.

I piled the papers together again to put them back in the box but as I opened the lid to dump them inside a glint of silver caught my eye. A key. I quickly moved over to the safe and sat down on my knees to test it out. It took some wiggling but the safe made a clicking sound and the door propped forward stiffly, just enough for me to work my fingers in and pull it open.

I couldn't see inside without leaning my head down to floor level so I reached a hand in and felt around. My fingers grazed against something firm and I pulled it out for a closer inspection. It appeared to be a journal of some kind, leather-bound with a little ribbon that kept it tied shut. I set it down beside me and reached back inside to be sure I hadn't missed anything. Tucked in the back corner I found a silver-looking ring.

It didn't look particularly valuable. It was actually sort of tacky, a bit oversized, and the metal dull looking. At its centre sat a red gemstone. Could have been ruby, could have been plastic. I didn't really know enough about jewellery to be able to tell. I slipped it on my finger and then raised it to my face for a better look. In the centre of the stone was a little flaw just underneath the surface, a tiny pinpoint that was just a bit darker than the rest of the stone with what looked like little shards or cracks shooting out away from it. Costume jewellery, probably.

I gathered the book from the floor and returned to the desk to look it over. The black leather cover was peeling at the corners and the pages inside looked worn and yellowed. The handwriting belonged to my father, there was no mistaking that. Black and cursive and neat to a fault. The words, though, were unfamiliar to me. Definitely not English. Welsh, perhaps?

He'd been born in Wales shortly before the war but was raised in Cambridge after his parents died in an air raid. I had no idea he could speak or write the language, though. He never spoke about his childhood and didn't have even a slight accent so it was never something that was discussed. I felt quite impressed, though, like I'd just found out he had a secret talent that none of us knew about.

At the top of the first page was what I assumed to be a date. '*14 Hydref 1958*'. Dad would have been around 23 when he'd written it. I flicked forward a few pages and came across one in English:

> *27 April 1959*
>
> *I'm grateful to Mr Wallace for providing board and a place to work, but I don't think I shall ever get used to the city. It's loud and obscene and the filthy air hurts my lungs. I long for somewhere more familiar. Still, it is better to be busy and amongst people, than to continue feeling sorry for myself. I should never have visited. What was I expecting? Still, a hard lesson makes for a hard man.*
>
> *I must remember to ask about an advance on my wages. My trip to Hastings is approaching and I want to arrive looking like I've made something of myself. She'll like that.*

There were a few more pages written in English but before I could settle on one to read Lee came back to the study carrying two mugs of coffee.

"What's that?" he asked, setting the drinks down on the desk.

"A diary, I guess. It was in the safe." I held it out for him to take a look. "Did you know dad could speak Welsh?"

"He barely spoke to me in English," he replied, tossing the book back onto the desk, uninterested. "Come on, let's get out of here. We'll go to a bar instead. Pre-birthday drinks. What do you say?"

"It's not our birthday for a fortnight. Besides, we should really finish up here," I said, looking around the room at the mess we'd made.

"Come on, brother. Live a little."

I considered my options as he grinned at me, his eyes pleading with me to say yes. I knew I should stay and do what was asked of me but I was sick of being the reliable one. I wanted to be reckless for a change. I chose fun.

"Ok, let's do it," I said, a nervous smile breaking onto my face as I rose to my feet. He gave me an excited slap on the arm and dashed out the door as I grabbed the journal from the desk and slipped it inside my jacket. "But I'm only having one."

Two

The further we drove from our parent's house the more my anxiety levels increased. Being reckless was all well and good but I couldn't shift my mind away from the fact that we'd left the place in disarray and finished none of what we set out to do. Lee didn't care, obviously, but then it was never him that got it in the neck. Expectations for him had always been lower. By the time we got to his flat, I was in a mind to turn around and go back.

"You can leave the car here and we'll walk into town," he said as he turned the key in his front door. He lived closer to the local nightlife than I did so it made sense, but I didn't love the idea of staying at his place. He stepped over the collection of mail that his doormat was hoarding and ushered me inside.

He'd never been a particularly organised individual, which was one of the reasons I visited so infrequently and invited him to mine, instead. Clothes lay strewn about the place, dishes sat unwashed, pizza boxes littered the coffee table and a faint whiff of cigarette smoke clung to everything. It reminded me of some of the student digs I'd seen at university, only Lee never attended and should have long since aged out of the lifestyle.

He grabbed two stale-looking glasses from beside the sink and set them down on the counter as I brushed the dust off one of the stools to take a seat.

"Your favourite," he said, pulling the lid from a half-empty bottle of whiskey and pouring out two oversized measures. "Chin up."

Drinking with Lee always put me on edge. He'd had issues in the past with never knowing when enough was enough, and though he had seriously cut back over the last two years I was always worried that he was balanced on a knife-edge between habit and addiction. Still, any attempt to discuss the topic inevitably led to arguments and I wanted an easy night, so I raised the glass to him and knocked it back.

"Right," he said, slamming his glass down on the counter. "Let's find you something to wear." He walked behind me and pushed me up off the stool, nudging me towards his bedroom.

"Lee, tell me you don't invite women in here," I said as he pulled a t-shirt from the laundry basket. He sniffed it and threw it over his shoulder to join the other items cluttering his bedroom floor. I moved to sit on the edge of the bed and then thought better of it.

"Come on, get changed," he said, turning his attention to the wardrobe. With the amount of clothes that had been discarded on the floor, I was surprised that there were any left to keep inside it.

"Why can't I just wear this?" I asked, pinching my shirt at the chest.

"Because you look like you're ready for a night down the bingo with all the other pensioners."

I looked down at myself and sighed. I'd only intended to spend the day cleaning so fashion wasn't a particular concern when I was getting ready, but the beige button-up I'd chosen had definitely seen better days.

"Here," he said, throwing a shirt at me, "put this on. And this."

I took my shirt off and replaced it with the items he'd given me; a white vest with a pink short-sleeved shirt, and tucked them into my jeans.

"And you can't wear them." He pointed down to my trainers and I kicked them off to join the rest of the mess on his floor. "They won't let you in with those."

He dug about for a pair of boots, which I had to admit were actually really nice, if not a bit uncomfortable, and I stared at myself in the mirror to check myself out. I looked more like him than ever, but I didn't entirely hate it.

"Are you sure it's not a bit much?" I asked, normally opting for more muted colours.

"No way," he said, coming beside me to fuss with his hair in the reflection. "You look great, honestly."

"I'm still not sure we should even be going out. I've got so much work to catch up on."

"Tom, it'll wait," he said, shaking his head at me. "We own the business now. We can do what we want. Stop being so boring."

"I'm not boring!" I snapped, a bit harsher than I intended.

Surprised by my outburst, he grabbed me by the arm, not roughly, but enough to make me pause, and turned to face me with a furrowed brow. "What's wrong? You know I don't mean anything by it, right? I'm just fucking with you."

I pulled my arm away, feeling a little guilty. "I know. Sorry. I'm just…" but I trailed off, unable to pinpoint exactly why I felt so touchy.

"I don't think you're boring, Tom. I know you're not. You just need to chill out a bit. Come on, let's go. You'll have a great time."

He covered himself in aftershave, swung a jacket over his shoulder and motioned me out of the room.

"Just have fun," I told myself as I reached for the door handle, and with a final deep breath, I headed out into the evening.

"Drink! Drink! Drink!" Lee chanted at me a few hours later as I downed another pint amongst a crowd of revellers. We'd hopped from bar to bar until coming to a stop in a converted church where the DJ sat nestled in what used to be the pulpit and drinks were poured from an exaggerated-looking altar. When I finished my beer I raised the glass over my head and cheered, and the crowd cheered back. My plan to have just one drink was long out the window but I surprised myself by having a really good time.

"Mr Jacob, I didn't know you had it in you." I turned on the spot to see Nia, one of the office juniors coming through the crowd. She'd joined the firm a couple of weeks before Dad passed away and seemed to have taken a bit of a shine to me.

"Call me Tom," I said, my speech slurring. I may have been her boss but I hated the formalities, especially outside the office. Though I'd never really socialised with anyone outside of work and they'd never seen me in this sort of state, thankfully.

"Ok, Tom, do you want a drink?" she asked.

"Yes! More drink!" I shouted to another cheer from the group as I stumbled back and forth.

"Let's get you sat down, shall we?" I felt Lee's hands around my waist, guiding me to one of the chairs.

"Now who's boring?" I asked with a raised eyebrow.

He laughed as he steadied me into one of the seats and then shimmied in beside me.

"You're really throwing them back," he said, cradling a half-empty pint glass. He'd matched me drink for drink but seemed to be having an easier time remaining sober. "It's nice to see you having fun."

"It's been a while, hasn't it?" I replied.

"Since you've had fun or since we've had a drink together?"

I contemplated this for a moment. "Both," I said, finally.

"I've missed it," he said, giving me a longing look, then he jumped to his feet and pulled me from my chair. "Come on, the night's not over yet."

I could barely stand upright as he dragged me back to the centre of the bar and I had to hold on to his shoulder as we walked. The music seemed to have gotten louder and was booming through the old building as lights flashed around in time to the rhythm. It was all adding to my dizziness, though, and by the time we came to a stop I felt like I might throw up.

"She's not taken her eyes off you since she got here," Lee leaned in and shouted to me. I followed his gaze to Nia who gave me a flirty smile and a little wave from the bar and I quickly looked away again, embarrassed. "Should I tell her or do you want to?"

I saw her start to make her way over to us carrying two bottles and I spun around looking for somewhere to escape to avoid the inevitable awkward conversation, tumbling a little as I did.

"Steady there, brother," Lee said, grabbing me as I fell into a table sending someone's drink flying to the floor. He kept a hand around my shoulders to steady me, keeping me in Nia's sights.

"Do you want to dance, Mr Ja- I mean, Tom?"

"*I don't dance*," were the words I was aiming for but most of the consonants seemed to have disappeared from my vocabulary so I shook a finger at her instead. Even if I'd wanted to, the room was spinning far too quickly for me to stay on my feet and move with any sort of rhythm.

"I'd love to dance," Lee said, immediately noticing my discomfort and extending his hand to Nia. "If that's ok?"

She looked unsure at first but then flashed a huge smile and tucked her arm into his. He was the perfect wingman, if wingmen were supposed to step in and take the girl you weren't interested in off your hands.

"I'm going to go outside for some air," I shouted over the beat.

"Do you want me to come with you?" he asked, but I shook my head at him and he gave me a nod as he moved off towards the dancefloor.

I wandered towards the exit, swaying from side to side as I weaved between the huddle of bodies drinking and dancing until I finally made it outside. The whole street felt like it was spinning and with the rush of fresh air, I leaned my hand against a lamppost and vomited onto the pavement causing some passers-by to jeer and start clapping.

The release helped the feeling of sickness in my stomach but did nothing for the dizziness and as I turned around to go back inside I walked straight into a large man who spilled his drink down my shirt.

"Watch it you daft twat," he snapped as I drunkenly waved him off and swayed along the pavement. I brought my hands up to my chest and wiped myself down, catching sight of the ring I'd found earlier in the day sitting on my wedding finger. I'd completely forgotten I had it on and the lights from inside the bar were making it look as though the red stone in it was glowing.

"You're not coming back in here, mate," the doorman said as I staggered back towards the entrance. He was tall and burly and looked like someone you shouldn't argue with, so of course, I did.

"I am," I said, trying unsuccessfully to push past him. "My brother's still in there."

"I won't tell you again," he said, putting his hand on my chest. "You've had enough, now piss off."

He crossed his arms and stood firm, blocking the doorway from me, but I ducked to the side and tried to sidestep him. With reflexes faster than my own he gripped me by the collar, dragging me several feet to the side of the building and pushing me down onto the ground in the deserted alley that ran alongside the church.

"If you come back again, I'm going to break your legs," he shouted. He stared down at me for a moment, making sure I wasn't going to try anything stupid, then disappeared back to the front of the building leaving me lying on the tarmac.

It took some effort but I managed to get myself to my feet. The whole world felt like it was spinning and I leaned my hands against the side of the church hoping that it would keep me upright. The ring caught my eye again and I glanced between it and the gold band on my right hand that had been a gift from my parents for my 21st birthday. It still looked like it was glowing, but this time there was no light in the alley that it could be reflecting. I felt almost mesmerised by it, as though I didn't quite want to look away, and it felt like it was pulsing.

"Tom?" My brother shouted my name from around the corner and I pushed myself back from the wall to go to him. I fought the urge to be sick again as my eyes spun around in different directions but it was no use. The whole alleyway began to turn sideways.

No, not the alley. Me.

I was passing out.

Three

There's an odd state that everyone has felt at one time or another that exists somewhere between dreaming and waking up. You're not fully conscious of everything around you yet, but you know you're no longer entirely asleep, either. I felt like I was stuck there.

The first thing that stopped me from falling back into a deeper slumber was the realisation that I was wet. Memories of the night before and how much I'd had to drink slowly crept back into my brain and I was filled with a sudden hope that I hadn't pissed myself.

But it couldn't be that. Even with my eyes closed, I could feel that I was drenched from head to toe. I opened a single eye to get my bearings and immediately closed it again. Too bright.

Wait, was that…?

I opened it again and waited for my vision to adjust. Above me, partially obscured by some grey clouds, was the sun. I brought a hand up to shield my eyes and opened the other to make sure I wasn't mistaken. I was definitely outside.

Have I been in the alley all night?

I tried to raise my head to look around but the hangover had already begun to kick in so I had to take it slowly. I looked left and then right and then immediately closed my eyes again.

"Where the hell am I?" I said out loud, then prayed really hard that it was a dream.

I checked again. Nope. Definitely real.

"We're in a fucking field, Lee!" I shouted, annoyed at myself for getting sucked into his antics again. When he didn't respond I looked around once more but there was no sign of him.

I rolled myself over and pushed myself up onto my hands and knees. I had to pause for a second to hold back the feeling that I might be sick again, but once it subsided I rose to my feet for a look around.

The field was empty but for a small building at the very top end, so I began to make my way towards it hoping I might find a phone or someone who could give me a lift home. My bones ached and every movement hurt, and every step of the way I plotted how I was going to kill Lee for getting me into this mess. *How did we even get here?*

I paused for a minute and tried to retrace my steps. I remembered being at the bar, going outside and being in the alley. I lifted my hands up mimicking the memory of leaning against the building, and my eyes were immediately drawn to the ring on my left hand. *Had it been glowing?* I twisted it around on my finger and stared at it in confusion. It looked totally normal, now.

As I got closer to the building it became evident that I wouldn't find anyone there with a phone. Rather than a house, as I'd expected, the building was some sort of barn. At the side of the building was a long stone trough that appeared to be gathering rainwater. Despite my reservations, I needed something to take the rotten taste out of my mouth so I rushed towards it and began to drink. I had only taken a small sip when a noise from inside caught my attention. It was slight, no more than a whisper, but I could definitely hear voices.

I stepped up onto the trough and pushed my head against the shutters to try to peer inside. The crack between the boards wasn't very wide, but I could make out the shape of at least one person standing in the middle of the room.

I shuffled along the stone trying to get a better view but the smooth edge wasn't enough to keep my grip and my foot plunged down into the trough sending up a murky residue from the bottom. "Shit," I shouted, and the voices from inside fell to a hush. I managed to retrieve my sodden boot just as the door to the barn swung open and two men came running out.

"Hey, I was wondering if-" but before I could continue one of them came bounding towards me and punched me square in the face.

I don't know how long I was out but when I came to I was resting up against the wall of the barn with a taste of blood on my lips and a throbbing in my nose.

The two men were standing nearby whispering to each other so I kept my head tucked into my chest and pretended to still be unconscious while I worked out what I should do next. I tried to sneak a peek at them but could only see some worn-out brown boots topped by trousers, one pair black and the other brown. It didn't give me much to go on.

The fatter man with the brown trousers halted his whisperings to kick me in the shin and I let out an involuntary moan of pain which caused the thinner of the two men to rush forward, grabbing me by the chin and raising my face to his. His brown eyes stared directly into mine and he shouted something at me in a language I didn't recognise. His warm breath and spit covered my face as he yelled and his eyes were filled with rage.

I deliberated whether I should speak up or just stay silent. Judging by the look on his face when he stopped yelling, he was expecting some sort of response, but I had no idea what he'd said to me or wanted to hear.

He turned to his friend and shouted something and the man ran off through the clearing on the other side of the barn. With his friend gone he turned his attention back to me, tightened his grip on my face and screamed at me again.

"I don't know what you're saying," I shouted through squeezed cheeks, and for a moment the look on his face flashed with confusion before he reached into his pocket and extracted a penknife. Flicking it open with his thumb, he brought it to my cheek, digging the tip of the blade into my skin.

"What did you hear?" he demanded in a thick Welsh accent.

"What? Nothing. I was just-" but I cut myself off as he increased the pressure of the knife against my face. He dragged it ever so slightly downward and I felt a small split in my skin begin to open. "Stop! I don't know what you want from me."

I raised my hand up to the cut on my face and his eyes widened. He grabbed hold of me, roughly pulling at my fingers as he tried to pull the ring from them, and I fought to get my hand away from him.

"Who are you?" he demanded. "Where is Elinor?"

"I don't know who you're talking about," I protested and he spun his arm out, connecting his elbow with my cheekbone and making my head smack against the barn wall. He reached for my hand again, this time bringing the knife to my finger as though he were about to cut it off me and I let out a loud scream. The barrage of attacks was leaving me feeling woozy and I was beginning to fear that this man might actually kill me.

He dug the point of the blade into my skin near the knuckle and I fought to push him off. Behind him, the trees rustled and I prayed that it wasn't his friend coming back to help him finish the job but instead, a young woman stepped out carrying a rifle. My attacker immediately fell back away from me and scrambled to his feet, hiding the knife behind his back as he turned to face her.

Keeping the rifle aimed at his chest the young woman came stomping through the grass and stood between us with her back to me. She began to shout at him, and though I had no idea what it was that she was saying, her tone was indication enough that she wasn't happy.

After a few moments of arguing the man raised his hands in surrender, laughed at the woman and then strutted off in the direction his friend had taken. She stared after him to make sure he was gone before turning to face me, allowing me a good look at her for the first time.

She didn't look very old and she wasn't very tall but her face was stern and I knew immediately that I wouldn't want to cross her either. Her red hair was tied up in a loose bun with little curls sticking out at odd angles and her pale skin had reddened with her anger. After we'd given each other the once over she held out a hand to pull me up.

"Thank you," I muttered as I got to my feet, realising I stood at least a foot taller than her. I brushed myself down and patted around the top of my jeans, relieved to find my wallet still in my back pocket and that he hadn't robbed me while I was out cold. "Do you know where I can get a taxi?"

She tilted her head to the side and popped out her bottom lip, looking at me with a sort of curious pity, then pulled a handkerchief from her cuff, spit in it and aimed to rub it under my nose. I tried to protest but she batted my hand away and proceeded to dab at my face whether I liked it or not.

"English!" she finally spoke. "If I'd have known that I'd have left you to it." Her strong Welsh accent made each word sound like she was half talking, half singing and she flashed me a huge smile to let me know that she wasn't being entirely serious. "I suppose that explains the clothes. You're a funny lot."

"I could say the same to you," I retorted, eyeing her up and down. Tucked into a long woollen skirt she was wearing a long-sleeved shirt that she'd fastened at the neck with a brooch. It put me in mind of my grandmother. Over the top of her outfit going all the way down to her ankles was an apron, long since faded from its original white, and she had it tied so tightly at the waist that it looked like it was pulling her inwards in the middle. I couldn't imagine it was at all comfortable.

"Yes, well I don't have the luxury of wearing inexpressibles," she said, pointing at my jeans, "but you… that's really quite something." She made no attempt to hide her laugh as she stared at me up and down and I felt silly again about being in Lee's clothes. I knew I should have worn my own. "And that shirt. That's what they're wearing in London these days, is it?"

She laughed at me again then hoisted her skirt and began to walk off. "Come on then."

I followed behind her but the effects of the hangover and the beating made keeping up with her difficult. "Can you slow down a bit?" I called out. "I'm also a bit hungover."

"That's how you ended up in my field, is it? One too many drinks? And will you be leaving again soon or should I put you to work?"

"No, I'll be gone soon, don't worry. I just need to work out where I am and find my brother and then I'll be out of your hair."

"Cwm Newydd."

"I'm sorry, I only speak English. I don't know what you just said."

"That's where you are."

"Is that near Cardiff?"

"Aberystwyth is about 10 miles west."

"Ok, I've heard of that. I couldn't point to it on a map, but I've at least heard of it."

"Tell me, Mr…?" she came to a stop and waved her hands around as she said it, waiting on a name.

"Tom. Jacob. Tom Jacob."

"Tell me, Tom Jacob, how is it you find yourself in the middle of a field in a village you've never heard of, in a country you obviously don't live in, being set upon by a man who doesn't even speak the same language as you, all while dressed like, well, like that?"

I opened my mouth to speak but realised I didn't really have an answer. "One of those nights, I guess." I shrugged my shoulders in defeat and she laughed at me again.

"I'm going to like you, Tom Jacob. Come on, let's get you inside and dry." And with that, she turned heel and marched off down the path to wherever it was that she was taking me.

"That man," I said as we walked. "Did he tell you why they attacked me?"

"Not really. Not that Arthur Morgan needs much of an excuse to go around hitting people. That man thinks he can treat the people in this village however he likes just because he lives in the fancy house up on the estate. Well, not on my land he can't."

"He mentioned someone called Elinor," I said, coming to a stop to catch my breath. "Asking me where she was."

The girl looked over her shoulder at me and then walked a few steps back to close the gap between us.

"Elinor is the girl he was to marry. About two weeks ago he comes shouting through the village telling anyone that'll listen that she'd been taken. Said he'd turned his back for just a second and then she was gone. Vanished. Ever since then he's been going around accusing people of whisking her off. And now you show up out of nowhere and he seems to have decided to start taking it out on you, too.

"If you ask me, I reckon she's run off. Especially with Jack Hopkin going missing, too. They were always sweet on each other, them pair. They were going to marry until their fathers called it off, but everyone knew they were still in love. Mrs Wilkes says she saw them canoodling amongst the gravestones over in the church, too," she paused for a second considering this. "But then, you don't really want to listen to what Mrs Wilkes tells you, the nosy old mare. Anyway, everyone but Arthur knows it. Eloped, probably. He just won't admit it. Too filled with pride, that one." She threw her arms up in a shrug and then her face suddenly became more serious. "He's not a nice man, you know. If he thinks you've got something to do with it, he won't let it go. You can be sure of that."

"But I wasn't even here two weeks ago," I said. "Why would I know anything about it?"

She sighed and began to walk off again. "We're not on the main road here. People don't generally come down into the village unless they need to. Two people go missing and then you show up. You can see why he might be making assumptions."

"But you came to help me. How did you know I wasn't dangerous?"

She seemed to find my question amusing.

"I can't pretend to know much about criminals, Mr Jacob, but I've enough sense to know that if you commit a crime in a place where you're the only outsider, you don't hang around waiting to be caught and drawing attention to yourself dressed like that. Besides, if I'm being totally honest it was less about saving you and more about having the chance to wave a gun at Arthur. I've never liked him. Nobody does."

She had a point but if those people had run off then it was none of my business. I just wanted to get home.

"I'm Mair, by the way," she said as I tried to keep step with her. She walked like she was ten minutes late for something and I began to get a stitch in my side. "Not that you bothered asking."

She shot me a grin over her shoulder that reassured me that she was teasing me rather than offended.

"Is it far?" I tried to make it sound like genuine curiosity but I was mostly concerned with how much longer we'd be walking. Years behind a desk had made me more unfit than I'd realised.

"This is it up here," she said, pointing to a quaint little cottage with whitewashed walls at the end of the lane. A bit further on I could see some more buildings and what looked like a pub judging by the sign hanging over the door. Perhaps I'd be able to get a taxi from there.

"Right, in you go." She held open the wooden door and then stood aside to let me enter, and I had to duck to get under the doorframe. Catching my first glimpse of the inside of her home I stopped dead, blocking the entrance. "Jesus," I let out under my breath.

I don't think I'd ever seen so much and yet so little in such a small space, and everything so old fashioned. No TV, no stereo, not even carpets on the cold stone floor.

I couldn't tell if the room was meant to be a living room or a dining room or a kitchen or some sort of mix of all three. It had a large open fireplace, flanked by two doors on either side of it, and a third door which I assumed went out to the back of the house. Trinkets and utensils were scattered all around making the place look cluttered and the only area that seemed clean and free from junk was an old wooden table at the back of the room with two chairs on either side of it that looked like they could fall apart at any moment.

"Well don't just stand there you daft fool," Mair jabbed me in the back, edging me into the house. "Get inside or we'll catch a death."

The door clicked shut behind me as I entered further into the room. I stood on the spot and turned circles trying to take it all in while Mair looked at me like I'd lost my mind.

When I was a child, we went on a school trip to a museum. It had relocated loads of old buildings from around the country and then restored and rebuilt them within the grounds so that we could see how people used to live years before. That's what her house reminded me of.

"Oh my god," I exclaimed, raising a hand to my forehead. "I get it now. This is a museum, isn't it?" I felt quite smug about working it out.

Mair, busy jabbing at the fire with a poker, looked over her shoulder at me and cocked an eyebrow. "You do say the strangest things. Now come, let's get a look at you." She began to mutter to herself in Welsh and tapped a finger on her chin then spun on her heel and darted off through the door to the left of the fireplace.

"Here we are," she called from behind the door. She'd left it open only a crack and I could just about make out a small bed tucked into the corner of the room. "You look to be about his dap."

"His what?" I called back but got no reply.

"Put these on," she said, flinging open the door and scurrying back towards me with a pile of clothes. "They may not be a perfect fit but it's the best I can do and they're dry at least. You can change in there."

"Really, you've been great but I should be going," I protested, but she pushed the clothes into my hand and nudged me towards the doorway.

I entered the room she had exited and pushed the door shut behind me. The bed was covered with lots of sheets, neatly made but none matching, and a solitary thin pillow. Plonking myself down on it, I hugged the clothes close to my chest and looked around the room. Behind the door was a chest of drawers, upon which sat a candle. I looked above me to the ceiling but there was no light fitting to be found. A small window to the side of the bed let in the room's only light and was decorated with a single curtain.

What the hell is going on here? Where am I? How did I even get here?

Having no answers to the questions that plagued me I stripped down to my underwear and looked through the clothes Mair had given me. They weren't exactly my style but I wasn't in much of a position to complain and I was at least grateful that I'd be able to travel home in something dry. The off-white shirt was long enough to be a nightdress and hung loosely down to my thighs but I pulled it on anyway and did up the single button at the neck.

The brown trousers she'd given me, despite being a heavy woollen material, were surprisingly comfortable. I had to shimmy them down my waist a little to try and give me some extra ankle coverage and they were a bit loose at the waist but otherwise, they didn't look too bad. A bit more hipster than my usual taste, I had to admit, but at least I was dry.

"How are you getting on in there?" Mair shouted from the other side of the door.

"The trousers are a bit big," I responded. "Around the waist I mean."

"Top drawer," she called back, and I turned to the dresser.

Expecting to find a belt, I slid the drawer open and saw three pairs of suspenders. Having no other option, I slipped them on and pulled them tight.

"In for a penny…" I said, grabbing the final item of clothing Mair had given me; a waistcoat in a similar colour to the trousers. With my boots back on, I was set. Granted, I looked like an extra from a period film but I'd be back to my own wardrobe soon enough.

Before I headed back to Mair I slipped my wallet and the two rings into my trouser pocket and checked out my reflection in the small mirror nailed to the back of the door.

The bruising around my eyes was starting to come out and my top lip and cheek were stained red with blood.

I ran my fingers through the stubble that was setting in on my face. I quite liked it, though I couldn't remember the last time I wasn't clean shaven. My hair was a mess but I tried to smooth it out with my hand to make myself look a little more presentable.

"There, now isn't that better?" Mair said as I swung the door open and walked back into the main room. She paused near the fireplace and smiled at me, proud of her makeover efforts. "Right, sit, I've got you some food," she said, handing me a bowl and motioning towards the table. "It's stew."

I took a seat opposite her and looked down at my bowl. There was evidence of vegetables in there. Carrots, it looked like, and maybe some meat, but the gravy looked like water. It didn't look particularly appetising but the feeling in my stomach left me too hungry to care so I grabbed my spoon and proceeded to dig in.

"So where are you from, Tom?" she asked, holding her spoon but making no effort to eat. "London, is it?"

"Cambridge," I said, taking a bite of stew. It was as bad as it looked and I struggled to swallow.

"It's all the same over that way I suppose," she said.

"I really need to get back as soon as possible. Is there a train station nearby?"

"Aye in Aberystwyth. You can change in Machynlleth and it'll take you right on through to Shrewsbury."

"Shrewsbury?!" I shouted. "Well, I suppose it'll have to do. How soon can I get there?"

"Monday, now, I should imagine. Unless you want to walk, but that'll take you a day at least and I dare say you'll get yourself lost."

"Why Monday? Why not today? Does nobody around here drive?" I could feel the snappiness in my voice and Mair looked less than impressed with my tone.

"The carriage for town already left this morning and it doesn't come through here on Sundays."

"You've got to be kidding me! How far up the bloody valleys have I ended up?" I threw my spoon in my bowl and cupped my hands over my eyes, frustrated.

"Now look here," Mair pointed her spoon at me, her accent getting thicker and her tone more serious, "you're not 'up the valleys' you're in West Wales and you won't be going nowhere with that attitude. Trying to help you I am. *Duw Duw.*"

I felt bad and a little embarrassed for snapping at her. She was right, she'd been nothing but helpful since we met. "Sorry. And thank you for letting me borrow the clothes. They're really nice," I said, hoping to break the tension. "Are they your husbands'?"

"Dear Lord, no. I'm not married. I haven't got time for all that. They belong to my brother."

"Oh? Will he be home soon?"

"No, he works over in the mine and boards with a family near the site. He comes home when he can but I don't see him as much as I'd like."

She looked sad about that so I aimed for something lighter. "And what about your parents, do they live in the village?"

"Dead."

I really wasn't doing well.

"My dad passed three years ago," she continued, "and Mam went the following winter. It's just the two of us now."

"I'm sorry to hear that," I said, pursing my lips into a sympathetic smile. "I just lost my father two weeks ago."

"They're all resting now," she said, putting on a smile.

"It's a lot to deal with so young. How old are you?"

"Did your mam never teach you that it's rude to ask a lady her age?" she said with a smile before bringing her hand to the side of her mouth as though she was about to tell me a secret. "Let's just say I was born in 1864 and we'll see how good you are at your sums."

"You're funny," I said, taking a spoonful of soup with a giggle.

"Why's that then?" she asked, looking bewildered, and for a brief second it seemed like she was actually being serious. I stared at her but she remained blank-faced. "Come on, it's not that hard, is it? You can add up, can't you?"

If she didn't look so sincere, I might have thought I was being tricked but she appeared to be genuinely mystified as to why I wasn't taking her seriously.

"Mair, what year is it?" I hated myself for even asking but something about all this wasn't adding up. The clothes, the house, her birthday. I felt like I was going crazy?

"Oh, come on," she laughed. "Arthur didn't hit you that hard."

"I'm serious, Mair. What year is it?"

The smile left her face, replaced with a look of concern as though she thought I might actually be losing my mind right there at her dining table.

"It's 1889, Tom. October 1889."

Four

Mair's words rang in my ears like a siren and I felt like my heart might thud its way through my chest. I could feel the colour draining from my face and the overwhelming urge to vomit returned to the pit of my stomach. I scraped my chair back loudly against the stone floor and stood to my feet but the sudden weakness in my legs threatened to send me tumbling to the floor and I had to lean against the table for support.

"Tom, whatever's the matter?" Mair asked. She shot up from her chair, her face stricken with worry, and rushed over to put an arm around me. I stared at her looking for any sign that this might be some elaborate joke but I knew in my bones that it was not. I needed air. It felt like the walls were shrinking in and making the room smaller and smaller and I clasped at my throat, gasping for breath as though I might suddenly starve of oxygen and pass out.

Mair tried to ease me back into my seat but I knocked her back and made a dash for the door, clawing at my collar with every step until I got outside and fell to my knees. The contents of my pockets spilled over the ground as I lurched forward sucking in large gasps of cold air until, when I could hold it no more, I vomited onto the concrete.

"Come on, get it up," Mair said as she stood behind me stroking my back.

"I'm ok," I huffed out, surprised by the hoarseness of my voice. "Can I have some water?"

She took herself back inside the house and I picked the ring up from my belongings on the ground. "How?" I asked through a heavy breath, and I turned it over in my palm. I knew it had something to do with my being there. It had to. I slipped it onto my finger and closed my eyes, clutching my hands together as though in prayer, but when I opened them again I was still on the floor outside the cottage.

I clenched at my abdomen and gulped at the air to try and suppress my body's desire to vomit again. My palms heavy with sweat, I twisted the ring about on my finger a second time and wished really hard, but still nothing happened.

"Tom, you're white as a sheet." Mair crouched beside me and offered me a cup of water. "What's wrong?"

What could I even say? If I told her what I believed the truth to be, that I'd somehow travelled back through time more than a century, she'd have me carted off to an asylum. Silence was my best option until I could be surer of my circumstance.

"I'm sorry, Mair," I said, struggling to my feet. I'd never had a panic attack before but that felt as close to one as I'd ever like to get again. I took off the ring, grabbed my belongings from the floor, and shoved them back into my pocket. "I'll be alright in a minute. Hangover, I suppose."

She looked at me like she didn't quite believe what I was saying but didn't question me further. "Get some water down you and come back inside to sit down. You're putting a worry in me."

I brought the cup to my lips and over the rim I spotted a man marching up the lane in my direction looking not altogether impressed. "Um, Mair…" I said, and she followed my gaze.

"Go inside, Tom," she said, stepping out of the doorway and guiding me in with a pat on the arm. She pulled the door closed behind me and stayed on the other side of it.

I headed for the armchair near the window and sat, elbows on my knees and my head in my hands. *This can't be happening*. I took a few sneaky glances around the room before tucking my head away again. I desperately wanted to spot some clues that this was just an elaborate hoax but there was nothing. There were no modern items that I could recognise and cling to. No electricity, no phone, none of the comforts I'd grown up around.

Perched on a small table next to me was a photograph and I picked it up to examine it. I'd seen these types of pictures before, in books mostly, but sometimes in other people's houses showing long-dead ancestors looking stoic and serious. An older couple stared back from the frame, their faces devoid of any emotion, and in the bottom corner, stamped in faded ink, was a small watermark that read '*DB Photographers 1884*'. Reading it made my stomach churn over again and I quickly set it back down, no longer wanting to see it.

Through the window, I could hear Mair call out to the man in Welsh and his footsteps came to a halt outside the cottage. Some words were exchanged that I couldn't understand and then she opened the door and they both stepped inside.

He was an older chap, somewhere in his forties or fifties, with a stern serious look about him. His clothes were almost identical to the ones Mair had given me, though they looked considerably more worn out. He threw me a sideways glance and doffed his cap then waved off Mair's offer of a seat, deciding instead to position himself at the doorway, blocking it. I got the distinct impression he didn't particularly want to be there and wanted to be able to make his exit as quickly as possible once the time came. Mair came to rest a hand on my shoulder and for a moment they both stared at each other as though they were ready to square off.

"Tom," she said, not taking her eyes from the man, "this is Mr Hopkin. His son Jack is the one I was telling you about earlier."

"Good morning," I smiled at him, unsure what business he would have with me.

"I won't keep you long," he said, "I just want to know if you'd heard anything of my son."

His accented voice was low and monotone, not filled with the urgency or worry I would expect of a man whose son had gone missing, and with every word his eyes flickered around the room, never settling upon me for more than a second.

"I don't know anything about that, sorry." It was the truth and all I could offer him. He didn't seem to expect I would say anything different and he remained unmoved. "I'm not sure why you'd even think I would."

"Arthur Morgan," he said, still not meeting my gaze. "Came into the village talking about you. Says you know where Ms Lewis is. I thought if you did then you'd be able to point me toward Jack, too. Boy's going to get a belt when I catch hold of him, putting his mam through all this worry."

"It's Arthur what needs the belt," Mair chimed in. "Throwing his fists around at anyone he doesn't like the look of."

"That's quite a shiner," Mr Hopkin said, pointing with his hat toward my face.

"It was my welcome-to-town gift from him."

"He wants locking up, he do," Mair continued. "I mean look at him," she indicated to me, digging a finger into my shoulder and making me flinch. "There's nothing of him, he obviously can't defend himself."

"Actually, I-" I began to argue but was quickly cut off again.

"Well Tom might be scared of him, but I ain't," she continued. "Let me catch him in my field again..."

"I'm not sc-" I tried again.

"No wonder he can't wait to leave, poor thing."

"Mair said you were from different parts," the man replied, jumping in while Mair took a breath. "Long way from home, aren't you?"

"London," Mair added.

"Not London," I countered. "Cambridge. I'm just passing through and got a bit turned around."

"So, he'll be on his way again soon, I hope?" he asked, staring at Mair with a look that demanded she reply with an affirmative.

"He's getting the train to Shrewsbury on Monday," she replied.

"And where's he staying until then?" he asked, his voice suddenly rising in tone and volume. I was beginning to feel like they'd forgotten I was in the room.

"He can stay here," she said, folding her arms across her chest. "We've got the room."

"I don't think so, young lady," he bellowed back, taking a step towards us both. "Your father would die all over again, his unmarried daughter letting a strange man sleep under his roof. I'll not have it."

He stared at Mair as though she were a deer and he was going in for the kill shot. Not willing to be an easy target for him she burst into a tirade of Welsh, flapping her arms and spitting out words at an alarming rate. Mr Hopkin responded with significantly fewer but whatever they were they managed to bring her to silence.

"You'll come with me, son," he said, his voice returning to normal. "It's not far."

"Really, I don't want to be any trouble," I said, hoping my subtle protest might help to change his mind. He had been no less than polite to me but his cold and direct demeanour had left me with little desire to spend more time with him than I had to. I looked to Mair with pleading eyes hoping she had more battle in her.

"It's ok," Mair said as she forced out a smile, "Mrs Hopkin will see you right. She'll have you earning your keep in no time. And she's a far better cook than me. You'll be fine."

I tried to feel reassured but I had little desire to go. One look at the stern face of Mr Hopkin, however, told me there'd be no use protesting so I nodded in defeated agreement.

"I'll come down first thing in the morning and see that you're doing ok," Mair continued, "and I'll bring those wet clothes down once I've given them a good scrub."

"Keep them," I said, knowing that I wouldn't be able to wear them without drawing attention to myself.

"Well, I'll be down anyway to make sure you're keeping out of trouble."

I was tempted to give her a hug as I stood up from the armchair but I decided against it, unsure of whether or not it would be appropriate. As if reading my apprehension, she grabbed hold of me and threw her arms around my neck bringing me close to her. Mr Hopkin, perhaps unapproving of the gesture, cast his eyes away and stared at the window.

"You'll be fine," she whispered. "Now go on."

With nothing to take with me other than the clothes that I was wearing and the items in my pocket, I made my way to the door. Mr Hopkin uttered something in Welsh to Mair and then followed me outside, shutting the door behind him.

The walk was mostly silent with my efforts to engage in conversation going mostly ignored apart from a few grunts and nods, so I decided instead to use the opportunity to try and get my bearings and make a mental note of the area.

When we reached the bottom of the lane I spotted the pub that I could see earlier. The sign above the door indicated that it was called The Farmers Arms which surprised me given the fact that it was in English while everyone I'd met so far preferred to speak in their native tongue.

The village itself was fairly pretty, the kind you might see on a postcard, and I was struck by just how small and secluded it was, surrounded by hills on all sides with a single road that came down one side and then up and out of the village on the other. In the centre stood a beautiful old church with a huge square tower. The crumbling stone walls that surrounded it were tall enough that I could only just see the tops of the headstones that were dotted around the churchyard. There was even a little school but it didn't look big enough to hold many children.

Mr Hopkin had no interest in being a tour guide and kept his pace straight and quick. We hurried along the main road on the only bit of the street that seemed to have any pavement and I peered through the windows of the row of small terraced cottages, maybe eight in number, that lined the road. They all looked much the same on the inside with everything they needed seemingly piled into one small living room. My nosiness came to an abrupt end, however, when I peered through one of the windows and found an angry-looking woman staring back at me.

Two men shouted a greeting to Mr Hopkin from outside a large white building with the words '*post office*' written on it in big black letters. He glanced over but made no effort to return their greeting, leaving me to flash a nervous smile in their direction as they stared on.

We'd caught the attention of quite a few of the locals as we walked. Some made fleeting glances while others turned their heads to watch as we went from one end of the street to the other. Perhaps it was the sight of someone new that caught their eye, or maybe Arthur had already informed the whole village that a stranger lurked among them. I couldn't be sure, but when I offered friendly smiles to some of them, I received only suspicious glances in return.

"It's just up by there," Mr Hopkin spoke for the first time, pointing at a little farmhouse sitting on a hill. The road we were walking along carried on beyond his property, up the hill and out of the village again, but we took a small path to the left that took us to the gate.

Throughout our walk, I'd kept anticipating that I would turn a corner onto more rows of houses and shops but it appeared I'd already seen everything there was to see. The place really was quite isolated in its own little valley and I could see why a strange face turning up would make for such exciting gossip. When there are only about a hundred people living nearby you probably become very aware of outsiders.

We approached the house and Mr Hopkin pushed through the gate, turning to hold it open for me. A sign on the post read '*Pen Castell Far*', the '*m*' having gone missing at some point previous to my arrival. The house was larger than the cottages in the village, though not by much, and was set amongst a patchwork of fields that stretched beyond it and up the hill. He led us around the side of the building, avoiding the front door, and came to a stop in a yard filled with outbuildings.

"Wait here a minute while I go and square things with Mrs Hopkin," he said, though something told me she would have little say in the matter, and he pushed through the back door into the house.

I wandered over to one of the barns and poked my head in through the door. It was filled with the smell of fresh hay and manure and I pinched my nose to block it out. A ladder rested against the back wall leading to a second floor, though there was no sign of what might be up there, and the walls were lined with various tools and bits of machinery. I felt sorry for anyone who had to lug all that equipment around. Spending all day in the fields doing manual labour wasn't the life for me, of that I was sure.

"Come on then," Mr Hopkin called from behind me. I turned to see him hanging out of the doorframe and staring out at the field, once again avoiding any sort of eye contact, and by the time I reached the door he'd already ducked back inside. I exhaled, nervous about what I was getting into and reminded myself that I would be home soon and that all this would be behind me. I just had to keep on hoping.

The back door needed a good nudge to fully open and it let out a long screech as I pushed through it. Inside the room, a kitchen, cabinets and dressers lined the walls and a long table sat at the centre filled with flour and dough and surrounded by eight chairs. There was a basin on one of the worktops, though no sign of taps or running water or any of the modern appliances I'd come to be used to in my own time.

Behind the table, standing in front of a huge metal stove that was set back into an alcove, seven faces stared back at me, all lined up from oldest to youngest like a somewhat poorer version of the Von Trapps.

"Come on, we don't bite." A woman that I assumed to be Mrs Hopkin motioned for me to come further into the room and I walked to the side of the table opposite them and offered a nervous smile. I felt like I was in a board meeting about to be appraised and evaluated, though if I were ever faced with this many solemn-looking faces in a boardroom I would probably assume I was about to be fired. None of them, barring Mrs Hopkin, looked very happy to be there.

Mr Hopkin, having done his job in escorting me there, appeared to lose all interest in the matter and sat himself at the head of the table and brought a newspaper up in front of his face. His wife, a short and plump woman with dark, greying hair, had a warmth about her that everyone else in the house appeared to lack, and continued to smile at me as I looked around.

"Hello, I'm Tom." I sported my best friendly smile as I raised a hand to wave at them but the children's faces remained unchanged and unimpressed.

"I'm Mrs Hopkin," the woman said with another broad smile. "It's lovely to meet you." She indicated to the girl on her left, "This is Ellen. We call her Nellie."

The girl looked to be about 20 and was the oldest of the children. She was dressed all in black with a white apron, her dark hair tied up at the back, and she put me in mind of a maid, or those waitresses you see in themed tea rooms. She was tall like Mr Hopkin, though she appeared to suffer none of his harsh facial features and eventually smiled at me once we were introduced.

"This is Elizabeth," Mrs Hopkin continued, "and we call her Betty. She's sixteen." The young girl smiled, then blushed, then dropped her eyes down to the ground in apparent shyness as she clasped her hands together in front of her.

"That there is Edward, otherwise known as Teddy. He's fifteen and our little labourer. Helps his dad out on the farm, he does." The young boy looked at me wholly unimpressed then folded his arms defiantly and pursed his lips into a frown. I gave him a slight nod of the head as a greeting but he immediately cast his glance sideways.

"And on the end there we've got the twins, Sophia and Howell." Sophia smiled at me curiously, a cheeky twinkle in her eye as she sized me up, but Howell kept his eyes low, obviously wary of the stranger who'd found his way into his home. Each of the twins seemed to have developed one or the other parent's genes, with Sophia being short and somewhat plump, just like her mother, while Howell towered several inches above her, tall like his father and stern-faced.

"And what do they call you then, little man?" I asked, given that nobody in the house appeared to use their actual names.

"Howell," he said, as though I'd asked the most absurd question ever put to him. Nellie and Betty both began to laugh and Mr Hopkin shot them a look that made them stop and straighten up again.

"And how old are you two?"

Sophia stepped forward and crossed her arms on the edge of the table, leaning in as she spoke. "We're ten and Mam

51

says we have to speak English to you, but that's alright because we have to speak it in school anyway and Mam says it would be rude to speak Welsh if you can't understand what we're saying about you."

"That's not quite what I said," her mother replied, looking a tad embarrassed. "Right, you lot, back to your jobs and let the young man sit down. I'll get us some drinks."

Nellie, the eldest daughter, took a seat at the table while her siblings filed out into other areas of the house. I followed her lead and sat opposite her and watched as she began to work the flour on the table.

"So, what do you do?" I asked, trying to strike some conversation.

"She's our big achiever." Mrs Hopkin beamed with pride as she set some glasses and a jug down on the table. "Got herself a job at the post office after only one application."

"I'm just a junior postmistress," Nellie interjected with an embarrassed smile. Her voice was soft but filled with confidence and she had less of an accent than the rest of her family. "I'd rather have liked to train to become a nurse, but…" she trailed off, and both she and her father cast awkward glances at one another.

"You won't be a junior for long my love," Mrs Hopkin said, taking a seat beside her.

They both talked as they worked the flour, turning it into a dough with barely a look down at what they were doing and then kneading it into loaves. They must have done it hundreds of times over the years and they made it look easy. I couldn't recall ever making bread. Our loaves always came ready-made and sliced. I'd never considered how much of a luxury that was.

"John tells me you're from London, Tom. Do you work?"

"I do," I said. "I work for a publisher in Cambridge." I stopped short of telling them I owned the business or arguing about the location.

"Fancy. And what brings you to Cwm Newydd?"

I paused to consider what to say next. The truth was out of the question and I obviously had no real business in being there so I was forced to make something up. "I was on my way to see family," I lied, "but we stopped for some air and I wandered off and got lost. It was dark and I walked for a few miles before eventually falling asleep in Mair's field."

I hoped it would be convincing enough to avoid further interrogation but they both looked as though they thought I might be simple.

"That's very… unfortunate," Mrs Hopkin said after a moment and Nellie's mouth curled into a smirk that she tried to contain. They definitely thought I was stupid.

"Will Nan make it tomorrow?" she asked her mother, changing the subject.

"I should think so, love."

"Is that your grandmother, I asked?" causing both women to burst into laughter. Even Mr Hopkin seemed to find it amusing.

"She's my sister," Nellie said. "Her name is Hannah but we call her Nan."

Of course they did. Why wouldn't they? Maybe I could start calling myself Steve while I was there.

"She's a housekeeper up at Felin Fawr, the big house up on the estate," said Mrs Hopkin. "She boards there with the others but she comes home when she can and we see her at church on Sundays if she's able. It's Nellie and Gethin's first reading of the banns tomorrow."

"You're getting married? Congratulations."

Nellie smiled brightly, nodding her head. "At the end of April."

"And a fine lad he is, too," Mr Hopkin piped up from nowhere, suddenly entering the conversation. "School teacher, he is."

Mrs Hopkin stood from the table and clapped her hands of any remaining flour. "Right, show Mr…"

"Jacob," I say.

"Oh, fancy that," she said with a smile. "My maiden name was Jacob. Show Mr Jacob where he will be sleeping while I get these stoves ready."

Mr Hopkin stood up, folded his paper and handed it to me. "You'll need that," he said.

I stared at it for a moment wondering what he meant. It was written in Welsh and the only things on it that I could understand were numbers. I tucked it under my arm anyway and followed him outside, wondering where he might be taking me.

In the yard, Mr Hopkin walked to the barn and motioned me inside. "We haven't got a lot of room in the house," he said, "and I can't very well have a stranger bedding down with my girls so this will have to do." He pointed up at the hatch leading to the second floor. "I will send Betty out with some sheets and a pillow for you. You'll understand why we can't give you a lamp," he added, motioning to the bales of hay.

I tried not to seem ungrateful but I couldn't help wishing Mair had won the battle and I'd been able to stay with her. At least I'd have been able to have a bed.

"What do I need this for?" I asked, waving the newspaper.

"That," he said, pointing to a small square building set several metres back from the house, "is the privy."

I'm sure my thoughts were written all over my face as he spoke but I tried to act like shitting outside with no flushing water was the most normal thing in the world to me.

"See you at dinner," he said, then he turned and walked away.

It seemed cruel to make me sleep in the barn. Though I could understand his reasoning it was bitterly cold and I had visions of freezing to death before I could ever get home. With no other option, I climbed the ladder into the room above. It was small and cramped and sloping at the sides. I hated it. It was too dark to see much of anything and I was hesitant in my movements in case I tripped and fell back down the hatch, so I dropped to my hands and knees and crawled to some hay in the corner, slumping myself down in what would become my new bed.

It's just two days, I told myself. *Two days and then you can get out of here.* I was trying desperately to console myself but the truth was that I had nowhere to go. Even if I made my way to Cambridge what would I do then? I needed to find out how the ring got me here in the first place and then make it send me home again.

I pulled it from my pocket and slipped it on my finger then, exhausted, lay down on the hay and closed my eyes, praying I would wake up in my own bed.

Five

I shot up from my sleep as something crashed in the room below me. My head slammed into the rafters and I let out a loud "fuck," partly from pain but mostly because I hadn't woken up in my own bed as I'd hoped.

The previous evening Betty had brought me some sheets and a pillow, some Long Johns and a pair of woollen socks, then when I declined the invitation to come to dinner she'd returned with some bread. She could barely look at me the whole time she was there and turned bright pink when I thanked her, but I was truly grateful for her effort having not realised just how cold I'd get in the barn.

The source of my sudden awakening, Mr Hopkin, seemed to be indifferent to my desire to sleep and began to hammer away at something metallic in the room below me. I pulled the sheets up over my head and hid under the layers of blankets to drown out the noise. It felt like a fort, somewhere safe, and I wondered if I could get away with staying there until whatever cosmic powers had brought me to this place saw fit to send me back. Mr Hopkin, however, had other ideas.

"Get up," he shouted from below and I curled up tighter, hoping he would go away. Through the cracks in the roof, I could see only darkness outside which was a time of the morning that I had no desire to be part of.

"We don't ask twice in this house," he called again. "Come now or you don't get fed."

I rubbed a hand across my stomach realising just how hungry I was. I was in no mood to dine with the family the night before and had eaten only soup and a slice of bread in a day and a half. I wanted to sleep but I wanted food more.

"What time is it?" I asked, my voice hoarse from the cold air in the barn.

"It's a little after five, we thought you could do with a lie-in."

I pulled the sheets off my head with a sigh and admitted defeat. I slid out a loose board against the wall and hid my wallet and the two rings behind it then did my best to get dressed without falling through the hatch to the stone floor below. When I finally looked presentable, I made my way down the ladder but by the time I reached the bottom the barn was empty.

The kitchen was alive with activity as I crossed the yard and the smell of bacon beckoned me inside. The twins nearly took me off my feet as they darted in and out of the chairs and I yawned wondering how they had so much energy so early in the morning.

"Tag," Sophia shouted, clipping me around the head as I took a seat at the table. The two eldest daughters sat and chatted amongst themselves but each gave me a welcoming smile as I joined them. I noticed that Nellie was clutching onto a book with something about ailments written on the front, but she didn't seem to be paying it much mind.

"I hope you like eggs," Mrs Hopkin said, nodding towards a pan on the stove. With my limited knowledge of the time period, I'd been expecting to receive not much more than a bowl of gruel but spread across the table was a veritable feast. A bowl of fresh bread slices sat at the centre of the table, the steam rising from them an indication that Mrs Hopkin had risen far earlier than I this morning to make it. At each setting on the table was a plate holding a thin slice of bacon and a small knob of very pale, almost white butter, already starting to melt.

"Would you like some tea?" Nellie asked, holding up a metal pitcher. I gave her a nod and she poured the hot water into a tiny china cup before stirring in a spoonful of leaves and handing it to me.

Howell and Sophia, red-faced and giggling, continued to dodge in and out of the chairs until Mr Hopkin, without saying a word slammed a fist on the table causing everyone to jump. Knowing not to defy their father they quickly took a seat on either side of me and fell silent.

"Will you be joining us at church today?" Mrs Hopkin asked, setting a plate of boiled eggs down on the table and taking a seat opposite her husband.

"Thanks, Mrs Hopkin, but I'd rather stay here if you don't mind?"

"As you wish," she replied, giving me a smile. "Girls," she looked over at her eldest two daughters and raised an eyebrow. They immediately stopped talking and turned their bodies to the table, raising their hands to pray.

I kept my hands in my lap and looked down at the plate in front of me while Mrs Hopkin led a prayer in Welsh. I had no understanding of what she was saying but I didn't need to. I was silently making my own plea to be returned home.

I joined in with the chorus of '*Amen*' and the table burst back into life with chattering and movement as the household reached for their breakfast. Mr Hopkin, ever the wordsmith, cast a cantankerous eye over proceedings and

Mrs Hopkin watched on, ensuring everybody had their share before taking their own.

"Why don't you believe in God, Mr Jacob?" Sophia asked and I paused mid-bite as all eyes around the table turned to me.

"Don't talk with your mouth full," Mrs Hopkin replied to her daughter, saving me from an awkward conversation.

"No Teddy today?" I asked, noting their son's absence from the table and needing a change of subject.

"Not today," Mr Hopkin said without looking up from his plate. His tone told me I should leave the topic alone so I turned my attention to Mrs Hopkin instead.

"I really can't thank you enough for your hospitality, Mrs Hopkin. The food is lovely."

"I'm only sorry I can't do more for you while you're here," she replied. "It's nice to have another man about the house since Jack ran off with that… that tart!"

The table fell immediately silent and all eyes turned to Mrs Hopkin. It seemed like every time I opened my mouth I led us into another awkward conversation.

"LEAH!" Mr Hopkin bellowed, dropping his knife and fork onto his tin plate with a clang. He clenched both of his hands into his fists and set them on the table on either side of his breakfast. Mrs Hopkin, with a look of both embarrassment and indignation, opened her mouth as if to speak again but was pre-empted by her husband. "That's enough!"

"Mr Jacob." Sophia tugged on my sleeve to get my attention.

"You can call me Tom," I replied and the edges of her mouth turned up into a small grin. She set down her fork and rubbed her hands down her front, leaving a trail of crumbs behind, then raised her elbow onto the table, leaned her head into her hand, and began to speak.

"Do you live here now?" She gave me that quizzical look that I was becoming quickly familiar with and I braced myself for whatever she might come out with next. "Because Mam said she can't afford to feed the whole bloody village".

Mr Hopkin let out another loud sigh as the table once again fell silent. I glanced over to Mrs Hopkin who had gone bright red with embarrassment and brought her hands to her face in exasperation. I gave her a smile that I hoped would convey that I was not offended but it dawned on me that I had no way to repay their kindness. Or to pay for anything, for that matter. I'd talked of train tickets and travel but had no way to pay for any of it.

"You mind your tongue, young girl," Mrs Hopkin said, reaching over and giving her daughter a playful slap to the arm that made her giggle.

"No, I don't live here," I said, "but I'll be sure to pay my way just as soon as I can."

Mr Hopkin let out a cough and as I glanced over I caught him rolling his eyes in doubt at his wife.

"And maybe while I'm here I can help out around the house?"

"You don't have to do that," Mrs Hopkin replied with a wave of her hand.

"Honestly, I'd like to. Maybe you could teach me how to make bread?"

"Make bread?" Mrs Hopkin, looking mortified, choked back a piece of bacon and both Nellie and Betty covered their mouths to shield another giggle at my expense. I looked around the table at all the faces for a sign of what I may have said wrong this time. "I don't need no men under my feet in the kitchen all day. If you insist on helping then there's plenty what wants doing outside."

"That's sorted then, you can come with me," Mr Hopkin said, taking a final swig of his tea. He wiped his face with his napkin and threw it onto the plate of barely touched food. I looked down at my own plate with not so much as a crumb left on it and I was still feeling as hungry as I was before I'd sat down.

"Thanks again, Mrs Hopkin," I said as I followed her husband out into the back yard. The sun had begun to rise bathing the yard in an orange glow, and fog rose up over the wet fields beyond. I appreciated its prettiness but I would still have rathered been asleep than witness it.

"You know how to use a hammer?" Mr Hopkin asked. "There's a fence that wants mending."

My experience with tools beyond a year 9 woodwork class was limited to putting up a set of flat-pack shelves in my flat but how hard could it be? I nodded and he beckoned me towards the barn.

"Grab that," he said, pointing to a bucket of rusty nails on the ground. They looked like they'd been used before and then left out in the rain but I did as I was asked. It was heavier than it looked and I had to use two hands to pick it up which he seemed to find amusing. We walked past the privy and hopped over the stone stile into the field behind the house.

"Ever mended a fence?"

"No, sir."

"You'll soon learn," he said. "A hard lesson makes a hard man, that's what my father always used to say."

I came to a stop and his words rang in my ears.

"Something wrong?" Mr Hopkin turned to look at me and for the first time since we'd met his face appeared to show concern.

"Nothing," I said, shaking myself off and continuing on. "My father used to say the same thing, is all. He passed away a few weeks ago. Took me by surprise a bit."

"He sounds like a sensible man. I'm sorry for your loss, Tom."

It hadn't taken long to cross the field but the walk uphill had left me out of breath and the warm air from my lungs created a mist with every exhale. My hands were already freezing and turning red and I blew some warm air into them, longing for a pair of gloves.

"Hold this," Mr Hopkin said, handing me a mallet as we reached a broken bit of fence. A wooden barricade surrounded the whole field with posts every few metres that carried two planks of wood between them and at various points in the fence the planks had come loose making it easy for the sheep to escape.

"Now, come over by here with that hammer," he said, fishing a nail from the bucket and then lifting one of the planks up and holding it into place. "Give it a good whack."

"Are you sure?" I said, concerned I was about to be the cause of him breaking several fingers.

"We haven't got all day," he barked back.

I stepped up to the post and with no valid reason I could use to get out of it I brought the mallet up over my shoulder and set forth a blow to the nail which I hoped would connect. My eyes closed the second I felt it hit and I drew back my body into a clenched position waiting for the yelp of pain.

"Now, do it again."

I opened my eyes and saw Mr Hopkin ready with a second nail to fully secure the fence in place. This time I felt slightly more confident and watched as the nail slid into the wood with ease.

"Not hard, is it?"

"No," I said, feeling quite proud of my efforts.

"Good," he replied. "Now get a move on and I'll see you after church." Without another word, he wandered off back down the hill to the farmhouse and I looked around the perimeter of the field counting eighteen fallen planks.

"This will take me no time," I said, reaching for the bucket to begin my task.

"Glad to see they've got you working hard." I turned to see Mair making her way across the field towards me. The morning sun highlighted her red hair making it look like flames in the distance and she walked with her arms folded tightly across her chest.

It had been, at a guess, around an hour since Mr Hopkin had left me to mend the fences and I was getting through it in record time. Having finished in the field he'd set me to work in I thought I would buy into his good graces by continuing on into the next one and had almost mended every broken post I could see. Despite the cold air I was sweating from the tiring work and was glad for the distraction and company.

"You not going to church?" I asked, reaching into the bucket for another nail.

"Ah, it's too stuffy for me," she said, coming up beside me and resting her arms on the fence I'd just fixed. She stared off over the farmland and smiled. "I make peace with God in my own ways."

"I want to say thank you again for helping me yesterday. I don't know what I'd have done if you hadn't come along."

"Everyone needs a friend, Tom," she said, turning to face me with a smile. "And besides, now you owe me a favour."

"I sure do," I said. "Need a friend and owe you a favour, I mean. But I'll probably need more help from you before you find any use for me."

"Now why doesn't that surprise me?" she nudged me on the arm and laughed. Mair had a way about her that made me feel at ease. The Hopkins had all been kind and polite but Mair was less formal and rigid and reminded me of my friends from back home. I had a feeling we would get on well.

"It's a fine job you're doing here," she said, gesturing to the fence.

"Just doing my bit to keep Mr Hopkin on side. Got to earn my dinner."

"And I'm sure Mr Hughes will love it," she replied.

"Yeah? Who's that then?".

"He's the man who owns this paddock," she said, shaking her head at me with a massive grin.

I looked around the field and the twenty or so panels I'd already fixed and Mair burst out laughing. "Please tell me you're joking!" I said, raising my palms to my face.

"You're on the wrong farm, you fool. I saw you from down the bottom and wondered what the hell you were doing up here. Thought I better come and rescue you again!"

I plonked myself down onto the wet grass, exhausted and embarrassed. My hands were beginning to crack and blister from the cold wind and the twisting of the hammer in my palms so I was at least glad I could stop.

"Come on, *twp*, let's go have a break," she said, extending a hand to me.

"*Twp*?" I asked. "What's that?"

"Stupid," she said, and I couldn't help but laugh. I definitely felt '*twp*'.

We'd only been back at the farmhouse long enough for Mair to boil some water when the family bundled back through the door. Teddy, absent from breakfast, was with the family this time, though he only stayed in the kitchen long enough to say hello to Mair and then disappeared into another part of the house, once again ignoring me.

"Straight to get changed," Betty directed at the youngest two children as she followed them into the house. She glanced over at me and dashed straight through the door into the main part of the house, her cheeks flushing red again. I remembered going through a similar phase when I was about her age, not being able to talk to anyone unless I knew them and immediately losing my voice when faced with a stranger. If it weren't for Lee, who always had enough confidence for the both of us, I'd never have gotten to know anyone.

"What a lovely surprise," Mrs Hopkin beamed as she ambled through the door and spotted Mair at the table. "Are you staying for your dinner?"

"What're we having?" Mair asked, confirming her place at the table. She was obviously very close with the family.

"Mutton," Mrs Hopkin replied, "but it won't be ready for a while yet."

"How did it go at the church?" I asked Nellie as she entered the room in her Sunday best, the question making her face light up.

"Oh, it was perfect," she replied, filled with excitement. She untied the lace veil from around her head and set it down in her lap. Though freed, her tightly styled hair didn't move and it stood in stark contrast to Mair's whose wavy red curls seemed to have a mind of their own despite being held up in a similar style.

"It won't be long now and yo-" I began, but I was interrupted by a bang at the door that sounded as though someone was trying to batter their way inside. Mr Hopkin shot to his feet and marched straight through the door to confront whoever was outside and for a second I thought Mair was going to march right on out behind him.

All of the women of the house immediately rushed to the kitchen window to see what was going on outside and with the sound of anger intensifying I decided I would go out to try and diffuse the situation. On my attempt to stand from my seat both Mrs Hopkin and Mair put a hand on my shoulders and pushed me back down and Nellie shook her head at me as an indication to stay put.

"Who is it? At least tell me what they're talking about," I pleaded.

"It's Arthur," Mair replied, but she stopped short of translating what either of the men were saying to each other.

The commotion continued for several more minutes before Mr Hopkin came back inside, seemingly unscathed but red-faced and visibly angry. He began to converse in Welsh with the others and I heard my name come up a couple of times as they each took glances at me. I refrained from speaking up or interrupting and instead sat listening as though I had any clue what was being discussed until, as if suddenly remembering I was in the room, Mrs Hopkin came and put a reassuring hand on my shoulder. She cast a look over at her husband that indicated that it was time for him to stop.

"I've got a mind to go and speak with that boy's father," he said, switching back to English. "Talking to me like that in my own home. If he were my son I'd have taken the belt to him long ago."

"I'd like to see that," Mair added, moving away from the window and taking her seat again beside me. Mrs Hopkin sat down on the other side of me and took both my hands into hers and gave me one of those smiles that you give to someone just before you tell them something bad.

"We want you to know, John and I, that we don't think you had anything to do with Jack running away, no matter what anyone else might be saying in the village."

I looked around perplexed at all the faces staring back at me. "What? What are people saying? I've never even met your son, I promise." I felt feeble professing my innocence to a situation I knew nothing about, especially to the parents of the missing man, but the last thing I wanted if I was to be stuck here was to be accused of kidnap. Or worse.

"We know that, don't we John?" She looked up at her husband and he gave a nod but stayed silent. "But it seems Mr Morgan thinks otherwise. He's convinced you know where Elinor is. He's demanding that we put you out on the street."

"I wouldn't blame you if you did," I said.

"Well we aren't, you've no worry of that."

"Maybe If I just speak to him I ca-"

"There's no talking to him," Mair interjected. "He won't listen. The whole village knows that they've run off and as soon as they're settled we'll get a letter to say as much, just you watch. If it wasn't for..." she paused herself, looked at

Mr Hopkin and reconsidered her words. "Well let's just say we all thought they'd get together in the end and this is just how they've gone about it. Arthur needs to accept that."

I glanced over at Mr Hopkin, jaw clenched and eyes facing the ceiling and wondered what Mair was about to say.

"Right, that's quite enough of this nonsense," Mrs Hopkin said, letting go of my hands. "This food won't cook itself."

I stood from my chair ignoring the looks from everyone around the table and walked out into the back yard. Before the door had even had time to close behind me, Mair was following me through it.

"Don't let him upset you," she said as I paced around the yard.

"I don't care about him," I said, pointing off into nothingness. "I just want to go home and I don't want to bring any trouble to the farm while I'm stuck here. They've already lost a son and now they have an extra mouth to feed and village busybodies to fend off. It isn't fair." I was trying not to raise my voice but I could feel myself getting louder and angrier with every word.

"Who does he think he is coming up here and threatening them? Telling them who can and can't stay under their roof?" I ceased my pacing and turned to face Mair head-on. "Fucking wanker," I spat out.

She looked a bit taken aback by my language at first but then her eyes went wide and her lips turned up into a big devilish grin.

"Well," she dropped her voice to a whisper and leaned in close to me, her eyes darting around to make sure nobody could hear her, "that *fucking wanker* is the son of the man who owns half of the land around these parts. Most of the people in the village are just tenants on his land and know better than to speak back. There's also the fact that the local constable is Arthur's cousin and you've got yourself a family who think they can do as they wish and a village too afraid to tell them otherwise."

I indicated to the house behind us. "Does he own this place?"

"No, and it's a good job for everyone that he doesn't or you'd all likely end up on the street but that doesn't mean he won't try to make things difficult for them and you."

"I still think I should go and speak to him."

"You'd only make things worse. You'll be gone in the morning and then you won't have to ever see each other again."

I considered her comment for a moment. The carriage into the city would be arriving the next day to take me away but I had no money and nowhere to go. "Actually," I said, "I was thinking of maybe staying for a little while. Just until I can earn enough to pay back Mr Hopkin and buy a ticket home. Assuming they let me, anyway."

"Of course they will," Mair smiled at me. She looped her arm into mine and began walking us back towards the house. "And if they don't, we'll sneak you in at my house until you're on your feet again. I suppose that means I'm going to be stuck looking after you for a few more weeks?"

I smiled and looked down at her. "I'm afraid so."

As we reached the back door I could hear footsteps running along the cobbles beside the house. Expecting the return of Arthur, I put myself between Mair and whoever was approaching and prepared myself for a fight, but the man who rounded the corner was unfamiliar to me. He was coated with sweat and panting heavily and as he came to a stop, he rested his arm on the corner of the house to catch his breath.

"Ioan?" Mair questioned, puzzled to see the man standing before us. "What're you doing up here?"

"It's the mine," he panted. His eyes went wide and I watched as Mair's face changed to a look of dread. "It's blown, Mair. The mine's blown."

Six

It was already dark by the time the first casualties arrived in the village. Mr Davies, the landlord at The Farmers Arms had opened his rooms to receive some of the men being brought from the mine but had become quickly overwhelmed by the number of injured people needing space so Mr Williamson, the schoolmaster, agreed to open the school building as an overflow makeshift hospital.

A group of men from the village had organised a rescue party and headed to the site of the explosion to see how they could help. I offered my services but Mr Hopkin suggested it might be best that I stay to look after Mair on account of me being unfamiliar with the area and not knowing the language, so we quickly made our way to the school to see what we could do to help.

The main road of the village was chaotic. People dashed around in confusion as they waited for confirmation about their loved ones while men in carts brought injured men and bodies to be treated and identified. In the yard outside the school, Mrs Hopkin and another woman had set up a table with jugs of clean water and were taking turns ripping bed sheets that people were bringing from their homes, organising them into strips of bandages to be used for dressing wounds. A few metres away another group of women formed a production line from the entrance of the school and were transporting desks out of the building to

71

make extra room in the classrooms. With most of the men helping in the rescue efforts, it was left to the women to move, carry, tend to the sick and collect clean water from the well outside.

Mair, her face grief-stricken, wandered in circles around the premises in search of updates. She had begged to be allowed to go with the men on the rescue operation, and I had no doubt that she would have clawed on her hands and knees in search of her brother had she been allowed, but Mr Jones, who had organised the first group, would not hear of it.

In the field next to the school, placed carefully in rows, the bodies of the deceased that had been carted to the village were being placed under blankets in an effort to not distress the wounded and bereaved further, while also giving people a chance to identify their husbands, sons and fathers. As soon as the first bodies were moved there Mair rushed over.

"I can't lose him too," she said as she pulled back the sheet on a body lying on the ground. A young man lay underneath, his face covered in dirt and blood. Mair took a sharp intake of breath and brought her hand to her mouth at the sight. "Owen Thomas," she whispered before hurriedly covering his bloodied face back up, "I went to school with him."

I grabbed her at the shoulders and raised her to her feet. Her body trembled, a mix of cold and shock, and she shook me off to move to the next body in the line. I wanted to tell her that it would be ok, that her brother would be fine, but as the number of sheets in the field increased it was feeling more and more unlikely.

As more people arrived in the village the noise in the school yard turned so loud that it was nearly impossible to distinguish one voice from another. People were shouting out from all sides, barking instructions or calling out for loved ones in the hope that someone may answer back. The wails of the injured carried on the wind and sent shivers across my skin but it was the cries of anguish from those reunited with the bodies of their relatives that were the worst sounds of all. I didn't need to understand their words to know what they were all thinking and feeling.

Mair moved further along the row peeling back sheets and staring down at the bodies of friends and neighbours and every time she did, her face filled with the same look of relief that it was not her brother, and a sadness that it was somebody else's.

"Tom, come quickly." I turned to see Nellie at the entrance to the school beckoning me over. As soon as we'd gotten word of what had happened she'd fallen straight into action and called for the organisation of the classrooms to receive the wounded, proving herself to be a competent and confident leader. Mair gave me a nod to let me know she would be fine and I ran to where Nellie stood. "I need your help inside," she said as she rushed back into the building.

Her aprons were covered in blood and her hair had come loose and fallen in little waves down past her shoulders but was kept out of her face with a veil tied at the back of her neck. It was a stark contrast to the composed and well-kept demeanour she always presented.

"Where are all the doctors and nurses?" I asked as we rushed through the corridor weaving in and out of people, some coming and going in their efforts to help while others stood waiting for updates on the men inside the classrooms. The building was small which left it feeling cramped and I was struggling to get through the mass. There were only two classrooms that I could see, and Nellie led me to the furthest one. "Shouldn't a doctor be taking over here and treating the wounded?"

She came to a stop outside the classroom and turned to face me. "These men can't afford doctors," she said, exasperated, "and even if they could there is only one and he's at the mine. We are all they've got. Now, are you going to help me or not?"

Her usual smile and charming demeanour were gone, replaced with determination and self-assuredness and she clearly had no time for my questions. I nodded affirmatively and she walked inside the classroom.

Twelve men were being treated in the room, lying on the floor amongst sheets and bandages as young women whizzed around trying to treat them. Some had lost consciousness but most were crying out in agony or shock and I tried to avoid making eye contact with them in case they could sense the fear in me.

"I only have a little first-aid training," Nellie said, kneeling beside a man and pulling back his sheets, "but I know this leg needs setting."

I looked down and then immediately away wishing I'd mentally prepared myself for the sight. Protruding from the man's leg and covered in blood was the splintered end of his shin bone which had pierced his skin and torn a hole through his trousers. I offered him a reassuring smile and he stared back at me with gritted teeth and heavy breaths as he tried to stop himself from screaming.

"Take his shoulders, Mr Jacob." She grabbed scissors and cut at his trousers exposing his entire left leg and the many cuts on his skin. She said something to one of the other women in Welsh who proceeded to place a wooden rod into the man's mouth and his eyes went wide with panic. "This is going to hurt," she said, and I wasn't sure if it was me she was telling or the patient.

He writhed in pain as she put her hands near the wound and I pushed on his shoulders to stop his attempts to sit up and pull away. When she wrapped her hand underneath his calf he let out a blood-chilling scream and I looked away immediately unable to meet his terrified stare.

"Now," Nellie shouted, and without looking I pushed down hard on the man's shoulders. He let out another gut-wrenching scream and the sound of crunching bone echoed across the room. A second later his body became limp and he passed out.

"He'll wake up soon enough," she said, grabbing two bits of wood that were piled beside her and affixing them to his leg as a makeshift splint. A girl of about twelve years old ran over to her offering bandages and she took a handful, setting them down in her lap, then she made a command in Welsh to a woman standing nearby who nodded her head and disappeared down the corridor.

"Tom, take these and apply pressure to that boy's head." She handed me a pile of bandages and pointed to a young lad sitting on the floor near the corner of the room. His face was featureless through the soot but he couldn't have been much older than ten.

With the bandages in hand, I kneeled in front of him and offered a reassuring smile, but his expression remained unchanged, terrified. From behind me, a girl brought a bowl filled with water and cloths, though neither looked particularly clean, and I began cleaning his face as best as I could to get a better look at him. He had a cut above his eye that was bleeding into his eyebrow and running down the side of his face but seemed otherwise unharmed.

"I'm Tom," I said, wiping the cloth across his cheek. "What's your name?"

He took a moment before finally replying. "Daniel."

"We're going to get you cleaned up and you'll be right as rain, ok? Do you remember what happened?"

"I don't know," he said. His voice was shaky and quiet and his eyes remained fixed in the distance. "I ran to the cage to go up top for help and then there was a bang. Next thing I know, Mr Granville was putting me in the cart and bringing me here."

"It looks like you've taken quite a bump to the head," I said, noticing the lump forming above his eye and cautiously running the wet cloth over it. "Your mother and father will be here looking for you shortly and then you can go home and rest."

"My father was still down there, sir," he said, and for the first time, his eyes began to fill with tears. He wiped them away with his cuff, smearing more dirt across his face. I had no idea what to say to him that could make any of this any better.

"Did you go to this school, Daniel?"

He shook his head again. "I'm from Pisgah. I don't know anyone here."

"Me either. Maybe we can be friends, eh?"

"Ok," he replied, his voice slightly firmer.

I folded a stretch of bandage into a square and pressed it over the cut causing him to wince. "I need you to keep this pressed nice and tight to your head, can you do that for me?" He nodded, replacing my hand on the bandage with his own. "If you need me just shout, ok. I'm Tom, remember." He gave me another nod and I made my way back to Nellie who was still bandaging the man with the broken leg.

An anxious calm had fallen over the room as the women went about their work and the injured passed out or passed away. Most of the ones who remained awake had fallen into a sort of stunned silence and their vacant eyes bore holes in the ceiling as they replayed what had happened to them in their minds.

"You've quite a knack for this," I said, reaching Nellie as she gently wrapped a cloth around the man's splints. "How do you even know how to do any of this?"

She sat back and dragged the back of her arm across her forehead, wiping away the sweat. "Books, mostly. And the Order of Saint John. We're a remote village, miles from a hospital, and most of the menfolk work in mines. They sent a group here to train people in the art of first-aid in case of an emergency and I volunteered my services. I was turned away at first but I reasoned that if all the men became injured in such an emergency then it would leave us back to square one, so now here we are."

"Well, you seem to have it all in hand. You're a natural."

"I would have quite liked to go to the infirmary in Aberystwyth to train as a nurse," she replied, keeping a perfect focus on the job before her as she spoke, "but father wouldn't allow it so I applied at the post office instead."

"Another carriage has arrived," a woman shouted from the doorway, bringing an end to our conversation.

It had been over two hours since the last large intake of injured men had arrived and everyone had become a bit unsure if there would be more. A man named David who had ridden the previous wagon to the village had told us that two other neighbouring towns had set up similar operations to our own, but with all of them miles apart and with no idea of how many injured men there were, we didn't know how many or who to expect.

The room became frantic again as the temporary nurses rushed to make room on the floor and seconds later the frenzied voices of the rescuers began shouting through the building as they carried men and boys into the hallways on makeshift stretchers

"Tom, tell them we can take two more in here and the others are to go into classroom one," Nellie said as she jumped back into action.

I did as I was ordered and ran to the corridor to direct the men to the various rooms. Eight more miners were stretchered through the corridor in various states of injury. Six went to the first classroom while I ushered the remaining two towards Nellie. The first man we received was unconscious though appeared to have only minor injuries. The appearance of the second man, however, made even Nellie take a moment to compose herself.

In what must have been a consequence of the blast, most of the man's clothing had been torn off leaving him naked but for a few loose threads of material where he'd worn extra layers. What was left of his clothes was charred and fused to his skin and most of his hair was gone too. His screams echoed through the room as though he were being tortured and one of the women closed the classroom doors to stop his wails from reverberating down the corridors.

"What can we do?" I asked, wanting to do something, anything, to ease his pain.

Nellie stood from her observation of the man and turned to me, bringing her head close to mine. "There's nothing we can do," she said in a whisper. "I don't know enough to treat him and he's so badly burned. He won't make it."

For the first time that day, the pressure looked like it might overcome her and her eyes began to glisten as tears formed at the corners.

"Laudanum, maybe?" she said with a defeated shrug. "It'll ease the pain a bit but not by much and it certainly won't be a cure. If nothing else it might make this a bit easier on him."

Before she could even reach for the bottle the man's cries stopped, dropping the room into an eerie silence, and we all turned to face his now lifeless body. Nellie immediately grabbed a sheet from her pile and covered him over then motioned to have his body taken away. As two women attended to the deceased man, she reached for the jug of whiskey that she'd been using to help with pain, pouring a little into a glass and knocking it back.

"Let's not mention this to Father," she said, holding her glass out at me with a quivering hand. I gave her shoulder a light squeeze and then left her to her thoughts.

Laying in the spot nearest the doorway was our other new patient. I wanted to give Nellie some respite so I decided to see what I could do by myself and headed over. He was unconscious when I reached him but the rise and fall of his stomach at least assured me that he was alive. I lifted his arms, checking for cuts, and tilted his head side to side to make sure there was no blood coming from his ears. I wasn't sure if that was standard procedure but I'd seen it done on television shows and it seemed a good way to check for any problems with his head.

One of the straps on his suspenders was broken and I lifted the free side of his shirt to look at his stomach. It seemed whatever had caused his suspender to snap had given him quite a blow to the side. From just under his armpit, down the side of his stomach and around to his back, a large red bruise had formed that got darker as it curved underneath him.

I ran my fingers along the outline of the bruise and he let out a sharp gasp and jerked his body away from my touch. Startled, I pulled my hand back and looked at his face to see him staring back at me. The whites of his eyes were stark against his soot-covered skin.

"Hello," I said, trying to remain as calm as possible. "I'm Tom. You're going to be alright. Can you tell me your name?"

"Gwyn," he said, his voice hoarse.

"Nice to meet you, Gwyn. Are you in much pain?"

"You're English," he replied.

"I am. I came all this way just to take care of you," I joked, hoping to keep him at ease. He managed a small grin before coughing and wincing in pain.

"Is it just your side that hurts?" I asked.

He nodded and I motioned for someone to bring me some cloths.

"I think he's broken a rib," I said to the young girl who came over to us. "Can you let Nellie know, please?"

Turning back to the patient I ran the cloths she'd handed me through the water and began wringing them out into the bowl, noticing for the first time how bloodied and filthy my hands were.

"That's my shirt," he said, cocking his head to the side and taking a better look at me as I dabbed the dirt from his face. "Fancy stealing from a dying man."

"You must be Mair's brother," I said with a smile, glad to know we would be able to give her some good news.

"No, Mair's my sister." He attempted a small laugh that brought with it some discomfort, making him twist his body awkwardly.

"We'll get something over to you for the pain in a minute," I said in an attempt to reassure him. "Mair will be glad to see that you're ok. She's been worried sick."

"Does she know you've been pinching from her washing line?" His lips curved up into a handsome smile that made his short beard crease into two large dimples on either side of his face. I rolled my eyes at him and looked away certain that my cheeks would flush red at any moment.

He reached up and grabbed my hand. I thought it was perhaps an effort to stop me from cleaning his face but he just held onto it and so I clenched my fingers tightly around his. Despite his attempts to joke with me, there was a fear that sat in his eyes and I braced myself for the inevitable moment when the panic and realisation of the situation would set in.

"You're alright," I said, hoping to keep him calm. "The worst of it is over and Nellie will get you fixed in no time."

He remained silent and for a moment we just stared at each other, completely still, offering silent comfort to each other. It was only as Nellie approached us a few moments later that I finally pulled my hand away.

"Here, take this for me, Gwyn," she said as she came up beside me. She squeezed two drops from a dark bottle into a glass and poured some whiskey over it. She passed it to me and put a hand behind Gwyn's head, propping him forward slightly while I raised the mixture to his lips. "That should help," she said, and then she scurried off again.

He swallowed the mixture and scrunched up his face in disgust as it washed over his tongue. When he was done he opened his mouth as if to prove that it was gone and I let out a little chuckle at the silliness of it. "So, what brings you to Cwm Newydd, Tom?

"Just on the lookout for unguarded laundry lines," I replied with a smirk. "I need some new socks for a complete set before I can move on to the next town."

"Well hopefully you don't find them too soon," he said and another silence fell between us as he smiled at me.

"GWYN? GWYN!" Mair's voice echoed down the corridor and she was soon at the door demanding to be let in. The women guarding the entrance made a valiant effort to keep her in the corridor but neither was a match for Mair and she barged her way through and over to where we sat.

"I'll leave you to it," I said as she gripped her brother's hand and began talking to him in Welsh. "It was nice to meet you, Gwyn."

His eyes trailed me as I rose to my feet. "See you soon, I hope."

Another two bodies were being taken out as I looked around for what I could do next. Piles of dirty bandages lay strewn across the floor and bowls of bloody water were dotted around where people had been treated, leaving me having to tiptoe around them to get to the back of the room. Spotting Daniel with his hands in his lap instead of on his wound as instructed, I made my way over to him

"I thought I said to keep that pressed to your head," I said as I kneeled beside him. He had his back against the wall and his head leaned against a bookshelf. I reached for his hand that lay upturned on the floor beside him, the bandage I'd given him sitting loosely in his palm, and the instant I touched him my blood ran cold.

"Daniel?"

I leaned in and gave him a little nudge to the arm, but he didn't move.

"Daniel, wake up, buddy," I pleaded.

I gripped his shoulders and shook him firmly but his eyes stayed closed and his head rocked back and forth, lifeless.

"Daniel, please wake up," I begged and I felt the first tears begin to run down my face. Despite my pleas, he remained motionless and I sank to the floor beside him. I scooped him up and held him close to me, his arms falling to my sides, and I sobbed for him. I sobbed for all of them as I rocked back and forth with his young body in my arms in the corner of classroom two.

When they came for Daniel's body they didn't bring a stretcher with them, instead, Mr Jones cradled him and carried him out by hand. He was the youngest of the victims. Fifty-three men and boys lost their lives in total, eighteen of them from our village.

Seven

In the aftermath of the disaster there was a quiet over Cwm Newydd. The days had brought constant rain, the grey skies the perfect backdrop to the mood of the people mourning their loved ones. In the village, people went about their business in silence, nobody quite knowing what to say to anybody else and it seemed even the birds had dimmed their song in quiet respect.

Having no mourning attire, and no money to buy suitable clothing, Mair had insisted on lending me more of her brother's clothes and I had summoned me to the cottage to collect them.

When I arrived, she had set aside some space in her front room for a large barrel that she'd filled with steaming water, and was ready in her aprons.

"What's this about?" I asked, confused.

"I mean it in the nicest way possible, Tom, but you smell. Have you changed those clothes since I gave them to you?"

I brought my arm up to my face and took a sniff. She was right and I was mortified. Mrs Hopkin had given me one of Jack's old shirts when mine got covered in blood but otherwise, I'd spent four days in the same clothes. I didn't like to ask Mrs Hopkin to wash them and had no idea how to do it for myself without a washing machine.

"Straight in there to change. "I've laid some clothes out ready for you."

I manoeuvred around the clutter of the living room and entered the room that I'd changed in when I first met Mair. All was as it was before, except this time the bed was occupied.

"Making a habit of taking my clothes," Gwyn said, smiling at me from the bed as I entered. I'd completely forgotten he would be there so his presence in the room took me by surprise."

"Gwyn, how are you feeling?" I asked.

"Sore," he said, pulling back the blanket to show me the bruising on his ribs. It had turned from red to a blueish purple.

"Make sure your sister looks after you," I said.

"Seems like she's looking after the both of us." He nodded towards the pile of clothes Mair had left on the dresser for me and I followed his gaze. "Airing out my best funeral suit for you too, she is. You must be her new favourite. She does love having someone to fuss over."

"I'm sorry," I said, feeling bad about having to commandeer his wardrobe again. "I don't have anything else to wear and she insisted."

"It's fine," he replied. "I won't be needing them anyway. They're all yours."

Feeling a little embarrassed for having to change into his clothes while he was right there, I turned my back to the bed and began to undress. When the silence became unbearable I tried to make small talk.

"Has the doctor been to see you yet?" I asked as I unbuttoned the shirt Mrs Hopkin had given me and dropped it to the floor. I could see his reflection in the mirror that hung from the back of the door, looking at me as we spoke.

"Not yet, but I don't think we will call on him. Nellie said there isn't much we can do for a cracked rib and we could do with saving the sixpence now I won't be working."

With no option for privacy, I dropped my trousers to the floor and stepped out of them.

"What the devil are those?" Gwyn suddenly shouted. "I've never seen drawers like it?"

I turned around unsure what he was referring to, to see him pointing back at my underwear. I hadn't considered what my elasticated black boxer briefs might look like to someone who'd never seen such a garment.

"They're, um," I stuttered, "they're a new style everyone is wearing in Cambridge. I guess they haven't reached Wales yet?" I don't think I sounded particularly convincing but it was the best excuse I could come up with.

"I should hope they never do," he laughed, then winced from the pain it brought. "They can't be at all comfortable, all tight like that."

"They're all I have," I admitted with a shrug.

"Here, take some of mine from the second drawer, and for goodness sake don't show them to my sister."

I laughed as I rummaged through the drawer he'd directed me to for something more period-appropriate.

"And these are better?" I asked, turning to him and holding up what could best be described as knee-length bloomers."

"Yes," he said, as I turned away from him to put them on. "Much better."

I quickly changed into the rest of the outfit Mair had set aside, which was nearly identical to the one that I had just removed, but with a slight colour difference, and scooped up the waistcoat, shirt and trousers that she intended to wash.

"I hope you feel better soon, Gwyn," I said as I reached for the door.

"Already do," he replied, and I made my exit, leaving him to rest.

"Grab that dolly," Mair said as I re-entered the living room. I looked around, bewildered, with no idea what she was talking about. "The stick," she said impatiently, pointing to an item that looked like a miniature stool attached to a broom handle. She proceeded to give me a lesson on how to do laundry. When she was done she took the clothes outside and squeezed them through a contraption of rolling pins and then brought them back in and hung them up around the room to dry.

"Can't I just bring them to you every time?" I said with a cheeky grin as we hung the last of the items.

"Don't even think about it," she replied, throwing a peg at me. "Now, your suit is ready and you can take that with you. Gwyn won't be coming in the morning, so you can escort me to the church. Be here first thing."

We attended a total of fourteen funerals over the next two weeks. Most took place in the village but we also travelled together to Pisgah for the burial of Daniel and his father. With so much going on, discussions of my leaving still hadn't been raised and I continued to sleep in the barn. The Hopkins didn't seem in a rush to send me on my way, though, which worked out well for me because I still had nowhere to go.

I'd created a new routine of putting the ring on each night, twisting and turning it until I fell asleep in my sheets in the hay. Then each morning I'd wake up in the same spot and the disappointment would set in again. I'd even spent an evening with a bottle of Mr Hopkin's whiskey thinking that perhaps I needed to be drunk for it to work but all I got for my efforts was a hangover. Whatever had made it work the first time wasn't working anymore and I'd begun to lose hope.

A few days after the last miner's funeral, a meeting was called at the church and it was decided that the harvest festival, which had been postponed due to the incident at the mine, was to be rescheduled as a low-key affair to raise spirits throughout the village. The fields had long since been cut and the church given their portion of produce for the season, but not wanting to miss the opportunity to take even more from the people, the vicar organised for the barn in the field adjoining the church to be decked out for a muted celebration.

Mrs Hopkin got straight to work planning, baking goods and organising the household with jobs. Mine was to help gather scrap wood and kindling along with two other men from the village to be built into a bonfire and I used the excuse to call to Mair's house, which I'd found myself doing quite frequently since the disaster.

"Thomas! What a surprise," she said with a roll of her eyes as I let myself into the cottage.

Despite her teasing, we'd grown quite close and it was at her insistence that I stopped knocking on arrival and just let myself in. I had a feeling, though, that she was just tired of getting up and down to answer the door to me all the time.

She had her head buried in a book at the table and I made my way through the clutter of her home to take a seat. "Good Housekeeping?" I asked and she looked at me confused. I knew immediately that she wouldn't get the joke but I chuckled at the effort nonetheless.

"Holmes," she said, shutting the book and setting it aside. "So, what bad luck have I brought on myself to receive this visit? I wasn't expecting to see you until tonight."

"I'm on a mission to find things to burn on the bonfire." I looked around the room and back to her with a smirk. "Your living room was the first place I thought of."

"And maybe we could sit you in the middle of it," she replied with a slap to my hand. "I'm sure I've got something in the yard, let me go look. Make yourself useful and put some water on to boil."

She disappeared through the door to the back of the house while I moved to the stove to prepare a pot. Mrs Hopkin would never let me anywhere near the stove at the farm but Mair made sure I learned quickly how she takes her tea and I'd gotten quite used to the slower way of doing it. I'd still have preferred to have a kettle and a teabag but the end result was much the same.

I'd only just poured the water from the jug when Gwyn called out from the bedroom, taking me by surprise. "*Mair, allwch chi fy helpu?*"

I set the pot over the heat and took the few steps to the bedroom door and poked my head in. "Oh shit," I said, seeing him sitting in the tub. I quickly retreated and pulled the door closed. "Sorry, Gwyn. Mair's out the back. I'll go get her."

"It's ok," he called back. "You'll do. Come here."

I took a deep breath and then edged back into the room keeping my eyes on the ceiling. "What's up?" I asked, trying to be casual while he sat naked in the portable tin bath. It was like an elongated bucket with handles at each end that he barely seemed to fit in it. It certainly didn't hold enough water to keep him covered.

"I can't get out," he said and I began to laugh. "I'm not stuck, you arse. It's my ribs." He flicked his hand through the water splashing me as I tried to duck out of the way. "Give me a hand."

"I dunno, maybe I should just leave you there," I joked.

"How could you be so cruel to a wounded man?" he said, pouting his lips at me. "Come on or I'll waste away."

I edged towards him and grabbed hold of his outstretched hand while trying to keep my eyes averted. He let out a sharp moan as I pulled him to his feet and in my fear that I'd hurt him I almost let go of his hand.

"Can you grab me the towel?"

"Are you ok?" I asked as I handed it to him. "It sounded like you were hurt."

"It's not so bad," he said, twisting his body to me and showing off the bruise on his side with no shame or embarrassment about his state of undress. The bruise had shrunk but still looked fairly sore. "It hurt a lot less than when Mair tried helping me. What a performance that was. Walked in here backwards, she did. I ended up having to tip myself over the side and climb onto the bed just to get to my feet."

I laughed again as I imagined the scene, though I felt a little bad for his struggle. "Well, I'm happy I could help. Do you need anything else?"

He stepped out of the tub and ran the towel over his hair leaving a puddle of water at his feet. "I'll shout if I do," he said with a smirk, and I turned for the door.

I pulled his bedroom door shut and leaned up against it, closing my eyes and letting out a long breath. If it weren't for the sounds of Mair shuffling around outside I may have just stayed there and let my mind run wild but I turned back to the fire instead to prepare the tea.

I stared around the room while I waited for her return and had an overwhelming urge to start tidying up. The house wasn't dirty by any means but the clutter that covered every surface and every inch of floor space made my skin itch and I wanted nothing more than to get it all organised and ordered. My compulsion was only quelled when she barged back through the door with her arms filled with a pile of wood so high that I couldn't see her face over the top of it.

"Do you think this will do?" she called from behind the stack. "I'm not helping you carry it down there, mind."

"It's more than enough," I said, relieving her of the pile. "I think I'll skip the tea though, and get this moved now if that's alright? You're both coming later?"

"Aye, we'll be there," she replied.

"You're not cooking, are you?" I asked with a wink as I headed for the door.

"Get going," she shouted after me, "before you get one of those boards across your backside."

Work on the bonfire had begun in earnest and within an hour I'd managed to build it over eight feet tall and nearly as wide. My fellow wood gatherers, Jenkin and Robert, had dropped their hauls off and then sat on the grass refusing to speak in English so I'd roped in Sophia to come down and help me complete it.

"I thought it would be taller," she said in her usual direct manner as she squinted up at it from beside me.

"I can't get up any higher," I replied.

She hitched her skirts up and began stomping towards the pyre. "Well, I can."

I grabbed her by the shoulders to pull her back and she let out a huff. "I don't think your mother would be too happy to have you climbing over that."

"No, I would not," Mrs Hopkin said as she came up beside us with a tray of small loaves. People from the village had already started to gather in the barn, decorating it with ribbons and figures made of straw and tables had been set up inside for the food, most of which seemed to be coming from the Hopkin's pantry.

"I can do it," Sophia protested. "Howell climbs on things all the time and he's rubbish. Please, Mam?"

Mrs Hopkin's eyes went wide and a single stare at her daughter brought her to silence. "I wish I'd had more notice," she said, holding up her tray to me. "I haven't made nearly as much as I'd have liked."

Teddy and Betty walked by with another two trays of food and I raised an eyebrow to Mrs Hopkin. She shifted uncomfortably and stared down at the loaves. "I better get these set down before Mrs Greenslade takes up the whole table with her apple pies. She will insist on showing off. You two stay out of trouble."

I looked down at Sophia who gave me a mischievous grin as her mother walked off towards the barn. "I could do it, you know," she said. "Climbing isn't just for boys."

"And neither is tag," I said, and I pushed her onto the grass and ran off into the field. In an instant she was on her feet and chasing behind me, laughing wildly. I sprinted through the grass weaving in and out of the villagers on their way to the barn before coming to a stop just seconds before a head-on collision with Arthur Morgan.

I stood straight, keeping my eyes on him as he stared at me with a smirk across his face. A second later Sophia ran behind me and whacked me in the back making me shuffle forward another step, almost colliding with him. He immediately reached up and put his hands roughly on my chest and said something in Welsh causing Sophia's mouth to drop open.

"That's a horrible thing to say," she said, grabbing hold of my hand as though to protect me. "Say sorry, right now."

He looked down at her with a snarl. "Run along, little girl," he said, and she stepped forward and kicked him hard in the shin.

He raised the back of his hand to her and I pulled her behind me, stepping forward again into the path of his swing but he pulled back before it connected.

"Hitting little girls? Is that what you do? Such a big man."

"Maybe I should hit you again," he said, and the smug look on his face made me want to hit him back right there in front of everyone. He let out a nasally snort and took a step to the side but turned to face me as he walked off into the field. "I'm sure I'll get another chance soon enough."

"I probably shouldn't have kicked him," Sophia said as we watched him walk off.

"Probably not," I replied. "But well done, anyway." I smiled at her and she let go of my hand and scampered off into the field.

Wanting to avoid an altercation I decided to steer clear of the barn for a while and I leaned against the open gate and watched the last of the villagers coming down the lane. The sun had already gone down beyond the hill casting a blueish-grey shade over the village as the evening set in and some of them were carrying lamps to light their way. Amongst the many faces, I noticed Nellie and her fiancé heading toward me and I reached out to give them a wave.

I'd had a chance to briefly meet Gethin over the previous few weeks but each time I saw him we were at a funeral which had left little option for us to become properly acquainted. He seemed a nice chap, and totally smitten with Nellie, but there was an aloofness to him that made me wonder if he perhaps found himself a little out of his depth in the village and on the farm. It was something that I could identify with and, short on friends, I hoped it might be something we might find we had in common.

"Waiting for someone?" Nellie asked as they approached.

"Just watching the world go by," I replied.

Gethin held a hand out to me, which I shook, envious of the fact he'd worn gloves as I stood there freezing in the chilly Autumn air. "You look cold, old boy," he said. "Come, we'll find some seats close to the fire ready for when they light it."

Inside the barn, people had already made a start tucking into the food and drink. Several of the residents had made pies and pastries, loaves and stews and there were two large urns filled with cider made from apples grown in the village. A separate table had been set aside where offerings were collected for the church and Mr Davies from the pub sat beside it playing tunes on his recorder while people clapped along. For the first time in weeks, everyone seemed to be having fun.

I sat at a table with Gwyn and Mair, Nellie, Gethin and Betty and tried to relax while Arthur cast glances in our direction for the duration of the evening. He had placed himself in the centre of the barn not eating, not drinking and not really engaging with anyone, and I was left to wonder why he'd even bothered to show up. A woman had sat with him for a while who seemed to enjoy his company and when she finally left his side she made a beeline for our table.

"*Noswaith dda*, Ms Griffiths," she said to Mair as she dragged a seat from the next table and sat down in the gap between us.

"*Noswaith dda*, Mrs Wilkes," Mair replied, but her tone was blunt and she didn't make eye contact, instead sitting with her arms folded and her eyes trained on me. Mair's face had a way of perfectly expressing whatever thought happened to be in her head at any given time. Right then it was telling the world that she had no patience for Mrs Wilkes but the woman either didn't notice or didn't care.

She was dressed in all her finery, head to toe in black and her skirt ruffled outwards taking up much of the space between us. Had it been any other colour it could have passed as a ball gown and its elaborateness stood in stark contrast to everyone else's modest attire.

"*A phwy efallai y byddwch chi?*" she said, extending a hand to me and my eyes darted around the table for help.

Mair rolled her eyes back and shook her head. "She wants to know who you are."

"I've heard so much about you." the woman said, switching to English.

"Then you know he doesn't speak *Cymraeg*," Mair snapped and Gwyn turned away to mask a laugh.

"Doesn't he speak for himself?" she asked, letting out a small chuckle. "How peculiar."

The wrinkles around her eyes and mouth lifted as she smiled and her long nose and angular features reminded me of the Wicked Witch of the West, the thought of which caused me to involuntarily smile back.

"I hope it's good things you've heard," I said.

"Well…," Mrs Wilkes trailed off, offering no further explanation. "I should imagine you'll be leaving us for London again soon."

Mair looked furious and opened her mouth to speak but Gwyn immediately yanked her arm to stop her. Mrs Wilkes just continued to stare at me, studying my face as though trying to work me out and the more I stared back the more she continued to grin at me.

A commotion in the corner of the barn pulled both of our eyes away and without a word to any of us, Mrs Wilkes darted from her seat to go and investigate. I recognised the sound of the shouting immediately and watched as Mr Hopkin stood up and dragged Teddy from the room by his scruff in front of everyone.

Teddy still didn't particularly like having to speak to me and for the most part I kept out of his way, but I'd noticed on the days where I helped out around the farm that his relationship with his father was particularly strained and his Mr Hopkin had given him more than his fair share of clips around the ear when he spoke back.

I didn't know if it was just the angsty awkward attitude of a fifteen-year-old or if there was something more deep-rooted, and it wasn't my place to ask, but whenever the two of them were in a room together it was almost certain that sparks would fly and it seemed this evening was to prove no different. His feet barely touched the ground as his father dragged him across the barn and threw him through the door.

Their voices trailed off as they got further across the field and Nellie and Betty both sat in silence looking embarrassed. "I better go and see what's wrong," Nellie said with exasperation and both she and Gethin got up to go after her father.

Mair leaned in close to me and whispered into my ear, "He's a good man, Mr Hopkin, but he's not half hard on that boy. He can do no right." When she pulled her head away again Sophia popped her face in between ours.

"Are you two going to kiss?"

Mair recoiled looking disgusted and Betty and Gwyn both broke out into laughter.

"Mam says he's sweet on you and that's why he keeps coming around to your house all the time."

I cast my eyes towards Gwyn and then immediately looked away when I spotted him staring back.

"He comes to my house," Mair said, scooping Sophia into her arms and tickling her, "because he hasn't got any friends and I'm the only one who will put up with him."

"I'm his friend," she replied, smoothing back the long blonde hairs that had come loose when Mair attacked. "It's not his fault that he's English."

"Well thank you very much," I said as everyone around the table began to laugh. I sort of admired her lack of filter, even if I did seem to catch the brunt end of it more often than not.

"Come on," Betty said as she rose to her feet. "They're about to light the fire."

It didn't take long for the barn to empty and we were soon sat in groups around the bonfire as Mr Davies stepped up to light it. It took a few tries but the wood eventually caught, bringing warmth to the crowd and casting an orange glow over everyone as embers floated skyward.

An older man, who had been propped against the door of the barn knocking back pints of cider for much of the evening, took advantage of the break in the music and began to sing. By the time he'd hit the second line of his song most of the people sitting around us had joined in.

"You know they've had too much to drink when they start singing," Mair said, getting up from the ground. "I'm going to get more food before I end up throwing myself on the fire."

I listened in awe of the growing choir around me as their voices all came together as one. "It's beautiful."

Gwyn smiled and scooted along the grass getting closer to me. "It's called *Myfanwy*. She was a rich and beautiful Welsh maiden who longed to be adored. A poor bard wrote a ballad of her beauty and his love for her but she rejected him for another and he wandered the woods for the rest of his life singing songs of unrequited love."

The sound of a hundred voices singing in unison seemed to echo off the hills and fill the air around us and it felt electric. "I've never heard anything like it," I said, and I had to turn my head from him as my eyes began to well up and goosebumps covered my skin. There was a sadness to their voices, despite their beauty, and while I didn't understand a single word of what they sang it filled me with a longing for home.

"Tom, are you ok?"

I turned to face him and forced a smile onto my face. "It would have been my birthday today," I said.

"*Would* have been?" he asked curiously.

"I mean it *is* my birthday."

"I can't believe you didn't say anything. Does Mair know? Or Mrs Hopkin?"

I shook my head and tried to smile again. "I didn't feel like celebrating. It's just making me realise how much I'm missing my brother. It's his birthday too."

"Twins?" Gwyn said, looking surprised. "And how old are you today?"

"Twenty-seven."

"Ah, I remember twenty-seven," he said, as though it were lifetimes ago. "They were good times."

"How old are you, then?" I asked curiously.

"Twenty-nine."

I laughed and gave him a nudge in the arm. "Old man."

"Not too old," he replied with a wink. An easy silence fell between us as we watched the fire and listened to the end of the song. He had a way of making me feel at ease and the more I got to know him the less sad I felt about being stuck there.

"Shall we go and find my sister?" he asked, and I gave him a nod and sprang to my feet.

We found Mair back inside the barn sitting alone with a mountain of food and looking happier than she'd been all night. "The singing's stopped then? It'll be fighting next, just you watch."

"I see Arthur is still sucking the fun out of the room," I said as we sat. We all turned to look at him at the same time and he sent a sneer in our direction and then aimed it at Betty as she brushed past him to get some food.

"Tom's got something exciting to tell you," Gwyn said, and I looked over at him unsure of what he was talking about.

"You're going back to London?" Mair replied, pretending to act excited. "You've worked out how to do your laundry? You've learned how to count change?"

"It's his birthday."

"Oh my god, Tom, why didn't you say?" she replied holding a hand to her mouth to stop the contents from spilling out. "I feel bad for teasing you now. Almost."

"It's your birthday?" Betty asked excitedly from the food table, and as she turned to face us some food slipped from her plate onto Arthur's leg leaving a streak from her knee to his boot.

"I'm really sorry," she panicked, and as she reached out to wipe it off he bolted upright sending her stumbling back, terrified.

"You idiot," he shouted. Betty's nose scrunched up and her face glowed a hot red and she looked like she was about to cry.

His raised voice caught the attention of some of the people outside who began to wander back in to see what was going on. The audience only seemed to make him angrier and he took a step toward her in a rage. I instinctively kicked an empty crate from the floor into his path and as his foot slipped through the wooden slats it rebounded against his shin and he stumbled forward, tumbling to the ground in front of everyone.

For a moment you could hear a pin drop but the silence was broken when Mair slammed a hand down on the table and began to laugh hysterically. As Arthur stood up and brushed himself off several others joined in too and with a look of contempt he fled from the barn followed quickly by Mrs Wilkes who rushed off after him.

As soon as he'd made his exit Betty rushed back to the table and sank low in her seat as though she was trying to disappear from view.

"Are you ok?" I asked, and she nodded, appearing more embarrassed than anything.

"He won't forget that in a hurry," Mair added.

"That's what worries me," I replied.

As the night wore on and the fire died down the people of the village made their way home leaving just a few of us left to enjoy the evening. Mrs Hopkin had allowed Betty to stay out on the provision that I didn't let her walk home alone and just a little after eleven we began the trek back to the farm.

"Did you have a nice night?" I asked as we crossed the street near the school. Betty gave me a nod and the briefest of smiles before turning her head away and staring off into the dark. "I've never been to a harvest festival before. We don't have anything like it in the village I'm from."

"Do you miss London?"

"I'm not from Lo-" I began as she burst into a fit of giggles and covered her mouth in an attempt to hide it. "Oh, she jokes," I said with a surprised laugh. "I'm learning more about you every day."

"Thank you for letting me stay with you this evening," she said. "I had a marvellous time."

"It must have been nice not having to look after the little ones for a change" I replied.

"I don't mind," she said, nervously. "I rather think that that's my lot. My parents need help and Nellie and Nan are always so busy with work."

"But what about what you want?" I asked, but she fell silent and looked away again.

The first few drops of rain began to fall as we left the road and took the path to the farm. We picked up our pace to avoid the incoming downpour and as we got to the gate a figure stepped out in front of us.

"Betty, go inside," I said as Arthur's face came into view.

He stepped into her path, blocking her route to the house and she dropped back beside me. "I'll scream," she said, and her voice had more confidence in it than I'd ever heard.

"You think you can make a fool of me?" he asked, ignoring Betty's threat and moving slowly towards us. "Do you have any idea who I am?"

"Not really," I replied, which only served to anger him. He clenched his jaw and took another step toward me.

"I mean it," Betty said.

"I'm just here to offer a friendly reminder that I can make things very difficult for all of you in this rat-infested shithole." He barged between us, knocking us both out of his way. "Just remember that."

"Hasn't this gone far enough?" I called out as he walked away, and he spun on his heel and raced back towards me making Betty jump back with a yelp.

"You've no idea," he spat back. "This is far from over."

"I don't even know you," I said, exasperated with the situation. "Whatever your problem is, you need to get over it. This is ridiculous."

He reached out and grabbed my collar with both hands, pulling my face just centimetres from his. Every breath made the skin on my face clammy and I could feel his heartbeat against my chest. Betty immediately started hitting out at his arm with the sides of her fists but he didn't acknowledge it at all, just kept his focus on me.

He leaned into my ear, resting his cheek against mine, and whispered, "I know you know where she is."

I pulled my head away and he forced his hands against my chest and pushed me back, sending me onto my arse through the gate. "We'll talk again soon, Tom."

As he made his retreat down the hill Betty came to my side and helped me to my feet.

"Shall I go and get father?" She asked as she came to my side.

"No," I replied, brushing myself off. "I'm going to deal with him myself.

Eight

I woke up with a start to the sound of a bell ringing.

"Milk," I shouted, then pulled the sheets up over my head to try and get back to sleep.

Every morning the cart would pull up at the gate beside the barn and the bell would ring for Teddy to run out with the urns to get them filled by the milkman. Billy the Milk, they called him. In fact, I'd come to realise that nearly everyone in the village was given some sort of title to distinguish them during discussions.

Dai the Pub, Printer Rhod, Fat John who lived two farms over and Thin John, otherwise known as Mr Hopkin. Then there was Thomas the Steps because his house was the only one in the village that had steps to the door, and Morgan Twice on account of his name being Morgan Morgan. Even Nellie was known around the village as Nellie the Post. I dreaded to think what I might have been known as.

The bell rang again and I threw the sheets off me in a huff. "Teddy, get the bloody milk," I shouted, and then it occurred to me that I was never usually asleep when Billy did his rounds and also it was a Sunday. We didn't have milk on a Sunday.

"Shift your arse," a voice called out from below and I scrambled from my sheets and hung my head through the hatch, spotting Gwyn standing below. He smiled up at me and I immediately began fighting against gravity as I tried to smooth my hair out to look less like I'd just woken up.

"What are you doing here?" I asked. "What time is it? Where the hell did you get a bell from?"

"We're going on an adventure," he said with a grin and I couldn't stop myself from smiling back at him. "Unless you want to go to church with the rest of them?"

I quickly threw my clothes on and as I reached for the ring to stash it in its little cubby, I realised that I'd gone to bed for the first time without putting it on. An immediate feeling of guilt hit me but I shook it off and climbed down the ladder to Gwyn.

"New shirt?" I said. I immediately wanted to kick myself for noticing and crawl back under the sheets for saying it out loud, but he just smiled and waved it off. "So where are we going?"

"I thought I'd give you a tour of the village."

"I've seen it. There's only about twelve houses and a pub."

He laughed at me and swung the barn door open. "But you haven't had a tour of all the secret spots and fun stuff."

Intrigued, I smiled again and followed him out into the yard. "Are you sure you're ok to be walking so much?"

"I'll be fine," he replied and he managed to climb the stile onto the road without too much difficulty. "Now, over here we've got some sheep. Don't get close though, they've got razor-sharp teeth."

"Ooh, terrifying," I joked. "So where are we really going?"

"Just seeing where our feet take us," he said as he climbed the stile into the field on the opposite side of the road.

The ground had gone soft and soggy during the rain overnight and my boots and the bottom of my trousers had gotten caked in mud almost immediately. I took a slow path across the hill trying to avoid the soggiest areas but every time I put a foot on the ground I wondered if it would be the step that sent me flying on my arse.

"If you fall, you're going to hurt yourself," I said.

"Ah, I'll be fine," he replied. "Us Welsh were made to walk these hills. It's you city boys that need to be careful."

Just as he said it my right foot slipped and while I managed to not crash straight to the floor, I did end up crouched over with both hands on the ground. Slushy mud squished through my fingers as my legs and arms started sliding outward from my body. Every time I tried to get some traction to propel myself upright, I just slipped more and was seconds from going face-first into the dirt.

"Well, well," Gwyn said with a chuckle as he tucked his arm underneath me. As he pulled me upwards he let out a small moan and I tried to take my weight from him quickly.

"Are you ok?" I asked, brushing the mud from my hands. He gave me a nod but I wasn't sure how honest he was being. "We can go back?"

"No, no, it's fine. Just a twinge. Come on."

We made our way across the field chatting about life in the village and I told him an edited version of what life was like back home. He told me about the people who owned the land we were on and showed me where a pig had chased Mair across the field when they were kids. Everything he spoke about had such passion behind it and it was obvious how much he loved the place. I could have listened to him talking for hours.

Our route took us out of the field and across the most southerly farm in the village which sat about half a mile south of the church. A lot of the buildings looked run down and most of the fields stood empty of both crops and livestock, but it was obvious that someone still lived in the house.

A few metres up the road from the farm we came to a clearing in the bushes where a slight path had been trodden into the ground. We followed alongside it for about a minute as it meandered along a small stream before coming to a stop where the water hit a drop and cascaded into a small waterfall about two metres deep.

"It's pretty here," I said as I made a seat for myself on a rock.

Hills flanked us on either side and a long valley stretched out nearly as far as I was able to see. It seemed to have every touch of landscape imaginable, with trees and lowlands, hills and streams, and I couldn't believe somewhere so beautiful was right on our doorstep.

"It's one of my favourite places," he replied. "I wanted to show it to you. My dad used to call it '*Y bryn i'r nef*'.

"What does it mean?" I asked, bringing my attention back to Gwyn.

"The hill to heaven."

I tried to imitate what he'd called it in Welsh but it came out a mess and I could feel my cheeks burning up as he laughed at me. "Have you always been able to speak English?" I asked.

"Now that's a long story," he replied.

"We've got time."

"Ah, here we go," he said with a smile, and he settled in on the rock beside me and began to talk. "My mam insisted that we learn to speak English but my father was dead against it. She thought it would give us better prospects as we got older but my dad thought it shameful. It was bad enough we had to speak it in school, he didn't want it anywhere near his house."

"Why is that?" I asked. Sophia had said something to me when I first arrived about speaking English at school and Mrs Hopkin seemed less than pleased about it, but I'd never considered that it was some sort of rule.

"Your men up in London. Nobody speaks Welsh in schools anywhere in Wales. Not openly, anyway. Mair took to English really quickly. She's a smart one but she hated it. She was very much on my dad's side and didn't see why she had to speak differently to everyone else. One day she got caught speaking Welsh when we were at school and had to wear the Not. Got a whipping from the mistress and a whipping from my dad. He might not have wanted her speaking English but he didn't want her breaking rules either."

"What's a 'Not'?"

"A heavy lump of wood on a rope. They'd hang it around your neck if they caught you speaking Welsh and make you wear it for the day. Then, at the end of the day, anyone wearing one would be lined up at the door for a whipping on the knuckles. You didn't do it twice."

"That's awful."

"It was the same at church. We were never a very religious family but my father wouldn't be preached at in English so he used to cart us off every week to the Methodist chapel in Pisgah until they started using Welsh again in the church in the village.

"But what about the rest of the village? Don't they feel the same?"

"Some do. Most just want an easy life. Not everyone has the means to go elsewhere and for lots of people, it doesn't matter what language their prayers are in as long as someone's listening. My father was just stuck in his ways. When I went to work in the mine and he found out that we couldn't speak Welsh there he was furious. If our farm was still up and running he'd have dragged me home within a day, but we needed the money."

I shifted about, uncomfortable on the rock but engrossed in his stories, and unintentionally got closer to Gwyn. Rather than move over, however, he seemed to move towards me a little and I felt a rush of nervousness flutter in my stomach.

"Wouldn't it have made more sense to speak Welsh at work?"

"The mines bring people for work, and people come from all over. Most of the ones in this area are owned by Englishmen so it was English speaking only."

"No wonder your father was mad."

"He wasn't the only one. There were and are many like him, trying to push back, to keep our traditions and customs and language. We were all raised on tales of what was and what could be and our words, our language, is the most important part of all."

The change of perspective made me suddenly understand why some people, like Jenkin the previous day, had been so hesitant to speak to me in English even if they could. Why should they?

"Teach me," I said, taking both of us by surprise. I hadn't entirely thought it through and I'd blurted it out on impulse but I meant it, especially when that wide smile of his spread across his face.

"What? Now?"

"Just some basics. Even if I can only say 'hello' and 'thank you', it would be a start."

"Well, I'm no teacher, that's for sure." He rubbed his forehead like he was already regretting it and I gave him my best pleading eyes. "But I guess we can give it a go. And I'm handy with a cane if you get out of line."

We sat next to the stream for over an hour while Gwyn tried to teach me some words and phrases but it seemed like we spent most of the time laughing. Mostly it was him laughing at my efforts to pronounce strings of letters that seemed to have no logical reason for being next to each other, but the time flashed by in an instant. When the church bell rang from the village and he said it was time to go I found myself disappointed to have to leave.

"We should come back here sometime," he suggested as we started to walk back along the stream.

"I'd like that," I replied.

We walked in silence for a little bit and every time I turned to him he seemed to be deep in thought so despite craving the chance to prolong our discussions I remained quiet and gathered my own thoughts. Since I'd first met Gwyn we'd become fast friends and I liked the time we spent together. More than that, I'd come to look forward to seeing him. The day spent walking and talking with him had been my favourite in a very long time and really solidified the feelings I'd had since I'd arrived in Wales that I'd been doing my life before I got here all wrong.

"Tom," he said firmly, finally breaking the silence as though he were about to say something serious. He stopped in his tracks and turned to me, setting his foot down in a particularly boggy patch of grass. As if it was happening in slow motion his eyes immediately went wide as his leg went out from under him. I instinctively reached out to stop him from falling but he grabbed hold of my arm awkwardly and his whole weight pulled down on me, sending us both crashing into the dirt.

Every inch of me was covered in mud and the more I rolled around trying to get enough grip to stand upright, the worse I was making it. Gwyn groaned beside me and I swiped the sludge from my face and saw him gripping his side. Without thinking I scrambled towards him and ran my hand along his stomach, bringing my face close to his.

"Oh my god, are you ok?" I asked.

"I'm fine," he said, and he burst out laughing. "It only hurts a little. You look ridiculous."

"You don't look so great yourself," I said, eyeing him up and down. He'd gotten just as filthy as I had and as we scanned the damage, we both noticed my hand still rubbing up and down on the side of his body.

"We need to get cleaned up," I said, pulling away quickly. "I can't go home looking like this. I don't even have anything to change into."

"Come on," he said. "Pull me up. We'll go to mine and get sorted out."

Around an hour later we were back on the road towards the farm. Mair was out when we got to the cottage so we quickly changed out of the filthy clothes and Gwyn heated water for a bath. He was a perfect gentleman, leaving me alone in the room while I got cleaned up, and then he let me borrow even more of his clothes to go home in.

"You really didn't have to walk me back," I said as we neared the gate. "You must be worn out."

"It's ok. I left my bell there anyway," he said, and we both burst out laughing.

"When we got to the back door I paused and turned to face him. "I've had a really nice day."

"I'm glad," he replied, with that smile that kept making my stomach flutter. I turned to push the door open and he leaned in close behind me. "Happy birthday."

A crowd of cheers went up as I stepped inside the kitchen and I froze on the spot, overwhelmed. Mrs Hopkin stood front and centre and immediately grabbed my face, planting a kiss on my cheek.

"Happy birthday, my love," she said. She kept my face gripped in her hands as she leaned back to take a look at me. "You kept us waiting long enough. He was supposed to have you home ages ago."

"My fault," he said, stepping into the kitchen behind me, and she swiped at him with her tea towel.

The rest of the family had all gathered around the table and even Teddy looked less annoyed by my presence than normal.

"I hope you like carrot cake," Mair said, ripping away the cloth that had been covering it on the table.

"You didn't make it, did you?" I said with a grin.

"I don't like you that much," she replied.

"Well, it does need to be edible," Mrs Hopkin said with a cheeky wink. "I did what I could. I didn't have much in the pantry, what with it being a Sunday and you keeping it a secret." She raised her eyebrows at me and it was all the telling off that I needed for not informing her.

"How did you know?" I asked, and all eyes turned to Betty. She giggled nervously then tucked her hands behind her back and dropped her head low.

I felt overwhelmed by the effort they'd all gone to on such short notice and I couldn't stop myself from grinning wildly at everyone. Little white ribbons hung around the table and stretched from the cabinets on either side of the room and on either side of the cake were two plates filled with sandwiches.

I hadn't known any of them for very long but the kindness they'd shown me made me a bit emotional, so I looked at them all staring at me and said proudly with all of my chest, "Dolf," causing the whole room to erupt into laughter.

"Close enough," Gwyn said, giving me a pitiful tap on the back. I turned to him in confusion but it only seemed to make him laugh more.

"I think you mean, '*diolch*'," Sophia said, and I brought my hands up to my face to hide my embarrassment.

"A toast to the old chap?" Gethin called out. He handed me a drink and everyone raced to pick up a cup.

"Dolf," Mair said, raising her glass in the air and the whole family fell about laughing again.

Once we'd demolished the cake the twins had insisted that we play a game. I was unsure of the types of games they might play so I deferred the decision to Howell, who ran from the room and came back with a strip of cloth. He'd chosen blind man's buff.

Unwilling to let her dishes be at the mercy of an idiot in a mask, Mrs Hopkin had ordered us all outside into the yard to play and within moments of stepping foot on the cobbles, Nellie was tying the cloth around my face.

I don't know who it was that grabbed me but they spun me round and round with such force that I worried I might be sick. With the final spin, I was let loose and I had to take a second to let the dizziness subside so that I didn't fall over and smash my head against the floor.

I heard the first clap and I spun around in the direction of the noise, throwing my arms out and reaching wildly to catch someone. Another clap came from the opposite side and I spun again to a chorus of giggles. Every time I thought I was getting somewhere I'd hear a shuffle of feet and another clap in the distance and get turned around again.

By now the family were all laughing and I was finding it easier to track their voices, but they moved faster than I could and I still thrashed about without hitting a target. This continued for several minutes until suddenly I could hear the clicking of heels on the cobbles getting closer to me.

I moved towards the footsteps and clasped my hands onto someone. "Got you," I shouted, and all the laughter around me ceased. I pulled the blindfold from my eyes and a young woman stood in front of me that I'd never seen before.

I took a step back from her as I tried to catch my breath. "I'm sorry," I said, a little embarrassed, and she raised her hand up and slapped me across the face.

Nine

The yard erupted into a fusion of voices as everybody started shouting in Welsh and fussing around me. I brought a hand up to comfort my now reddening cheek and kept my eyes locked on the woman who'd hit me. Despite the obvious anger on her face, she looked like she might burst into a flood of tears at any moment but she remained resolved, jaw clenched and like she might strike out again.

Our staring match was only broken when Mair stepped forward and hooked the woman by the upper arm, yanking her away from me. With her focus now broken, she began to shout back at the crowd leaving me watching on and understanding next to nothing of what was happening.

Mrs Hopkin was the first to break into English, finally giving me some words I could cling to. "Hannah Mary Hopkin, you apologise to that boy this instant."

The woman, now identified to me as the Hopkins third child and second daughter, otherwise known as Nan, took little notice of her mother and yelled back at her in Welsh causing the crowd to devolve into rows once more.

Gethin and Gwyn looked at each awkwardly and backed away from the mass towards the barn, neither wanting to get involved. Mair had no such hesitancy, though, and put herself between Nan and Me leaving us standing at the centre of a cluster of Hopkins.

"What the hell are you playing at, you stupid girl?" Mair shouted at her.

"I've been dismissed," she screamed back, and the first tears inched their way down her cheek. "I've lost my post and it's all because of him."

Mrs Hopkin rushed to her daughter's side and wrapped a loving arm around her shoulder that seemed to soften her for a moment and she tucked her head against her mother's neck as she wept. "What do you mean you've been dismissed?"

Nan pulled her head back and stared at her mother and Mrs Hopkin raised a sleeved hand to her face to wipe away the tears. The yard had fallen silent as they waited for her explanation and I searched around their faces feeling suddenly like an outsider again, hoping to find a look from someone that told me that I wasn't somehow to blame. Avoiding the tension, Betty grabbed Howell and Sophia and dragged them into the house. I wanted to go with them.

"They came to my room this morning and told me to pack," Nan blurted out. "No notice, no pay and no carriage home. I've had to walk all the way from the estate."

"And how is that Tom's fault?" Mair chimed in, her tone still snippy. She folded her arms across her chest and raised her eyebrows to the girl and Nan scowled back. I got a distinct impression there may have already been an element of tension between the two women before today but it was no time to ask. "How do you know it wasn't that mouth of yours getting you into trouble again?"

Nan pulled away from her mother and stepped up to Mair. If these women had been from my own time they'd almost certainly have been hair-pulling by this point but propriety kept them at arm's length and they battled with raised eyebrows and sneering lips instead.

116

"If you must know, Mair, though I don't understand why you make it your business, they told me. They said that while *he* was living here there was no longer a place for me."

"Nan, I'm so sorry," I said. I extended a hand to her as though it might offer some comfort and show her how bad I felt but she just looked at it in disgust.

"I'm going up there," Mr Hopkin said. He'd remained fairly quiet throughout, which was not unusual by any means, but he also liked a strict order and his non-interference as the yard fell into chaos was a source of confusion for me. Perhaps he didn't want to get involved in what he saw as a 'woman's matter', or maybe he thought I deserved to be slapped, but I found it interesting that his ire was piqued only when his decision to have me stay at the farm was mentioned.

"John, don't you go looking for trouble," his wife called after him, but he ignored her pleas and set off across the field towards the gate.

"I'll go with him," Gethin said, edging across the cobbles towards us. "I'll see to it that there's no bother." He kissed Nellie on the cheek and jogged off after his soon-to-be father-in-law.

"Let's get you inside," Mrs Hopkin said, and she guided her daughter towards the house. The rest of the family and Mair followed behind leaving me standing in the yard feeling guilty and stupid. When the last of them disappeared into the kitchen I turned towards the barn, storming past Gwyn and slamming my way through the doors.

My feelings quickly turned to frustration and I kicked a bucket of nails sending them scattering along the floor. With my fists clenched I let out a long low yell that echoed off the walls and I slumped down against a bale and threw my head into my hands.

I looked up when the door to the barn squeaked open again and Gwyn took a few steps toward me. "It's not your fault, you know." He leaned against the hay and eased himself to the floor beside me and I hid my head away again. He was only trying to be nice but I didn't want to hear it. Every time something seemed like it was going well, something else came along to make me hate it there again.

"Tom."

"What?"

"It's not your fault."

"Then whose fault is it?" I snapped, thumping my fist down on the ground. He reached out to grab my hand but I snatched it away before we could connect, no longer in any mood for pleasantries. "I'm sick of it here. I'm sick of Arthur fucking Morgan. I want to go home."

Gwyn looked despondent and let out a sigh and the guilt that made me feel just made me more annoyed. "I'm sorry you feel that way," he said and he made to get up from the floor.

"Don't go," I said, grabbing his arm. "I didn't mean to have a go at you. I just don't understand what his problem is."

"Arthur never came to school with the rest of us," Gwyn said, turning his body towards me. "His family could afford tutors and he stayed at home so he didn't have many friends. His family would bring him down to the village every so often but he was a spoiled little brat who never knew how to play well with others. Everything had to be his way and he would run to tell on us over the simplest of things.

118

Eventually, nobody wanted to play with him and he stopped coming.

"A lot of the property in the village is owned by his parents. As he got older he would walk around the village as though he owned it all and whenever someone would upset him they'd get a knock at the door telling them that rents were going up or that new tenants had been found. Everyone became too scared to answer back and 'no' isn't a word he hears very often, I'd imagine. He wanted you out of this house and didn't get his way, so now he's in a frenzy. He's got no power over you and that makes him mad, so he's taken it out on Nan, instead.

His words brought some sense to the situation and I felt a little easier. I'd met men like Arthur before, so sure of their own importance that they treated everyone else like dirt, but ultimately, they were always miserable underneath it all. Still, I had no sympathy for him. He'd brought all his misery on himself and he could wallow in it as far as I was concerned.

The barn door creaked again and Sophia ducked her head in. "Mam says you're to come inside."

Not wanting to go a second round with Nan and fearing that I'd likely be given my marching orders so that she would be able to ask for her job back, I shook my head at the young girl. "I'll come in a little bit later," I said, and she scooted off back to the house.

I'd barely had time to open my mouth to respond to Gwyn when the door flung open again and Sophia reappeared. "Mam says that if you make her come out here to get you herself then you're going to get a clip round the earhole." She seemed to find this particularly amusing and struggled to recount her mother's words without breaking out into a grin.

"I think it would be wise not to test that," Gwyn said and I feared he was probably right.

When we entered the kitchen, the room was silent and everybody looked miserable. Mrs Hopkin sat on the far side of the table nearest the stove with Nellie and Nan on either side of her, both with their eyes down. Mair sat alone opposite them, arms crossed, chin up and ready for battle. Whatever was about to go down, I hoped that she was on my side.

"Sit down, Tom," Mrs Hopkin said and I perched myself on the chair next to Mair and leaned forward over the table. A pot of tea sat at its centre, Mrs Hopkin's cure-all, but everyone's cups remained untouched. "Nan has something to say."

She kept her head down so I couldn't see her face and let out a huff. "Sorry," she mumbled, only just loud enough for me to hear.

Mrs Hopkin slammed her palm down on the table and Nellie bolted back in her seat. "So help me, Hannah…" she said, leaving her threat hanging in the air.

Nan shuffled forward, straightening herself in her seat and finally met my gaze. She looked just as pissed off as before, but it seemed that the likely cause this time being forced to apologise to me. I didn't want it. I didn't even particularly feel like I deserved it, and sitting there in silence waiting for it made me feel even more awkward because I didn't want any of them to think that I expected it.

"I'm sorry, Tom," she said again, this time with a little more gusto. I offered her the beginnings of a grin hoping to convey to her that it was ok. I didn't love being smacked in the face but at least I could say I was used to it since I'd arrived in the village.

"I understand," I said. "You really don't need to apologise."

"She does," Mair piped up and Nan cast another snarly glance at her.

Mrs Hopkin rolled her eyes in Mair's direction but conceded. "She's right. You had no right to hit Thomas."

"But-"

"No buts," her mother interrupted firmly. "You weren't brought up like that."

"I'm sorry, too," I said, and Mair swung around in her chair casting her unimpressed gaze over me.

"What have you got to be sorry for?" She said, poking me in the arm. "It's Arthur that wants to be sorry. Throwing his weight around again."

"But if I wasn't here…"

"If you weren't here he'd find someone else to pick on," Mrs Hopkin interjected. "He's never had a kind word for this family. It's a wonder she got a position there in the first place."

"My mother is right," Nellie spoke up. "Ever since that business with Jack and Elinor, he's been looking for trouble. His feud with you is just another way to take aim at this house."

I felt a little reassured by their words but Nan remained indignant. "And what am I to do now?" she said, throwing her arms in the air in a somewhat overly dramatic fashion.

"We'll just have to see what tomorrow brings," Mrs Hopkin replied. "Things are always better in the morning."

It was more than an hour later when Mr Hopkin returned to the house. Mair and Gwyn had already left to go home and Nellie had disappeared into the sitting room with her nose buried in one of her medical books. I'd remained at the table, where I spent most of my time if I wasn't sleeping in the barn or helping Mr Hopkin in the field, and racked my brain for things to talk about.

Mrs Hopkin was deep into the preparation of that evening's dinner and Nan had remained with us in the kitchen boring holes into me with her stare. She had refrained from any more outbursts but the tension between us remained frosty so my attempts to speak with her went mostly ignored.

I was about to give it another try when the kitchen door slammed open and Mr Hopkin barged in, closely followed by Gethin. He tore the cap from his head and launched it at the hook on the wall, missing it, then went immediately for the cupboard where he kept his whiskey.

"That swine," he shouted, slamming the bottle down on the counter. "I'd like to wipe the smile right off his face."

"What happened?" Mrs Hopkin asked. She kept her distance and stayed near the pantry while she spoke and Nan moved over to the next seat as he approached the table.

"He had some unsavoury words to say about Jack," Gethin said, taking a seat beside me. "Most of it was quite unrepeatable."

"How dare he." Mrs Hopkin stood tall and pushed out her chest, furious at the idea of Jack receiving criticism. "My Jack is worth ten of that man."

Mr Hopkin knocked back the contents of his glass and poured himself another. "Is he? Running off the way he has, making you worry. That's not much of a man."

"John!" Mrs Hopkin looked deeply upset by his comment but he didn't turn to acknowledge it. He took a big gulp of the whiskey from his glass, slammed it down on the table and then stood, tucked the bottle under his arm and stormed out of the room.

"Whatever's the matter?" Nellie asked as she crossed his path entering the kitchen, but she didn't wait for or expect an answer. "Are you able to stay long?" she asked Gethin as she took a seat opposite us.

"I'm afraid not, darling. School tomorrow."

Gethin's job as a teacher meant that we didn't see much of him throughout the week. He lived a few miles away in the next village and worked in a school that was even further afield but he was hoping to move to Cwm Newydd once he and Nellie were married in the spring and would then commute until a post opened up in the village school.

Aside from the Morgan's, he was the only person I'd come into contact with in the village who showed any sign of having a significant amount of money, and he travelled back and forth in his very own small carriage. I couldn't quite understand why he wanted to move here but until they were married Nellie had to suffice with infrequent visits.

"Are you ok, Mrs Hopkin?" I said as she came to sit with us at the table. Her husband's words about their son seemed to have upset her more than I think any of us realised they would and she leaned on the table with her head in her hands.

"Nan, finish those potatoes," Nellie commanded. Her sister rose from her chair with a sulk but didn't protest.

"Can we get you anything, Mrs Hopkin?" Gethin asked.

"I'll be alright," she said, mustering a smile, "I just need five minutes. Tom, could you be a dear and go and ask Mr Hopkin for the key to the coal shed?"

I got up from the table with a nod and made my way across the kitchen and into the sitting room. With no sign of Mr Hopkin, I went through the passage, past the front door which I'd still yet to see ever be used, and up the stairs to the second floor.

I'd been staying at the farm for nearly a month and in all that time I'd never ventured upstairs. In fact, I'd only ever been beyond the kitchen into the sitting room one time. Despite having more space in their house than most people in the village, the Hopkins seemed to live entirely in the kitchen.

The stairs creaked and groaned as I climbed them and I had to be extra careful not to lose my balance on the steep, thin-cut steps. At the top I was faced with three doors, each leading off to different bedrooms that I assumed were distributed between the sons, daughters and parents. At full capacity there would be nine people living here, and even though it was bigger than most of the other houses in the village I still found it hard to believe that they could fit everyone in.

"Mr Hopkin?" I called out, not sure which room he might be in. I waited for a moment and the door to my left creaked open and Sophia poked her head out.

"He's in there," she whispered. She pointed to the door on the other side of the stairway and then brought her finger up to her lips indicating silence. "He's sad."

"Thank you", I whispered back to her and she closed the door again.

"Mr Hopkin," I said again, knocking on the door Sophia had pointed to. I reached for the doorknob, turning it gently in case he was asleep, and pushed my head through the opening. Staring straight back at me, Mr Hopkin sat in an armchair at the bottom of the room next to the window. He motioned with the bottle of whiskey for me to come in, and I edged into the room.

I came to a stop beside the bed and stared out of the window at the view down over the village. Rain was coming down against the glass but the sun still managed to peek through the clouds, casting a golden shimmery hue over the fields as it began to set. It was quite a spectacular view and I couldn't imagine there were many better ones in the village.

"Mrs Hopkin needs the key for the coal shed," I said. I eyed up the bottle he was cradling. In the short time he'd been gone he'd already drunk more than half of it.

"She thinks I don't care," he said then took another swig, his monotonous tone unchanging despite the alcohol.

"I don't know what you mean," I replied.

"I'm not a cold man, Thomas. I care very much."

"Do you want me to go and get Mrs Hopkin?" I asked, unsure what to do.

A silence filled the air between us as we both contemplated what to say next. When he finally spoke, his voice sounded weak. "I just want him to come home." He lifted the bottle and took another swig then shifted his gaze to the wall behind me. "Why won't he come home?"

I turned to follow his stare and saw, hanging over the bed, an old black and white framed photograph of Mr and Mrs Hopkin surrounded by their children. Something about it was immediately puzzling to me and I could feel my brow furrow as I tried to work it out.

I crooked my head and took a curious step forward as my eyes darted between the solemn-looking faces of the Hopkin family. It took a second for my brain to register exactly what I was seeing and I wasn't sure I even believed my own eyes at first, but there, standing proudly at the back of the photograph with his hand on Mrs Hopkin's shoulder, my father stared back at me.

Ten

My mother and father were married in Cambridge on July 22nd 1965. I remember this, despite it being six years before I was born, because their anniversary was the same date as my mother's birthday. She would often joke that it was the only way she would be able to get my father to remember either occasion, and she was probably right.

On the mantelpiece in our sitting room at home, in an ornate silver frame, stood the only picture from that event that I'd ever seen. My mother, having turned 24 on that day, stood in the centre, her train running down the church steps and her face partially obscured by a veil, but not enough to hide the wide smile on her face. To her left, towering over her and looking decidedly less impressed by proceedings, stood my father, his dark brown hair parted at the side, his crooked smile looking forced, and on the back of his right hand a scar shaped like an anchor that he'd always maintained had come from an accident with some old printing machinery when he was younger.

It was that same scarred hand, adorned with the very ring that I'd found in the safe, that was resting on the shoulder of Mrs Hopkin in the portrait over her bed. The man staring back at me, though younger than in any picture I'd ever seen of him, was undeniably my father, John Jacob. He had the same eyes, the same features, and even the same parted hair that he would sport until the day he died. There was no denying it and I was frozen to the spot struggling to accept it.

It was only when Mr Hopkin coughed from behind me that I even remembered that I was not alone. "I need to go," I said, springing into action and bolting from the room and down the stairs.

"What on earth is the matter?" Mrs Hopkin called out as I barged through the kitchen and out into the back yard.

I went as fast as my feet would take me. Rain was slashing against my face as I bolted down the hill towards the village and the sun had almost completely set, darkening my route, but I didn't mind my step. I just ran. When I reached the pub I spun right, up the hill past Mair's cottage and all the way up to the top field, hopping over the fence and through the grass until I was right back where it all started; the field I woke up in.

I don't know if I'd intentionally brought myself there or if I'd just run out of village to run through, but I came to a stop in the centre of that field and screamed at the top of my lungs. They could probably hear my voice at both ends of the valley by the time I'd stopped screaming but I let out every last bit of tension and anger and frustration I'd been holding onto since I'd arrived. And then, exhausted, I fell to the ground.

Had I finally cracked? The rain was lashing down, soaking me from head to toe, and I was lying in the middle of a field in the middle of nowhere screaming into nothingness. The more I tried to reconcile my thoughts the more convinced I became that I must have gone mad and I was soon hysterical with laughter. I just couldn't stop myself. Each time I considered what had happened to me, what I'd seen in that room, the puzzle pieces that were starting to slowly fit together, my chest would heave and my shoulders would shake and I'd roar with laughter again. Despite the rain, however, and despite the laughs, I was also very aware of the tears I was shedding at the same time. I was incredulous at the absurdity of it all and devastated by the loss of everything I thought I knew.

"What's so funny, then?" a voice called out from the distance.

I turned my head, the grass brushing against my face, and saw Gwyn walking in my direction. He was slow, more careful of his footing this time, and holding onto his ribs as he moved. I knew he'd hurt his side more than he was letting on earlier, the liar. When he reached the spot I was lying in, he slowly lowered himself down on the grass beside me.

"You wouldn't believe me if I told you," I said, bringing my hands up and rubbing the rainwater from my face.

"You went past that window quicker than lightning." He stared off over the village as he talked, a pensive look on his face. Finally, after some silence, he said, "I was glad to see you again, Tom."

I raised myself off the ground and sat properly beside him. "I've ruined even more of your clothes," I said, pointing to the mud that was now caking the back of my legs and likely the back of my whole body.

"That's ok," he said, and he reached over and put his hand on my knee. Unlike our previous connections that ended as quickly as they started, this time he let his hand stay there. "It's Mair you'll have to grovel to."

The rain began to ease off to a drizzle and we looked out over the village as the final moments of sunlight disappeared beyond the rooftops.

"It's a nice night," he said. "Don't you think?"

I moved my hand across my leg just slightly so that our fingers were lightly touching. "Yeah," I replied, staring off over the village. "It's a lovely night."

By the time I arrived back at Pen Castell Farm, everybody had already eaten and the youngest children were in bed. I crept into the kitchen looking for food and hoping not to disturb anyone, only to find Mr and Mrs Hopkin sitting at the dining table. They stopped talking as soon as I entered the room and both looked at me with concern.

In all the fuss of the previous month, I had continued to stay in the barn without any discussion of my intentions to remain and when I saw them both sitting there, especially with all that had gone on and Nan returning home, I was suddenly worried that I may have outstayed my welcome and was about to be given my marching orders.

"Sit down, love," Mrs Hopkin said, her usual smile nowhere to be seen. My heart sank, but Mr Hopkin not having his head in the paper at the table made me most nervous of all.

I took a seat opposite them and prepared myself for the news. I knew I could go to Mair's house if I absolutely had to but it was cramped enough already with just two of them living there. With me moving in as well and bringing no money to the pot I knew I'd just be a burden. At least at the farm I'd be able to work for my supper.

"You ran out with the winds of God earlier," Mrs Hopkin started. "Do you want to tell us what upset you? Only, John said you were fine until you saw the photograph in the bedroom and-"

"If you know anything about Jack's whereabouts, now is the time to tell us," Mr Hopkin interrupted, his face reddening. I could see he had little patience for this conversation or his wife's delicate approach and my reaction had obviously made him suspicious.

"We're not accusing you of anything, love," Mrs Hopkin chimed in, "but Christmas is right around the corner and we want him home with us. If you've any idea where him and that girl have disappeared to, please, we just want to know."

Her face was filled with anguish and I knew she was looking to me to put her mind at ease but what could I say? *'Sorry Mrs Hopkin, but you know your son who you saw last month as a 23-year-old? Well, I buried him six weeks ago aged 63. Oh, and it was also 109 years from now in 1998. Also, he was my father. Sorry I didn't mention it sooner but I only just found out myself.'*

I wanted to put an end to their worry but I knew I couldn't tell them the truth. I wasn't even entirely sure what the truth of it all was but if I told them what I thought I knew they'd throw me out for sure.

"I saw him," I said, beginning my lie. "It was just before I got to the village. I'd stopped for food and met a couple on their way to Cardiff. I only spoke to them for a minute but they seemed happy and normal and it was miles from here so I didn't make the connection. It wasn't until I saw the picture that I even knew what Jack looked like. I've never been upstairs before. I'm so sorry, Mrs Hopkin, I promise I didn't know."

Mrs Hopkin brought a clenched fist up to her mouth and closed her eyes. I wasn't sure if she was praying or about to cry but I was instantly wracked with guilt about my deception.

"They both seemed happy," I continued, hoping my lie might bring them some peace. "And he said his name was

John," I added, because that's what I'd always thought my dad's name to be.

"Well, that's his name," she replied. "We named him after his father but we called him Jack all his life. Nobody ever called him John."

"I really am sorry," I said again. "If I had any idea, I would have told you sooner." I justified my lie by telling myself I was doing something good for them and that at least now they wouldn't be worried that he was lying in a ditch dead somewhere.

"At least we know they're safe and together," Mrs Hopkin said, turning to her husband and forcing a smile. "At least we know that."

Mr Hopkin, who had remained quiet throughout while he considered my every word, suddenly bolted up from this seat. My initial fear was that he was about to tackle me to the ground but he instead slammed his fist into the table causing a teacup to bounce from the force and shatter on the floor.

"I bloody knew it," he bellowed. He grabbed for his hat and marched to the back door. "I'm going to wring his bloody neck when I catch hold of him."

As I turned back to face Mrs Hopkin I spotted Teddy hiding behind the door to the sitting room, listening in on the commotion. When he caught my eye he darted off towards the stairs.

"Where will he go?" I asked.

"To the pub most likely until he's calmed down."

"I should go and get my things," I said, getting up from my chair.

"You'll do no such thing," she said sternly. "Sit yourself down."

She opened the stove and took out a plate of leftover bread slices and put it down in front of me then fetched a broom from the pantry and began sweeping up the broken cup, making quick work of the mess on the floor.

"Will Mr Hopkin be ok?" I asked as I picked at the bread. She eased herself down opposite me, clinging to the broom as though it might try to escape.

"You won't meet two men more alike than Jack and his father," she began. "You might have noticed that Mr Hopkin can be stubborn and set in his ways, well Jack is exactly the same. Every day with them two you can feel a storm brewing, neither of them willing to budge. John wanted Jack to work the farm with him but he'd no interest in fieldwork. Never did. One day after a row in the pens Jack marched right down to Rhodri Thomas and got himself a job working the printers. He was in his element, but it sent his father grey. We needed him on the farm, see, I won't lie to you, but Jack needed to find out who he was on his own and John could never see it. Said duty comes before desire and threatened to put him out on the streets, but I wouldn't have had that and he'd have never done it. He just couldn't see why Jack wouldn't put the family and the farm first like he'd had to. Grandad Hopkin was exactly the same. The apple didn't fall far from the tree."

I listened intently as she spoke and thought of my father and how he'd raised us. It seemed unthinkable that he'd fought so hard against what was expected of him only to rule over Lee and me with the same rod. We'd grown up having it drummed into us that we'd continue with the business and our happiness about that wasn't part of the equation. As far as apples falling far from trees went, my father wasn't all that different from his own.

"And what about the girl?" I asked. I remembered the name 'Ellie' had been scribbled on my father's papers. Elinor, perhaps? If it was the same woman then perhaps he'd tried coming back to the village or looking her up.

"Jack and Elinor were sweethearts but his father wouldn't allow them to court. Mr Hopkin and Elinor's father fell out about two years back, really nasty it was, and he wouldn't hear of it. As far as I know, Elinor's father felt the same way and the next we heard she was engaged to Arthur Morgan. He'd always had eyes for her and he hated our Jack.

"We all knew that Jack and Elinor used to sneak off together but Jack always denied it when his father asked. I suppose they'd rather run off and leave us all behind than be parted. Despite his bluster, John blames himself. Thinks if he'd just done things differently, he'd be able to build bridges. And on top of that, he thinks I blame him too."

"Do you?" I asked without thinking.

"Jack is a smart boy," she said, not answering my question. "He knows his mind and he knows how to mind himself. He'll be ok, and he'll be back soon enough once the real world sets in, just you mark my words."

She seemed to have contented herself with the idea that he was safe and would come home when he was ready, which only made it sadder that I knew she would likely never see him again.

Figuring that it was my best shot to gather information, I decided to probe a little further. "I noticed the ring Jack was wearing in the picture," I said, trying to remain cool. "That's how I was sure it was him. He was wearing it when we met. Is it a family heirloom?"

"I should be so lucky," she said, laughing at my question.

"Oh? So where did it come from?" I was trying not to sound too keen, but she was happy to talk and didn't seem suspicious of my asking.

"Well, I only know what I've been told, but years ago before they fell out, John and Mr Lewis were fishing down near Devil's Bridge when they found an old man unconscious beside the river. They brought him around and gave him tea and by way of thanks, he gave them a pouch with a red gemstone inside. If you ask me, it was just some fancy glass, but they wouldn't hear of it. Thought they knew better, see. They squabbled and argued over who should have it and what it might be worth until they were barely talking to each other anymore except to argue over that bloody stone.

"Before long everyone had had enough of the bickering. They confided in Billy Cotter, God rest his soul, who took the stone until they could sort out their differences and decide who should have it. Thinking he was helping, Mr Cotter cut the stone in two. He set one into a ring and gave it to John, and the other into a necklace and gave it to Mr Lewis, but rather than thank the poor man it just caused even more arguments. Billy died just a few days later and they still couldn't put their differences behind them, but with no stone to argue over they just refused to speak to each other anymore and haven't since."

My ears pricked up at the news of the necklace. If there was another stone then perhaps it would give me more of a chance of getting home. I'd just need to get my hands on it to try.

"So, where's the necklace now?"

"I'd imagine it's still around the neck of Elinor Lewis, where it's been since it was made." Her words made my heart sink. She raised herself from the table and made her way to the stove, putting some water on to boil. "But I'm telling you now, it's not worth the money it cost Billy Cotter to set them. It's a shiny bit of junk and it's been nothing but trouble since the day it was found."

My head was spinning from the revelations laid out by Mrs Hopkin. If Elinor was wearing the stone when she disappeared then did she make it to the future with my father? Was she the woman in Brighton that he spoke of in his diary? Even if the stone was worth nothing there was certainly something powerful about it. Did Elinor and my father know what it could do? Did they plan it? My ending up here was random, but did it have to be? Was there a way to make it work at will? I suddenly had so many questions that I had no answers to.

"What's Devil's Bridge?" I asked as Mrs Hopkin set out some cups at the table, settling on a question she'd be able to answer. Maybe I could go there to find the stranger who offloaded the stone.

"It's not far," she said, pouring us out some tea. "They say that the bridge was built by the Devil himself in return for the soul of a maiden but he was tricked into taking the soul of a dog instead and cursed the area. Years ago, when the bridge needed repairs, the workmen were too superstitious to knock it down for fear of angering the Devil, so they just built a new bridge right over the top."

A shiver went down my spine as she recounted the story and, probably entirely by coincidence, the kitchen lamps began to flicker, making Mrs Hopkin laugh.

"All stuff and nonsense," she said, taking a sip of her tea. "Everyone tells a different version of the tale and that's the one my mother told me, but you can make your own mind up if you ever see it. It's only a few miles away."

"Maybe I can visit sometime," I said, and she smiled at me. I decided to bite the bullet. "Mrs Hopkin, if it's alright with you I think I'd like to stay for a while. I know things are tough right now, but if you can give me food and a bed then I'll work the farm for free until we're all fixed."

"And what of your family? Won't they expect you home for Christmas at least?"

"I like it here," I said, surprised that I was beginning to mean it. "And to be honest I don't have anyone to go back to. But it's ok for you to say no. I'll understand completely."

"You're welcome here for as long as you like, and I know John could do with your help. He's been very impressed by your work so far."

"Oh? He never said anything."

"It's just his way, love. If he's silent then he's content. It's when he speaks you need to mind yourself."

"Thank you," I said, bringing her hand up and kissing it.

"Oh, get off, you," she said, playfully batting me away. "Now, away to sleep, you've got an early start."

I set my cup down and headed for the back door.

"Oh, and Thomas," she said, causing me to turn around, "bring your stuff in with you tomorrow. You can have Jack's bed while he's away."

I gave her a final smile and pulled the door closed behind me.

Sleep that night was hard to come by. Around an hour after retreating to the barn I'd heard Mr Hopkin return to the house. His slow shuffling steps had caught my attention, an indication that his drinking had continued, and I'd momentarily considered going to talk to him about the events of the evening. Unsure of what his temperament might be, however, I thought it a conversation best saved for when sober and away from tools. It was a good decision, it seemed, because within minutes of going into the house I could hear him begin to shout about something and it went on for quite a while.

I blocked out the noise and tossed in my makeshift bed, uncomfortable with my position and uncomfortable with my thoughts. Had I ever really known my father? And with all the information that had been revealed to me, could I ever really judge him with the same harsh eye as I had done for my whole life, knowing what he'd been through? Or was it worse because he knew how it felt?

Was that huge event in his life something that just happened to him unjustly or did he have some control over the ring that I wasn't aware of yet? And did any of it justify the man he became or the father he turned into?

I tossed again, my mind turning to the lie I'd told the Hopkins about their son. As much as I'd tried to justify it to myself, I couldn't help feeling guilty at the false hope I'd given them. But how else was I to explain my reaction to the portrait? Seeing my father was the last thing I'd expected and the truth was out of the question. They didn't seem to doubt me, which I was grateful for, and it would at least be one less worry for Mrs Hopkin.

Mrs Hopkin. The name echoed in my brain.

Tom Hopkin. Thomas Hopkin. Is *that* my real name?

I swirled the name on my tongue, the name I should have had if my father hadn't changed it. I quite liked it. Not that it made any difference now, of course. Why did he change it, though? A final act of defiance towards his father, perhaps?

138

I was pulled from my thoughts by the sound of the kitchen door swinging open and someone coming outside. I sat up from my bed, worried that Mr Hopkin may be wandering around drunk and would end up falling over something in the yard, so I threw on my shirt and climbed down the ladder to the floor below.

With no candle to light my way, it was difficult to see in the barn. Moonlight shone across the stone floor from the small window next to the door but it cast a murky glow that made me unsure of every step I took, not entirely sure at what point my foot would connect with the ground. Upon reaching the door I pulled it open gently, worried that he might be slumped behind it, and poked my head out to get a better look.

"Are you ok, Mr Hopkin?" I called out, my voice barely above a whisper.

"Go away, Mr Jacob," a voice in the shadows said back, but it wasn't Mr Hopkin.

I pushed the barn door open further and stepped outside wishing I'd had the forethought to put my boots on. The air was freezing and every hair on my legs felt like it was standing on end. I scurried over to where the voice had come from and found Teddy sitting on the cobbles with his back against the house. Just enough of the light from the moon fell upon him that I could see he was fully dressed, despite being long past his usual bedtime.

"What are you doing out at this time of night?" I asked, sitting down beside him. The cold floor immediately made the backs of my legs numb and I shuffled around uncomfortably.

"I'm leaving," he said, wrapping his arms around his knees for warmth. "Jack did it, so can I."

"You haven't gotten very far," I said, giving him a playful nudge in the arm.

"Piss off," he spat back.

I'd never heard him swear before. I'd never heard him say much of anything. Since I'd arrived at the farm he'd avoided me like the plague.

"What would your father say if he heard you speaking like that?"

"I don't care. I hate him and I hate this house."

"No you don't"

He looked up at me for the first time, his face filled with anger and he looked like he'd been crying.

"What do you know? You don't know anything about me."

"Well, that's because you never talk to me. If I didn't know any better I'd think you didn't like me."

"I don't."

His frankness made me laugh, which only seemed to make him more annoyed.

"Is it something I've done?" I asked.

"You're not him, you know. You can't just come in here thinking you can take his place.

"Jack?"

"He should be here, not you."

"Oh, Teddy," I said, putting a hand on his shoulder that he shrugged away. "I'm not trying to replace your brother. I'm sorry you feel that way. I bet you miss him, huh?"

"He was supposed to take me with him. He said one day we'd get away from him but he's left me here on my own."

"Get away from who? Your father?"

"He hates me. Nothing I do is ever good enough. I'll never be good enough for him or this stupid farm and he tells me every day."

"Running away won't make things better."

"What do you know? He wouldn't care if I was gone."

"You know, Mr Hopkin reminds me of my father. We didn't live on a farm like this but I still had to do as I was told. I wanted to be a policeman but he insisted I follow in his footsteps instead and work for the family business. He was hard on me. He was even worse to my brother. But he loved us. In his own way, he loved us very much, I'm sure. He just didn't always have the best way of showing it. He was a lot like your father in that respect. Never really good with words. But that doesn't mean he didn't feel it. I think your father would miss you very much if you were gone, just like I know he misses Jack.

"I know it isn't always easy, but you have to cut him some slack, too. It's not easy being him either, you know. He has all of you to look after and the farm to run. He has to make sure there's food on the table and a roof over your head. It's a lot for one man to deal with on his own. He's not being hard on you because he doesn't love you. He's being hard on you because he needs you to learn. You'll be the man of this house one day and it'll be your job to make sure your family is taken care of. He's not perfect, he's just scared of it all going away."

Though I talked of Mr Hopkin it was my own father who filled my thoughts and the more I tried to reason with Teddy the less sure I was about whether it was him I was trying to convince or myself. For the first time, perhaps ever, I felt that maybe I understood my dad a little better. Maybe I even forgave him a little. I'd spent so many nights growing up feeling the same way as Teddy did but looking from the outside in brought a clarity I'd never considered before.

"Aren't you running away from home?" Teddy asked, interrupting my thoughts. "I know you're staying here now. I heard you talking to my mother earlier."

"I don't have anything to run away from," I told him. "My father is gone now. We can't ever make things right. You can, but only if you stay."

"I just want him to be nice to me," he admitted. "Jack is gone and Howell is useless and he never treats the girls like he treats me. It's not fair."

"Well now that I'm staying a little longer I'll be able to help out and you'll have less to do. And maybe if you quit ignoring me we could even be friends."

"Maybe." He wiped his eyes with the back of his sleeves and rested his arms on his knees. "I'm sorry I told you to piss off," he said, finally turning to look at me.

"That's ok. I won't tell if you don't." I offered my hand and he shook it. His lips ticked upwards, not quite a smile, but it was a start, and then he used my hand to pull himself up to his feet.

"I better go back in, Mr Jacob. Sorry, again."

"Call me Tom," I said, getting to my feet. My legs had turned ice cold and my limbs had gone numb, leaving me feeling like I might fall over if I tried to take a step. "Get yourself up to bed and I'll see you bright and early, yeah?"

"Ok," he said, turning and heading for the back door.

There had been something cathartic about my chat with the young boy, as though a weight had been lifted, hopefully for both of us. Once I was sure he was safely back inside the house I made my way back to the barn.

"Thank you, Tom," I heard as I pushed open the barn door.

I turned back to where the whisper had come from and glanced around in the darkness. Leaning out of the pantry window and bathed in moonlight, Mrs Hopkin smiled across the courtyard at me having heard my discussion with her son. I nodded my head in her direction and then disappeared inside the barn, finally exhausted.

Eleven

It was still dark when I made my way for breakfast the following morning and the cold air had brought with it the first flurries of snow, which coated the fields and made them sparkle in the last remnants of the moonlight. The house was already alive with activity and I could hear the voices of Mr and Mrs Hopkin and the clattering of pots and pans as she prepared breakfast from across the courtyard.

Rather than the familiar sounds of the family chatting, the voices coming from inside the house were tense and fraught with anger, so I hung back and waited in the cold morning air. I tried not to eavesdrop but it was difficult not to hear the worry in Mrs Hopkin's voice as she fretted about the empty shelves in the pantry and I was once again left feeling guilty for my lack of contribution whilst being fed by them each day.

As I edged closer to the door to try and hear more of the conversation it swung open leaving me caught in the act. Betty stepped out and crashed straight into me, but instead of turning crimson like she normally would, she just looked fed up.

"We need more water. Can you help me?" she asked. She wouldn't meet my gaze, but this time it felt like it wasn't her shyness that was stopping her.

"Is everything ok?" I asked as we collected pails from the shed. "Your mother sounded upset."

"It's Nan," she replied. "Well, not her specifically, but her return." She dropped her buckets down in front of the water pump with a crash and brought her hands up to her face, exasperated. "Mama is worried about how she will feed everyone. Christmas is coming and income from the farm is always low in winter. I hate seeing her like this."

Whether they blamed me or not I had to accept that at least part of the responsibility for Nan's dismissal lay with me. My presence also meant an extra mouth to find food for, so I had to do something that would make things right.

"Betty, I have to go. Will you be ok with the water on your own?"

"Yes, of course," she replied as I began making my way back to the barn at pace. "But where are you going? You haven't had breakfast yet."

"I know," I called back to her. "Tell your parents I won't be eating today. I've got some errands to run. I will be back this evening."

"But what about-" she called out, but I was too far away to hear or worry about the rest of what she said. I had formed a plan.

"Is your brother home?"

"Well, hello to you too?" Mair said, looking up from the pot she was stewing over the fire as I entered the cottage. "He's just getting dressed."

"I need to go into the city and I have no idea where to go or how to get there, so I thought you and Gwyn could take me. What do you say?"

"Today? You've got no chance. Do you think this house just runs itself? I've got far too much to do."

I looked around the room, everything exactly as it was the last time I was there and every other time before that, and wondered what it was she actually did with her time.

"Don't mind her," Gwyn said, coming out of his bedroom. He had a towel thrown loosely over his bare shoulders and his face was wet, his beard looking neater than I'd seen it since we first met. The bruising on his side appeared to have changed colour again, this time filled with yellows, and it was now not much bigger than a handprint. I was glad to see him healing well. I was glad to see him at all. "She's just fussing because she has a gentleman caller today so I was about to go out myself."

I turned to Mair and raised my eyes, pretending to be shocked. "Miss Griffiths! The scandal."

"Don't you start," she said, throwing a cloth at me. "Mr Jones is just coming to escort me to the post office."

"Mr Jones who helped get the men from the mine?" I asked, remembering the old man who had taken charge of the rescue efforts. I scrunched up my face in disapproval. "He's got to be thirty years older than you."

"Not him, *twp*, his son, Ioan. And it's all perfectly innocent so you can both stop making faces unless you want to feel the back end of my spoon," she said, waving her ladle at us. The wet contents from it flung off, making a stain on the front of her shirt. "Aw, look what you did now." She shot us both an unimpressed look and rushed off into her room.

"So how about it then?" I asked, turning my attention back to Gwyn. "Will you come with me to Aberystwyth? I really don't think I could make it there and back on my own. I haven't left the village since I got here. If you don't have other plans, that is."

"You know, you don't have to make excuses to come over here," he said with a cheeky grin.

I rolled my eyes, pretending not to like his teasing. "Is that a yes, then?"

He glanced at the clock on the mantel, "We will have to go now if we want to get the bus."

"The bus?" I asked, confused.

"Well, you don't plan on walking, do you?"

The bus was, of course, nothing like I might have expected. Once Gwyn was dressed we'd made our way through the village, past the pub and up the road out of Cwm Newydd, reaching the top of the hill just as a large horse-drawn wagon made its way down the lane towards us. Gwyn, on the promise that I would pay him back, covered my fare, tossing some coins to the driver before we hopped on the back.

The inside of the wagon was cramped. Long wooden benches ran along either wall and a thin, hay-covered gangway through the middle left little room to move. The only other passenger onboard was an old lady who was asleep at the front, but it seemed like it could become very crowded quite quickly if many more people got on along the way. I looked out of the window as we pulled away from the village, excited to see the city for the first time.

"You still haven't told me what the big emergency is," Gwyn said. He'd sat opposite me when we boarded, though the benches were so close together that we were having to sit with a knee between each other's legs in order to face each other.

"This," I said, reaching into the pocket of my waistcoat. "I'm going to sell it."

I handed him the gold ring I had received as a birthday present from my parents years before and he turned it around in his palm, studying it.

"That's heavy," he said, bringing it up to his eye and peering through it at me. "Where did you get it? It must be worth a fortune."

"It was a birthday gift from my parents when I reached twenty-one."

"You didn't tell me you were rich," he joked, handing me back the ring. "And here you are borrowing money from a jobless man. Have you no shame?"

I struck my knee out, knocking his away playfully. "I'm not rich," I said. "Do you think I'd be wearing another man's clothes if I had money of my own?"

"They look good on you."

I turned to look out the window, an embarrassed smile forming on my face from the compliment. We were in the middle of nowhere. There was the occasional farmhouse but otherwise nothing to be seen for miles. I'd been told the village was isolated but I'd had no idea just how far away we were from any other civilization.

"Why do you want to sell it?" Gwyn asked, bringing my attention back into the vehicle.

"It's for the Hopkins'. Money is getting tight and I need to pay my way. I'm helping where I can but mended fences and clipped ewes don't put food on the table or coal in the fire. Selling the ring should cover me for a few weeks, hopefully."

"Are you sure you want to?"

I looked down at it clutched in my hand and thought of my parents. I'd hardly taken it off for the last six years but I barely noticed it anymore and if it could help the Hopkins then selling it would be worth it.

"I don't need a ring to remember them by," I said. "It's just stuff"

The carriage hit a bump causing the woman at the front to grunt and shift in her seat, before going straight back to sleep. Gwyn reached for his ribs, the jolt causing him some pain, and I instinctively reached out and put my hands on his waist.

"Are you ok?" I asked.

He looked up at me, his face just inches from mine, then glanced over to the woman at the front of the bus.

"I'm good," he smiled, and his eyes locked on mine.

We hit another bump and I shot back in my seat, the woman now fully awake. She glanced out the window and then banged on the front of the carriage. A few moments later she moved to get off and Gwyn and I had to exit to allow her to pass.

"Jesus it's freezing," I said, drawing my arms across my chest to try and preserve some heat. The woman filed past us dragging her bags and walked off in the direction we'd come from. "I hope she's not too far from home," I said as we climbed back aboard.

"We're not far from the city now," Gwyn said, taking off his scarf and putting it around my neck. "We should get you some proper winter clothes."

As the carriage ambled along the road the hills and fields made way for more buildings and about 30 minutes later we were on cobbled streets. Snow had settled on the rooftops though the roads were mostly clear so we had no trouble passing through. As we headed downhill into the city I could see the sea and a row of tall buildings lined across its front.

Gwyn seemed quite amused by how excited I became by the views.

When we arrived on the main road I was surprised to see so many other carriages and people. Cwm Newydd had just one main road through the village and it was rare to see any carts or wagons on it, but the city was bustling like any other I'd seen in my own time and it felt exciting to be amongst civilisation again.

"This is us," Gwyn said as we pulled up alongside the entrance to a long pier. We stepped out of the back of the carriage and Gwyn shouted out, 'thank you,' to the driver in Welsh.

"I need to find somewhere to sell the ring," I said, looking up and down the street, "and somewhere to buy a coat."

"Over here," he said, grabbing me by the arm and pulling me into the road. Carriages were coming from both directions and in no particular order so we had to dodge amongst them to get to the other side of the street.

Being in front of tall imposing buildings again felt strange and I kept looking up to the rooftops as we walked along, not quite believing what I was seeing and trying not to bump into shoppers as I went. The signs were different and the contents weren't the same, but it was remarkable how familiar it all felt to my own time. The same chatter amongst pedestrians, people from all over the world, the noise of traffic, the hustle and bustle of people going about their day. If I closed my eyes I could imagine being right back home in Cambridge.

"This is it," Gwyn said, ducking into a shop doorway. I looked at the sign above the door. It didn't have a name but instead said '*Sellers of Silver*', and I followed him in.

Inside the shop looked like a warehouse that had had all of its contents picked up and shaken around, left to lie wherever they landed. Shelves on all walls went from floor to ceiling, filled with items I'd never seen before, and some that looked all too familiar. Rolls upon rolls of materials were stacked against walls and sacks of various goods were left in piles on the floor. Things were hanging from the ceiling that we had to weave in and out of and there were scales set around every few feet to weigh and measure the coming and going of goods.

At the back of the shop, a tall lanky man in an apron stood with a measuring tape around his neck and waved at us to come further in.

"What can I do for you today, gentlemen?" he asked as we approached. I was surprised to hear him speak English to us without any prompt. Most people in the village had been accommodating of my lack of language skills but tended to fall back into their mother tongue if they weren't speaking directly to me or were meeting me for the first time. Being greeted in English by a stranger felt both strange and exciting.

"I want to sell a ring," I said, fishing for it in my pocket. I handed it over to him and he brought it up to his face.

"Nice. Weighty." He put it in his mouth and bit it. "What do you want for it?"

"How about you tell us what you think it's worth?" Gwyn shot back, not allowing the man to undersell us. I knew it was worth a couple of hundred pounds in my own time but I had no idea how that might translate to 19th-century Aberystwyth. Fifty pounds perhaps? That seemed like a good amount, and a lot given how many items I'd bought at the post office for pennies.

"Follow me," he said, beckoning us over to one of the scales. He plopped the ring down on it and stroked his chin. "I'll give you 14 pounds and sixpence."

"Done," Gwyn said before I had any chance to consider. My heart sank a little, unsure about whether or not I was getting a good deal, but I knew if he'd only offered one pound I still would have had to take it. I just had to hope I made my money's worth.

"Are you sure that's good?" I asked Gwyn as the man disappeared to the back of the shop again.

"You won't get better," he replied. "That's nearly six months' wages."

When he put it like that, I felt a little better about the deal.

"Here you go," the shopkeeper said, returning to the scales. He handed me a small pile of coins and two large sheets of white paper filled with various squiggles and bits of writing, both with the word 'five' printed rather ornately in the bottom corner. I'd only ever been given coins to spend at the post office so seeing these notes, which looked as though he'd just written them out himself, was quite a surprise. They were so big compared to the fivers I knew from back home.

"Have a good day now," he said, tipping his cap to us and then disappearing back to his treasures.

We left the shop and followed along the street until we reached another establishment labelled 'Outfitters' above the door.

"Go get yourself a coat. I'll be back in ten minutes," Gwyn said, ushering me into the shop before disappearing out of view.

Before I'd had a chance to wonder where he was going a heavy-set man with a beard came upon me to ask if I needed help.

"I'm looking for a coat," I said, looking around the room. There was a section for suits along one wall, and trousers and shirts hung from railings on the other side, but I could see no sign of outerwear.

"This way, sir," he said, leading me to the back near the counter and till. "I think this would suit you just splendidly."

He reached through a rack and pulled out a long grey coat that had far more buttons than it needed. He held it up to me and it hung almost to my ankles.

"I was hoping for something a little shorter," I said, causing him to eye me curiously. He reached for another, this time in brown, that reached my knees. I screwed my lips up and tilted my head looking at it. "Anything shorter?"

He let out a 'hmph' noise and moved to another rack. "We have this," he said, pulling out a grey woollen jacket. "It's a new style. Hasn't really taken off."

I took the jacket from him and tried it on, its warmth immediate. I walked to a small mirror against one of the walls and admired myself. The fit showed off my broad shoulders and tucked in at the waist, highlighting my shape, which had improved greatly with the manual labour on the farm and the flimsy meals I'd been eating.

"I'll take it," I said, not taking my eyes off myself. I did the buttons up halfway and turned again in the mirror, checking myself from all angles. "And I'll need some socks, trousers and a new shirt. And a new waistcoat, too, please."

The shopkeeper, excited about the prospect of my multiple purchases, set about gathering styles and sizes. It wasn't until I was at the counter with a big pile of clothes that I suddenly became worried that I wouldn't have enough money to pay.

"That's two, two and one," he said, handing me a paper bag filled with my items. I had no real idea what the numbers meant so I gave him one of the five-pound notes hoping it would be enough. He put it through the till and handed me enough change that I could have bought it all again. I thought back to all the money I'd spent on fashion over the years and suddenly wished I'd been sucked back in time sooner. I'd have saved a fortune.

"Got everything you need?" Gwyn asked as I exited the shop. He was leaning on the door frame smoking a cigarette, a small bag tucked under his arm.

"Did you?" I asked, motioning to his purchase.

"Just a little something for Mair," he said. "Are you hungry? I'm starving."

I'd skipped breakfast that morning and my stomach was rumbling from the lack of food. I nodded and he smiled, motioning for me to follow him.

"We come here every time we're in the city. They have the best cakes."

We stopped outside a shop just up from the outfitters and the smell wafting out from inside was incredible. Through the window, I could see trays and trays of candies and sweets, cakes and chocolates. I put my hands on the glass and pushed my face right up to it, savouring every sight and smell.

"You are allowed in, you know," a woman called from behind the counter inside. Gwyn was already halfway in and followed him through the door.

"Two pics, please," he said to the lady at the till, knowing exactly what he was there for. I was too busy staring around in wonder to have any idea what I might want.

"What'll it be?" The old woman shouted over to me.

I was spoiled for choice and let my stomach run away with me. "I'll have six of those," I said, pointing to a pile of chocolate bars with a rather disturbing image of Father Christmas printed on the front. "No, eight. And two shillings worth of that." I pointed to what looked like peanut brittle near the weighing scales and was hypnotised by the sticky toffee casing. Whatever it was, I needed to try it. "And I'll take a bag of those nuts as well, please."

"You're going to make yourself sick," Gwyn said, coming over and grabbing my hand. Into my open palm he placed a small, round cake.

"It's not for me," I said. "It's for the Hopkins. What's this?" The cake was warm and smelled amazing, I could see some fruit inside it and it was coated on top with sugar.

"It's a pic," he said. "Welsh cake. Try it."

I took a bite, the cake crumbling around my mouth as I did, and the warmness of it made me close my eyes to savour every bit. Mrs Hopkin had proved herself a great cook but nothing she had served was as good as this. Maybe it was the sugar, which she rarely seemed to have in the house, but after weeks without any of the food I was used to I was pretty certain this might have been the best thing I'd ever eaten.

I held up the remnants of the cake to the woman at the counter, with my mouth still half full. "And I'll take nine of these."

"No wonder you never have any money," Gwyn said, popping the last of the cake into his mouth.

"I forgot how much I enjoy shopping," I replied. When the woman had collected everything I paid for my items and took the bag from the counter. "I need to pick a gift for Mr and Mrs Hopkin. Any ideas?"

"You could try in Rowlands," he said, pointing me to a store a few doors down as we exited the shop. The snow had started to come down heavier and the skies were beginning to darken from the clouds. "You've got ten minutes or we won't get the bus back," he added.

"Hold these," I said, handing him my bags. "I'll be real quick."

I rushed off along the pavement to where Gwyn had pointed and came to what might pass in my own time as a department store. Through the windows I could see sections for clothing and homewares, books and furniture. Surely I'd find something in there.

The shelves were filled with knick-knacks and trinkets, though I wasn't seeing anything that seemed like an appropriate gift or that would say both thank you and Merry Christmas at the same time. I walked along an aisle browsing the various ornaments on offer, but nothing caught my eye and I was beginning to give up hope.

As I was about to cut my losses I spotted a small china cup and saucer set nestled among some kitchenware on one of the shelves. It was small and delicate looking with little pink flowers decorating it, and I felt sure that Mrs Hopkin would love it. Then, to make sure Mr Hopkin didn't feel left out I grabbed a few other little items and a small bottle of wine from a rack near the counter.

When I got back outside the shop Gwyn was huddled in a closed doorway sheltering from the snow. "All done?" he asked as I made my way towards him.

"I think so. Now I just need to sit."

"Well now's your chance," he said, pointing to the carriage that we'd rode in on that was parked on the opposite side of the street. "Let's go."

By the time we were back on the hill overlooking the village we were in complete darkness and a thick layer of snow had covered everything, reflecting the light of the moon and making the valley look like the perfect Christmas scene.

"Thank you for today," I said to Gwyn as we walked through the lane towards the pub. Despite my protestations about aggravating his ribs, he'd insisted on carrying some of my bags for me from the carriage.

"You don't have to thank me. I've enjoyed myself. We should do it again."

"I'd like that," I replied. "Though maybe next time don't let me spend so much. I've only got about six pounds left."

"There was no stopping you," he laughed and gave the bags a shake to remind me of my spree. "Just make sure you don't lose that money."

"I won't. I'll give some to Mrs Hopkin and keep the rest for when I need it. Oh, and I owe you the bus fare, too. I nearly forgot."

"Keep it," he said. "You can pay next time. That'll mean we have to go again."

We reached the bottom of the lane next to the pub. Gwyn needed to take a left while I was headed straight on through the village, and we both came to a stop.

"Do you want me to walk you to the farm?" he asked.

"No, you should get going. It's been a long day. You need rest."

A second passed by that felt like an eternity while we just stared at each other, smiling. The snow was coming in thick, the cold air making his cheeks glow red, and I don't think he'd ever looked more handsome than he did right then. I stepped towards him, unsure of my next move, but whatever it would have been was interrupted by someone coming out from inside the pub.

"I should go," I said, motioning my head towards the farm. "It's getting late."

He smiled and held out my bags to me. As I reached for them, he locked his fingers into mine and held our hands together for just the briefest of moments.

"Goodnight, Tom," he said with a smile as he took a step backwards and began his departure.

"*Nos da*, Gwyn," I replied. I was a little unsure of my words but he flashed me a grin for my effort

"Not bad," he said, taking another step back before turning and walking towards the lane. "Not bad at all." Then he rounded the corner and was out of sight.

I stared after him for a moment and then hurried along the street through the village, snow creaking and crunching underfoot and a smile on my face that was making my jaw ache. Everything seemed still and quiet, the residents all settling down for the evening to keep warm in front of their fires, and I couldn't wait for tomorrow to come to make my excuses to go visit Mair's house again.

"I come bearing gifts," I announced, bursting through the kitchen door to the farm. Everyone was at the table having just eaten dinner.

"You're back earlier than I thought you'd be," Mrs Hopkin said, obviously surprised by my entrance. "Betty said you didn't want food and we've nothing left. Shall I cook you something?"

"No, Mrs Hopkin, you stay where you are." My spirits were higher than they'd been in a long while and I swept around the table with a huge grin on my face.

"Are you drunk?" Teddy asked, causing all the children around the table to laugh.

"I am not, but I'm feeling very festive," I replied. I put my bags down on the counter amongst the pots and pans that were waiting to be cleaned. "I have brought gifts. If that's ok with you, of course, Mr and Mrs Hopkin?"

"I don't see why not," she replied, eyeing me curiously. Mr Hopkin gave me a nod so I reached into my bags and pulled out the bag of pics.

"Cakes for everyone," I said, ripping the bag open and laying them out on the table. The children seemed excited by the sugary treats and everyone reached in to help themselves. Once they were done Mrs Hopkin took one for her husband and then one for herself. "And I don't know what this is," I said as I placed the peanut concoction down on the table, "but it looked too good to leave in the shop so I hope I got enough for everyone.

I made my way around the table to Mrs Hopkin. Her eyes were wide, not from the treats, but from seeing her family enjoying them so much, and I sat in the empty chair next to her.

"I don't have much," I said, reaching into my pocket, "but I sold my ring to help out and I want to give you this." I handed her about five pounds worth of coins and clenched her fingers shut over it before she could refuse.

"We can't take this, Tom, it wouldn't be right," she said, a look of consternation on her face.

"I insist. You've been good to me. Let me pay my way, even if it's only a little bit."

She looked to her husband who gave another nod of approval and then threw her arms around me for a hug, squeezing me tightly and rocking me back and forth.

When everyone else had gone to bed that night, I snuck out to the barn and up the ladder to my makeshift bed. I opened the little cubby I'd made to hide the ring and my wallet and carefully placed the tea set and chocolate gifts for the family beside them and covered them over again, ready to give to them out on Christmas Day.

When I went back inside the house I made my way to my new lodgings in the room at the top of the stairs, and for the first time in weeks, I fell asleep in a real bed.

Twelve

The week leading up to Christmas had been one of the busiest since I'd arrived and it had been all hands on deck at the farm. The days had become incredibly short on available sunlight so not only was there more work but also less time to do it in.

Mr Hopkin had insisted on making sure all the fields were ploughed, despite the increasing snow, and with no engines to help get the muck turned, Teddy and I were left to do most of it by hand. That was on top of housing all the livestock, all the extra feeds and rebuilding a stretch of wall along the north road.

By the time Christmas Eve rolled around we were exhausted but it brought a flurry of excitement to the farm. Even Mr Hopkin appeared to be caught up in it, telling Teddy and me that he would take over farm duties until the New Year to allow us an extended break. Teddy, who had been working harder on maintaining a good relationship with his father, even went so far as to throw his arms around him for a hug. Most surprising of all was that Mr Hopkin seemed delighted and hugged him back, showing a level of affection I'd never seen in him before.

Mrs Hopkin had been busy all morning in the kitchen preparing food for the next two days so Teddy and I were tasked with choosing, cutting and retrieving a tree suitable for decoration in the sitting room.

The snow was coming down thick and fast as we headed to the bottom field and the trees were so thick with snow that it was nearly impossible to tell a good one from a bad one. He didn't pick the one I would have gone for but it was a strong choice with a good triangular shape and we shook the snow off to reveal thick, fluffy branches.

"You're not bringing that thing through here. You've got no chance," Mrs Hopkin shouted with barely a look as we scraped open the kitchen door with the tree in hand. Her arms were covered in flour and there were ingredients and utensils spread all over the kitchen. "Get around the front with it."

On her orders, we dragged the tree around the building and stood at the front porch shaking it loose of the fresh layer of snow that had settled upon it. Teddy banged the door and we huddled close for warmth until we heard the latch go and the door swing open.

We'd barely got it upright in the living room when the noise of carriage wheels on the cobbles in the yard signalled the arrival of Gethin. Mrs Hopkin greeted him with frantic shouting as he opened the back door, sending a chill through the house and blowing flour up into the air. Avoiding her wrath, he quickly ducked into the living room to join us.

He had brought a box with him that he set down near the fire and he began to extract its contents. It was overflowing with ribbons and coloured card and within minutes he had the twins sitting quietly and making decorations for the living room.

"Will you escort me to the village to collect Nellie?" He asked once the tree was in place. It wasn't entirely straight but the lean gave it a bit of added charm. At least that's what I told everyone so that I could stop trying to correct it.

"I'll grab my coat," I said, grateful to be asked. The house was becoming too crowded and with the kitchen out of bounds, there was a distinct lack of somewhere to sit and a high risk of being stuck in a small space with Nan, which I wanted to avoid. She'd reached a point where she could now talk to me without her voice being filled with bitterness but our conversations remained on a strictly necessary basis and there was no polite chit-chat to be had.

"You seem to have settled in well," he said as we exited the house and made for the gate. The snow had eased a little making it easier to see where we were going but it was several inches deep which made walking difficult. Within seconds my feet were soaked through and I wanted to be back by the fireplace.

"It's different here. Quiet. But I like it. How about you? Are you looking forward to moving to the village?"

"Well…" he said, and I wasn't sure if the pause was to disguise his feelings or because he was holding the gate open for me but he didn't elaborate further. "How are things now with Nan?"

"Better," I replied, a little confused by the sudden change of subject. "Not perfect, but civil at least."

"She's upset, but not with you. Not really. You know what women are like. She will be fine soon enough and you two will become great friends, I'm sure."

"I hope so," I replied.

"She's pretty, too, don't you think?"

"I haven't really noticed. She looks a lot like Nellie, I suppose."

"Maybe you should ask to accompany her to church in the morning."

I stopped in my tracks on the road, finally cottoning on to where he was leading the conversation, and began to laugh. His skills as a matchmaker, as well as being way off base, were considerably lacking in subtlety. "Are you suggesting I show an interest in Nan?"

"It wouldn't be the worst idea, would it? Then we could all be stuck in this village together," he joked.

"Well, for starters," I said, beginning to walk again, "she is eighteen and I am twenty-seven. It wouldn't be appropriate. And even if it were, I don't think we'd be interested in each other in that way."

"Oh, you have eyes for someone else, then?" he asked.

"I didn't say that."

"Yes, but you haven't denied it. We're friends, you can tell me. Who is it?"

"Mair," I called out, seeing my friend coming towards us from across the road and grateful for an excuse to end the conversation with Gethin. "Are you looking forward to tomorrow?"

"I can't wait," she said, joining us on the pavement and wrapping her coat tightly around her. The bottom of her skirts were caked in snow and even with the extra layers and her huge bonnet, she must have been freezing. "We've been going up to the farm every Christmas night for as long as I can remember and Leah's mince pies will be more than welcome after whatever semblance of a dinner I make tomorrow."

"Not a strong cook, Miss Griffiths? You'll have to practice hard if you're to find a husband." Mair gave him a sideways glance and an arched brow which made me break into laughter.

"What's brought you out in this weather?" I asked as we continued through the village.

"I've been at the graveyard paying my respects to my mam and dad. I'd have gone this morning but there was no way I was going out in that blizzard. Did you see it?"

"I was cutting the tree down in it," I replied.

"I should have known you'd be doing something stupid," she said with a grin. She linked her arm to mine and pulled me close causing Gethin to glance at us and give me a knowing nod. It was obvious that he thought Mair was the one I had eyes for but I did nothing to correct him.

By the time we reached the post office, Nellie was already waiting outside and a layer of snow had settled on her.

"You made it," she said, kissing Gethin on each cheek and then scanning around to make sure nobody saw her do it. Their courtship, and the etiquette of it, fascinated me. So different from the couples of my own time, Nellie and Gethin were expected to adhere to a strict set of rules until they were married. Naturally, those rules were sometimes bent, and her kiss on his cheek was particularly brazen, but they were never left alone together and he'd never spent the night which seemed completely alien to me.

At the entrance to the pub across the street, a group of carollers had gathered to sing hymns and a small crowd had encircled them. We walked over to watch them and Gethin threw a shilling in an upturned hat they had laid out, earning smiles from them as they sang.

"How did your courtship go?" I teased Mair, careful not to be overheard.

She looked up at me sternly. "How did yours go?" she replied, cocking an eyebrow and giving me a smirk.

"I, uh, I…" I spluttered, suddenly lost for words. "Very funny."

"Everyone else in this village might be stupid," she said, keeping her eyes locked on the singers, "but you should know better to think anything gets past me." She looked up at me, rolling her eyes and shaking her head. "You two have been making eyes like silly teenagers for weeks now. You're many things, Tom Jacob, but subtle is not one of them. Just be mindful."

Her words made me nervous. The era wasn't known for its accepting nature and there was trouble to be had if the wrong person became suspicious but she seemed surprisingly nonchalant and I felt somewhat relieved that I might finally have someone to discuss such things with, even if it did involve me admitting to a crush on her brother.

I wanted to play it cool but I couldn't help the slight grin that spread across my face as I tried to act coy. "I honestly don't know what you mean."

"I'm sure you don't," she replied, turning back to look at the carollers.

"Besides, I think Gethin thinks we may be sneaking around, you and I."

"You wish," she scoffed.

"Hey!" I said, giving her another nudge in the side. "What's wrong with me?"

"You're perfectly delightful," she said sarcastically, "but I have my sights set elsewhere."

"Mr Jones?"

"Not likely. He's a handsome man but so terribly boring. One walk to the post office and I was ready to jump in front of the next stagecoach. If only he wouldn't speak," she said with a sly grin.

"So, who is the unlucky man?"

"That, Tom, you will just have to wait and see."

"Nellie is ready to get back now," Gethin said, coming around the crowd to us. "Miss Griffiths, do you need an escort home?"

"No, thank you. I'll be fine. Tom, I'll see you tomorrow," she said, hugging me before departing.

Once dinner was eaten and Gethin had said his goodbyes the family all gathered in the sitting room to decorate the tree. I'd been lucky to get a seat near the fireplace and watched as the children hung the ribbons and paper chains they'd made around the room and on the tree. It was nothing like any Christmas tree I'd ever seen before but despite having none of the razzle-dazzle I was accustomed to, the effort that had gone into acquiring it, making the decorations and having everyone join in to decorate it, made it my favourite of all the Christmas trees I'd had.

Along the mantel, Mrs Hopkin had set out a row of Christmas cards that kept catching my eye. Far from bringing joy, they were some of the most terrifying images I'd ever seen. One or two had traditional snow scenes but the majority were adorned with oddly shaped animals and people who looked terrified. One, sent by her sister who lived in London, had an image of the Devil on it, all horns and cloven feet, holding a small chubby boy upside down by his ankle with the words 'Merry Christmas' written above it. It was quite possibly the least merry thing I'd ever seen.

As I watched the Hopkins come together to decorate the house I began to think of my own family and what they might be doing.

I'd been in Wales for two months and without realising it, I'd stopped feeling as though I was stuck and had come to be quite settled. Free of the shackles of the office and expectations at home, I'd begun to think of them less and less and the realisation of that filled me with guilt. I'd even stopped going back to the barn so frequently to try on the ring. Did I even want to go back anymore? My life had changed so much and though I hated having to admit it to myself, I was happier than I'd been in years.

I wondered if they missed me. Was time continuing on as normal now that I was no longer a part of it, or had it stopped the second I'd travelled through it? If life was continuing without me, then what would things be like?

I stared at the brandy in my hand and thought of my dad and his scotch; how he would offer us a drink each Christmas Eve as we sat down to watch old films and how the smell of mum's cooking filled the house. As children, Lee, Sophia and I would sneak down to see if the presents were there, expecting bikes and consoles, new clothes and the latest gadgets. We never wanted for anything but I never realised the important things that we didn't have until I met the Hopkins.

I hoped that Lee had the good sense to go home to Mum for Christmas and they weren't both spending it alone, their first without dad or me. Mostly I hoped that whatever they were doing, they weren't worried about me or missing me too much.

"Why are you crying, Mr Jacob? Are you ok?"

Howell brought me out of my thoughts and I looked up to see the whole family staring at me. I wiped at my face. A small tear had run down my cheek, but I flashed them all a smile.

"I'm good. Sorry, yeah, I'm good. I was just thinking about my family."

I was trying to play it off, but Mrs Hopkin looked concerned and came over to hug me, making me well up again. This woman, my grandmother, no more than fifteen years older than me, had been looking after me as though she'd raised me herself.

"Merry Christmas," I said, squeezing her tightly. "Thank you for everything."

"Tom should do it," Sophia said, pulling my attention from Mrs Hopkin.

"What should Tom do?" I asked.

"Put this at the top." She handed me a star that had been made using twine and twigs and pointed it to the top of the tree where it was meant to hang.

"I can't," I said, looking around the room at all the faces. "One of you should do it."

"Go on, son," Mr Hopkin said, giving me a nod and a smile that filled me with joy.

I nervously took the star from Sophia and then reached up and hooked it over the tallest branch, eliciting claps from the rest of the family.

"Right," Mrs Hopkin said, "who's ready for presents?"

"I'll be right back," I said, before running to the barn to collect the gifts I had bought for the family. When I returned there was a small sack in the middle of the room filled with gifts that the family was eager to open.

"I didn't know what everyone would like," I said, taking my seat next to the fire, "But I wanted to get you all a little something to say thank you for having me and making me so welcome."

I felt a little silly reaching into the bag to give everyone bars of chocolate but the way their faces lit up in appreciation made any concerns disappear and I was glad that I didn't come empty-handed, even if my gifts to them were small.

"Mrs Hopkin, I got you this. Well, it's sort of for both of you." I handed her the box with the tea set inside and she opened it gently, as though afraid to damage the cardboard. "I'm sorry it's not wrapped."

"It's beautiful," she said, lifting a small teacup and twirling it around in her hand, admiring the pattern. "John, have you seen this?"

"And to make sure you've got something to put in it, this is for you," I said, handing the bottle of wine to Mr Hopkin. He examined the label and nodded in approval, then reached out and shook my hand.

The Hopkin children began to reach into the sack, searching the gifts for tags with their names on them. Tin soldiers for Howell, a new doll for Sophia, clothes and hats for the elder children and bags of fruits and nuts for everyone. They were all so pleased to receive anything at all, and they all lavished their parents with hugs and kisses in gratitude.

"We didn't forget you," Mrs Hopkin said, reaching behind her for a small bag of gifts. "These are from all of us."

I thought I might end up crying again as she handed me the bag, something I'd found myself doing more in the last two months than I had in the ten years prior. I tore through the wrapping as everyone watched. The first gift was new socks, which I don't think I'd ever been more grateful for. Next, I pulled out two bottles of beer, bags of fruits and nuts and then finally a book of Welsh words and phrases, which got a laugh from everyone when I held it up to show the room.

As the family began to sing a rendition of *Silent Night*, I watched the fire roaring beside me, and as I considered the effort and money that must have gone into my gift, I smiled to myself, more content than I'd been in years.

On Christmas morning I received a lie-in for the first time since I'd arrived there, not waking up until the bells started to ring down in the village calling the residents to prayer.

Once dressed and washed I accompanied the family to church for the first time and as I walked through the village I couldn't help feeling an immense sense of pride. I wore the new clothes that I'd bought in Aberystwyth, saving their first outing for this very occasion knowing that everyone would be dressed in their absolute best.

"Looking very smart, Thomas," Mair said when we met at the gate to the church. "Doesn't he look dashing, Gwyn?"

"Very smart, indeed," he replied with a smile. His clothes were the finest I'd ever seen him in, fitting his shape perfectly and showing off the thick upper arms he'd developed from his job down the mine. I smiled back at him, impressed, and began the walk into the church. Betty, more comfortable with me each day, hooked her arm to mine and accompanied me into the service.

We filed into the pews on the left side, sitting several rows back from the front, while Mair and Gwyn took seats on the right. The service went much like any other I'd been to in my own time, though I understood very little of it. Some of the hymns were sung in English so I mimed along but spent most of the time glancing over at Gwyn. He didn't seem particularly focused on the songs either and spent just as much time glancing back at me, making me grin each time he did.

Exiting the church was a much slower affair as people from the village stopped to wish each other well and Betty once again took my arm to accompany me out.

"*Nadolig Llawen*," Mrs Wilkes said to me as we reached the door. I'd heard it enough to know she was wishing me a Merry Christmas so I said it back, eliciting a raised eyebrow and a smirk from her in return. "Have you met Mr Morgan?" she asked, ushering Arthur towards me. I hadn't noticed him at the church so was taken aback by his sudden appearance before me, and Betty became visibly uncomfortable. Mrs Wilkes, of course, was fully aware of the animosity between us but I refused to be baited in front of everyone on Christmas morning and gave him a forced, but polite nod. He muttered something that I couldn't understand but it caused Mrs Wilkes to snigger and they walked off towards the gate.

"What was that about," Mair asked, coming up behind me.

"Just Mrs Wilkes popping by on her broomstick," I replied.

She looked at me, confused. "I don't get what you mean," she said, but I waved it off.

"It's no matter. Today is not the day for worrying about Mrs Wilkes or Arthur Morgan and their games."

"Will we see you after dinner?" Betty asked.

"Yes, lovely," Mair responded, reaching out and squeezing Betty on the arm. "This one wins at all the games but this year I shall thrash her."

Betty smiled and went bright red. She dipped her head, unable to look at any of us and I began to guide her off before she exploded with embarrassment.

"See you after dinner," I called back, but Mair was already nattering away to someone else.

"I love the snow," Betty said, almost so quiet that I didn't hear her. "It's always so sad when it melts away."

"Then we should build a snowman before it's all gone. We can do it while the food is cooking. Teddy and the twins can help."

"But what about dinner?" she asked. "I'm supposed to help my mother."

"Nan can help with that. She knows her way around a kitchen and I'm sure she'd rather be doing that than standing in the cold with us. It's about time you had a little fun."

She thought on my words for a few steps and then clutched my arm tight. "We'll do it right in front of the house," she said excitedly, her smile beaming as she quickened her pace to get home. "And everyone will be able to see it from the village."

As soon as we were back on the farm she ran off to change and gather up her siblings. The snow had subsided overnight but we still had over a foot of it layered across the whole front field. In no time at all the body of the snowman had been built, leaving us red-faced from the cold and exertion. Nellie and Howell, not wanting to risk frostbite, watched from the bench under the front window while Teddy, Sophia, Betty and myself rolled around the balls to build it higher. When it was almost complete Sophia ran off to collect coals for his face.

"Hey Teddy," I called out. As soon as he turned to me I launched a snowball at him, catching him off guard and covering his face in snow.

"I'll get you," he said, bending down to pick up a handful of snow and giving me time to dash off.

As I tried to dodge an incoming attack from Betty a snowball caught me in the side of the face making my ears ring and turning my cheek numb. I turned in the direction it had come from to see Mr Hopkin laughing to himself for catching me off guard. The children, unaccustomed to seeing their father being so playful, immediately started pelting him with snow, causing him to duck and dive to avoid them.

"Dinner is ready," he shouted, running around the side of the house away from the onslaught.

Mrs Hopkin had provided us with a feast. I'd never had goose before but it looked and smelled delicious and I couldn't wait to try some. The table was laid out like a banquet with the goose sitting proudly in the middle surrounded by roast potatoes, vegetables and two huge gravy boats filled to the brim. Off to the side she had set a plate for Jack in the hope that he might return for Christmas with his family, though none of us acknowledged it for fear of upsetting her.

"Merry Christmas," Mrs Hopkin called out and raised her glass.

"Merry Christmas," we all cheered back, raising our glasses along with her.

Once a prayer was said, Mr Hopkin gave the nod for everyone to tuck in and the table came alive with chatter and excitement. By the time we had finished we'd eaten our way through more food than I'd seen since I arrived there, and it was all cooked beautifully. For the first time in a long while, I was actually too stuffed to move.

By the time Mair and Gwyn arrived, we'd retired to the sitting room with brandy and the games had already begun. The children had pushed the furniture around to create more space but by the third round of charades, I needed a rest and was desperate for a place to sit.

"Care to join me outside to smoke?" Gwyn asked, approaching me with two drinks in hand. He knew I didn't smoke but I wasn't going to refuse time with him so I followed him out to the yard.

The cold air caught my breath as we stepped out into the darkness and snow had begun to fall again. I wrapped my arms around my body to keep myself warm and wondered why Gwyn had really asked me to join him instead of smoking inside as he had done before.

"I got you a little something," he said, reaching into his inside pocket. The snow was coating his hair and lashes, causing him to blink and shiver as he spoke. He pulled out a small bag and offered it to me. I looked at it, then up at him and gave him a curious look wondering what it might be. "Open it."

Inside the bag was a small silver pocket watch dangling from a chain and it looked far more expensive than what he should be spending on me. I looked down at it in my palm and watched the hands ticking forward counting quick seconds, though the moment between us seemed to last much longer.

"Gwyn, it's beaut-" I started, but he grabbed my arms and pulled me towards him, kissing me hard on the lips right there in the yard. I instinctively froze and then relaxed into his embrace, kissing him back.

It was better than I could have ever imagined. I'd spent so long longing for it that I could hardly believe it was happening and I wrapped my arms around his shoulders, drawing him closer.

"I've wanted to do that since I met you," he said when our connection finally broke. I stared at him, and smiled, wishing it hadn't taken him so long.

"I've got something for you, too," I said, grabbing his hand and leading him to the barn. He followed behind me up the ladder and I reached into my secret cubby to retrieve the small bag which contained his gift. "It's not much but this is for you. It seems a bit rubbish now compared to your gift but I hope you like it."

He opened the bag and pulled out the book that I had bought for him while we were in Aberystwyth.

"It's A Christmas Carol," I said. "It's my favourite. I thought you might like it but if not, I can change it."

"I love it," he said, then he leaned in and kissed me again, pushing me down onto the pillow as he did.

A little while later, leaving Gwyn where he lay, I threw on my shirt and rushed back to the house to get us drinks and grab my coat under the pretence that we were still outside chatting and smoking.

"Are you two alright?" Mrs Hopkin asked as I reached for two glasses and filled them with brandy. "You've been outside for a while."

"Just putting the world to rights," I replied. I snuck a glance over at Mair who raised a disbelieving eyebrow at me. "And Gwyn is trying to encourage me to smoke cigarettes."

"It's bad for you," Mair said. "I don't care what they say."

"I'll bear that in mind," I replied. I grabbed my coat from the hook and then hurried back across the yard into the barn.

"Gwyn, I can't climb the ladder with the drinks," I shouted up through the hatch but got no response. "Gwyn? Gwyn?"

Worried that he'd gotten cold feet and run off I set the drinks down on the floor and rushed up the steps to the second floor.

"Tom, what's this?" he asked, his voice shaking. He was sitting on the hay with a blanket strewn across his middle and my wallet upon it. In his hand he was holding out my driving licence with my picture displayed clearly on the front next to my date of birth; 1971.

Thirteen

Every single hair on my body stood on end as a wave of pure fear washed over me like a cold shiver, freezing me on the spot. I looked at my licence in his hand and my mind raced with all of the possible ways that everything was about to go wrong.

"Gwyn, I can explain," I said, though I had no actual idea how I could and I left the statement hanging there without anything to back it up. I tried to reach out to him but he moved his arm away from me like he no longer knew who I was anymore.

"What even is this?" he asked, trying to bend the plastic card between his fingers. "Why does it say you were born in 1971, Tom? And all these other dates…? They're years from now. I don't understand what this is?"

He waved the card at me and then threw it at my chest, getting angrier the longer I went without explaining myself.

"You wouldn't understand. It's hard to explain."

"So, you're not even going to try?"

"I don't know what to say, Gwyn. You won't believe me and even if you thought that I was being truthful you'd still think I was mad. You should just go."

I didn't want him to leave but I had no way to explain myself and in a return to form it felt easier to push him away than to just be honest about things.

"I'm not going anywhere until you explain yourself," he said. His voice was getting louder, though he did reach out and put his hand on mine which gave me an element of relief. My heart was already racing and I didn't think I could handle seeing him get mad at me as well.

"I don't even know where to start."

"Anywhere, Tom. Start anywhere. Just be honest with me."

"I'm not from here," I blurted it out, deciding to just be truthful with him and deal with the consequences later.

"Well, I know that."

"No, I'm not from *here*," I said, waving my arms all around me. "This time, this year. I don't know how I got here. I was born in 1971. I was living in 1998 and then I woke up one day a few months ago and I was here, in Wales, in this time, with no idea how I got here."

"If you're not going to tell me the truth then I'll leave," he said, reaching for his clothes.

"Look," I said, shoving my fingers into the back of my wallet and pulling out a photograph. "This is me with my brother and sister and my parents." I held up the photograph taken years earlier, in full colour and replete with eighties hair and clothing. He took it in hand and studied it, looking between the photograph and my face as if trying to confirm it was really me.

"I don't understand," he said, rubbing a hand across his eyes.

"I swear to you it's the truth. I was out with my brother and I'd had a bit too much to drink. I passed out and when I woke up I was in your field. I thought my brother was playing a prank or I'd wandered off, but then I met your sister and saw your house…"

"But how?"

"I don't know." I reached over to the cubby, grabbed the ring and held it out to him. "I'm fairly certain it was this."

"That's Jack's ring. I've seen it before."

I contemplated for a second about how much I should reveal, but I figured having come this far I may as well just get it all out.

"Jack hasn't run away with Elinor. At least I don't think so. I think he travelled forward to my time. Well, to some time before I was born. And then he met my mother..." I trailed off and he looked at me, eyes widening. I held out the photo of my family again for him to see. "He's my father."

"Jesus!" he said, raising the photograph close to his face and studying it. "It looks just like him. Older, but just like him."

"Not *just* like him. It *is* him. He died a few months ago, in 1998, when he was 63 years old. I found this ring in his belongings and when I put it on it started glowing and I ended up here. Elinor had a necklace that was made of the same thing. I think she might have gone through time, too."

"This is too much," he said, rubbing his brow. "How? Wait, so the Hopkins are your grandparents?"

"Yes. I didn't know at first, I swear. I saw a photograph in their bedroom and my father was in it. That's why I was running the other day when you came and found me in the top field. That's when I found out."

"And that's what you said I wouldn't understand?"

"Exactly."

He rubbed at his temples while he digested the information I was giving him and he looked like his brain might come running out of his ears at any moment. Now and then he would shake his head at me and then return his gaze to the photograph and I wasn't sure if he entirely believed me, or even if he could or wanted to.

"Look," I said, rummaging through my wallet. Bank cards, this one expires in 2001. My video hire card, issued 1997." I flung the cards towards him hoping it would help convince him.

"What's a video?"

"It's like a little plastic box you use to watch movies. It's… Look it doesn't matter, do you believe me or not?"

"I do. I do. I just…"

"What?"

"It's just a lot to take in."

I reached out and took his hands in mine. "I swear I'm telling you the truth."

His fingers wrapped tightly around mine and he gave me a slight smile, though I could tell he was still apprehensive.

"How do you go back?"

"I don't know. I don't know if I even want to anymore. Do you want me to go?"

"That's not fair. I don't want to stop you from being with your family."

"Well, I sort of am with my family," I joked, which made him smile. "And even if I wanted to go, I can't. It doesn't work anymore. My father never managed to get back here and I can't spend every day looking at it hoping it will work again. I guess that's why he had it locked away in the end, and why I've left it up here out of sight."

"Will you tell them?" he asked, motioning his head towards the house.

"The Hopkins? No. They wouldn't understand. I contemplated telling your sister when I first got here, but I kept it to myself. I didn't want to end up carted off to an asylum." He smiled again but remained silent and kept his head low. "Are you ok, Gwyn?"

"Just thinking," he replied.

"About what?"

"I'm nearly 112 years older than you." His smile turned into a laugh which eased the tension in the room somewhat.

"Well, you look good for it."

When we heard footsteps coming along the floor of the barn downstairs we looked at each other in shock and terror. Gwyn, still undressed, scrambled for his clothes while I stashed away the contents of my wallet which were strewn around us, not wanting to explain either situation to whoever was approaching. He managed to get his trousers on just as Mair popped her head through the hatch next to us.

"Jesus," he said. He seemed to relax a little but my heart still felt like it might beat through my chest. "You frightened the life out of me."

"I don't know what you two think you're playing at," she said, her face furious as she moved her head to look between us, "but I'd think you'd have more sense than to be doing whatever this is right under their noses. Have you no bloody sense?"

"We weren't doing anything," I tried feebly to protest.

"And I suppose my brother's shirt just fell off, did it? Get dressed and get inside and stop being so bloody ignorant."

I'd never seen Mair so mad and I felt bad about having snuck away from the party for so long, but it was quickly side-lined when I realised how cool her reaction was to what she saw. Perhaps she was more progressive than most. Or maybe it was nothing new. Had Gwyn had many partners? Was I jealous?

"NOW!" she shouted, retreating back down the ladder.

Gwyn must have been able to see the fear on my face and he moved on his knees towards me and kissed me on the forehead. "It's ok," he said, face inches from my own. "She's ok. Come to mine tonight. We've both got some things to explain, I think."

Back inside the house, Gwyn made excuses for us that we had been debating some recent politics and lost track of time. Having no clue about any politics of either his time or my own I stayed as silent as possible and nodded along. Luckily, everyone seemed either too drunk or too high-spirited to pay much mind to the finer details.

As the festivities began to wind down and people started retiring to bed, Gwyn made a show about carrying on the party back at his house as an excuse to justify my leaving to go with him. Mair almost threw a spanner in the works by inviting Nellie and Nan to join us, but both declined in favour of their beds which left just the three of us walking through the village in the snow back to their cottage.

"What were you thinking?" Mair finally broke her silence as we walked past the church. "Of all the places. Have you no sense?"

She walked between us for the duration and I couldn't help wondering if she was concerned we might not be able to control ourselves and would start making out in the street.

"You can't stay mad at me for long, dear sister," Gwyn said, his usual charming demeanour even more exaggerated by the alcohol. He linked his arm through hers and she shot him an unimpressed look.

"And what if it had been someone else who came looking for you, eh? How would you have explained that?

"But it wasn't, was it? You worry too much."

"Ten years, Gwynfor! I worry about you being hauled in front of the magistrate and locked up for ten years. And you," she said, turning to me. I'd been attempting to stay silent and unnoticed while she delivered her lecture, but I had no such luck. "Are you trying to get yourself tossed out into the street? Do you think Mr Hopkin would have been so forgiving if he'd walked in on you?"

I remained silent. I didn't have anything that could counter what she was saying that was in any way defensible.

"You two will be the death of me," she said, finally linking her arm into mine and connecting us all together. "If I catch you both being so stupid again…" She left her threat hanging in the air, the message loud and clear.

When we reached the cottage Mair set about lighting lamps and bringing the fire to life while Gwyn poured out three drinks. I removed my coat and headed for the armchair near the window, drawing the curtain closed before I sat.

"Why are you so…" I struggled to find a word, "forgiving?"

Mair sat on the floor holding a log for the fire and considered my question for a moment.

"It's not my job to forgive, Tom. I can't say I understand it, but I suppose I don't need to. We all love differently and I don't think God made anyone wrong. As long as my brother is safe and happy, I've no business poking my nose in."

I was impressed with her attitude. I'd met people less tolerant and progressive even in my own time and I was sure her stance was not one imitated by many in this one. It made my respect for her grow even stronger.

"Right," Mair stood up and brushed the dust from her hands, "I need to get out of this dress so I'm going to bed. Don't stay up drinking too late."

She gave us both a kiss on the cheek and then left for her bedroom.

I turned my attention to Gwyn. "How does she even know?"

He handed me a drink and grinned at the question. "I was about nineteen, I think. Mair would have been about fifteen. I'd come home from the pub, drunk. Far drunker than I'd ever been before or since. I'd spent a year pining for Billy Evans and for some reason I saw fit to tell her about it. I woke up mortified and tried to take it back but she was wise enough to know better. You're the only other person I've ever spoken about it with.

"So, you don't make a habit of getting caught then?" I said with a smirk.

"Not if I can help it," he said, setting his glass down and edging towards me. He put his hands on either arm of my chair and leaned in for a kiss. I brought my hands up to his face and ran my fingers through his beard, enjoying the feel of him being so close.

"Come with me," he said, pulling me up from the chair and leading me to his room.

About an hour later I lay in Gwyn's bed watching the snow falling outside the window. He'd gotten up to get drinks and I waited amongst the sheets for his return, lost in my thoughts. My mind kept running through the events of the evening and I felt changed. Relaxed. At peace. I couldn't even remember the last time I wasn't worrying over something but since I'd arrived here things had made me different. I wanted to see my mother and brother again but I felt sure now that I didn't want to go back. Or at least, I didn't want to go back to how things were, living to work and constantly feeling stressed out and uptight. I was finally, for the first time in a long time, allowing myself to enjoy life, even if it was a life that had been thrust upon me.

Gwyn soon returned to the room with drinks, naked but for a thin sheet around his waist, and climbed back into bed beside me.

"I'm freezing," he said as he wrapped his arm around me. I lay, still in my thoughts, propped on a pillow with my arms behind my head, basking in the moment.

"What do you miss?" he asked as if reading my thoughts. He ran his fingers back and forth across my chest giving me goose pimples all over my skin from his touch.

"Normal clothes" I replied. "And flushing toilets. Oh, hot showers, definitely. I want a shower so bad. My car. Indian food. I love Indian food."

"What about your family?" he asked, making me realise I'd left them off my list.

"Them, too, obviously. My brother, especially. I think this is the longest we've ever been apart."

"Is he like you?"

"We look alike but that's about where the similarities end."

"What's it like where you come from?"

"It's different, but sort of the same. People don't change, I've realised, but everything is faster, busier. Everybody drives cars, with engines, no horses, and they fill the streets. If we had a car we could get to Aberystwyth from here in about fifteen minutes."

He stopped stroking my chest and raised his eyes to me. "You're teasing me."

"I'm not. And if we need to go further, to other countries, we fly on aeroplanes. You could be all the way over in Spain within three hours."

"No, now I know you're lying," he said, playfully slapping me on the chest.

"I don't know how to explain it. After the war, everything changed. Technology developed quicker than ever and the church had less say in things. The last, or next, one hundred years are hugely different."

"What war?"

I wasn't sure at first how much I should reveal, thinking perhaps that to know might somehow change things, but given that he would be in his 50's by the time the First World War started I could see little harm in telling him the truth, and so I gave him a rundown of events as best I remembered them from what I was taught at school. He sat up and listened intently as I recounted stories of the Wars, the rise of the Third Reich, the fall of monarchies and the endurance of our own. I told him of movies and music, the hippy movement and the labour struggles of the eighties. He was awed by the advancements in technology, though I was pretty sure when I told him about the moon landings he thought I was making things up again.

"And what about us?" he asked. "Would we still have to sneak around in secret?"

"Things are better, but there's still a long way to go. It's not illegal anymore and some countries are even talking about legalising marriage. You might still get some stares, but mostly nobody cares and it's not so strange to see couples living together openly."

"Unmarried?" he asked, as though the thought of it was the most shocking thing he'd heard so far.

"Yes, unmarried. Women too. Single parents or unwed couples are all quite common."

"Well, I don't know about Cambridge, but I can't see that taking off in Wales," he said, in utter disbelief.

I laughed and tucked my arm around him, "You'll see."

"But I won't, will I?" he said, suddenly turning to face me. "Whether you stay or go I'll still be here in this time. I'll be long dead before any of that happens."

"Don't think like that. I'm here now."

"But for how long?"

I didn't know how to reassure him because I didn't have any of the answers I knew he wanted. I pulled him in close to me and lay my head against his as I considered what to say next, but before anything came to mind, we'd both fallen asleep.

Fourteen

By the time New Year's Eve rolled around the snowfall had subsided and most of what was on the ground had melted, which meant a return to work at the farm. Gwyn and I had agreed to only see each other occasionally so that we didn't raise suspicions. It was getting harder to explain his frequent visits to the farm, and my disappearances to his house when I should have been working was leaving jobs undone, much to the annoyance of Mr Hopkin.

Earlier in the day during a discussion with Gwyn, he'd told me that unlike in my own time it was not customary to have celebrations on New Year's Eve and instead all festivities would take place the following day to welcome in the New Year. I confirmed this with Mrs Hopkin, who informed me that we would be having another large family dinner followed by a small gathering of friends in the evening, to which Mair and Gwyn would be invited.

I hatched a plan to get some time alone with Gwyn and mentioned to Mrs Hopkin that it was traditional where I came from to spend the evening of New Year's Eve in the pub, which I had hoped would allow me the chance to be out until late without question. What I had not reckoned with, however, was Gethin deciding that this was a custom that he would very much like to adopt and deciding to join me.

Gwyn had found the whole situation quite amusing but argued that it was better to spend time together in the company of others than not to spend time together at all, so we planned to meet in The Farmers' and hoped that we could either make excuses to leave early or that the Gethin would do so instead.

By mid-afternoon, Nan and Betty were busy helping their mother sweep out the hearths of each fireplace, in what I was told was an effort to usher in good luck for the coming year. The superstition must have extended across the whole house because by the time we left for the pub every surface, nook and cranny was sparkling, all the washing had been done, every item in every room put into the right spot, and the whole place was gleaming. It looked better than I'd ever seen it.

Nellie, who seemed a tad put out by Gethin coming along with us for the evening, had tried to convince him to stay and spend time with her, which I wholly encouraged, but he stood firm and she was left reading one of her medical books in the sitting room with a sulk on her face.

When we got to the village Gwyn and Mair were waiting outside for us and I could barely contain my smile at seeing him as I walked toward them.

"Out for a stroll, Miss Griffiths?" Gethin asked as we approached.

"In this weather?" she replied. "I don't think so."

Gethin looked gobsmacked. He was a nice chap but he seemed to have clear ideas of what people's roles and expectations were, and drinking with a woman was obviously something he never anticipated doing. "You aren't planning to come inside, surely?"

"Watch me," she said, and she pulled the door open and strutted into the pub. Gwyn just shrugged and shook his head. I knew he'd have had little say in the matter.

The pub was like most others I'd been to in old villages, with an overabundance of wood panelling, a few tables dotted around with stools and some comfier looking seats with cushions over in the corner. Dai, the landlord, stood at the bar with a towel over his shoulder offering service with a smile to anyone who approached but the sight of Mair had him rattled.

"You can't drink in here, Miss Griffiths," he said, leaning up against the bar.

"She is," Mair replied, loudly indicating to a woman on the other side of the room. "Besides, I'm not here to drink, I'm here to make sure these men stay out of trouble, so I'll be having lemonade. In a proper glass. And you can bring it over." She placed herself down on a stool before he could protest and I grinned at her audacity.

"You better vouch for your sister, Gwynfor," he said, getting Mair's glass ready. "We don't want no women in here causing a scene. You know how they get."

"I'll mind her, Dai," he called back, and it seemed that Mair's battle was won.

"This is quite peculiar, isn't it?" Gethin said. He sat down looking at Mair, bemused. "Wouldn't you rather be in the snug with the other ladies? Do they have one of those here?"

"I'm quite fine where I am, thank you," she replied.

"Right," Gwyn said, changing the topic, "What're we drinking?"

Dai had a good selection of ales and liquors on the shelf behind the counter, some of which I even recognised from my own time, but the dust that gathered over most of them was a good indication that the local clientele didn't have much taste for anything other than tankards of ale. I considered getting a glass of gin, but the suggestion caused the whole table to fall quiet and stare at me as though I'd just spoken a foreign language, so I quickly passed that one off as a joke and said no more about it.

The evening hadn't brought much custom to the bar, and after over two hours of being there, only one other small group had taken up space at one of the tables. Despite my urgency to escape the pub and find my way back to Gwyn's bedroom, I had found myself enjoying the evening. Mair was in fine form with her wit, which kept the table in fits of laughter, and every now and then I would feel Gwyn's foot brush against mine which kept the anticipation ramped up for our eventual liaison.

Gethin had appeared to be enjoying himself throughout the evening but as time wore on I had been running out of things to talk to him about so it came as a bit of a relief when he checked his pocket watch and faked a yawn for our expense, indicating that he was ready to leave.

"It's been fun gentleman, Miss Griffiths," he said, standing up and giving a little bow to the table, "but I should be on my way."

"Enjoy the rest of your evening," I said, standing to shake his hand and wondering if I should have perhaps protested a little to at least make it seem like I wanted him to stay.

He put on his coat and scarf and made for the door. As he pulled it open Arthur Morgan walked in and we immediately caught his attention. Gethin tipped his hat to him and then ducked out the door into the night while Arthur made his way to the bar.

"That's all we need," Mair said, loud enough for him to hear. He ordered a drink and then turned and flashed her a smile. For a second I thought she might get up to give him a piece of her mind but she continued to stare at him, the disgust written all over her face.

Once served, he picked his drink up from the counter and moved to sit at the table right next to us. He had the whole room to choose from but it seemed he wanted to make a point. "Gwynfor," he said with a tip of his hat, completely ignoring my presence. His greasy smile seemed entirely forced and though he was sitting alone he acted as though he owned the whole room. Everything about him, from the way he sat to the way he held his drink reeked of arrogance.

Gwyn was aware of all the issues I'd faced with him and remained silent when he'd attempted to greet him.

"You used to keep better company, Gwyn," he added, determined to get his reaction.

"And where are your friends?" I asked, unable to stop myself from biting back. He let out a snigger and said something in Welsh that caused Mair to clench her fists and Gwyn bolted up from the table, his chair scraping against the concrete sending a loud noise out across the bar.

Arthur got to his feet in equal time and the two men faced off with each other. Mair and I jumped from our seats and each grabbed one of Gwyn's arms, lowering him back to his seat. Dai shouted out in Welsh from behind the bar with a gesture of his thumb, which I deduced meant something along the lines of 'settle down or get out.' Arthur took his seat again but his smirk remained and his eyes never left us.

"What did he say?" I asked, unsure of how offended I should be. Gwyn looked enraged and clenched his hand so tightly around his tankard that I thought he'd put a dent in it.

"Something disgusting," Mair replied. "Because *he's* disgusting." She made sure he could hear but it only caused him to snigger again.

We all sat in silence for the next few minutes, Gwyn and Arthur never taking their eyes off each other, until the call for last orders rang through the bar. Taking it as his cue to leave, Arthur knocked back a final swig of his drink and got up from his seat.

"Have a good evening, Mr Jacob," he said as he passed. "I'll be seeing you soon." He barged my shoulder as he moved toward the door and this time I was the one who got up, intending to follow him outside and have it out once and for all. Gwyn and Mair both grabbed me by the arm and Arthur sauntered out sporting his slimy grin once more.

"This has to stop," I said. "I've done nothing to him. If I'm going to stay here, we can't keep going in circles like this every time we see each other. The man is mad. I'm going to have it out with him."

"You'll do no such thing," Gwyn said firmly, putting his hand on my knee under the table. "Leave it be."

We finished our drinks in silence and made our preparations to leave. As we were gathering our coats the group who had been sitting at the other side of the pub made their exits, leaving just the three of us inside along with Dai.

"You're still coming back to ours, yes?" Gwyn asked.

"If it's ok with Mair?"

I looked at her as she tied her bonnet, and waited for her reaction. I knew she wouldn't say no but I didn't want to put her in a position where she might feel awkward in her own home.

"As long as one of you makes tea before bed. I'm parched. And I'll take breakfast in the morning as well," she joked. "Let's start the New Year as we mean to go on."

"With you being waited on, you mean?" Gwyn said, cocking his eyebrow up at his sister.

194

"Exactly," she replied.

Dai came from around the bar to see us out, ready to lock up upon our exit. "See you soon, folks," he said, but as he swung the door open two police officers walked in, forcing us all back into the pub.

They took slow steps as they walked inside, looking around the room before planting themselves between us and the exit. I recognised one of them immediately. He'd been with Arthur when he'd tried to cut my fingers off after first arriving in the village.

"Looks like you've been serving after hours, Dai," he said.

"Of course not, gentlemen," Dai replied, flashing them a nervous smile. "It's only ten past the hour. They were just finishing up and leaving."

"We're just going on our way, Graham," Gwyn spoke, attempting to get past him, but the second constable put his hands up to stop him from leaving.

"That's Constable Morgan to you, Mr Griffiths."

Morgan, of course. Mair had told me that Arthur's cousin was the local policeman. It was immediately obvious that his arrival here wasn't a coincidence.

"We need you to come with us," he continued, and his colleague reached out for Gwyn's arms.

"What are you doing, get off him!" Mair shouted as she tried to reach her brother. In doing so she barged past Graham Morgan, accidentally knocking him backwards into the wall.

"And we'll take this one for assaulting an officer of the law," he said before turning his attention to me. "Now, do we have to restrain you or will you come of your own accord?"

"Come for what?" I argued. "We haven't done anything. We've been here all night."

I waited for a response but he had no interest in saying anything further. Gwyn was still being held by the other officer but he gave me a nod to let me know he was ok, so against my better judgement I made my way out of the pub with the policemen.

"You can't do this," Mair protested as a pair of cuffs were attached to her wrists. "We haven't done anything wrong."

"Resisting arrest as well, Constable Johnson. See to it that it's all recorded for the magistrates."

"Shut up, Mair," Gwyn scolded as his hands were being bound. "Just say nothing."

"I think that's wise," the other officer said.

"Don't let me catch you serving late again, Dai," Graham said, then he grabbed me by the collar and marched me through the door.

Outside the pub, a carriage was waiting for us and I watched as Gwyn and Mair were put into the back of it. Graham spun me around to put cuffs on me and I spotted Arthur sitting on the wall of the church smiling over at us. As they put me in the back of the wagon and bolted the door, he flicked a cigarette to the ground, gave us a wave and then walked off into the darkness.

The inside of the wagon smelled damp and musty and I could barely see the faces of my friends. In stark contrast to the omnibus that we had travelled in a few weeks earlier, the jailer's wagon was surrounded by bars that let the cold air blow through, leaving us all shivering. "Where are we going?" I asked.

"The city," Gwyn said. "He mentioned the magistrates so we're to appear before the courts I'd imagine."

"For what?" I asked, incredulous at the idea.

"Whatever he decides we've done wrong, I suppose."

"He can't just make up charges," I said, and I began trying to pull my wrists apart to get my hands free.

"He's a Morgan, Tom. He can do what he likes."

"This has got Arthur written all over it," Mair said, her voice filled with rage. "The... the fucking wanker."

Enough light from the moon was breaking through the bars for me to see Gwyn raise his head to look at Mair, and then turn his eyes to me.

"I suppose you taught her that?" He asked, and I had to stifle a laugh.

I leaned my head back against the railing, exhausted and annoyed. The bumps in the road removed any hope of sleep and so I sat, staring, and hoped that whatever fate befell me, it didn't involve a trip to the gallows. If Mrs Hopkin was right and you should start the New Year as you meant to go on, then this didn't bode well for the time ahead.

Fifteen

"Name?"

The officer at the desk blew out a cloud of smoke with his words as he asked for my particulars. Ash was falling from his pipe as he scribbled on a piece of pre-printed paper, which he scrubbed away with the back of his hand leaving streaks of black across my information. He didn't even look at me. Didn't care to.

It was still dark when we'd arrived at the station in Aberystwyth. The wagon had taken a different route to the bus we'd travelled on previously and I found myself in an area of the city that I'd never seen before. The rusty sign clinging high in the corner of the building we had stopped at read, '*Great Darkgate Street*', but it didn't help me get my bearings.

As soon as we were taken from the back of the carriage Mair had been escorted off through an entrance at the side of the building while Gwyn and I were marched up the steps at the front and presented to the duty officer.

He blew out another plume of smoke that got caught in my throat, causing me to cough. With my hands constrained I was unable to cover my mouth and flecks of spit splashed over the man's form. Finally, he looked at me, rather annoyed. "You are hereby charged with drunken behaviour, assault and resisting arrest. Do you have anything to say for yourself?"

"Not guilty," I replied, and the left side of his lips curled up in a snarly grin.

"That is for the courts to decide. Please empty your pockets into this." He reached for something below him and then placed a small wooden box on the desk. Unable to reach my pockets, the officer behind me dug his hands into them, roughly grabbing for the contents before spilling the coins and pocket watch I was carrying into the tray. "You'll now be held at Her Majesty Queen Victoria's pleasure until you are put before the courts in two days hence."

"Two days?" I shouted as I was dragged away down a side corridor. I tried to look back to see if Gwyn was ok but I received a smack to the side of my head for my efforts and was pushed through a huge metal door which slammed shut behind us.

"Where are we going?" I asked, but no reply came. We turned left and started down another corridor. It was dark and dingy with green tiles lining the walls and no windows to let in any light. At the end of the corridor was a row of holding cells and Graham marched me to the furthest one.

He smirked as he shoved me inside but said nothing while he undid my handcuffs. I wanted to plead my case but I knew it was pointless so I just watched as he locked the heavy steel door behind him, leaving me alone.

The room was damp and cold with the bare stone walls providing the minimum of shelter and the tiny window, too high up for me to see out of, not yet letting any sunlight in. Two benches lined the walls, not wide enough to sleep on and too hard to be comfortable, and in the corner near the door was a metal bucket. The smell coming from it let me know exactly what it was to be used for and I took a seat as far away from it as I could.

I waited alone in the dark for around fifteen minutes before I heard footsteps in the hallway again. When the cage opened, I allowed myself a brief moment of hope that perhaps someone was coming to tell me that it had all been a terrible mistake and that I was free to go, but the arrival of Gwyn and the re-locking of the door dashed that small bit of hope to pieces.

"Did they hurt you?" he asked, rushing over to me on the bench. I stood to greet him and he raised his hands to my face, kissing me, before drawing me into a hug.

"I'm fine," I said. "What about you? Are your ribs ok?" I pulled his shirt up to take a look at him, running my hands across his stomach. He didn't appear to be any worse off than before but I knew he wouldn't tell me if he was in pain.

When I was sure that he was fine I sat on the bench and tried to get comfortable. The room was thin enough that I was able to put my feet up on the one opposite and Gwyn sat alongside me with his head in his hands.

"I hope Mair's alright," he said. "I don't like that they took her off."

"It's Mair," I said, trying to sound reassuring. "She'll be fine. You know she can look after herself."

"I just hope her mouth doesn't get her into any more trouble."

"What do you think he's doing this for? Arthur, I mean."

He leaned back against the wall and let out a long sigh. "Because he can."

"What will happen to us?" I asked, worried I might be spending the rest of my life behind bars.

"Neither of us has been in trouble before. Arthur might be able to get his cousin to do his dirty work but neither of them is a judge and neither of them can decide our fate." He paused for a second before adding, "At least, I hope not, anyway. If we're lucky we might get a fine."

"But they took all my money."

"Mine too," he said. "If they're honest men we'll get it back."

"If they were honest men, we'd not be here in the first place."

It was several hours before anybody came back to check on us and we were both irritable from the lack of sleep and the discomfort of the cell. Hearing the jingle of keys in the corridor outside, both of us bolted upright and stared at the door in anticipation.

When it swung open a man stood before us that I didn't recognise. He was younger than the men who had dealt with us the previous night and his face seemed friendlier as his eyes flicked between us.

"Jacob? Griffiths?" he asked, as if we weren't the only two men in the cell. "Come with me, please."

Leaving the door wide open he turned heel and headed down the corridor. Gwyn and I gave each other a glance before rushing out and following behind him until we found ourselves back in the area of the station where we'd had our charges read to us.

"Wait here, please," he said, then he made his way to a door on the opposite side of the room. When he pulled it open Mair was standing behind it and she immediately bolted toward us. In her outstretched hands she carried a heavy-looking paper bag which whacked into my shoulder blades as she flung her arms around me. She leaned back and looked at me with glee, then, taking hold of my face she planted a kiss squarely on my lips.

"My love," she wailed dramatically. She stepped back again and squeezed my face pushing my lips into a pucker. I raised an eyebrow at her and her smile spread wide. "Oh, my love, I missed you. I thought I'd never see you again."

I glanced at Gwyn who looked as surprised as I was and Mair threw her arms around my waist and held on to me tightly.

"Thank you, constable," she called over my shoulder. "We will see you bright and early tomorrow morning." Then, linking her arm through mine she dragged me towards the door and into the street.

As soon as the door slammed closed behind us Mair let go of my arm and powered down the steps to the pavement. "You owe me twenty shillings," she said, pointing a finger at me before she began to walk off down the street.

"What for?" I asked, trying to keep step behind her.

"For posting your bail, Thomas."

"But how are you out here?" Gwyn asked.

She stopped and turned around pushing the bag she was carrying into her brother's chest. "The man they sent me off with was a fool. He saw me in my fancy dress and wanted to know how a respectable lady such as myself ended up in custody so far away from home, so I told him the truth. Well, some of the truth, anyway. I said I was an innocent lady out fetching my idiot brother and my darling fiancé home from a 'soirée' when the police arrived and in all my protestations they'd gotten me confused as a troublemaker and carted me off. I cried a bit, said some things about God and my dead parents and he suddenly became ever so obliging and let me go with a warning not to get mixed up with delinquents."

"So, they're letting us go, too?" I asked.

"Not on your life," she replied. "Over an hour I spent this afternoon trying to convince that man to let you out. Tried all ways to tell him that you were upstanding citizens and that it was all a big misunderstanding, but he would have none of it. When he got sick of my nagging he finally agreed to bail. Your release came at the cost of twenty shillings and I want it back from one of you."

The smile on Gwyn's face widened as she'd revealed her tale, impressed, though probably unsurprised by her audacity. "So, what now?"

"You're still in court tomorrow as planned. You're to meet the constable outside at 8'o'clock sharp and if you don't show up they'll arrest you as runaways. It's the best I could do."

"I could kiss you," Gwyn said, grabbing his sister and squeezing her.

"Well, I'd rather you didn't."

"What's in the bag?" I asked.

"Your stuff. But I don't know if all the money is there or if they helped themselves to any. You better hope they didn't."

Mair walked on and I took the bag from Gwyn to look inside. The watch was there alongside a handful of coins. There didn't seem to be anything missing that I could tell. By the time we reached the far side of the promenade, I'd put everything back into my pockets and discarded the scrunched-up bag.

"We're here," Mair said, coming to a stop in front of a large building that looked out over the water. The sign outside said 'The Queens Hotel', and it was one of the biggest buildings I'd seen in the city, with huge windows overlooking the ocean and a grand entrance leading inside.

"Why are we here?" Gwyn asked, casting me a confused glance.

"I'm not going all the way home and coming back again when we can just stay here for the night," Mair said. "Gwyn, go in and book us two rooms. Tell them we're all siblings, here to visit family. Make sure they know I am to have a room of my own. I don't need them thinking I'm some sort of forward woman."

With our story set, we climbed the steps and entered the building, all trying hard to look like we belonged. Despite the events of the previous 24 hours, we all still looked fairly respectable in our celebratory finest, and Gwyn didn't seem to be having any trouble making the reservation for us.

"Three bloody pounds" he whispered when he got back from the reception desk.

"Be glad it wasn't more," Mair replied. "Now, where are the rooms?"

We followed Gwyn through the lobby of the hotel which was much grander than anywhere I'd visited since arriving in Wales and offered a sense of classic luxury. Plush carpets covered every floor and the walls were adorned with the finest artwork and furnishings. Three pounds seemed like a fair price to pay.

As we descended the stairs Gwyn smiled at me and it occurred to me that we would have a room to ourselves, warm and comfortable, for a whole night. Arthur Morgan may have drained our pockets with his little escapade but I definitely owed him a thank you for creating the perfect getaway for Gwyn and me.

"Mair, you're along here. 106," he said, handing her a key and pointing down the hallway off the first staircase. "If you need us, we're just on the other side of the doors in 112."

"I won't need you," she said with a wide grin. "I won't be getting out of that bed until morning." She gave us a wave and disappeared through the double doors to her room, leaving us alone.

"Shall we?" Gwyn asked with a smile, holding open the doors on the opposite side of the landing for me.

When we got inside our room I felt like I'd died and gone to heaven. By modern standards, it was lacking some of the essentials I'd have normally enjoyed, but compared to the barn or Jack's lumpy bed it was a relative palace.

The walls were decorated with an ornate red and white wallpaper that covered the whole room, with curtains that matched it hanging from both windows. Between the windows on the wall was a small radiator, which I ran towards and rubbed my hands along as though it were an old intimate friend.

"Oh my god. Heat!" I said with excitement. It was only warm, at best, but I didn't care. We had a heat source that didn't involve seventeen blankets and an open fire and for that I was grateful. Gwyn came up behind me and wrapped his arms around my waist and I leaned my head back against his shoulders. "Not yet," I said, pulling his hands away. "I need to see the bathroom first."

"I don't think I've ever seen you this excited," he called after me as I headed to open the bathroom door.

"Oh my god," I called out, thrilled by the contents of the room. A sink with running water. A bathtub with its own taps. A toilet. A real-life, working, flushing toilet. "I don't think we can ever leave here," I said, poking my head through the door.

Gwyn was lying on one of the single beds, his waistcoat removed and his shirt buttons open to the waist, and I suddenly lost all interest in the bathroom.

"How's the bed?" I asked. There were two in the room, singles, though neither of us had any intention of using the second one.

"Come and find out," he replied, smirking and tapping his hand on the little bit of space beside him.

I didn't need any more persuasion. I kicked off my boots and climbed up the bed over him, kissing up the length of his chest as I went. When my lips met his he grabbed at my shirt, pulling it up and over my head, then spun me over, nearly toppling us off the bed in the process. I pulled him in close to me and he tucked his head into the crook of my neck.

"We should stay here forever," I whispered.

It couldn't have been any later than 6 a.m. when Mair came banging at our hotel room door to wake us for our day in court. My sleep had been uneasy, thinking of all the worst possible outcomes, so I was already awake by the time she arrived. Gwyn, who seemed to have no such trouble getting rested, lay beside me with his arm thrown over me and his chest pressing against my back.

"One minute," I shouted, as I untangled myself from his embrace. I grabbed a shirt and threw it over my head then ran to open the door before the people in the other rooms started to complain about the knocking.

Mair looked immaculate as she waded into the room and shook her brother awake. The comfortable rest had obviously done her good and she bounced around the room with an upbeat excitement as though we were going on an excursion instead of spending the day in front of a magistrate.

When we arrived outside the court the constable who had issued our release was waiting to escort us in. We sat in the courtroom for a little over 20 minutes, waiting and watching while other men took their turn in the dock, a rotation of criminals coming and going for all to see. Mair wasn't allowed in with us and was instead directed to wait with a group of other women in the foyer, which greatly displeased her.

Most of my fellow criminals were being tried for petty crimes and alcohol seemed to be a contributing factor to the majority of cases. There was no sign of a jury or barristers anywhere in the room and the judge, upon reading the notes of each case, swiftly issued down his sentences. Most were not even asked for a plea, their guilt merely assumed.

The presiding judge, Lord Chambers, seemed to have little care for either the crimes or the men standing before him. He gave a distinct impression throughout every proceeding that he would rather be elsewhere but I was comforted by the fact that he appeared to be fairly lenient, with most men receiving only fines.

I was glad of his quick work and didn't want to spend any more time there than was necessary. The room was horrible, dark and musty, with wall-to-wall wooden panelling that looked like it needed replacing many years before. His words echoed around the room making him sound more intimidating than he probably was and as he looked down from his podium I couldn't help but feel small and completely at his mercy.

When it was my turn to be seen I was escorted to the dock and made to stand opposite the judge for sentencing.

He looked down at me from his seat only to confirm to himself that I was actually there and then returned to scribbling away on the document before him.

"Thomas Jacob, you stand before me accused that on the night of December 31st, eighteen hundred and eighty-nine, you did knowingly engage in drunken behaviour, committed an assault on a fellow citizen and resisted the attempts of a constable to subdue you. How do you plead?"

When the topic of the court case had come up the previous night, Gwyn and I had agreed to plead guilty to the charges brought against us because he thought they were petty enough that we may get away with only a fine. Pleading not guilty and going to a trial by jury would mean calling in Arthur Morgan and his corrupt cousin to testify against us and would almost certainly result in us being imprisoned. Admitting guilt was the lesser of two evils.

"Guilty," I said, begrudgingly, knowing it to be false and that I had done nothing wrong.

"In light of your having no previous record of ill behaviour, and your acceptance of responsibility in this matter, you are to be issued with a fine of six shillings, to be paid to the clerk of the court no later than 24 hours hence."

He returned his gaze to his desk and gave a wave of his hand to dismiss me. The constable at my side led me out of the room and I gave a nod to Gwyn on my way out. As we exited the room I heard his name being called out by the judge and hoped he would not receive a punishment more severe.

In the waiting room outside the court the number of women who were waiting had dwindled, but among the remaining sat Mair. She was being talked at by a woman that she was paying no attention to and when she saw me, she got up and walked across the hall, leaving the woman on the bench mid-sentence.

"I got a fine," I said as she hugged me.

"And what about Gwyn?"

"He's up now."

We didn't have to wait long for him to appear, thankfully. Mair spotted him first while I was counting through the coins from my pocket. She rushed over to hug him and he flashed me a smile over her shoulder. I felt like I could exhale for the first time since we arrived there and I wanted so badly to be able to hug him, too.

"How much?" I asked as he made his way over to where I stood.

"Eight and six," he replied, and I dug through my pocket for more coins. He'd received an extra charge for disturbing the peace which resulted in a heftier fine but I was happy to pay it if it meant we could get out of there and go home. Despite having the chance to spend a night with Gwyn in a posh hotel, where for a brief moment it was as though we were like any other normal couple, I knew I would be glad to see the back of Aberystwyth and be back in the familiar surroundings of Cwm Newydd, where I planned to finally have it out with Arthur Morgan once and for all.

When we arrived back in the village we were all exhausted and had spent much of the carriage journey in silence. Gwyn asked that I spend the night with him again, and tempting though his offer was, I knew I'd have to face the music and explain myself to the Hopkins sooner rather than later, so I declined. I did, however, accept his offer to escort me home. Mair, tired and hungry, flatly refused an offer to join us and with a half-hearted wave she disappeared up the lane to the cottage.

Mrs Wilkes stood outside the post office as we passed through the centre of the village, waiting on her daily sources of gossip and intrigue. When she spotted us, she came rushing over, a wide grin across her face, and when neither of us acknowledged her approach, she stepped into our path to stop us in our tracks.

"*Prynhawn da*, gentlemen," she said as she cast her eyes between us. She was twirling a black parasol over her right shoulder, though there was neither sun nor rain that she needed shielding from. "That was some nasty business at the pub, wasn't it? I could barely believe my eyes when I looked out of my window and saw the constable dragging you off."

She emphasised the last few words as an elderly couple walked past us on the pavement, causing both of them to cast us disapproving glances and Mrs Wilkes' smile to widen.

"Just a misunderstanding, Rachel," Gwyn said, and his use of her first name caused her smile to dim somewhat.

"Hmm, quite," she replied, arching her eyebrows as though she knew better. "I do hope Constable Morgan wasn't injured. I heard there was quite a scuffle."

"And I'm sure you've wasted no time in telling everyone as much," Gwyn shot back. His patience was wearing thin and I pulled on his arm to get him to move on.

"Was there anything in particular you wanted, Mrs Wilkes?" I asked.

"Just being neighbourly," she responded, her smile now back to maximum. "Do have a good day, gentlemen."

She held an arm out to allow us to pass and then scurried down the pavement to find her next victim as we headed up to the farm.

"I'll see you tomorrow, yeah?" I said to Gwyn as we reached the front gate. I stared up at the house and the small hill I would have to climb to reach it. Once again, I'd brought embarrassment to the Hopkins and I was dreading their reaction when I returned home.

"I'm going to walk you to the house," he said, pushing through the gate and holding it open for me.

"I can make the last few steps on my own," I said. "You should go get some rest."

His gorgeous smile spread across his face and he reached up to rub the back of his neck. "But I can't kiss you goodbye out here, can I?"

When we approached the side of the house, I noticed the barn door was swinging in the wind and I walked over to push it shut. As I did so, I saw the latch had been broken, apparently forced from its hinge. I peered my head inside but there was no sign of anyone in there.

"That's odd," Gwyn said, examining the latch.

"The ring!" I whispered, remembering my stash on the top floor of the barn. I burst through the door and ran for the ladder. I climbed as fast as I could, careless in my ascent, and my feet slipped on the rungs as I went. When I reached the top I scrambled through the hatch and across the makeshift bed to the cubby I had made to hide my belongings. My heart raced as I pulled the sheets back and looked inside.

It was empty. Both my ring and my wallet were gone.

"Where is it?" I shouted as I tore through sheets and hay, hoping to find it among the debris that I was leaving behind. Gwyn came up beside me and began to help me look. When it was nowhere to be found I slumped down and threw my head into my hands.

"It's him. It's got to be." Gwyn looked at me and I knew he was thinking the same thing. "Arthur's got the ring."

Sixteen

On Gwyn's insistence, I agreed that I would wait until the following morning before heading out in my search for Arthur and my belongings. He'd spent over an hour sitting in the barn trying to calm me down and though I knew he was right, he wasn't making me feel any less anxious. When he was finally sure that I wouldn't rush off into the night, he said his goodbyes and left for home.

When I got back to the house, Mr and Mrs Hopkin were sitting at the table with Nellie and Teddy, and all discussion ceased upon my arrival. I immediately made my apologies to Mrs Hopkin, who ushered me into a seat and began boiling a pot on the stove for tea.

"So, you're a crook now?" Teddy asked, barely able to contain his excitement over the subject.

"Enough of that," Mrs Hopkin said, slapping him over the back of the head with her tea towel. Even Mr Hopkin let out a little snigger, amused at the predicament I'd found myself in.

"Does everyone know?" I asked. I felt embarrassed and unable to find much humour in the situation.

"There's been words in the village," Nellie said. "They were discussing it in the post office. I came straight home to let everyone know where you were."

"We were worried sick," Mrs Hopkin said. She placed a cup down on the table in front of me and scooped in a spoonful of tea leaves. "We're just glad you're alright."

"It was Arthur," I said, feeling no shame in pointing the finger firmly in his direction. "He set the whole thing up. We didn't do anything wrong."

"I'm just glad it was only you and not Gethin as well," Nellie said as she took a sip of tea. She immediately glanced up over the rim and looked horrified. "I don't mean…"

"It's ok," I said. "I'm glad he wasn't involved, too. But I swear, we did nothing."

"We know, son," Mr Hopkin said.

"So, you didn't smash the pub up?" Teddy asked, disappointed that I wasn't a master criminal.

"Where on earth did you hear that?" Mrs Hopkin asked.

"That's what Mrs Wilkes told Nan," he replied, shrugging his shoulders.

I rolled my eyes and shook my head. "Nothing was smashed up. And Mrs Wilkes needs to learn to mind her own business."

"She's always been close to the Morgan's," Mrs Hopkin said. "Got a real soft spot for Arthur."

"I don't know why," I replied. "He's awful."

"It was probably him that broke into the barn," Teddy said. He leaned back in his chair and folded his arms, his mind already made up on the matter.

"I was meaning to ask about that," I said. "What happened?"

"We came back from church yesterday and the lock was broken off." Mr Hopkin shifted in his seat, angry with the situation. "Nothing gone, as far as I can tell, but it's me that'll have to pay to fix that lock."

"Like we haven't got enough to be worrying about as it is," Mrs Hopkin chimed in.

I didn't tell them that my things had gone missing and he made no mention of the ring or wallet which reassured me that nobody from the house had taken it, but it didn't make me feel any less anxious about the fact that it was even more likely to be in the hands of Arthur.

"If you don't mind," I said, setting my cup down on the table, "I could do with getting some sleep. I'm going to go up to bed."

My sleep was restless. My mind raced with panic about the situation and I laid there trying to dream up more lies that I could tell to cover my tracks should Arthur decide to reveal my secrets. I tossed and turned, struggling to get comfortable and shut my mind off until finally I heard the birds begin to chirp outside and wondered if I'd even managed to get any sleep at all.

I'd promised Gwyn that I would wait for him to come with me to Felin Fawr to confront Arthur, but I couldn't wait any longer. The anxiety was driving me mad so I got up from the bed and got dressed. I was going to go there immediately.

I could hear Mrs Hopkin down in the kitchen preparing breakfast but I had no appetite for food. I needed to get this done. I crept slowly down the stairs so that I didn't wake anyone up, and tiptoed through the living room while trying to work out an excuse as to why I needed to leave before eating.

Seemingly wise to my intentions, I pushed through the door into the kitchen and was faced with Gwyn, who was sitting at the table drinking tea and awaiting my early arrival.

"Here he is," he said. His tone was neutral but he looked less than impressed with me.

I sat on the chair nearest the door and started putting my boots on, and Mrs Hopkin flashed me a smile and put a cup down beside me before disappearing into the pantry, leaving us alone for a moment.

"I didn't know you'd be here so early," I said, my voice no higher than a whisper.

"I can see that," he snapped back. I hated when he was annoyed with me. "Do you think I'm stupid?"

Our glares at each other were interrupted by Mrs Hopkin coming back into the kitchen. "Will you be back in time for dinner? I'm making a stew. I dare say you'll be hungry after working on that old barn all day."

"The what?"

"It shouldn't take us too long, Mrs Hopkin. I'm just glad Tom offered to help."

"Quite right, too. You shouldn't be overdoing it or you'll crack another rib."

"Yes," he said, turning to face me again. "I really should be taking it easy."

"Well, you stay here then," I said, rising to my feet "and I'll go and do it by myself."

"No, it'll be better if I'm there," he said, also standing. He looked as annoyed as I felt. Mrs Hopkin, sensing something was off, had also come to a stop and just stared at the two of us while we glared at each other. Had it not been for Nan bursting into the kitchen I don't think any of us would have backed down first.

"Was it something I said?" She asked as I reached for the back door and stormed out of it. Gwyn was close behind me but I was in little mood to talk and I walked off ahead. I avoided the path to the gate and instead crossed the field behind the barn and hopped the fence onto the top road out of the village.

"Do you want to tell me what that was all about?" Gwyn asked from a few steps behind me. I'd heard him struggling with the fence and I wanted to go and check on him but my stubbornness wouldn't allow it and I'd continued walking off.

The wind at the top of the hill was bitter and it seemed to be getting stronger as we walked. The rain and snow were holding off, at least, but I'd rushed out without my jacket and I was already regretting it. I knew the estate was about three miles away, but I'd never been there, or even to this side of the village. I was just hoping the road would lead me to where I needed to go and I wouldn't freeze to death before I got there.

"You don't have to come with me," I said. "I don't want you getting caught up in my shit, Gwyn."

"I want to be there for you," he called back. "You shouldn't go alone. You don't know what he's capable of."

"I don't care, Gwyn. I'm sick of it."

"Look at the bother we've been in for the last few days. You think he couldn't make things even worse for everyone if he wanted to?"

"I don't care. I want my things back and I'm going to tell him to leave me alone."

He grabbed me by the arm, stopping me in the middle of the road and shook me. "Stop! You're being reckless rushing in like this." He stared right at me but I wouldn't meet his gaze, determined not to let him talk me out of going. "He's already beaten you, had us arrested, broken into the barn and had Nan dismissed. What do you think he'll do next if you keep provoking him?"

"Provoking him? Gwyn, I've done nothing! I'm not going to be bullied and I'm not going to have this hanging over me, waiting for him to tell everyone about me. I'm going to have it out with him and you can either come with me or do us both a favour and go home."

We walked in silence for the remainder of the journey. I kept wanting to say something, to apologise for being so snappy with him, but I knew my stubbornness would not allow it. As bad as I felt inside, I knew that if I opened my mouth to speak I would give him the same short temper as before, and I wanted to at least save him that.

When we approached the gates to the estate and I saw the house for the first time I was amazed by its size and grandeur, and then mystified as to why someone due to inherit it, who could spend their days living amongst its opulence, would devote so much time to terrorising the people of the village.

"We can just go back," Gwyn said as we stood at the bottom of the long driveway. I looked at him and then at the house. My mind was made up long before we'd even got there and I wasn't about to change it. I marched on up the driveway to the front door and started banging on it with my fist.

"Yes?" A suited man answered the door, a butler I assumed, and he looked at me with immediate disdain. I stood firm, refusing to allow him the belief that he was better than me even if he did work in a fancy house.

"Arthur! Where is he?" I tried to see into the house behind him but could see nothing but fancy furnishings. The man's demeanour remained unchanged and he stared at me in silence. "I want to see him now!" I demanded.

"I'm afraid you will have to return at a later date," he said, and then he moved to close the door. I reached my hand out to stop him from shutting me out and he stared at me in disbelief.

"You tell him to come out here now," I demanded again, keeping force on the door so that he would have to acknowledge me.

"Mr Morgan has left on business and won't be back for some days."

His face was filled with disgust which annoyed me even further. I was sure that the whole house was now aware of the commotion I was making on their doorstep but I didn't care.

"I'll need you to let go of the door," he said sternly, putting some force behind it.

I didn't want to let go. I didn't want this to all be for nothing but I knew deep down that Arthur would have no fear in facing me. If he was in there he'd have come out and he'd have loved every minute of it.

"Come on, Tom, let's go," Gwyn said, pulling my arm away from the door. The butler took the opportunity to slam it in my face leaving me on the doorstep with nobody to argue with but Gwyn. In one of the windows, I could see two young women in uniform staring out at me and I turned away before I shouted something at them that I'd regret later on.

"What the hell did you do that for?" I shouted at Gwyn, turning my ire on him. I stormed off down the driveway to the gate before he could answer. "You should have stayed out of it."

"What were you going to do? Stand there all day and night until Arthur comes back? Didn't you hear him? He'll be gone for days. What good were you doing?"

"That's not the point, Gwyn."

"Then what is the point? Why don't you explain it to me?" He stopped me again and we stood face to face in the road. I felt sure the people in the house were still watching from the windows but I didn't care anymore.

"He's got my ring and I want it back!" I tried to keep my voice level and calm but it was seething with anger.

"Jesus! That fucking ring," he shouted, raising his hands to his head. "Why do you even care? Let him disappear if that's what's to happen."

"You don't get it," I screamed at him.

"No, I think I do." He replied, pointing a finger in my face. "I'm not stupid, Tom, no matter what you might think."

"Gwyn, I don't thi-"

"You think just because I didn't grow up with... what are they called, cars? And moving pictures and fancy schools that I'm some sort of simpleton? That I don't know someone trying to run away when I see one? I don't need your expensive education to know there's life beyond this valley. Beyond this time."

He dropped his voice to a low growl and came close enough to my face that I could feel the warmth of his breath. He was furious. I'd never seen him like that before and I didn't like it.

"You want that ring because you want to be able to run away the moment things get uncomfortable for you. The second you find out how it works you'll be gone. Do you think I don't know that?"

"Gwyn, that's not-"

"I can't do this, Tom." His voice had changed from anger to sadness and I tried to reach out to him but he moved away to the other side of the road, turning his back on me.

"What's that supposed to mean?"

"We can't see each other anymore."

"You don't mean that." I reached out again and grabbed his arm but he shook me off. He raised his hand to his face, biting at the tip of his thumb as he thought about his next words. I wanted more than anything to just connect with him but he could barely even look at me.

"If you find that ring then you'll leave the moment you work out how to get back to your own time. And even if you don't, what do we have? A lifetime of sneaking around? Of stolen moments hoping nobody catches us? A life lived in secret? Is that what you want? And what of me? Should I spend the rest of our time always wondering if you wished you were somewhere else? One big argument and you disappear, never to be seen again. I can't do it. We shouldn't do it to each other."

"But I want to be with you." I could feel myself beginning to cry and I looked to the ground, embarrassed. Finally, he softened, coming towards me and putting his hands on my face.

"This isn't your time," he said softly, raising my head to look him in the eyes. "Things are not as simple here as they are for you back home. You could never walk down the street and hold my hand, or proudly be with me without anyone paying any notice."

"But I don't care about any of that." I was now openly sobbing, my eyes pleading with him to change his mind.

"You should care," he said, wiping tears from my face.

"But what about all the things you said? About how you felt?"

"I meant it. You know I meant it. I think you are amazing. But when that ring went missing, I was glad. I didn't know I would be, but I was. And then seeing how desperate you were to have it back… Your heart isn't here. I wish things were different."

"They can be. Don't do this," I pleaded.

"We have to, Tom."

"Don't say 'we'. You're choosing this."

"Then *I* have to."

I threw my arms around him and I wasn't sure if I'd ever be able to let go but he kissed me on the top of the head and gently pulled himself away. I couldn't bring myself to look at him so I turned and I ran and I didn't stop until I reached the farm.

"Did you wait until all the morning jobs were done before returning?" Nan said to me as I crossed the yard behind the barn. She was standing at the pump filling pails with water and I took my frustration out on the closest one, kicking it across the cobbles and spilling the contents everywhere.

"What on earth is wrong with you?" She angrily called after me, but I ignored her and carried on my route, swinging open the barn door and then slamming it behind me.

I hadn't even reached the ladder when the door swung open again and she stood at the entrance with her hands on her hips. "Do you want to tell me what that was about?" She demanded.

I didn't want to speak to her. In fact, she was probably the last person I wanted to speak to, but she stood firm, her foot tapping on the concrete as she awaited my response. Her face was stern and I saw in her what I used to see in my father when he would give me a dressing down. I'd never noticed how similar they were before and now I was realising it I felt even less inclined to speak to her.

"I don't know how they do things where you come from, but around here it's bad form to ignore someone when they speak to you."

"Fine. I'm sorry I kicked your water over. Now, will you please leave me alone?" I reached for the rungs on the ladder and began to climb but I stopped myself after a few steps and rested my head against the wood. "Look, I'm sorry. I didn't mean to take it out on you, I'm just having a bad day. It's not your fault."

"I should say it isn't," she replied, remaining firm. She was making it really difficult for me to not get snappy with her again and I took heavy breaths to compose myself. "Well?"

"Well, what?" I asked.

She moved to a bale of hay against the wall and sat down on it, arms folded, and waited. She had no intention of leaving until she got an explanation so I reluctantly stepped down off the ladder and sat across from her.

"I assume you don't go around kicking things without good reason."

I didn't know what to say. I couldn't tell her what happened with Gwyn or explain about the ring but I realised that I needed to get everything off my chest. She wouldn't have been my first choice of therapist but she was there and seemed willing to listen, so I talked.

"I suppose I've just realised today that I can't have everything that I want." It was vague but it was at least true.

"Have you ever wanted two things at once but ended up left with neither?"

"Yes," she replied, "I wanted a good position and a steady income, and now I don't have either of those things."

I rolled my eyes at her, not able to go over that again, but her face softened and she gave me a small grin so perhaps she was being only partly serious.

"Forgive me, but I must ask. Does this have anything to do with a certain lady friend?" I looked up at her and said nothing. I was curious to hear what her thoughts might be so I allowed her to believe what she wanted to believe. "Has there been a falling out?"

"Let's say it was about someone else. Just hypothetically. I'm not from here and I never planned to stay for even this long. Certainly not forever. I can't promise them that I'll never want to go home but it's far too early to make a promise to stay, and unless I do, hypothetically, of course, then nothing can happen. So now I'll never know if it would have developed into something that made me want to stay here for good. Does that make any sense at all?"

I felt like I was rambling but she thought on my words for a few seconds then dropped her hands into her lap, shifted herself upright and looked me dead on.

"If you are unable to provide certainty to a person, should you expect them to wait for you until you make a decision? Should they spend every day wondering if that is the day you decide you'd rather make your life elsewhere? It seems to me, if you'll allow me to be honest, that *you* are the one who isn't being entirely fair in this circumstance. If you are unable to provide a guarantee then it seems the honourable thing to do is to walk away until you can make a decision that you will stick to."

She was rubbish at this. I didn't ask for wisdom, I needed her to lie to me. She should have been telling me that I was allowed to take as long as I wanted and that it was ok to be torn and confused. I wanted reassurance and comfort.

I hated that she was right.

Seventeen

In the two weeks since Gwyn had ended things with me, my main focus was to keep things together and act as normally as possible around the farm. Mr Hopkin didn't seem to notice any changes and kept me busy with work but Teddy picked up on it and continuously followed me around asking me if I was ok. It was sweet that he cared but the constant reminders that I was not, in fact, ok, became irritating quite fast.

I'd only seen Gwyn once in that whole time. I'd popped to the post office to run an errand for Mrs Hopkin and saw him coming out of the pub with a man I'd never seen before. He was more than a little worse for wear and decided to come over to talk to me, and with nowhere to run to I had no option but to face him.

He remained polite throughout our brief chat but as soon as I was able, I made excuses to leave. I wanted more than anything to stay, to listen to anything he had to say on any topic at all, just so that I could spend time with him, but I couldn't. It hurt all over again to be so close to him and yet feel so distant, and I was worried that I would say something that I shouldn't, or that he would say something that I didn't want to hear. Running away was easier.

I had to change my whole routine to get him out of my head. I missed seeing him every day. I missed the way we would sneak off to spend time alone or make excuses to see each other. I missed his smile and his laugh and his touch. The more I thought about it, the more work I took on until I started to think about him a little less each day.

Despite what had occurred, I still saw a lot of Mair. The day after Gwyn and I argued she came to see me to check that I was alright. I wasn't entirely certain what he had told her, but she placed the blame squarely at his feet and I did nothing to contradict that.

She suggested that I go to see him and try to raise his mood. He'd been down, apparently, but I had mixed feelings about it. It was his decision that brought us to this place but I hated the idea of him being sad. I'd heard that he'd been drinking a lot, too. Nan had mentioned seeing him come from the pub one afternoon, and Nellie and Gethin had also seen him sitting on the floor outside one evening. He told them he'd been cut off by Dai and told to go home but had been too drunk to make it any further than the pavement.

I asked Mair about it and she hinted that he'd been drinking at home too, but I got annoyed and changed the subject. I didn't like the implication, intentional or otherwise, that I may have played a part in him picking up a bottle instead of working through his emotions like the rest of us had to.

I'd returned to Felin Fawr twice since my first visit in the hopes of confronting Arthur. At first, I was told that he was still not back from his trip and the door was shut in my face again, but on the next visit, they didn't even answer. After several attempts to get the attention of someone from inside, I returned to the farm, defeated.

I'd asked around the village for information about his whereabouts but nobody had heard from him in weeks. Even Mrs Wilkes had no information, or at least none that she would part with. The whole situation just made me even madder. Gwyn wanted us to be apart because he couldn't guarantee I wouldn't leave, and Arthur having the ring and being out of town ensured that I had to stay. Either way, I was losing out.

And so I continued throwing myself into work on the farm, picking up every job and errand that needed completing and being more productive than I had been since I started helping out there. I'd mended fences and gates, repaired a leak in the cow shed, re-ploughed the fields ready for spring and even made a start on building a new coop for the chickens.

Inside the house had been no different. I'd fixed two of the beds, installed new shelves for Mrs Hopkin in the kitchen, and built a dollhouse with Sophia and a bookcase for all of Nellie's medical journals. There was nothing that I wasn't willing to do to keep myself occupied.

The chicken coop was proving to be my biggest job of all. They were always running around the yard and the field in front of the house, and more than once we'd had to hop the wall to get them back in off the road. The coop they'd been housed in since long before my arrival was one good gust of wind away from collapsing down on them, and foxes were also becoming a problem, so I'd set about making something better.

Mr Hopkin gave me a budget of fifteen shillings to get supplies from the hardware store in the city and it was enough to build something big and solid with money left over to get some chicken wire for a new fence, too.

I was in the middle of finishing off the roof of the new coop when I looked down the field and saw Gwyn approaching from the gate. I was achy and tired and really didn't want to have to face him but I knew I couldn't keep running away, either. I stood from my work and hit my hammer against my palm, not considering that it might have seemed threatening given what had gone on between us, and waited to see what he'd come for.

"You ok?" he asked, leaning on the coop. I stared at it nervously, hoping my creation was as sturdy as I'd intended it to be.

"Yeah, you? How are those ribs?" I asked, pointing the hammer in his direction.

"Better," he said, rubbing his hand along his side. The motion caught my attention but I kept my eyes trained on his face.

And then there was silence. Conversation for us had never been this difficult but I had nothing to say and no idea why he'd come when I was finally starting to feel a bit better about him not being around.

"Is there something I can help you with?" I asked. I didn't intend for it to sound so cold but I knew that it did and did nothing to correct it.

"I just wanted to see you."

That annoyed me even more and this time I couldn't help sounding angry. "What for?"

"To see how you're doing." He left another awkward pause and I could feel my frustration building. "I still care about you."

"How is your friend from the pub?" I didn't want to ask, I knew I shouldn't ask, but I couldn't stop myself from spitting it out. I was jealous when I saw them, and even though I was certain there was nothing to be jealous about, I was still jealous now that I was thinking about it again.

"Don't do that," he said. The way he shook his head at me made me feel as pathetic as I probably sounded and it filled me with anger.

"Don't do what?"

"He's a friend."

"So was I." I hated how petty and jealous I was coming off but I just couldn't stop myself.

"He's *just* a friend," he clarified. "There's nobody else. There hasn't been anyone else. There's only you. It'll only ever be you."

His comment took me by surprise and I dropped the hammer on the ground, narrowly missing my foot. We both reached for it, though he got there first, and I immediately got a twinge in my neck making me recoil in pain.

"Your neck giving you gip?" he asked, handing me the hammer. He brushed his fingers against mine and I pulled my hand away quickly.

"What are you doing here Gwynfor?"

"Gwynfor? I'm Gwynfor now?" I was being petty again, but I was already past trying to control or contain it. I kept my gaze on him, waiting for his reply. "I already told you. I just wanted to see you. I miss you."

"Well, I didn't ask for any of this." I rubbed my neck, trying to ease the ache, but it seemed to be travelling to my head and giving me a migraine and I was losing patience with him again.

"I'm sorry. I shouldn't have come," he said, and I let out an annoyed sigh. Seeing him was both wonderful and enraging and I hated how much it was messing with my emotions.

"Is this funny to you?" I asked, waving the hammer and making him step back. "Coming up here acting as if everything is normal after you've avoided me for weeks." I reached for my collar, suddenly feeling hot, and undid the buttons.

"I never wanted to not be friends."

"And I never wanted to *only* be friends," I was trying hard to keep my tone even and my voice down so that I didn't bring attention from inside the house, but it was a struggle. "You chose this and now that you're feeling sorry for yourself you think you can just stroll on over here."

"I should go," he said, turning his back to me. "This isn't what I wanted."

"I'm leaving," I blurted out, making him stop and turn back to face me. My body felt like it was on fire and sweat was beginning to pour down my face. I shook off my coat, nerves obviously getting the better of me, then straightened up again as he approached. "I'm leaving the village."

I'd been contemplating it since my discussion with Nan but seeing him again, then watching him turn to leave me once more, was more than I could bear and it made the decision clear. If I had to keep doing this it would hurt too much and I'd never feel better. I had grown to love the village and the Hopkins but with no Gwyn to keep me here and no ring to get me home I would have to start a new life somewhere else.

"What? Why?" he asked.

"I can't stay here. I can't keep seeing you. I'm going to look for work and make a fresh start somewhere new."

He rubbed at his temples, frustrated with the turn of events. "I don't want you to go."

"Well, it's not up to you," I said, wiping the sweat from my brow. "I just thought you should know. Now, if that's everything then I've got work to do."

He stared at me for a minute looking defeated, then gave me a begrudging nod and turned to walk away.

I reached up to mop more sweat from my forehead. My head was pounding and I thought my legs were going to buckle as I watched him walk away. I already regretted it.

"Gwyn!" I yelled out as my legs started to give way. I clutched onto the coop to steady myself as he turned back around. I tried to call out to him again but this time I couldn't get his name out. A look of panic overcame him and he started to run back but I was already on the ground before he got to me.

I awoke in a bed that was not my own. For a moment I thought perhaps I was somehow back in my own time but as the fog cleared and my eyes focused, I could see Betty sitting in the chair next to the window. Someone had brought me to the master bedroom of the Hopkins farm.

"What happened?" I asked as I attempted to turn my head. I felt like hell and my whole body ached.

Upon hearing my voice Betty rushed from the chair to the door. "He's awake," she shouted, and seconds later Mrs Hopkin, Nellie, Nan and Gwyn all shuffled in and gathered around the bed. They all looked down at me with concern, though I struggled to focus on any one of them in particular.

"Ok, give him some room," Nellie said, taking charge and popping a thermometer in my mouth. The only one I'd known to ever be in the house was used on the cattle and I prayed she'd washed it first. Before she even read the results I knew I was burning up. My body felt like it was on fire but I was shivering as though I'd been left outside naked in the snow.

"You've got a fever," she said to me, putting the thermometer into the pocket of her apron. She poured a glass of water from a jug on the nightstand and placed it in my hands. I didn't have the energy to sit upright so I had to try and take sips without pouring it over my face. "How long have you been feeling unwell?"

"Just today, I think. What's wrong with me?"

Nellie moved to the front of the room and pulled the curtains closed, blocking out the last rays of sunlight that were peeking in through the glass and allowing me to see a little clearer. "You're probably just overworked and run down, which has let a fever take hold, but we should call for the doctor to be safe."

"Honestly, I'll be fine," I said as she felt around my forehead. "There's no need for a fuss."

"You'll do as you're told," Mrs Hopkin said, grabbing my hand and giving it a light kiss just above the fingers. "Rest, and I'll bring you some soup." She tried to force a smile but I could see the concern in her eyes.

"Ok, everybody out," Nellie said, ushering people to the door. "Let's give him some room."

"Gwyn, can you stay for a moment?" I asked.

My request elicited a curious look from Mrs Hopkin but she left us alone and shut the door. The second the room was empty he grabbed my hand and leaned in to kiss my forehead.

"Don't," I said, turning my head from him. I was glad of the affection but I was also worried that I might have something that could infect him.

He got to his knees beside the bed, keeping my hand clutched in his. As he got closer to me the redness in his eyes became obvious. He'd been crying. "Please don't be like that, Tom," he said.

"No, it's not that," I said, trying to reassure him. "I mean, you shouldn't be doing that, but I also don't want you to catch anything."

"But Nellie said it's just a fever," he argued.

"But it might not be. I learned enough at school to know how rife these times are with diseases. I don't want to risk it. Go, wash your hands." I pointed to the bowl of warm water with a flannel in it that had been left beside the bed, and he reached for the soap on the nightstand.

"Don't go," he said as he dragged the cloth through his fingers.

"I'm not going to die, Gwyn!"

He stopped what he was doing and looked at me again. I'd never seen him look so worried. "No. I mean don't leave. I couldn't bear it if you did."

"Gwyn, I-"

"No, let me finish," he interrupted. "When I saw you falling to the floor I knew instantly I'd have done anything to make sure you were ok. Every minute that you were out I prayed for you to be safe and well. I don't know what I'd do if I lost you."

He reached out to take my hand but I moved it away. "You can't touch me, Gwyn. Not until we know what's wrong and that you can't catch anything."

I felt like I was becoming paranoid but if I had an infection that he could catch then he needed to keep his distance. His touch was all I wanted but it wasn't worth the risk.

"I don't need you to decide now," he continued, stepping back away from me. "We can talk about it when you're well. I just wanted you to know that I'm sorry."

The bedroom door swung open before I could reply and Mrs Hopkin scuttled backwards through it carrying a tray filled with soup and two fresh jugs of water.

"Nellie says you're to drink until you can drink no more. There's a pot under the bed if you need it." She laid the tray over my lap and turned for the door. "I'll let you know when the doctor arrives."

I looked at the soup and felt immediately queasy. I had no appetite for anything, only a desire to get warm and stop shivering. I pushed it away and Gwyn moved it over to the dresser.

"It's so cold," I said, pulling the blankets from my waist up to my neck and curling my body up to gather some warmth.

"You've got a fever," he said, pulling the blankets back off me and leaving me lying there in just my long johns.

"Who undressed me?" I asked, curious about how I came to be out of my clothes. "And who brought me inside? And why am I in this bed?"

Gwyn smiled and sat himself down in the armchair, helping himself to spoonfuls of my soup.

"I tried to lift you but it hurt my ribs so I called for Teddy and Mr Hopkin. They brought you in and Leah said to put you in this bed so you'd be more comfortable."

"And my clothes?"

"You were filthy and sweating. Betty helped me strip you down. I thought her head was going to explode. She got so red seeing you in your underwear. You need to mend those buttons."

I clenched my eyes closed, embarrassed by his teasing. "She'll never be able to look at me again, poor girl. Has anyone told Mair?"

"No, I haven't been home since you collapsed."

"She probably thinks you're in the pub," I said without thinking, causing him to frown. I didn't want him to think that Mair had betrayed his confidence. "I mean, I've just seen you coming in and out of there a lot lately."

"Yeah, well, it turns out I couldn't drink away my thoughts of you."

I tried to smile at his comment but all I could muster was a cough. My throat had been sore since I woke up and coughing felt like I was dragging splinters up from my chest. He handed me a glass of water and I drank it down, the chill of it making me shiver more. I longed to get under the blankets for some warmth, despite the sweat that was leaking from every pore of my body.

With a knock at the door, Nellie popped her head into the room to see how I was doing. She gave Gwyn a stern look for eating my soup and then turned her attention to me.

"How are you feeling?" she asked, putting the back of her hand against my forehead.

"I'm cold. He won't give me my blankets back." I felt like a whiny child.

"Well, he's right. You need to cool down, not warm up. Have you been drinking the water?" I pointed to the empty glass beside me and she nodded in approval and then reached for the jug to fill it back up. "Make sure you get through both jugs by the time I next check on you. We've sent for the doctor but I don't know how long it will take for him to arrive, I'm afraid."

"How long until he will be back on his feet again?" Gwyn asked.

Before she could open her mouth to respond, Mrs Hopkin let out a piercing scream from downstairs, causing both her and Gwyn to rush from the room.

Using all of my strength I leaned over and grabbed the dresser, using it to steady myself as I raised to my feet. As fast as I could, which was not very fast at all, I made my way downstairs, holding on to anything available along the way to help keep myself upright.

Panicked voices were coming from the back of the house and most of the family were gathered at the doorway of the living room looking into the kitchen. I grabbed Teddy's shoulder for support and tried to see what had caused the scream and he put his arm around my waist, helping to keep me upright.

"He can't breathe," Mrs Hopkin cried out. She pushed her way through the children and moved further into the kitchen, allowing me to move into the space she had left. With the better vantage point, I peered over Nan's shoulder and saw Howell on the tiles, eyes bulging as he clasped at his throat gasping for breath.

Eighteen

The wait for the doctor was agonising for the whole family. Minutes ticked by into hours and there was still no sign of his arrival.

When I had fallen ill earlier in the day, Gethin had been sent out of the house and down to the village to find Doctor Rees. When he got to the doctor's house he was informed that he was away to attend an emergency with no mention of when he would return. With no surgeries to speak of, and the nearest hospital in Aberystwyth, he had been forced to turn his carriage around and head back to his own village in the hope that his local doctor would be available to take up the case. Now, with no way of informing him of the latest developments and the dire situation that Howell had found himself in, we were all left to pray that he did not come back empty-handed.

Nellie, as expected, had immediately jumped into action to have Howell lifted from the cold stone floor, and Mr Hopkin, with no care for the meal being prepared by his wife, swept the table clean of its contents, sending bowls, dishware and food crashing to the ground to allow space for the boy to be laid out and examined.

Red marks ran down Howell's neck where he had maniacally clawed at himself while struggling for oxygen, leaving several cuts that needed to be tended. By now exhausted, his body had become limp and he no longer writhed, though this seemed of little comfort to Nellie who was concerned by his shallow breaths and continued to feel around his throat for lumps and blockages. She had initially suspected choking, followed by mumps but there was no swelling to be found, and no reason, she informed us, that it would suddenly starve him of oxygen when he had appeared well only moments prior.

In the time since her son's collapse, Mrs Hopkin had become a nervous wreck and was screaming for the safety and well-being of her child. She had been with him when he went down and it had been the suddenness of it, and the resulting bang to his head on the stone floor as he fell, that had caused the scream we had heard from upstairs. Once Nellie was certain that there was no damage done from the fall, Mrs Hopkin was ordered from the room and escorted to a chair in the sitting room by Nan and Betty where she continued to wail, sending echoes of her cries across the house. Despite their efforts to calm her, she could not be consoled and continued to make attempts to get up and return to her son.

Nellie tore at Howell's shirt and pressed her ear to his chest. His breaths were shallow and weak and she seemed at a loss for what to do next. She paced, then tapped her chin, then paced some more and continually asked for silence, even though nobody dared speak for fear of breaking her concentration. Beside the stove, she had stacked all of her medical books, which she would periodically pick up and skim through. Seemingly unable to find what she was looking for, or not knowing what it was that she *should* be looking for, she would return them to the pile and begin pacing again.

The effort of bringing myself downstairs had left me feeling weak so I'd pulled a chair in front of the back door and sat myself down. I still felt as though I was freezing, though I continued to sweat, leaving Gwyn constantly wiping at my face with one of Mrs Hopkin's tea towels. Nellie had suggested I return to bed to rest, but I couldn't stand being upstairs not knowing what was happening and she was too distracted to argue, so I stayed put.

"Betty!" Nellie suddenly shouted. Everyone in the room turned their attention to her and Betty ran from the living room to her side. "I need you to chop some ginger. Lots of it. And I need you to boil water. We'll need at least enough for two jugs."

Betty did as she was asked, putting two large pans of water on the stove to boil and grabbing all the ginger root from the pantry that she could find.

"What the hell is this going to do?" Mr Hopkin asked impatiently, raising his hands in exasperation while Betty began chopping. He had remained mostly silent throughout but had joined Nellie in her pacing several times. He seemed willing to defer to her in the situation, though shared little understanding of anything she was doing and his impatience was growing.

"It's to help him breathe," Nellie replied. "He's struggling for air. One of my books says that ginger can be an aid when you have trouble breathing and it's the only thing I can think of. I don't know what else to do."

Mr Hopkin didn't look convinced but there was little he could do to argue if he wanted his son to have any chance of survival and nobody else had any other suggestions that could help.

Gwyn turned his back to everyone in the kitchen and dropped his voice to a whisper. "Is there anything you know that could help him?"

I shrugged, wracking my brain for anything that could assist Nellie. I'd watched a show once where a doctor was caught in an emergency without any supplies and stuck a pen into a man's throat when he was choking, but Howell didn't seem to have anything lodged in his airway and I wasn't about to suggest to his parents that we should stab him in the neck. There was nothing that I could offer to help.

When the water had boiled Betty tipped in the chunks of ginger and gave it a stir, which gave the room a scent that reminded me of Christmas. I'd been expecting that Nellie would have him drink it, but she instead directed Betty to pour it into two large tin jugs and placed one on each side of Howell's head. She continued to stir at them, wafting the steam towards her brother in the hope of clearing his airways. It didn't seem to make his breathing even out but it did quieten down the rasping and gurgling sounds he had been making, which Nellie considered a good sign.

"Drink," Gwyn said, handing me a glass of water. "You need to look after yourself too." I grabbed the glass and took a gulp but my throat was sore and each mouthful felt like I was trying to swallow a snooker ball. Still, he wouldn't allow me to stop until it was all gone.

"I think you should go back to bed," he said, but he already knew that I wouldn't be moving from the kitchen until I was sure that things were ok.

"Is he going to die?" Sophia asked. In all of the commotion, I hadn't even noticed that she was sitting on the floor beside me, tucked into the corner of the room and with her hands up over her ears. Either forgotten or deemed to be no obstacle to the movement of the adults, she had been left there to watch as events unfolded, terrified at watching her brother's struggle.

"I'm sure he'll be fine," I said, but the outlook was not looking good. With no idea what was causing it and no sign of the doctor, I was beginning to worry that he might not last very long.

Gwyn came to kneel in front of her and brushed a hand through her hair. "We just need to wait for the doctor and then everything will be fine. You've got nothing to worry about."

She reached out to hug him, and as she did the sleeves on her dress pulled back revealing a rash on her arm. The irritation of the material moving along her skin caused her to scratch at it and as she lifted her sleeve to do so it revealed an open sore, about the size of a penny, that was deep and oozing.

"Sophia, what's that?" I said, grabbing her arm. I raised her sleeve as far as it would go and saw the rash had spread right up to her shoulder, flaky and dry. There were another two sore spots, though they were sealed over and looked more like blisters, angry and ready to break under the slightest pressure.

"Nellie, I think you should take a look at this," I called out. Sophia retreated from my grasp and began to cry. She tucked herself as far back into the corner as she could get, as though she had just been told off and was avoiding punishment. "It's ok," I tried to reassure her, but she pushed her face into her knees and curled up tightly.

"What is it?" Nellie said. She dropped the towel she'd been holding over Howell's face onto the table and made her way to us.

"She has a rash. It looks sore. It's all up her arm."

She crouched down next to Gwyn and tried to take hold of Sophia's arm but she tucked it tightly to her chest and wouldn't budge.

"Sophia, *cariad*, I just want to have a look." She tried again, but the girl was unmoving, probably frightened half to death. It wasn't helped when Mr Hopkin, short on patience at the best of times, bellowed something in Welsh at her so loudly that it even silenced the cries of his wife in the next room. Sophia, now more upset than she already was, filled the newly created silence with loud sobs that made her shoulders shake.

Nellie cast her father a disapproving look and he turned for the cabinet that the whiskey was stored in, poured himself a large measure and knocked it back in one gulp.

"Sophia, I need to look at your arm. You're not in any trouble, but I need to see it," Nellie tried again.

Without moving her head from her knees, she slowly inched her arm forward for Nellie to inspect. She pulled the young girl's sleeve up and looked at it curiously for a moment, her eyes roaming the length of Sophia's arm as she tried to work out what had caused the rash.

"What is it?" Gwyn asked.

"Is it something to do with what's happening to Howell?" I added.

She flapped an arm to silence us and continued her inspection. With a small amount of effort, she pried free Sophia's other arm and raised the sleeve. It was red but it didn't appear to be as flaky or dry as her other arm and there were no sores. When she was satisfied with her assessment, she pulled up her sister's skirts and Gwyn and I averted our eyes into the kitchen while Sophia's legs were inspected.

"Nothing there," she said, covering her back up. "When did your arm get like this, Sophia?"

"Today. At school," she said, raising her head to look at Nellie. Her eyes were red from crying and her blonde hair was matted to her face.

"And did you tell your mistress?" Nellie asked.

Sophia shook her head and her eyes began to well up with tears again.

"Did you see anyone else with the same rash?"

Sophia stayed still for a moment then nodded her head and pouted her lips as tears began to stream down her cheeks once more. "Emma Jones and Derek Evans have it too. Miss got cross and sent them out so I was too scared to tell her."

Nellie brushed her sister's hair behind her ears and smiled at her before rising to her feet and rushing to the table where Howell was lying. "Get his slacks up," she said to Betty as she began to inspect his arms. Betty came around the table and rolled the legs of his trousers up to his knees and Nellie moved her attention to his lower extremities.

"I can't see anything," she said, putting her hands on her hips and biting her bottom lip. "Perhaps scarlet fever?" But she didn't seem entirely convinced. She returned to her books, flicking through pages faster than she could read them.

"We're here," Gethin announced, barging through the back door and nearly sending me flying from my seat. He stopped short at the sight of Howell laid out upon the table but was immediately ushered into the sitting room and out of the way. A moment later the doctor stepped in, closing the door of the kitchen with a loud bang.

He was an elderly gentleman, at least in his late sixties, and dressed more like he was going to attend a dance than to perform medical duties. His dark hollow eyes were framed by a grey beard on the lower half of his face, coloured by yellow tobacco stains around his mouth, and a large top hat on his head. His red waistcoat was highlighted by a gold pocket watch that hung from a chain and his suit, with tails, was the kind I'd seen on the men who were drinking in the hotel lobby in Aberystwyth. I wasn't entirely certain, but there seemed to be a faint aroma of alcohol about him, too.

Nellie, who had once again proven herself invaluable in an emergency, stepped forward to greet the doctor and provide the information that she had gathered, but he sidestepped her and moved toward the table.

"Now, what do we have here, then?" he said in an accent I was unfamiliar with. It didn't sound either Welsh or English. He placed his large leather bag down on the counter next to the back door and unclasped it, causing both sides to fall open and reveal at least a dozen miniature bottles. Nellie once again attempted to speak but he raised his finger to his lips, looked at her and made a shushing noise. Uninterested in what she had to say, he turned his attention to Gwyn.

"You, boy, what do we know so far?"

Gwyn, unwilling to be drawn into the doctor's misogyny, deferred back to Nellie, who this time spoke whether the doctor liked it or not.

"It struck Mr Jacob first," she said, pointing towards me. "He went down in the garden during the afternoon with a fever. I gave him fluids and recommended bed rest."

"He doesn't appear to be resting now, Miss Hopkin," the doctor snarked, but she ignored it and continued.

"Then this evening my brother struggled to breathe. It appeared as if he was choking. I boiled ginger root to help the air pass easier to his lungs but his breathing is still shallow. We've also found a rash on Sophia. I checked Howell over and he doesn't have it, but hers is sore and weeping. I thought perhaps it was scarlet fever."

He stroked his beard and considered her findings.

"Come here, little girl," he said, beckoning Sophia with a single finger towards him. His bedside manner left much to be desired. She was hesitant at first but Gwyn held her hand and walked her over to him. The doctor raised back her sleeves roughly, causing her to wince in pain. He let out some mumbling noises and then returned to his bag and extracted a small metal tongue depressor. Gripping Howell's face, he pulled his jaw down and inserted it into his mouth. Howell, delirious with fever and still struggling to breathe, barely acknowledged the doctor's attention and remained still on the table.

He wiped the depressor against his sleeve, and then, turning to Sophia, he kneeled down and popped it into her mouth. I had to stop myself from telling him that even *I* knew he should be changing or sterilising it first, but he continued on with little concern for potentially spreading any disease that we might have.

"Did it occur to you, Miss Hopkin," he said, rising to a standing position, "to check inside their throats?"

His accusatory tone annoyed me, as though he were expecting Nellie to somehow know every step of a diagnosis when without her Howell would likely already be dead.

He stepped towards me, depressor at the ready, and I swatted it away as he raised it to my face. I stuck my tongue out and said 'ahhhh' so that he could get a look at my throat without me having to be at least the third recipient of his instruments' probing.

"If you had cared to look, Miss Hopkin," he said after a long pause, "you would have seen the white spots and membranes forming in the throats of the patients. You have an outbreak of diphtheria on your hands."

I had little knowledge of the disease and even less idea of its severity, but I was pretty sure that it was something I'd been inoculated against as a child. That fact led me to worry less about its long-term effects on myself, but I was pretty sure it didn't bode well for everyone else in the room who would have received no such vaccine. I wasn't even sure if there was a treatment for it in these times.

Nellie, now racked with guilt for missing something that none of us knew to look for, raised her hand to her mouth and clutched her nose in an attempt to stop herself from crying. When the doctor gave her another disapproving glare she rushed out of the kitchen and bounded up the stairs to her room.

"You have very mild symptoms," he said to me while he fished around in his bag for items. "Your fever will break and I expect you'll be back to normal in a day or two."

He pulled out a small glass jar, the label of which I couldn't read, and handed it to Mr Hopkin.

"The girl is to rub this into her arms twice a day to fight the rash. If she develops a fever, you must keep her cool and rested. No solid foods for at least two days. She has only a small whitening to the lining of her throat and I suspect it will feel a little sore for a day or two, but there is little to be done about that I'm afraid."

Everything he said was in a very matter-of-fact manner and nobody seemed particularly happy with his demeanour, but they remained silent and heeded his advice.

"What of Howell?" Mrs Hopkin cried. She'd risen from her seat in the living room and come to stand in the doorway of the kitchen waiting for news of her son. The doctor looked at her but ignored her pleas, returning his attention to Mr Hopkin.

"It is unlikely your son will last the night." Mr Hopkin's shoulders dropped as though the air had been knocked out of him and Mrs Hopkin let out a wail and buried her head into Nan's breast. "If he does, then he might just stand a chance of pulling through, but I suggest you prepare yourselves for the worst."

Sophia ran to her mother and clung to her skirts, sobbing loudly at the news. Betty and Nan tried to remain strong while they comforted their mother, but both were visibly shaken. Either forgetting himself for a moment, or simply not caring, Gwyn put his arm around me as I tried to take it all in.

"Two drops of this in some water every hour," the doctor said, handing a small bottle to Mr Hopkin. "I can do no more."

With a tip of his hat, he grabbed his bag and left the house, followed quickly by Gethin who was tasked with returning him to wherever he came from. The rest of us were left to wait.

Nineteen

Howell's laboured breathing was the only sound that penetrated the silence of the kitchen in the minutes after the doctor left. I stared at the broken dishes strewn across the tiles, processing all that we'd just been told, knowing everyone else's thoughts were the same as my own.

When she could sit and think no more, Betty sprang from her chair near the stove and began to slam Nellie's books down on the counter. The thuds of the heavy tomes awoke the room from its daze and we watched as she began frantically flicking through the well-worn pages of maladies and cures in the vain hope of finding something that might prove the doctor's prognosis incorrect.

When she could find nothing of use she slammed her fists into the pages and let out a scream that rose from the depths of her belly. Teddy attempted to comfort her but she batted his arm from her waist and stormed off into the pantry, her face red with anger, and slammed the door with a force that caused the windows to rattle.

When Nellie returned to the kitchen a few moments later she had recomposed herself and was ready to work. I caught her eye as she moved around the large wooden table in the centre of the room and though she remained stoic, she carried a fear for what the night may bring.

"Teddy," she said, her voice somewhat shaky, "you're to go to the schoolmaster's cottage and inform him of what's happened. He will need to issue a notice to all parents at first light."

"But it's after midnight," he replied. "He'll be asleep."

"Then you must wake him. We have no time to delay."

Teddy grabbed his cap from the hook on the wall and after a final glance at his brother on the table, he rushed through the door and into the night.

The breeze that rushed in through the opening added to my chill and I brought a shivering hand up to feel my forehead. Still burning. Nobody seemed to notice, or care, that I was sitting amongst company with no shirt on, and I wished I had a blanket I could wrap around me for more heat, but I knew neither Gwyn nor Nellie would allow me anything that might raise my temperature.

"Betty, prepare two beds in the boys' room," Nellie commanded as she tied a fresh apron around her waist. "Teddy will need to sleep down here tonight so that they can rest. We don't need him getting sick too."

"What can I do?" Nan asked, wanting to be of use.

"Clean," Nellie replied. "Get this floor swept and cleaned away. I need space."

Sitting beside her son, Mrs Hopkin clutched his hand in hers and brought it to her face, then began to pray. Tears filled her eyes, running down her cheeks and over his fingers as she whispered words in Welsh asking God to save her son.

After giving her mother a moment, Nellie approached and crouched down beside her. "You can't do that," she said softly, trying to take Howell's hand away from her mother's grasp.

"HE'S MY SON!" Mrs Hopkin screamed, her face reddening, and she turned her shoulder to her daughter, blocking her from separating them.

Undeterred, Nellie moved closer and put her arms around her mother, leaning her head onto her shoulder. "We need to make him comfortable. You don't want him lying on this table all night, do you?" she reasoned. This time Mrs Hopkin said nothing and Nellie looked up to her father. "Can you carry him to bed please?"

Mr Hopkin laid his half-empty glass of whiskey down onto the counter and then scooped him up and carried his motionless body out of the kitchen. Mrs Hopkin kept hold of his hand and followed them from the room, and Sophia chased after them a second later, not wanting to be away from her parents or brother.

"How are you feeling?" Nellie asked, turning her attention to me. She looked exhausted and I knew I couldn't have looked much better.

"Don't worry about me," I said. "I'll be fine." I tried to get up but Gwyn put a hand on my shoulder and held me firm in my seat.

"What are you doing?" he asked.

"I'm going to make tea," I replied. "We could all do with it."

"Not likely," Nellie said, and she moved to the cupboard where her father stored his various bottles, extracting a large decanter filled with brandy. "Gwyn, some glasses, please."

He released his grasp on me and began searching the cupboards for any cups that hadn't been swept and shattered on the floor, eventually laying four out onto the counter into which Nellie poured some of the largest measures I'd ever seen.

"Now, for you, this is medicinal," she said, handing me a drink, "but for me, it is just long overdue." She raised her cup to nobody in particular and knocked it back in one. Her face screwed up and she let out a shiver from the alcohol, then placed her cup down on the table. "I should go and check on Howell."

Gwyn held out a glass for Nan but she scrunched her nose up at it and shook her head, so he poured hers into his own, knocked it back and dragged the back of his hand across his mouth.

"Don't like brandy?" he asked as he set his glass down on the counter beside the bottle.

"We snuck some out to the barn once," she said, resting her chin on the top of the broom as she talked to us. "It was my idea, of course, but Nellie didn't need much persuading. I don't remember much of what happened after the first few sips except that I had the most awful case of vomiting. Nellie got so afraid that she'd be in trouble that she dragged me out into the field and left me there. My head hurt for days after that and now even the smell of it makes me queasy."

Gwyn laughed as he poured himself another. I was nursing mine, taking small sips and trying to hold it down. It ran down my throat like lava but it warmed my chest and helped me to stop shivering so much.

"Do you need anything else?" Nan asked. She'd set the broom down in the corner of the room and moved towards me, though she seemed careful not to get too close. When I shook my head she pulled her apron off and tossed it into the basket near the door. "Then I'll see if Betty needs any help."

Gwyn watched as she entered the living room, pulling the door closed behind her. At the sound of the latch catching on the clip, he put his glass down and came to lean in front of me, bringing his face in line with my own. He reached out, sweeping my hair across my forehead then tracing his finger through my stubble and down to my chin before dropping his hand to my own and holding it tightly.

"I want to kiss you," he said and I tried to laugh at the idea, though it sounded more like a singular raspy breath of air escaping my throat. I was still in my undergarments and sweating profusely. I looked and felt disgusting.

"Don't," I said, partly from feeling too ill for sweet talk and partly because I still wasn't sure if his sweet talk was something I wanted to hear.

"Please, Tom, I said I'm sorry."

"It's not the time, Gwyn, not with everything that's going on."

"Don't you see?" he said, clenching my hand tighter. "It's exactly the time. We don't know what's going to happen. What if you get sick like Howell? I couldn't bear to lose you and you not knowing how I feel."

"You're not going to lose me."

"So, you're going to stay?"

"I didn't say that. I mean, I'm not going to die."

"You can't know that, Tom. None of us can."

"But I do know that," I replied, and his face became confused. "Where I'm from, diphtheria is pretty much non-existent. They've found treatments and cures. I've had a vaccine for it. I guess I'm just sick because it's been so long since I had it, but I'll be ok. My body can fight it off."

I was only half sure that what I was saying was correct but I needed him to believe it. More than that, I needed myself to believe it. He seemed confused by what I was telling him but as the words sunk in, so did the relief, and he dropped his head to rest on our clasped hands.

"So, you'll be ok?" he asked.

"Yes. But that doesn't mean that *you* will be," I said, pulling my hands away from him. "You need to stop touching me. And keep washing your hands."

I leaned back, exhausted, and rubbed at my eyes trying to wake myself up a little.

"Come on," he said, getting to his feet. "You need to get back to bed. You look awful."

"Thanks," I said, raising an eyebrow at him. I got myself up onto my feet and Gwyn rushed to get his hands under my arms to keep me steady as he guided me to the bottom of the stairs. Once he was sure I had reached the top safely he disappeared back into the kitchen.

"How are you feeling?" Nellie asked as I entered the bedroom. She, Nan and Mrs Hopkin were all sitting on Teddy's bed staring at Howell, watching for any sign of change. I climbed into my bed on the other side of the room, pulling the single thin sheet I'd been left with up to my chin, and propped myself against the metal bar that stood in for a headboard.

"Like I could sleep for a week," I replied. "How is he doing?"

Howell was pale and his breathing shallow. Whatever the doctor had spotted in his throat was causing him to gasp and gurgle with every breath and it sounded painful. His eyes were closed but I wasn't sure if he was sleeping or unconscious and I didn't want to ask which it might be. I wasn't sure I even wanted to know.

"There's been no change, which I think is perhaps a good thing," Nellie replied. "He's certainly no worse."

"Is Betty looking after Sophia?"

"She's gone to lie down," Nan replied. "She's beginning to feel unwell now, too."

"Why?" Mrs Hopkin spoke up, removing the handkerchief she'd been holding to her mouth. "Why did Sophia not tell us she was sick? If her school mistress knew there was something in the air then why did she not tell anyone? We could have done something. We could have had more time."

"You can't think like that," Nellie said. She put her hand on her mother's knee as some sort of reassurance but it did little to alleviate her anguish.

"And that doctor..." she continued. "No heart. No heart at all."

"I did find him pretty blunt," I added.

"Drunk, he was," Mrs Hopkin said, her face filled with contempt. "Gethin had to fetch him from a billiards room. Disgusting."

A noise came from the hallway causing everyone to look up, and Gwyn poked his head around the door and then stepped inside. It was getting cramped in the bedroom and I could feel myself getting hotter for the first time all night.

"Good timing, Gwyn," Nellie said, taking to her feet. "I need you to help me lift Howell upright. We have to give him his medicine."

She poured out a glass of water from the jug on the nightstand and removed the small bottle from her apron that the doctor had given as medicine. There was a small pipette in the lid for administering dosage and she raised it to her face to inspect the contents. When she removed the lid the smell of urine filled the room, making me heave.

"What is that?" I asked, bringing my hand to my nose.

"Ammonia," she said, squeezing the contents of the pipette into the glass destined for her sick brother.

"NO!" I shouted, startling everyone and using all my energy to propel myself up from the bed. "You can't give him that."

Everyone turned to look at me as though I'd lost my mind, but I knew I was right about this. I'd only ever heard of ammonia being toxic and dangerous and used in cleaning chemicals. I could think of no scenario where poisoning the boy would be in any way beneficial to his health. I looked at Gwyn hoping he understood the pleading in my eyes to mean I knew something that they didn't and that this would be a bad idea.

"I, er, I think Tom, er, might be right," he stuttered, shifting his gaze between me and Nellie, trying to read my mind and defend my outburst while having no clue what was causing my alarm.

"Whyever not?" Mrs Hopkin asked, wondering why I would stand in the way of her child receiving his medication.

"The doctor is wrong," I pleaded. "It won't help. It will make him worse."

I had no idea how I could make them listen to me, but I knew that I had to, somehow.

"Well, I think the doctor would know more than you, don't you?"

Mrs Hopkin, her voice stern, was visibly upset with my outburst and her face was reddening at an alarming rate, while Nellie stood frozen, unsure of whether to continue or hear me out.

"My friend," I said, making something up on the spot. "He had the same condition. They gave him ammonia, too. It stripped the lining right out of his throat. He never talked again and spent the rest of his life in constant pain."

I had no idea if anything I was describing was near to what the actual effects of the substance were but I knew I needed to be shocking enough that they would pay attention to my words so that they would reconsider giving it to Howell.

"He's right," Gwyn said. He looked unsure but played along. "Mair uses it for cleaning. It took the pattern right off the pots."

I didn't know if he was telling the truth or not but his siding with me was seemingly having the desired effect. Mrs Hopkin sat with her mouth wide open and Nan looked horrified by my tale. Nellie, who was still holding the pipette over the glass, had now been put in the most difficult of conditions between heeding my words against or giving her brother what she considered might be life-saving medicine.

"Plus, the man was obviously drunk," Gwyn chimed in, as if needing to hammer the point across. "Who knows if he even picked out the right bottle? It doesn't seem like the right thing to give a small boy, does it?"

Mrs Hopkin looked mortified and I wondered if perhaps we'd overdone it a little. Without a word she rose to her feet and took the mixture from her daughter's hands. Rather than giving Howell the concoction herself, as I thought she might, she instead moved to the window, opened it and poured the liquid out onto the ground below.

"I'm trusting you, Thomas," she said, an outstretched finger pointed just an inch from my face. "Don't make me regret it."

The sounds of the farm waking up and coming to life as the sun rose over the valley roused me from a light sleep that I didn't remember falling into. The candle on the nightstand had long since melted to a stub, its light now replaced with beams of sunlight pouring in through the small window beside my bed, and a faint smell of ginger filled the air, emanating from the pots that had been left around Howell's bed all night.

The noise of me shuffling my pillow as I tried to get comfortable roused the attention of Mrs Hopkin, who turned her attention away from her son momentarily. Dark circles had formed under her eyes and she'd removed her mop-hat, letting her hair fall messily around her shoulders. I'd never seen her look so distraught. She hadn't moved an inch and neither had Nellie, who slept behind her on Teddy's bed, propped up against the wall.

"How is he doing?" I whispered, pulling myself upright.

"He's still sleeping," she said. She kept her back to me as she spoke but the sadness in her voice was unmistakable.

"Did Gwyn go home?" I asked, realising he was nowhere to be seen.

"He went downstairs with Nan. They're keeping busy."

I felt obliged to make small talk though her tone made it obvious she had no desire to speak, so I left her in peace and stared out over the yard, hoping the new dawn brought with it an easier day.

Teddy and Mr Hopkin were in the yard below collecting pails. The noise of the tins clattering filled the silence left by our lack of conversation and caused Nellie to stir. Startled, she immediately went to her brother to check on him. His breathing was still raspy but his chest appeared to be rising and falling at a greater volume than it had been when I'd fallen asleep and she seemed relieved by his progress.

"I've watched him all night," Mrs Hopkin said. She remained still and expressionless as she spoke, as though afraid that any slight change in her demeanour might affect his progress. "I've begged and pleaded with God to keep him safe."

"Come," Nellie said. "You need to eat something. Go downstairs. I can take over from here."

She attempted to bring her mother to her feet but Mrs Hopkin was not for moving and instead clasped hold of her son's hand again, causing him to stir.

"Howell?" she cried out, lurching forward and leaning over him.

"Mam?" His voice wasn't much more than a whisper and his throat was hoarse, but his call to her brought Mrs Hopkin to tears and she slumped down over him, scooping his body against hers.

"I'm here," she said as she gently rocked him against her chest.

"My throat hurts."

She raised her hand to his head, brushing his hair away and smiled down at him through her tears.

"I need to check you over," Nellie said as she stepped up to the bed. She felt his forehead first, assessing his temperature, then slowly eased him out of his mother's arms so that he could lie comfortably. Peeling the sheet away from his body she began to inspect his arms and legs. "Still clear," she said, finding no signs of a rash. She brought a hand to his face, pulling his chin back to inspect the inside of his mouth. "We'll need to keep an eye on this," she said. "He might be over the worst of it but he's not out of the woods just yet.

259

I'm going to go and check on Sophia and Betty and then I'll be right back."

As if on cue, Betty screamed out from the bedroom next door and Nellie ran out of the room towards the sound of her voice. I immediately jumped from the bed and followed her across the landing, aching from the sudden movement, and pushed behind her into the girls' bedroom.

In the corner of the room opposite the door, Betty crouched in a crumpled heap, sweating with fever and her face contorted with agony. Her body shook as she clawed at her chest and her mouth hung wide, but no more sound escaped her.

"Betty, what is it?" Nellie asked, her voice filled with panic as she rushed to her sister's side. She clasped her hands on either side of Betty's face and tried to make her eyes meet her own, but Betty's gaze was fixed across the room and her head remained firmly pressed against the wall. "Speak to me Elizabeth!" Nellie demanded again, to no avail.

I moved further into the room, looking around me, and immediately realised the source of Betty's anguish

"Get her out," I bellowed as Mrs Hopkin came into the room demanding to know what the fuss was about. I threw my arm in the air, pointing to the doorway, and Nellie quickly rose to her feet and pushed her mother out onto the landing.

For a moment it was as though everything stopped and I became acutely aware of every noise around me. The creaking of the floorboards as I edged toward the bed and the birds tweeting outside the window. Even the sound of my own breathing felt as though it was ringing in my ears and I had to consciously hold my breath as I edged closer to where Sophia lay.

It was her eyes that I noticed first. Had they been closed I may have been fooled into thinking that she was merely asleep. The sun coming through the window made them sparkle, two spots of colour in an otherwise colourless room, but they were cast upward towards the ceiling, unmoving, with all signs of that familiar cheeky twinkle now gone.

On her neck were the same red marks that we'd seen on Howell, a consequence of desperately clawing at her throat as she gasped for breath, unnoticed, while her family sat at her brother's bedside in the next room.

Twenty

Sophia's funeral took place on a sunny Tuesday morning, a day before what would have been her and Howell's eleventh birthday.

Arrangements had been delayed by over a week due to the sickness lingering in the house, and many other homes in the village had also suffered outbreaks and deaths, bringing another wave of sadness and despair over Cwm Newydd.

That morning we'd all gotten ready in relative silence. Sophia's body had been brought back to the farm in a small wooden casket the evening before and Mr and Mrs Hopkin had kept a vigil at its side for the whole night. It was the first time since Sophia had died that Mrs Hopkin hadn't slept in her daughter's bed, and may have been the only time in over a week that she and her husband had been able to bear being in the same room together. They hadn't been arguing, at least not in earshot of any of us, they just both fell into silence and avoided the other at all times.

Howell was hit particularly hard by his twin's death. He was on the mend, healthwise, though his voice remained hoarse, and he wandered aimlessly around the house having lost the other half of himself. It was easy to relate to, being a twin myself, which made it difficult to be around him sometimes. I could easily imagine his pain and grief, and it made me miss Lee more than I ever had.

When they brought Sophia's body home he was inconsolable and refused to go near her coffin. Every time he needed to get from upstairs to the kitchen, he would go out the front door and in through the back one, avoiding the living room and her tiny wooden casket entirely. During the few times that he would speak to any of us, he would tell stories about how Sophia was at school or visiting friends, not willing, or perhaps unable, to truly acknowledge his loss.

Nellie and Nan had taken over the running of the house when it became evident that their mother was in no mood for chores. She would come to sit at the table each day, dressed and ready for the day's work as though she had the intention of doing it, and then she'd stay there until the evening in near total silence until it was time to go to bed again. They cooked and cleaned and tried to keep as normal a routine as possible, working around their mother to keep the house in order while she sat and stared at nothing, lost in her thoughts. They tried several times to get her involved so that it would take her mind off things but she had lost all interest in anything and during the few occasions when she would break her silence it was to ask to be left alone.

Betty, who had been the last of us to fall ill, was taking the longest to recover. She'd been bed-bound for five days after that first night, fighting off infection and fever. It took another two visits from the local doctor before she began to show any signs of improvement. Nobody said it out loud, but none of us thought she was going to make it and now that she had it didn't seem like she would ever be quite right again.

Gone was the healthy teenager who spent her days rushing around after the children and blushing every time someone spoke to her. She had now become thin and frail, always short of breath and too tired to concern herself with embarrassment or shyness. The doctor had deemed her too unfit to attend the funeral but she had joined us in the living room as we gathered to say a prayer.

"We need to be making a move," Gethin said when the private service was complete. He began to usher the family out of the house but Mrs Hopkin wouldn't budge.

"Come on," Nellie said, wrapping an arm around her mother's shoulder.

Mrs Hopkin shrugged her off with such force that Nellie stumbled backwards, catching her elbow against the fireplace and letting out a yell. Gethin rushed to her but she shook her head to let him know she was ok as she rubbed her arm. She tried again with her mother, but there was no budging her, and she held on to the coffin tightly.

"They can't have her," she cried as she stared down at the wooden box that contained her daughter. "We're not going."

Gethin looked as though he was going to try again but Nellie ushered him from the room towards the front door and I followed them outside, unsure of what would happen next. She took her father aside for a word and then he disappeared back into the house.

I watched through the open door, unable to hear what was being said, but he slowly began to inch towards his wife as they spoke. Eventually, he put an arm around her and she collapsed into his embrace, letting out loud sobs that caused us all to look at the ground, uncomfortably avoiding each other's gazes as we listened to her grieving wails.

A crowd of mourners met us outside the church and lined the path from the gates to the doors before following us inside. So many people from the village attended that the pews were filled out and people were forced to stand at the back of the room to pay their respects.

Unlike the other funerals I'd attended since I first arrived in the village, this one was personal and we all struggled to keep our emotions maintained. Surprisingly, it was Mrs Hopkin who managed to hold it together best out of all of us, maintaining her composure throughout the whole service while the rest of the family wept for Sophia.

It was only when we got outside that she finally broke down. On the other side of the church wall was the school, and to honour their classmate, all of the children had lined up in the yard to pay their respects as we walked to the graveside. When she saw them, Mrs Hopkin became inconsolable and had to be escorted the remainder of the way by Teddy and Nan. Her wails continued until Sophia was lowered into the ground.

Over the next few weeks I busied myself in the fields, using it as a distraction from grieving and allowing myself to truly consider what it was that I wanted to do with my life. Sophia's death had made me realise how much I was leaving behind if I was never able to return to my family, but I'd come to love the life I had made for myself and didn't want to leave the farm. And then there was Gwyn.

I knew that I wanted to be with him, and perhaps my stubbornness was getting the better of me, but I didn't want to go through that pain again if he changed his mind a second time, and it wasn't fair to him if I ever found the ring again and faced the option of going home. I hated how torn I was.

Every time I felt like I was set on a decision, something would happen or someone would need help, or I'd see Gwyn and I'd convince myself that I should stay. And then I'd think about my family and how they must be feeling and I'd be filled with a determination to find a way home. A month after the funeral I was still no closer to making my mind up.

I'd spent much of the morning on the cart dragging the back field when I noticed Betty walking across the yard. She'd been coming out to the fields to sit with me while I worked quite a lot of late. Sometimes she would talk but mostly she just watched in silence as I completed my jobs. I enjoyed the company, even when nothing was said, but when she did speak, she was different. More mature. Out of all of us, she'd changed most of all.

I pulled the cart up next to her and jumped down, patting the horse on the rear and leaving it to graze as I joined Betty on the wall.

"It's getting warmer," she said, looking off over the fields. "Spring is almost here. The lambs will be due soon."

"More work," I replied. "Your father and Teddy will have lots to do."

"He has lost his love for the farm," she replied, talking about her father. She was right.

Mr Hopkin had relinquished most of his duties in the days leading up to Sophia's funeral and just sort of stopped caring, leaving the bulk of the work for me and Teddy to carry out. He'd join us occasionally if the mood took him, but it was rare and he spent most of his time in his armchair in the bedroom, looking out over the village and nursing a bottle of whiskey.

"It takes time," I said. "He will be in better spirits soon."

"And what of you, Tom? Will it not be more work for you, too?"

She turned her gaze to me, curious about my reply. I'd opened up to her during our discussions about how I was struggling to decide my future, and she would periodically enquire about the outcomes of my deliberations.

"I don't want to leave the family struggling," I said. "There's so much here to do. But at the same time, I think my family will want me to go home."

"You don't seem any closer to making your mind up," she replied.

"I don't know what to do for the best, Betty. I just don't want to let anybody down."

She reached over and took my hand in hers and focused her eyes on me. "Do you remember walking home after the bonfire at the harvest?

"When Arthur set upon us? How could I forget?"

"Before that. Do you remember what you said to me?"

I shook my head, all recollection of our conversation now gone.

"You asked me what it was that *I* wanted. What is it that you want, Tom? Forget your obligations and decide what it is that you want. What is going to make you happiest?"

She stood up from the wall and headed for the house, leaving me to contemplate her words.

"Tom," she called out as she reached the back door. "If you do decide your path leads you away from here then I shall miss you very much."

She gave me a final smile and then disappeared back inside the house.

Later that day I was stacking hay in the barn when the door swung open and Gwyn walked in. He was sporting his usual smile and looking particularly handsome and I was very glad to see him.

"Hello stranger," I said, sitting down on one of the bales.

Gwyn had made his feelings for me clear when I'd fallen ill, but not wanting to pressure me into making a decision he'd been giving me space since the funeral to come to a decision about what I wanted, promising that he would wait for however long it took. He'd stuck to his word, and I'd found myself missing him more and more.

"I thought I'd check in," he replied, taking a seat beside me. "It's been a few days since I last saw you."

"Ah, I'm still as beautiful as ever," I joked, flashing him a big grin.

"It's true," he replied. "And it's a good job that you are because you're incredibly dull otherwise."

"Shut up!" I said, hitting him in the arm and pushing him into the hay. I enjoyed his teasing and I'd missed it when he wasn't around. "Do you know what I like most about spending time with you?"

"What?" He asked, sitting upright again.

"Absolutely nothing!"

His mouth dropped open, feigning offence, and I burst into laughter again. He shoved me back onto the hay and I grabbed at his shirt, pulling him over with me. In an instant he was on top of my chest, his face inches from mine and the laughter came to an abrupt stop. We barely had time to lock eyes before our lips met and we were kissing frantically, our hands ravaging each other as we rolled around in a frenzy of pent-up wanting.

"Not here," I said, dragging him towards the ladder to the second floor. I didn't know if it was a smart decision, but I knew it was what I wanted right then.

As we were sneaking back out of the barn a little later, Teddy rounded the corner giving us both the fright of our life.

"What are you doing creeping around?" I snapped, half shocked by his sudden appearance and half terrified that he might have suspected what we'd been doing.

"Sorry," he said, dropping a bucket to the floor and looking just as surprised as we were. "I need your help. We need to make a start weaning the calves."

"Teddy, I've no idea about any of that stuff," I said. While I was proud that I could now officially call myself a labourer, if not an actual farmer, there were still elements to working the land that I was clueless about.

"I know," he said, giving me an impish grin. "This is how we get my father back to work."

A few minutes later I was on the landing of the farmhouse preparing for battle.

"Mr Hopkin," I called out and then walked straight through the bedroom door. If I'd knocked and waited, he'd have just ignored me. "Teddy says it's time to wean, but I don't know what to do."

He sat in his chair, as he did every day now, drink in hand and watching the world outside pass by. He didn't even look up to acknowledge me.

"The boy knows how to mix feed," he replied, never taking his eyes from the window.

"He says he's forgotten. That Jack did it last year and he can't remember what it needs."

"Not today."

"Mr Hopkin. John," I was pushing my luck being so informal but I pushed ahead anyway. "We need you back outside with us."

"Let it go," He gestured with his hands as he spoke, spilling whiskey from his glass. "Let it all go. What good is it anymore?"

"How will that feed the family?"

"Family?" He finally turned to look at me. "My wife doesn't talk anymore. Jack is gone. Sophia is dead. Betty is broken. Nellie is to be married soon and Nan can't wait to get a job away from here. And we all know Howell's not cut out for farming. Me and Teddy can't do it alone, even with your help. The house will come to a standstill soon. Let it go."

"Everyone else is already keeping this place going," I argued back, annoyed that he didn't seem to realise how hard everyone was working. "It's you who's come to a standstill and locked yourself away. We need you outside. The house is fine. Nellie is keeping it running as well as it ever has been."

"That girl's not meant for the kitchen."

"Well, we both know where she should be," I replied, pushing my luck once more. "She told me, you know, that you wouldn't allow her to train at the infirmary. You've seen her. She's incredible and it makes her so happy. You're the one who's made sure she'll never leave the kitchen."

He rose forward slightly, anger rising, before shaking his head at me and settling back in his seat, returning his gaze to the window.

"I'm not a monster, Thomas." His voice was calm, considered, and for a moment it even wavered a little. "I know they all think I'm a bad person, but everything I do, I do for them."

"Then why stop her from doing what will make her happy?"

"While she lives under my roof she follows my rules," he said, before stopping briefly to consider his thoughts. "But she won't live under my roof forever, and I need to make sure she is taken care of."

"What do you mean?"

"It will be Nellie's job to run a house and look after her own children one day. I did what I did because Gethin asked it of me. I've no desire to squash her dreams but her husband's wishes must come first and he asked that I deny her request. Once they are married they can argue it out amongst themselves."

"But he's not her husband yet."

"And he never will be if she's disobeying his wishes before they even stand before God."

"But they're not his wishes. Not in her eyes. Don't you see? He's letting you take the blame because he's too cowardly to speak for himself. Mr Hopkin, I mean no disrespect and I'm sorry to speak out of turn, but Jack already ran away because he couldn't take control of his own life, and Sophia, God rest her, will never know her own. Are you really going to stand by while Nellie lives a life set out for her by others? Watching as she grows more resentful and too old to start over? I know you want better for her. I know you do."

"It's done!" he shouted. "I'm not meddling in their affairs anymore."

"Then meddle in your own. You might be ready to watch this farm fall to ruin but the rest of us want to at least try."

I could see the anger spreading across his face and made my exit to re-join Teddy in the yard before things could escalate any further. There was nothing more I could do, but the sound of his glass smashing against the wall as I went back downstairs let me know that I'd struck a nerve.

Back in the yard, we set about gathering tools from the barn and I told Teddy about the conversation I'd had with his father and how I may have overstepped the mark.

"Couldn't have been that bad," he said, pointing back towards the house.

I looked up from the bucket I was filling to see Mr Hopkin, dressed in his overalls, exiting the back door. He grabbed a shovel that had been left leaning against the kitchen wall and began walking towards the pens. It was the first time I'd seen him outside in days.

"Let's hope he's not just out here to dig a grave for me," I said, making Teddy laugh. "Grab the barrow. We'll go make a start before he changes his mind."

He only spoke to give instruction, but he stayed out and worked with us for the rest of the day.

It was a start.

Twenty-One

Mrs Hopkin was still in the throes of the depression that had taken hold since Sophia had passed away, but with Nellie's wedding less than a week away she had begun to open up a bit and was distracting herself with preparations. She wasn't quite her old self yet, but she spoke a little more and had started helping the oldest girls around the house again. They were small but welcome steps.

The contributing factor to the turnaround in her mood came when Nellie suggested that perhaps it would be better to ask Gethin's mother to provide the food for the reception party. Mrs Hopkin took great offence to this and immediately placed a huge order for supplies down at the post office shop. I wasn't sure if Nellie knew which were the right buttons to press with her mother, but the smirk she gave when Mrs Hopkin grabbed her coat to walk down the hill was a good indication that the suggestion wasn't accidental.

The food order had been coming back to her in dribs and drabs and each day one of us had been tasked to go and collect the latest supplies. Today was my turn, and as soon as I'd finished the morning feed with the calves, she'd put a list in my hand and sent me on my way.

As I waited in line outside the post office, I saw Mair bounding down the lane from her cottage looking uncharacteristically cheerful. She was dressed very smartly for a Thursday morning and I was curious as to where she was headed.

"Mair." I called out to her with a wave and she flashed me such a warm smile it made me suspicious. "Where are you going?"

"I can't stop," she said. "I'm going to be late. Call around for tea this evening."

She darted around the side of the pub and rushed off up the hill without saying another word.

"She's been going for the omnibus nearly every day."

I turned around to see Mrs Wilkes had joined the line behind me. She did love to hang around the post office looking for gossip.

"Been watching her, have you?"

"One tends to notice patterns if they repeat themselves often enough, Mr Jacob."

"Or if you spend all day looking for them," I replied.

"And how do you spend your days, Mr Jacob? What do you look for? Or should I say, whom?"

She pursed her lips and raised her eyebrows at me, a look of smugness on her face. She was insisting on playing word games and I tired of it quickly.

"Will there be anything else, Mrs Wilkes?"

"I heard about your outbursts at Felin Fawr. I daresay much of the village has."

"I'm sure you've made certain of that."

I stepped forward as the queue moved towards the door and she kept close behind me, unwilling to unhook her claws.

"Such an ugly business."

"Well, if Arthur hadn't run off scared…"

"Scared?" She found my comment amusing and let out a very fake, very high-pitched laugh at my expense. "Mr Morgan has far bigger concerns, I'm sure. His new business venture is doing remarkably well by all accounts."

"Oh, he's still alive then?" I gave her a disappointed look and she seemed unimpressed by my remark.

"Quite alive," she replied, a bit more snappily this time. "And very much a success in his endeavours." She looked me up and down in my work slacks, covered in muck and threadbare, and let out a little snigger. "So successful, in fact, that he may never return. I'll be sure to pass on your regards in my next letter."

She stormed off across the street and I breathed a sigh of relief at her departure. I was growing to hate her.

If she really was in contact with Arthur then it meant he wasn't that far away, and I wasn't sure how I felt about that. It had crossed my mind, on the few occasions I allowed myself to think on it, that perhaps he'd somehow managed to make the ring work and that he'd zoomed off through time and out of my life. I'd also hoped, and felt little to no shame in it, that if that were the case, then he would find himself reappearing somewhere unfortunate, such as a cave filled with lions, or perhaps at the bottom of an ocean.

It was a fun thought, but I ultimately knew it wasn't possible. If he were missing then his family would have made it known and it would have been all anybody at the post office would have been talking about. If Mrs Wilkes was correct, however, then I still may never see him again, which left the subject of the ring, and my potential departure, very much up in the air.

"You don't look very happy," Gwyn said, falling in step with me as I walked back to the farm with Mrs Hopkin's sacks of food.

"I'm fine," I replied. "Mrs Wilkes…"

"Ah, yes. She has that effect on people. What did she have to say for herself this time?"

"News of Arthur," I said, and he suddenly looked as annoyed as I felt.

"He's back?"

"No, just living the high life somewhere and she wanted to make sure I knew about it."

"How do you feel about that?" He asked, and I came to a stop on the path.

"I don't know," I said with a sigh. "I'd gotten used to the fact that I might never see him or the ring again."

"And now?"

"I don't know, Gwyn." I was trying to keep my voice calm. I could feel myself getting frustrated but I knew it wasn't his fault.

"Do you still want to leave?" he asked.

I didn't want to keep him hanging on but I just didn't feel like I could give him a definitive answer. Betty told me to make a decision based on what it was that I wanted, but I hadn't had five minutes of peace to even think about what that might be. I decided to just go with the truth.

"I want to be with you, Gwyn, but I miss my family. At the moment I don't have a choice to go home, but maybe one day I will and it will be the hardest choice I'll ever have to make because I can't have both you and them. I don't want to make a promise to you that I might not be able to keep and I don't want you to lose your nerve and end things if you get scared that I might leave you. We have to both be certain. Does that make any sense at all?"

He brought a hand to my cheek and smiled at me. "Tom, I've never been more certain of anything. I choose you, every time, and I'll wait forever until you're ready. Take your time and think it through. Do what's right for you."

He gave me a wink and jogged off back down the road leaving me alone on the path to the farm. Betty's words ran through my mind over and over as I walked the rest of the way to the farm. *What is it that I want?* Deep down it felt like I'd already decided. I just had to bite the bullet and admit it to myself.

"Here you go," I said, dropping the sacks down on the counter in the kitchen. Mrs Hopkin gave me a nod in acknowledgement and carried on mixing whatever it was that was in the bowl in front of her. "Shall I make tea?"

"It's in the jug," she said. "You can pour me one out. I'd say I've earned it."

"Have you much left to do?" I asked as I took a seat at the table, trying to stay out of her way. It was nice to see her working in the kitchen again after so long. Smiles were still a rare sight, but the more she busied herself, the more the old Mrs Hopkin seemed to come through.

"More than I'd like and I haven't even started on dinner yet.

"It's a shame we can't have a takeaway delivered," I said.

"What's one of them?" she asked. She plopped herself down at the table and scrunched her nose up as she often did when I said things she didn't understand and I tried to figure out the simplest, most time-appropriate way of explaining it.

"Where I come from, back in Cambridge, there are shops that make dinner for you. You give them your order and then they deliver it, ready for you to eat."

"Well, well," she said, filled with shock. "Imagine that. I imagine there are a fair few wives out there who wouldn't mind being able to call on a service like that. I can't imagine the menfolk would like it much, though. Mr Hopkin is quite particular about what I put in front of him."

"Well, they wouldn't be able to beat your cooking anyway, Mrs Hopkin."

She smiled at me briefly, then, as though remembering that she shouldn't, her face quickly returned to neutral.

"I'm still waiting for you to teach me to make bread, don't forget."

"Oh, get out," she said, slapping my hand. "You can barely pour hot water in a cup, I'm not letting you near my ovens."

"Then you better start using them more often, then, because between you and me," I leaned in close and dropped my voice to a whisper, "Nan's a much better boxer than she is a baker."

Mrs Hopkin let out a laugh and brought her cup to her mouth to hide her smile. "Right, you, go and get washed and dressed. You're not sitting at my table in that state."

After dinner that evening I called around to see Mair as arranged. Her visits had been getting less frequent and whenever I'd tried to arrange for us to meet she would make excuses about being too busy. I'd mentioned it to Gwyn, wondering if perhaps I'd done something to upset her, but he said she'd been acting the same way with him and was spending a lot of time out of the house lately. He also reminded me that this was Mair, and if she was upset about anything then we would all know about it, so while it put my mind to rest, it also piqued my interest about why she was being so cagey.

"Will you tell her?" she asked, handing me a cup of tea and taking a seat opposite me in her living room.

I'd spent the time since I'd arrived getting her up to speed on Nellie's wish to train as a nurse, how she believed her father would not allow it and that it was actually Gethin who didn't want her to be too busy to look after him. Mair had insisted that we could go no further without tea and immediately set about boiling a pot.

"If it was me, I'd want to know."

"I can't," I replied, taking a sip and discretely spitting it back into the cup. Mair's tea making was better than her cooking skills but this was a particularly bad brew. "The wedding is right around the corner. I can't tell her. And what if I did and Mr Hopkin said I was lying? I'd look like a troublemaker. She'd never forgive me. She might not forgive me even if she believed me. It's always the messenger who gets the worst of it."

"Well, I would tell her," she said matter-of-factly. "And I'd have quite a few words for any man who told me what I could or couldn't do, as well."

"Honour and obey," I said dryly, giving her a raised eyebrow.

"Obey? Hardly. Men have it easy enough already without us bending over backwards to tend to their every whim. And they're not smart, you know. None of them. It's a wonder any of them can get dressed without a woman's help. If it's not their mother's, it's their wives. They go from one breast to the other."

She was getting redder in the face the more she talked, and her already fast speech was quickening with every sentence.

"Oh, they promise you the world, but you let them put a ring on your finger and suddenly they don't know how to clean up after themselves or make a sandwich. Or they stop you from becoming a nurse because it doesn't suit them, because God forbid they have to manage for themselves while a woman takes care of business."

"You're going to make some lucky man a very miserable husband one day," I joked. The truth was, although I teased her, I admired her for being so strong-willed in a time when she was expected to shut up and do as she was told. I was sure more women felt the same, even if few were as vocal about it.

"So, are you going to tell me where all this is coming from?" I asked. I put my cup down on the table next to the armchair and raised my foot onto my knee as though preparing for a counselling session.

"I don't know what you mean," she said, suddenly busying herself with something in her lap and ignoring my gaze.

"Oh, come on. Don't make me drag it out of you. I've hardly seen you for weeks. You've been avoiding me and you're always busy. Even Mrs Wilkes stopped me in the village to discuss your frequent trips on the omnibus."

"Mrs Wilkes," she said, her face filled with disgust, "needs to mind her own business instead of poking her nose into mine."

"And now," I continued, "you're suddenly free for tea and giving me the 'all men are bastards' speech. I know something is up. What's his name?"

She slumped back on the chair and let out a sigh. "There was someone," she said after a moment's pause. "We met at one of the funerals after the accident in the mine."

"Odd place to meet a man," I said, and she just glared at me. I held my hands up in apology and fell silent again.

"You know, I actually thought he might be different. We were reacquainted after Christmas and then met a few times more. All was well at first, but then he found out that the cottage was legally Gwyn's and he lost all interest. Told me today that I didn't have the prospects he'd expected and that things wouldn't work."

"So, what did you do?"

"Well, what could I do? I got the carriage home. What I wanted to do was slap him across his ridiculous face."

"I'm really sorry, Mair. That's terrible."

"Don't be. Love is a fool's errand. I guess I just became envious of everyone else having it for a moment." She was attempting to brush it off but as with everything Mair ever felt, the hurt of the situation was written all over her face. "Anyway," she said, changing the subject, "what of you? Are you still being pig-headed and threatening to leave?"

"Things have been really busy up at the farm and now with the wedding coming up I just keep getting delayed."

"Rubbish," she said, setting her cup on the saucer with a loud clink. "You have no obligations here. You and I both know it. You could set off this instant and John and Leah would think no less of you because of it."

"But I-"

"But nothing. You're staying because you want to stay. Don't get me wrong, I've grown quite fond of having you in the village so I'm in no rush to see the back of you quite yet, but we both know why you're staying."

"Is it that obvious?" I asked. This had quickly turned from a therapy session for Mair into me being forced to admit things to myself I was trying to keep buried.

"Will you just put him out of his misery? I love my brother, but if I have to spend another night seeing him come home with sad eyes while he mopes about the place like an old stray, I might be forced to have some strong words of my own, and we both know how out of character that would be."

"How much has he told you?" I asked.

"Hardly anything, which, might I add, makes it all so much worse. But I don't need to understand or know every last detail to know that you're both playing games that are making you miserable. You can't keep sneaking around and then saying that you're still leaving. That's not fair to either of you. You need to have it out with him and be honest."

As though he had been waiting outside for the perfect opportunity to barge in, Gwyn swung through the door with a massive smile on his face, bringing our conversation to an abrupt close.

"Receiving guests again, are we?" he said to his sister as he greeted her with a kiss on the cheek. He gave me a little wink as he threw his coat over the back of the chair and I felt an immediate knot in my stomach.

"What are you so happy about?" Mair asked. "What have you done?"

"Nothing," he replied, and another smile spread across his face. "Can't I just be happy to see my two favourite people? Who wants tea?"

He turned his attention to the stove and I watched as he fussed with the pots. He looked so at home in the kitchen and I imagined what life could have been like if I'd met him in my own time; this crazy wonderful man who had invaded his way into my every thought. We'd never get that chance to know, but we could make something work now, in this time. I wanted to try.

Mair was right.

It was time to stop running.

Twenty-Two

I spent the following two days desperately trying to get some alone time with Gwyn so that I could tell him how I feel and let him know my decision. Time was hard to come by, however, as preparations for the upcoming wedding were in full swing at the farm. When I finally managed to get an hour free to go and talk with him, Nan decided that we needed some bonding time and was pestering me to go with her and the rest of the family to pick flowers for the service.

Most of them had already left for the grove at the top of the hill but Nan had stayed behind to ensure my attendance. No matter how much I protested that I had things I needed to do she wouldn't hear of it, so with a sulk, I eventually gave in to her demands.

"I don't see why you need me to come," I protested as she pushed me through the kitchen door and into the yard.

"Because it's tradition," she replied, putting on her bonnet and making a quick march for the gate. "The wedding is tomorrow. We're all going, so you needn't argue."

"Your father isn't," I replied.

"Father has other things to do. Stop being so quarrelsome."

She rushed for the gate, her skirts flowing behind her and a large basket in hand, and I had to speed up to keep pace. It was unseasonably warm and by the time we turned to start walking up the hill I was already beginning to sweat, wishing she had at least allowed me time to change into something lighter.

"Mair will be there," she added, turning to me with a devilish smile on her face.

"What's that look for?" I asked.

"You will insist on playing the half-wit, Tom," she laughed. "Or do you think me one? You two are as thick as thieves, always whispering and visiting with each other. What else could it be if not courtship? I take it you worked things out, then?"

"I'm not courting Mair Griffiths," I said, laughing at how preposterous it sounded out loud. "We're just friends."

"If you insist," she replied, cocking up her eyebrows.

She didn't believe me but I didn't waste any time protesting. "How much further is it?" I asked, changing the subject.

"Not far. We need to go through there."

She pointed at a break in the hedge as we reached the top of the hill and I ran over, holding back the stray leaves and brambles so that she could pass through without ruining her clothes. On the other side we found ourselves in a large open field, surrounded by trees and covered in flowers, a sea of blues and pinks and yellows. I could hear the sounds of laughter in the distance, muffled by the sound of water running nearby.

I brought a hand to my eyes, shading out the sun, and stared across the field. "It's beautiful here."

"Over here," Nellie called out, waving across the field to us from a grove of trees.

We turned towards her calls, Nan linking her arm in mine, and crossed the field into a small opening under a canopy of trees where the rest of the family sat shaded from the warm spring sun. A river ran nearby, slicing the grove down the middle, and Mrs Hopkin had set down some blankets for people to relax on.

"I don't see much flower picking going on here," I said, taking a seat next to Betty, who was leaning against a tree with her head in a book. I was surprised she was able to make the walk. The hill had wiped me out and I had none of the ailments that she had, but she seemed well and content and gave me a warm smile as I joined her.

"All in good time," Nellie said. She reached into the basket beside her and extracted a small tin beaker, then filled it with lemonade and handed it over.

"Where are the boys?" I asked, noting the absence of Teddy and Howell.

Mair rolled her eyes at me and raised her hand to her face, extending a finger skyward. Many feet above us, balancing precariously on a thick extended branch, Gwyn smiled down at me with an excited wave, his hairy chest on full display. I hadn't expected him to be there, but seeing him suddenly made the trip worth it. Behind him, Teddy was waiting impatiently to get past while Howell, who hadn't made it quite as high as the others, clung to a lower branch with all four limbs as though his life depended on it.

"Are you ready?" Gwyn shouted, and Mair rolled her eyes again.

"That man will never grow up," she said as he jumped from the tree into the river behind her. He disappeared underwater for several seconds and then re-emerged a few feet downstream. A second later Teddy made his jump, a little closer to the edge than Gwyn had, causing us all to get caught in the backsplash.

"Lord, it's freezing," Gwyn said as he climbed up the side of the bank and came towards us. He'd rolled up his trousers to the knee and the water running from them left little puddles on the ground wherever he stepped. "You should go in," he said, grabbing his shirt from the ground and rubbing it across his chest.

"I'm happier just to watch," I replied, eyeing him up as he glistened in the stray rays of sun that managed to push through the leaves above us.

"I'm starving," Teddy said, bursting past Gwyn and kneeling down next to his mother. He rummaged through the basket and extracted a sandwich which Mrs Hopkin, with the reflexes of a cat, ripped from his hand before he could even raise it to his mouth.

"Get your brother out of that tree, now!"

Teddy burst out laughing as he spotted Howell wrapped around the branch with his face pressed into the bark but made no effort to retrieve him.

"I'll go," Gwyn said, and he nudged Teddy in the head as he walked past.

Nellie clasped her hands together and moved to the centre of the group, an excited smile on her face. "Ok, I want to fill both baskets with as many flowers as we can pick. Leave the red ones though, they're bad luck. Are you ready?"

Nan picked up the empty basket she had brought, tucking it into the crook of her arm, and then helped Mair to her feet. Excitedly, the three women walked out from under the trees into the meadow, gossiping as they went.

Betty hadn't looked up from her book the whole time that Nellie was speaking and they hadn't waited around for her to go with them. "Are you not joining them?" I asked.

"I think I'd rather stay in the shade," she replied, returning her gaze to the page. "I'll only slow them down."

"Here, Tom, help me with this," Mrs Hopkin asked, waving a bottle of her homemade lemonade at me with the cork firmly wedged into the top. I shuffled along the grass to sit beside her as Gwyn returned with Howell tucked under his arm.

"In you go," he said, walking straight past us and tossing Howell over the edge of the bank into the river. He turned around to us with a huge grin on his face, immensely proud that he'd drenched an eleven-year-old who was now flapping around in the water trying to get out.

"It's good to see you smiling again," I said as Mrs Hopkin watched on, laughing.

"It feels like it's been a while," she said, and I caught the warmth of her stare for the first time since we all got sick. "I think it's about time."

I threw my arm over her shoulder and drew her in close to me. She'd become like family. She technically was. Seeing her act more like her old self meant more to me than I ever realised it would.

Howell wasn't quite tall enough to pull himself up onto the banking, and unable to get a grip on the slippery grass he was repeatedly falling back into the river, causing Gwyn and Teddy to double over in hysterical laughter. Even Betty took her nose from her book to giggle at the situation. After several cries for help, I took pity on the lad and reached down to pull him out.

"Tom, what's that?" Teddy asked, pointing across the river through an opening in the trees. Foolishly, I followed the path of his finger and squinted against the sunlight as

Gwyn's palms connected with my shoulders sending me tumbling into the water below.

I immediately drew in a huge breath, swallowing mouthfuls of murky river water as I thrashed about trying to find the right way up. I finally broke through the surface, wiping my hair out of my eyes, and shot Gwyn an evil glare. Not that he noticed, of course. He was on his knees, pounding the ground with one hand and clutching his stomach with the other as he struggled to breathe through his laughter.

"Think you're funny, do you?" I shouted as I swept my arm through the river, spraying them all with water and making them all laugh even more.

The water was nearly up to my chest and absolutely freezing. I waded over to the edge, my boots weighing me down, and Gwyn stupidly reached out a hand to help me out. I immediately kicked my foot against the side of the river, using the ground as leverage to pull him in beside me.

"Payback," I said, quickly jumping onto the side of the bank and away from any retaliation.

I was soaked to the bone and my woollen trousers weighed heavy on my waist making it difficult to walk. As I reached for the bottom of my shirt, intending to pull it off and over my head, I heard Mair yell for her brother from the field, followed by the sound of hooves coming along the ground.

Gwyn jumped out of the water and ran over to me, alerted by the yells from his sister, as a figure rode up and blocked the entrance to the glade.

"You're trespassing," he said, and I had to put my hand to my eyes to block out the sunlight and get a good view of him. It wasn't until he swung his leg around and jumped down from the horse that his features became clearer and I saw that it was Arthur Morgan, back from wherever he'd been hiding since he'd had us arrested and stolen the ring from me.

"You've got some nerve," Gwyn said, taking a step towards him. I put my arm out to stop his path and Arthur smirked, unbothered by the thought of Gwyn's approach.

"We've been coming here for years," Mrs Hopkin said, coming to stand beside us. "The whole village has. You've no right."

"I've every right," Arthur snapped. He took a step towards her and Teddy jumped in front of his mother, putting a barrier between the two. "Now, I won't say it twice. Get off my land, old hag, and take your vermin with you."

This time I was the one who made a start for him and he reached for the rifle saddled at the back of his horse. Mrs Hopkin grabbed hold of my sleeve, pulling me to a stop and I waited to see what he would do next.

"Mama, let's just go," Betty said. I hadn't noticed that she'd even gotten up, but she walked slowly toward Arthur, unafraid of his threats. "There's a foul smell around here, anyway."

"That's right girl," he said, sneering at Betty. She grabbed Howell's hand and pushed past Arthur into the field as Nan, Mair and Nellie finally reached us.

"Go," I said, ushering Mrs Hopkin and Teddy towards the opening. "We'll collect your things."

Mrs Hopkin kept her eyes on Arthur as she walked past and Teddy made sure to keep himself between them until they were both out into the clearing with the others.

"As for you, freak," he said, taking steps towards us. "Your time is coming." He grabbed me by the wrist, and pulled me against him, bringing his face so close to mine that his breath caused a dampness on my cheek. "We're not done, you and me."

"I know you took my stuff," I said, pulling my face away from his and freeing my arm from his grip.

I caught a brief glimpse of Gwyn from the corner of my eye as his arm swiped past my face and his fist connected with Arthur's jaw. Arthur stumbled back a few steps putting space between us and Gwyn looked ready to go for him again. Mair called out from somewhere in the background as Gwyn went in for another swing, but this time Arthur sidestepped him and Gwyn's blow connected only with air.

He brought his hand up to his chin, twisting it as though trying to lock it back in place, then spat out some blood before turning to Gwyn with a sly grin. "You'll regret that one, Gwynfor."

"But it felt so good," Gwyn countered, spreading out his arms and inviting Arthur to fight back. "I'm not afraid of you."

"You will be," Arthur said as he mounted his horse again. "Now get out of my field." He pulled hard on the reins causing the horse to back up and let out a loud whinny, then he set off at a sprint through the field, narrowly missing Mrs Hopkin and her children as he passed.

Mair immediately made a beeline for us, hitching up her skirts and running through the tall flowers to the clearing. "Are you ok? What did he say?"

"We're fine," Gwyn replied. "Get them home. We'll be right behind you."

"But…"

"No buts, Mair," he snapped. "Go."

His sister turned heel and headed back to the Hopkins', gathering them up and leading them back towards the house.

"Is your hand ok?" I asked. As soon as Arthur was out of sight he'd brought it up to his chest and cupped it with the other, obviously hurt from punching that awful man.

"It's nothing. It was worth it."

"You shouldn't have hit him," I said as I began gathering the blankets and baskets left behind by Mrs Hopkin. "Last time you only stood up to him and he had us locked up. What do you think he'll do now you've smacked him in the face?"

"He doesn't get to put his hands on you," he replied. "Nobody does."

I smiled at him, glad to have him on my side, and tossed his shirt at him so that he could get dressed.

"It *was* quite impressive," I said with a wink as we made our way out of the grove, and he made a jokey flex with his arm before pushing me off into the flowers.

"My hero," I teased and he grabbed my hand, bringing me to a stop. I looked over to the rest of our group who were now at the far side of the field, disappearing one by one through the opening onto the road, and then turned my attention back to him.

"As long as you're here I'll always look out for you. I hope you know that."

"About that," I said, deciding that now was as good a time as any to tell him of my decision. "I-"

"Come on," Mair shouted, bringing our attention back to the opening at the edge of the field. She stood in the gap waving her arms and beckoning us toward her. "We're all waiting by here."

"I guess it'll wait," I said with a sigh, and we rushed off to re-join the group.

Twenty-Three

"Get a move on," Mrs Hopkin shouted at Teddy. Every time her back was turned he was picking at pastries in the kitchen and still hadn't gotten dressed. "We haven't got all day."

The farm had been alive with activity all morning as the family rushed around in preparation for Nellie's and Gethin's wedding, and Mrs Hopkin was buzzing from room to room trying to make sure everything was ready and in place for the day to go off without a hitch.

Teddy and I had been tasked with decorating the yard and laying out tables for the guests. With the house being too small to host a large group and the village not having any sort of community hall, the yard to the side and rear of the farmhouse was to host the reception, with the barn cleaned and swept out ready as a backup should the rain come. Luckily the hot weather of the last few days had graced us once more, and clear blue cloudless skies lay overhead.

We hung bunting in rows between the buildings around the yard and Mrs Hopkin had ensured that all the table cloths were boiled and bleached and laid out in pristine fashion across the tables, each one with a small posy of flowers picked the day before sitting atop them. All that was left to do was put out the food after the ceremony.

Mr Hopkin had risen earlier than usual and left the house for town, hitching one of the horses to the cart that we'd been expressly told was for farm use only, and leaving the rest of us to get the house in order. With less than an hour to go until we were due at the church, there was still no sign of his return and Nellie had spent the last twenty minutes shouting down the stairs in a blind panic that she would have nobody to give her away. When I walked into the kitchen her mother was shouting reassurances back up the stairs to her, but the look on her face told me she was just as concerned about his whereabouts as Nellie was.

"Are you not meeting Gethin at the pub?" Betty asked, coming into the kitchen and taking a seat at the table. She was dressed in a long white gown that had had to be taken in at the last minute to accommodate her constant weight loss, and her hair sat in a bun on top of her head, decorated with flowers and a few loose curls that fell around her cheeks. Nan had plastered her in makeup earlier in the day complaining that she looked too pale and her mother had washed it off again complaining that she looked like a 'forward girl'.

"I'm meeting them at the church," I replied. "Is your sister nearly ready?"

"Nan is just attaching her veil and then she will be. You're looking very dashing, by the way."

Not so long ago a statement like that would never have made it past her lips and she'd have flushed with embarrassment for just thinking it, but she eyed me in my attire and gave me a warm smile. I'd never been a fan of formal wear, always feeling like I looked like a child in grown-up clothing, but it did feel nice to be in something that wasn't caked in farm debris or tearing at the seams.

Gethin had chosen for us a grey pinstripe trouser with a dark morning coat and burgundy waistcoats, finished off with top hats and cravats. Upon first seeing it I complained to Nellie that I would look like a footman but she assured me it was the height of fashion and I had to admit that once it was on and all put together it did look rather good. I was more excited, though, to see what Gwyn would be dressed like. I hadn't ever seen him in formal wear before, except at funerals.

"If your father doesn't hurry up and get back here, I'm going to show him the pointy end of that poker," Mrs Hopkin said, breezing back into the kitchen from the yard.

"You're looking very beautiful, Mrs Hopkin." I'd never seen her so done up and with her hair neatly tied and her pink dress flowing around her she looked prettier than I'd ever seen her.

"Thank you," she said, doing a little curtsy as the bells of the church began to chime to announce the wedding.

"That's my sign to leave," I said, rising to my feet.

"You can't go without seeing Nellie first," Betty said. "You have to wait."

"I can't go anywhere without Teddy," I replied. We were meant to be walking to the village together ahead of the rest of the family to meet with Gethin, but he was taking forever to get ready.

"Look at the time," Mrs Hopkin said as she hurried off again and leaned through the kitchen door. "Teddy," she yelled. "If I've got to come up there you can look out."

"I'm here," he said, popping his head around the door frame. "I look stupid."

I could only see his head, but his hair, which was usually covered by a cap or ruffled up in a mess atop his head, was combed neatly with a side parting and stuck into place with pomade, giving it a greasy shine. It suited him.

"Get in here," his mother said, and he slowly crept into view. "You look wonderful," she added, grabbing his shoulders and kissing his cheek.

"Gerroff," he said, wiping his face.

"You ready?" I asked him.

"No," he replied, and though he tried to make himself look miserable he couldn't help but smile and I had to resist the urge to scuff a hand through his neatly coiffed hair.

Pushing him to the door I grabbed my hat from the table and began to follow him out. As he reached for the handle it flung open and Mr Hopkin burst through, red-faced and panting.

"I'm sorry," he said, and he leaned his hands down on the table to catch his breath. "Took longer than I thought." Mrs Hopkin began to berate him but he ignored her and ran through to the sitting room. "Nellie," he shouted up the stairs. "Come and see."

He rushed back through to the kitchen and ushered us outside, a big grin covering his face. In the yard stood his wagon, decked out with hundreds of flowers and wrapped in pink and white ribbons. The horse attached to it had not escaped the makeover, either, with its reins adorned in bows and a halo of flowers on its head which was tilting to the side and looked ready to drop at any moment.

As soon as she saw it Mrs Hopkin let out a gasp, bringing her hands to her mouth as her eyes began to well up.

"Do you think she'll like it?" he asked.

She threw her arms around her husband, kissed his cheek and then did a loop around the cart taking it all in. "John, it's beautiful."

"She's only going to the bottom of the hill, she could have walked," Teddy said, earning him a clip to the ear from his mother.

"Cost a pretty penny," Mr Hopkin said, "but it was worth it."

"Oh my God!" Nellie gasped from the doorway, and we all turned as one to look at her.

She looked stunning. Her white lace dress flowed with her every movement, tied at her waist by a thin yellow ribbon, with elbow-length sleeves that showed off just a hint of her arms above her evening gloves.

Her long dark hair had been tied up in loose curls, hidden in place by a lace veil that hung down to her waist and had been fastened behind each ear with a flower. Under the warm April sun, she looked as though she were glowing.

"You look incredible," I said, suddenly overcome with a feeling that I should bow to her, though I refrained for fear of looking like an idiot.

"What do you think?" Mr Hopkin asked, taking her hand and leading her around the wagon.

"I love it," she said, and she kissed him on the cheek.

"I've got one more gift for you," he said, reaching into his breast pocket and pulling out an envelope.

"I should wait," she said, pushing it back towards him, "until Gethin is here."

"This one is just for you," he said, causing her to look curiously at him. "Open it."

She took the envelope, tearing at the seal while looking at him for some sort of hint to its contents, but he remained silent, smiling at her as she pulled out a letter from inside.

"Dear Miss Hopkin," she read aloud, "We hereby invite you to commence formal training at Aberystwyth Infirmary beginning September 1890…"

She trailed off after that, her eyes widening with excitement, and she threw her arms over her dad's shoulders in an embrace that nearly knocked the flowers from her hand. Mrs Hopkin, who was by this point in a flood of tears with a grin like a Cheshire cat, joined them in their embrace.

"Come on everybody," she said, motioning to the group. "One last family hug before we send her off."

Nan, Betty, Teddy and Howell all gathered together with their arms around Nellie and her parents, and I watched from the side thinking what a lovely picture it would have made.

"And you, you soft mare," Mrs Hopkin said, beckoning me over. "You're a part of this family too, whether you like it or not."

I stepped up to join them with a huge grin on my face. I did like it. I liked it very much.

Outside the church I met with Gethin and his best man Dylan, who while pleasant, barely spoke a word to any of us. We stood, along with Teddy, and greeted guests as they arrived for the wedding.

Mair and Gwyn were amongst the last to reach the church, both looking beautiful in their formal wear. They walked towards us arm-in-arm and Mair, in a yellow dress decorated with white lace flowers embroidered all around it, leaned in to kiss me on the cheek. "You look so handsome," she whispered as she brushed past me into the church.

Gwyn, unable to say what was on his mind with so many other people around, gave me a knowing smile and a tip of his hat as he followed behind her. It was enough to put a smile on my face.

When everyone was inside Gethin and Dylan entered to take their places, leaving Teddy and me waiting for the bride to arrive.

"Looking good, Teddy boy," I said, giving him a light jab to the arm. "I didn't even know you knew how to wash."

He let out a little laugh and hit me back. He was shifting his weight from one foot to the other while he stared off up the hill for a sign of his sister.

"Are you nervous?" I asked.

"What have I got to be nervous about? It's not me that's got to marry him."

"You're going to miss her, aren't you?"

"Can't say I'll notice," he replied, trying to play it cool. I knew it must be tough for him to see another of his siblings leave home, as she inevitably would over the coming weeks, even if it was only to somewhere else in the village.

Before I could press the matter further the sound of hooves on the road brought my attention towards the hill and the carriage that was bringing Nellie to her groom. Behind it walked Mrs Hopkin, along with Howell, Nan and Betty, who looked as though she was struggling to keep up, though I knew that she would have refused any suggestion of joining her sister on the wagon.

Along the street, residents of the village who were not attending the wedding came to their doors to cheer on the bride through her procession. Even Mrs Wilkes had wiped the sour look from her face and managed to raise a smile for her. When they pulled up outside, Mr Hopkin helped lower Nellie to the ground and she waved to the people who had gathered to see her.

At the gates, a small crowd of children had gathered in anticipation. Mr Hopkin removed a small pouch from his pocket and gave it to his daughter who pulled on the string and tipped dozens of ha'pennies all over the floor, sending the waiting children into a scramble to see who could collect the most.

Once the pavement was clear she made the short walk from the gate flanked by her family. Mrs Hopkin kissed her on the cheek, and then she, along with Howell, Teddy and I went inside to await Nellie's entrance. Teddy and I took a stand alongside Dylan and stared towards the back of the church as the organ began to play and Nellie, holding on to her father, began her march down the aisle, with Nan and Betty close behind her.

I caught sight of Gwyn amongst the congregation and he gave me a wink and that huge gorgeous smile, and I began grinning back at the crowd, flushed with excited embarrassment. I'd still had no chance to talk with him about my intentions to stay so had resolved that I would do it at the reception before I had the chance to get drunk. Seeing him there, unable to take his eyes from me, just solidified my decision further.

As Nellie took her position in front of the vicar I, along with her father and the other groomsmen, seated ourselves in the front row and watched her become Mrs Ellen Evans.

At the reception, I was seated at a table near the bride and groom alongside Mair, Gwyn and a chap called Zachary, who I'd never met before. We took our seats and watched as Mr Hopkin, and then Gethin gave speeches to the crowd, and Gethin revealed that he'd booked a secret honeymoon to

Tenby, eliciting much excitement from Nellie and gossiping in the crowd.

Once the formalities were over the party got into full swing and it wasn't long until the wine was flowing.

"What a lovely day it's been," Mair said, arriving back at the table with a plate of food. She'd made a beeline for the buffet table as soon as Mrs Hopkin brought the food out and made sure to stack her plate high enough that she wouldn't need to return for a while. "Didn't she look beautiful?"

"I think everyone looked really good," Gwyn said, rubbing his knee against mine under the table.

"So, what do you do, Zachary?" I asked the stranger at our table. In our few opportunities to speak so far, he'd seemed funny and charming but had mostly been showing a keen interest in Mair.

"Please, call me Zack," he said with a friendly smile. "I'm a blacksmith. Well, an apprentice, but I've nearly completed my training."

"Oh? We could do with one of those up at the house," Mair said. She put her elbow on the table and rested her chin in her hand, flashing her big eyes at him. They'd been flirting for much of the day and since the wine was opened she'd gotten worse at disguising it.

"What do we need a blacksmith for?" Gwyn asked. "We haven't got any cattle or equipment anymore."

"Ow! Watch it," I shouted, as the boot that was meant for her brother connected with my shin, causing me to raise my knee into the table and making everything on it jump. I shot an angry look at Mair who sent the same face toward her brother, who in turn burst out laughing.

"That thing needs mending," she said, waving a pastry and indicating at nothing. "The one out the back."

"Oh, yeah," Gwyn replied, with exaggeration, "The thing."

I couldn't work out if Zack was too clueless to notice the situation, or just smart enough to take advantage of it, but he nonetheless agreed to escort Mair home that evening and take a look at whatever it was that she needed fixing. Gwyn and I, having the minds of school children, burst into laughter at the innuendo, causing more looks of disdain from Mair.

"Would you like to dance?" Zack asked, offering a hand to Mair, who rose to her feet and accompanied him to the centre of the courtyard.

Off to the side, in an area kept clear of tables, three people from the village sat with instruments playing music. The sounds of the violins, flute and pipes kept the spirits of the guests up, some of whom were filling the space with dancing, and all seemingly knowing the correct moves to each new piece of music. Men created arches with their arms that women danced under, and they bowed and curtsied and spun, all in time and rhythm with each other. The elegance of it seemed in stark contrast to what I normally saw when people danced at a wedding back home.

"Gentlemen," Nan called out as she approached the table with Betty. "I'm quite sure it would be improper for us to ask you to dance," she said with a smile, "so please do us the honour of not letting us stand alone."

Gwyn rose immediately from his seat and took Nan by the arm, escorting her with a smile.

"I don't know how to do it," I said, causing a laugh from Betty. "I don't dance."

"I'll show you," she said. "Come on."

Apprehensively I took her hand and stood from the table. Although I was just another body in the crowd, I couldn't help but feel like all eyes were on me and I began to sweat.

"Relax," she said. "Just watch what everyone else does."

She lined me up down the row of men and stood opposite me with the other women. Any concerns about her health had seemingly disappeared and as the music began she started, along with all the other women, to skip on the spot, tipping her feet in and out with every other jump. A second later the men began to move, imitating what the women had done, and I tried to keep up.

The couple at the end began dancing forward and met at the centre of our lines. They joined hands and did a spin before dancing their way to the other end, the rest of us moving forward a turn and repeating the moves over and over. By the time I got to the head of the line, my confidence was up and I reached out for Betty and spun her around as we danced in front of everyone.

"See, I told you it was easy," she said with a huge smile before pushing me off and sending me to the back of the line. I made it to the end without falling flat on my face and when we stopped and bowed to the women the onlookers gave us all a round of applause for our efforts.

"Are you ok?" I asked her as I took her by the arm and led her to her table. I was feeling pretty winded so I could only imagine how out of breath she must have been feeling.

"I'm fine. Thank you, Tom," she said with a smile. "That felt good."

I tipped my head to her and went to find Gwyn. He was standing over at the food table picking at it rather than just putting it on a plate and taking it to the table like everyone else.

"I'm going to grab my jacket and then we're going for a walk," I said, then headed into the house. In the kitchen, sitting alone at the table, I found Mrs Hopkin.

"Needing a break from all the festivities?" I asked, taking a seat beside her. Her face was a mixture of both happy and sad, and she stared down at her hand, twisting her wedding ring around on her finger.

"Just thinking about when I got married," she said, without looking up.

"How long has it been?"

"Twenty-five years in September. Feels like yesterday. Same church. Same vicar, even. We didn't have a party afterwards, mind you. We couldn't afford it back then. We came back here and sat around this table with our parents and had mutton. Then, when it was over, my mam and dad left and I stayed behind. I've been here ever since."

"What you've done for Nellie today, she'll always remember it."

"I just wish the whole family had been here to see it," she said, and she brought her hand up to her face, wiping a tear from her cheek. "Oh, ignore me," she said, as if snapping out of a trance. "I'm just having a moment. Let's get back to the party."

She moved, as though she was about to stand, but I took hold of her hand and held it in mine on the table. "Sophia is with us all every day, Mrs Hopkin. And Jack's not gone, he's just off and away. He'll be back soon enough, I'm sure."

"You remind me of him, you know? You even look like him. Sometimes I'll look up and the light will catch you just so, and I'll think for a moment that he's come home. I don't know what we'd have done without you these last few months. I'm glad you found your way to us, Tom."

"Well, I'm not going anywhere," I said, squeezing her hand and giving her a big smile. "This place feels like home now, so I'll be staying for as long as you'll have me."

"You're always welcome here, my love. Always. Now go, enjoy the party and get some food before Mr Hughes from next door eats all of those sandwiches."

I leaned in and hugged her then left her to her thoughts as I headed back outside.

"Come on then," I said to Gwyn as I passed, and he turned to follow me away from the party.

We strolled down through the farm gate and onto the road into the village. The sun was still high as we walked, but the sky was turning orange as night crept closer and the air had turned a little chillier.

"So, what do you need to talk about?" Gwyn asked as we walked past the school.

"I've been thinking. I've been thinking quite a lot, actually, about us and this place and what I want."

He began to smile and then stopped, unsure if he would be happy with what I was going to say next. I took a moment to pause, considering my words, and we came to a stop outside the church gate.

"I'm crazy about you, Gwynfor Griffiths. I've known it all along but I got scared that you'd get cold feet again so I told myself to stay away, but I can't. I don't want to."

His eyes went wide as a smile spread across his face and he grabbed my hand right there in the street.

"I'm going to stay. Here in the village, in this time. I'm going to stay and be with you in whatever way we can."

He looked like he was going to reach out and kiss me but I stepped away and darted my eyes back and forth reminding him where we were.

"Do you mean it? Really?" he asked, and I nodded. "But what about the ring? What about Arthur? If you get it back, won't you just want to leave?"

"I've thought about it. Over and over. I've kept myself awake at night thinking about what I would do. How I might never see my mother and brother again, or how I could return and never see you again. I love my family, but if I go back, I'll be doing it for them. If I stay, then it's for me, and I choose you. Is that selfish?"

"Not at all," he said, though I expected no different.

"But you can't get cold feet again," I warned. "I can't go through that again. Even if it has to be a secret forever."

"I promise," he said, and as though his face couldn't decide on an emotion, he burst out laughing as a tear rolled down his cheek. "Quick, let's go to the cottage and celebrate. We'll probably have half an hour before anyone notices we're missing."

"I'm freezing," I said, rubbing my arms. The chill of the late afternoon was really beginning to set in and I could feel goosebumps all along my skin. "I forgot to grab my jacket."

"Ok, you wait here," he said, his face filled with excitement. "I'll run back to the house and get it. I'll be five minutes."

He ran off along the street towards the farm and I watched him until the bend, hoping he wouldn't be too long. Not wanting to stand in the street, I pushed open the gate of the church and went inside, moving slowly among the headstones and keeping my arms around me for warmth.

I followed the path around the church to some graves at the back. Sheep were grazing among them, having escaped from the adjoining field where the wall had crumbled. Rather than being scared by my presence they just stared at me as I wandered through until I reached a small area near the north wall. A tree had sprung up there and toppled some of the older headstones that were surrounding it, and now grown so large that it cast the area in a cold shade.

On the ground amongst some tall headstones sat a small plaque marking the resting place of Sophia. The family hadn't yet been able to afford the proper headstone, so a small slate with her name on it was all she had for now. I knelt next to it, arranging some of the flowers that had been left there after the wedding, and began to talk to her about the day.

"She can't hear you, you know?"

By the time I realised that it was Arthur Morgan standing behind me it was too late. As soon as I spun around to face him the butt of his rifle connected with my face, knocking me out.

Twenty-Four

I awoke to an almost perfect blackness and no idea where I was. All I was certain of was that it was dark and damp and somewhere that I didn't want to be.

I'd been propped against a wall, my hands and feet tied, and my back soaked through with moisture from the coarse surface I leaned against. It was quiet, too. Only the sound of water dripping from above me cut through the hush of the space, hitting the stone floor and sending out frequent tinny echoes.

Pain shot through my head as I tried to move, a result of being hit in the face that had left me with a pounding headache and what I was certain was dried blood making the side of my face feel stiff and sticky.

I shifted around a bit, noticing that the rope that bound my ankles was looser than the one at my wrists, and tried shuffling my feet to see if I could break free. There was definitely room to manoeuvre.

"Help!" I yelled, hoping that I was close enough to civilization that someone would hear me. I continued to struggle against the binds on my feet as I shouted. The friction was wearing through my thin suit trousers and causing my ankles to burn and chafe but there was definitely more movement in my legs than there was before.

"Help!" I screamed again. I left a pause and fell still, trying to listen for noise or movement from outside. None came.

"Where the hell am I?" I wondered aloud. I was starting to panic trying to work out where Arthur might have taken me. It was broad daylight when he hit me and people were in the village. Someone must have seen him put me on a horse or into a carriage or something. Someone must be looking for me. What the hell was he playing at?

I brought my legs closer to my body and kicked and thrashed again with my feet. The ropes hadn't given way enough for me to free myself but they had loosened enough that I was able to twist my feet. I put the back of one foot against the heel of the other and pushed hard. My wedding shoes were tied tightly but with enough force I was able to round one off the heel and push it off. This time when I began thrashing, my right foot escaped the bond and pulled free.

After a lot of wrangling, I managed to get myself onto my knees, and with no small effort, eventually onto my feet. With my hands still constrained behind me, I felt around on the slippery stone surface of the wall and began taking side steps along its length in a quest to find an exit.

"You're going the wrong way," a voice in the darkness spoke out, frightening me half to death.

"Who's there?" I shouted, my voice cracking despite my best efforts to compose myself. "Arthur?"

"You won't get out."

The disembodied voice echoing around the room made me feel more uneasy than when I thought I was alone. Not knowing where he was or what he was doing filled me with genuine fear and I could hear my breathing get louder and faster as my heart beat overtime in my heaving chest.

"You could just let me go," I said, hoping I might be able to reason with him. "This has gone far enough, don't you think?"

Before the last words had even left my lips a rush of heavy, frantic footsteps filled the room. In a heartbeat he was upon me, screaming in my face. "TELL ME HOW IT WORKS!"

The hot air of his breath and spit covered my face and I recoiled, terrified by the sudden screaming that was shattering the blackened silence. I tried in vain to retreat but was firmly wedged between him and the wall.

"I don't know what you're talking about," I pleaded, and I could hear his footsteps stagger off as he disappeared somewhere into the cavernous space.

"The time for games is over, Mr Jacob." His voice was calm again, distant.

"How long have I been here?" I asked, trying to divert the topic.

"Too long, already."

"People will be looking for me."

"Mr Griffiths, perhaps?" There was a snark to his tone that made me uncomfortable. "You're a man of many secrets, aren't you Mr Jacob? I heard you at the church. The two of you make me sick."

His voice remained in the distance and I began edging along the wall again in the hope that if I could not see him, then he could not see me. If I could just find a door handle I might be able to free myself and get outside and start screaming for help until someone pays attention.

"I don't know what you mean," I said, taking another step right and being careful not to make a sound. If I could keep him talking I would have a better guess at where in the room he was lurking.

"Must we do this, Tom? Must we dance this dance where you act the fool and I hold the cards until you die of starvation?"

Was he capable of that? Unhinged he may be, but would he let me die?

I took another step. "What do you want to know?"

"The ring. How does it work?"

"I don't know."

"You're lying to me." He began to raise his voice again and I froze on the spot.

"I'm not, I swear. I'm just as much in the dark as you are."

"You're funny," he said, his voice calming again. It was closer now. "I've examined the contents of your purse. I believe them to be real." A second later he was on me again. He pressed his cheek against mine, bringing his left hand up and running it through my hair until he eventually grabbed hold of it. My face pinned, he brought his lips to my ear, dropping his voice to a harsh whisper. "Ask me why."

"Why?" I spat out, surprised by the sudden strength in my voice.

He pulled away from me roughly, sending my head back against the stone, and moved once again into the darkness. The return to silence as he contemplated his answer was even more unnerving than the sound of his voice and I took another step sideways hoping to find release.

"I received a letter some months ago," he began, and I could hear his steps pacing back and forth nearby. "It was from Elinor. She wrote to tell me that she was calling our engagement off." He laughed as though he could hardly believe she would have the impertinence. "She believed that she loved another and could not bring herself to marry me. I know you've seen my house, Tom. Jefferson told me all about your outbursts at the doorstep so you know what I was able to offer her. But it seemed she would rather scurry about with that dirty Hopkin bastard than live the life that I would provide. Now tell me, Thomas, does that make sense to you? No, I didn't think so, either. So I did what any aggrieved man in my position would do and I rode right over to her house to put her back into her place."

"Why are you telling me this?" I asked.

"DON'T SPEAK!" he screamed, and I could hear his pace pick up. I braced myself, expecting to be hit but no blow came and his voice returned to normal as he began to talk again. "When I got to her house her father, none the wiser about her letter, just let me walk right in and up to her room. She was preparing herself to go and meet *him*. I couldn't stand it, seeing her dressed like a whore for another man, that stupid necklace hanging down to her tits inviting everyone to look at her. It filled me with rage.

"I didn't kill her. I know that's what you're thinking. I could have. I wanted to. But I didn't." His tone was calm, almost pleading, as though he genuinely wanted me to believe that he was the wronged party, somehow. "I tried to reason with her at first, but you know what women are like. She became hysterical, telling me to leave. Me! So I grabbed her. I took hold of her wrists and I threw her onto the bed. She tried to get up. She even slapped me, but the rage had taken me over. If she wasn't going to be mine then she wasn't going to be anyone else's, either."

"So, you did kill her?"

"That's the thing," he said, rushing close to my face again and putting his hands around my throat. "She had such a small little neck, not like yours, and I held it so tightly that I was able to lock my fingers together as I gripped it. She wanted to scream, I know she did, but no sound would come. All she could do was gasp for air. I don't remember her ever looking so pretty."

He eased his grip on my throat, holding me now by just one hand, and he dropped his head to my shoulder, almost nestling into me as he chuckled softly. I felt sick feeling him against me.

"You're crazy," I said, and he shot upright, bringing his second hand to my throat once more and holding me hard against the wall.

"Do you know what's crazy, Thomas?" he spat through clenched teeth. "What's crazy is that as I pinned that harlot down, as she clasped at my hands to get me off, that stupid necklace she always wore started glowing. Can you believe that? Bright red it went, as though someone was shining a light right through it, and just as quickly as I noticed it, she was gone. Vanished. Now that's crazy, wouldn't you say?"

He released his grip and moved back into the darkness as I dragged as much air as I could into my lungs. The sound of his pacing started again and I took my chance to keep moving around the edge of the room.

"If you knew all along that I had nothing to do with her going missing then why have you spent all this time hounding me?"

"Are you a superstitious man, Thomas?" he asked, and his footsteps came to a stop again. "Something like that will make you question everything you ever thought to be real.

But who could I tell? Who would believe me? Despite the terrible way she treated me and the awful things she forced me to do in that room, I still loved her. Isn't that something? I loved her even though she's a witch."

"A witch?" I wasn't expecting that one.

"Jack pretended not to know anything of her whereabouts, of course, but I knew they were in it together. Out to get me."

"You're completely mad," I said.

"No, Thomas," he laughed. "They were mad for thinking they could fool me. The next day I saw him leaving the village, probably on his way to her, so I followed behind him, out of sight. When we reached the top of the hill, I set upon him and we fought. When he reached out to hit me, I grabbed hold of his wrist and could see that just like the necklace, his ring had begun to shine. I tried to prise it from his finger, and I'm pretty sure I broke a few in the process, but he would not give in. The coward turned and ran instead. Of course, I gave chase, but when I rounded the corner he was gone. Vanished, just like Elinor. Then, just a few days later, you show up out of nowhere wearing the exact same ring. Quite the coincidence, wouldn't you say?"

"Maybe people just don't want to be around you," I said snarkily. I was quickly losing patience with his paranoid tales of witchcraft and conspiracies. "What's your point, Arthur?"

I wondered if he had been like this before Elinor disappeared or if the sight of her vanishing in front of his eyes sent him crazy. Whatever happened to her, she'd had a lucky escape, that was certain.

"You didn't hide it well, did you?" he said, changing the topic. "It was almost like you wanted me to find it, to find you out. Was the truth getting too much to bear, Tom? Knowing that you took Elinor away from me?"

"What? Have you lost your mind? I didn't take her anywhere. She was already gone when I got here."

"SO THEN WHY DO YOU HAVE THE RING?" he screamed at me, rushing again towards my face. I cowered back as he grabbed my hair and banged my head against the stone wall causing me to cry out.

"How *is* your father?" he asked, his face inches from mine.

"Dead," I spat out. I had no energy left to play dumb and I wasn't going to give him the satisfaction of thinking that I was shocked that he'd worked it out.

"Well, that's something, I suppose," he said, and even through the darkness, I could tell he was smiling. "And that whore, is she your mother?"

"I've never met Elinor," I said, exhausted from going over it again. "I already told you this."

"That woman in your strange portrait… She looks like her, you know? Did he tell you about her?"

"He never mentioned her."

"Because he was ashamed," he shouted. "He knew she was rightfully mine."

"You can't just own a person. She didn't love you."

My head hit the wall again, but this time it was his hand pressed against my forehead that forced the connection and I let out another cry of pain. I was still reeling from the impact when he hit me in the stomach, winding me. I leaned forward in agony, my head coming into contact with his chest, and he grabbed me by the hair and raised me upright.

"Tell me how the ring works."

"I don't know," I said, and another blow connected with my gut. Tears had begun streaming down my cheeks as I sucked in huge gasps of air. If he'd not been holding me up I was sure I'd have crumpled to the ground.

"You got here, and now I want to get there."

"Get where?" I screamed. "I didn't choose any of this! Even if you could make it work for you, who knows where you'd end up. She could be dead already and then what? Have you thought any of this through? You need to move on. It's done."

He stroked the back of his hand across my cheek and I could feel the ring on his finger as it rubbed down my skin. When he reached my jaw he pulled back and punched me in the face, splitting my lip. I could taste the blood as it trickled into my mouth and I spat it out hoping it hit him.

"You will tell me," he said confidently. "Maybe some time alone will encourage you to do what's best."

He retreated into the darkness and a second later a door opened on the opposite side of the room. Outside I could see fields in the moonlight, but nothing that I recognised. I ran towards the opening but before I got even halfway, he'd pulled it closed behind him, leaving me locked in the darkness.

"Help me," I shouted, kicking the door trying to make as much noise as possible. "Somebody help. I'm in here."

When the door next unlocked, I was sitting on the floor in front of it, my voice hoarse from screaming for hours on end, and severely dehydrated. I'd continued to shout for a while, though my cries had gotten fewer and quieter as the night wore on until eventually, I just stopped. When it finally swung open I fell through it onto a pair of boots, ready to accept my fate.

Dawn had broken and the light from the sun rising over the field cast my assailant in shadow as he looked down over me. I closed my eyes as he leaned down, preparing to be beaten again or dragged back inside, but instead, he swept the hair from my face and pulled me into a sitting position.

"Tom, what the hell has he done?"

I opened my eyes again, blinking against the brightness, and saw Gwyn staring back at me, his face mixed with relief and distress.

"Where am I?" I asked as he made a start untying my hands. The ropes had cut me and I had to stop myself from pulling away from him as he tried to help me get loose.

"It's an old boarded-up cottage up on the estate. I heard you shouting but then you went quiet. I searched every building until I found you. I'm so sorry it took me so long. Where is he?"

"I don't know," I said, bringing my hands from behind my back for the first time in hours. Pain shot from my shoulders to my fingers and I had to move slowly to stop myself from crying out. "He's gone mad. Like, actually mad. I thought he was going to kill me. We need to get away from here. He knows everything, Gwyn."

He put his arm around me and lifted me to my feet and we began to make our way out into the open.

"What do you mean, everything?"

"Everything. About me, about us, about my father. He wants the ring so he can get to Elinor. It was her necklace, Gwyn. She disappeared like I did, like my father did. He saw it happen."

"Well, if he thi-"

From the side of the building, Arthur stepped forward, striking Gwyn across the face and sending him stumbling back. With all the energy I could muster I pounced forward, fist clenched. He lifted his hand out to block me and I lost my footing, taking him by the waist as I fell and sending us both crashing to the ground. We rolled around, fighting for dominance and hitting each other until eventually, he had me pinned beneath him.

I took a blow to the face, then another, then as he raised his arm to land the third Gwyn came from behind and grabbed it. Arthur turned to face him and received Gwyn's fist across his jaw which sent him spiralling sideward from on top of me. He scrambled in the grass to regain his footing but before he could rise Gwyn struck out with his foot, kicking Arthur to the side of the head and knocking him unconscious.

"We've got to go," he said, grabbing my arm and pulling me to my feet. We made it a few metres before I stopped and turned around.

"Wait!" I pulled free from his grip and ran back to Arthur. Dropping to my knees beside him I grabbed his hand, yanking the ring from his finger.

"Come on, let's go," Gwyn called out, and as I got back to my feet I stuck my boot into his ribs for good measure.

The rain had started to fall heavily over the valley and I was struggling to keep up with Gwyn as we made our way towards the treeline. I was still wearing only one shoe and it wasn't made for running through soggy grass. When I nearly lost my balance for the third time, he grabbed hold of my hand and pulled me into the woods at the edge of the field.

We created a clearing through the brushland as we ran, hitting away leaves and branches that whipped at our face.

More than once I had to pull my trousers free of brambles and they had torn beyond any repair that Mrs Hopkin would be able to manage. I had no idea where we were going but we continued to run until eventually the woods opened to a clearing and we stood over a steep drop down into the quarry below, where workers had already started their day. A long path worn into the grass trailed the edge of the cliff face round to the other side and down into the quarry and it looked like it might be our best way out.

"How did you know I hadn't run away?" I said, bending over with my hands on my knees to catch my breath.

"Because you promised you wouldn't." He let the statement hang in the air and I smiled, glad that he knew it. "I found your pocket watch in the graveyard and Mr Dennis said he saw you riding off with Arthur. I knew you wouldn't just go with him so I came looking."

"Where does everyone think I am?"

"I only told my sister," he said through laboured breaths. "I didn't want to cause a panic at the wedding so I came alone. I promised her that if I hadn't found you by first light then I'd come back and gather some men to help search. She was about ready to come looking herself."

"I'm just so glad you got to me," I said, grabbing his face and pulling him into a gentle kiss. "Take me home, please."

I hadn't noticed Arthur approaching as we embraced, but as we turned toward the treeline to make our way home, he was standing there, drenched, panting and pointing a pistol right at us.

"I'll be having that ring back now, Tom."

Twenty-Five

Arthur's face was bruised and bloodied and he held a hand across his stomach clutching onto his ribs where I'd kicked him. Despite his injuries he stood resolute, and the arm that pointed the gun to us never faltered. I had no doubt that if, or when he shot, his aim would be direct and on point.

I instinctively took a step back as he began to inch forward. His movements were slow and calculated, circling me rather than coming straight forward, until we were both standing just a few metres apart on the quarry's edge. I looked down at the jagged outcrop of rocks below, calculating my chances if I was to fall. If he decided to rush me, I'd have to think fast to get out of the way. The drop would kill me, that was for sure.

Putting some space between us, Gwyn had inched towards the clearing that Arthur had emerged from. A clear line into the woods had opened up but neither of us fancied our chances trying to outrun a bullet. We stood like three points of a triangle waiting for someone to make the first move. I wanted him at my side but at least the distance between us would make it harder for Arthur to kill us both, and for now, his focus was on me.

"This is only going to end my way, Tom," Arthur shouted over the noise from the quarry. He was flicking his gaze between me and the ground far below him as he spoke.

"You're going to give me that ring and tell me how it works, or you're going to the noose for the murder of Elinor Lewis."

"Don't be so stupid, nobody is going to believe I did anything to that woman."

"Do you know how far I had to go, Tom, to find someone that looked even remotely like her? Someone nobody would miss. How hard it was getting her back to this godforsaken village without anybody seeing her? The things I had to do to disguise the body? What do you think I was doing all that time I was away? She was nice, too. Stupid, but nice. And ever so friendly. But now she's just lying there with all of your strange documents alongside her waiting for a good local policeman to come along and find."

"So what?" I asked. "You're just going to frame me for murder because you can't handle that Elinor left you? It makes no sense. Face it, Arthur, whether she went with Jack or disappeared into thin air, she didn't love you. She didn't want to be with you. You lost."

His lips curled in and he waved the gun at me, his body shaking with rage. "I will blow your fucking head off," he screamed.

"And then what?" I asked. "You kill me and you'll never know how the ring works, then you'll have lost all over again."

"Then maybe I'll kill him instead." He swung his body around, turning the gun on Gwyn and I reached out with both hands and shouted for him to stop. "You think you can make a fool of me?"

He cast another look into the quarry but this time raised his free hand up and signalled to someone below. I glanced over the edge, trying to keep Arthur in my periphery. At the bottom of the path on the other side of the opening his cousin

Graham, the local constable, was beginning his ascent up the tracks to us, flanked by two other uniformed men.

"It's Graham," I turned and shouted to Gwyn. "He's coming up the path. It's all a set up."

The sight of his cousin made Arthur laugh arrogantly as he turned his attention back to us. "I always win. I'm Arthur fucking Morgan. The only way out of this is my way."

"You've lost your mind," Gwyn shouted. "Is all this really worth it?"

"Quiet, you filthy sodomite," Arthur barked, then he brought his eyes back to mine. "Will killing him inspire you to cooperate, Tom? Are your secrets worth his life?"

He cocked the gun and raised it towards Gwyn's face.

"No, stop!" I shouted, taking another step towards him at the rocks' edge. "I'll tell you what I know."

"Don't do it, Tom."

"That's more like it," Arthur grinned. "Give me the ring."

With his free hand he beckoned me forward and I took another step toward him. I looked over into the quarry as I moved, trying to stay away from the edge and mind my footing. Graham hadn't gotten far but it wouldn't take too long until he reached the top and we'd be surrounded on both sides.

I needed to get Arthur's attention back off Gwyn and onto me. This wasn't Gwyn's fight and I wasn't about to watch him die for me. "Why are you doing this?" I called out. "Is your pride really that important?"

"SHE WAS MINE!" he screamed, bringing the gun back towards me. "Nobody walks out on me."

"But she did. She's gone."

I knew I was antagonising him but I didn't care as long as he left Gwyn alone. I motioned with my head to try to encourage him to run off into the trees but he stayed rooted to the spot, not willing to leave me.

"Even if you find her, she's never going to take you back. You're going to be stuck in a time you don't know, rejected all over again."

"Tom, just shut up," Gwyn called out, afraid I'd talk myself into a bullet.

"I'd listen to your filthy lover if I were you. Now, give me the ring."

"Not until you put the gun down."

"Give me the fucking ring," he shouted. He aimed the gun slightly to my right and fired off a round that passed inches from my head. The shot echoed around the quarry and I recoiled from the sound, almost losing my balance. Gwyn shouted to me in the distance but his voice was nothing more than muffled noise and I brought my hands to my ears to try and block it out.

Down on the path below us, Graham stopped in his tracks and stared up at us on the rocks above. He raised a hand to his eyes for a better view and when he was sure that it was not his cousin who had received a bullet, he picked up his pace.

"You've lost your fucking mind," I shouted, leaning toward Arthur, filled with rage.

"Give me the ring," he shouted again. "Just hand it over and you can walk away."

"How do I know that I'm not going to end up in jail anyway?"

"You'll have to trust my word." He tried to make his voice sound reasonable but there was no way I was going to believe him now.

"That's not good enough. Someone is going to find that body sooner or later with all my things with it. I want to know where it is."

"Give me the ring and I'll tell you."

"No," I shouted. My only hope was that he was so desperate for the ring that it would give me some bargaining room. "Tell me and let Gwyn go and then I will give you the ring and tell you how to use it."

"For him to just run off to the body? I don't think so."

"You're still the one with the gun, Arthur, nobody is running anywhere," Gwyn said, inching towards us.

Arthur paused to consider his options. The rain lashed down around us, thick and heavy, making it difficult to see. I stared at the sodden ground beneath Arthur's feet at the quarry's edge and willed it to crumble away, to send him falling to his death, but it stood firm and so did he.

"She's in a shallow grave," he said. Rainwater ran down his face and sprayed from his lips as he spoke. "It's behind the barn in the top field, right where I first found you. Now, we had a deal. Hand over the ring and tell me how to get to Elinor."

There was no way that I was going to trust his word but I was low on options. I could die, I could go to jail or I could try to call his bluff. With the information I needed, I took a step back away from him and he moved closer toward me, pointing the gun at my head.

"I'm going to make sure you're telling me the truth," I said, taking another step back and holding my hands up in surrender. I kept my voice as calm and soft as I could. "And then you'll get the ring."

He cocked the gun again and took another step toward me.

"That's not what we agreed," he screamed. "Hand it over."

"Tom, what are you doing?" Gwyn called, but I couldn't take my eyes off Arthur. "Give him the ring."

"I'm not losing everything for this maniac. If he wants it, he'll have to prove he's as good as his word."

"Three..." Arthur shouted out as he took another step toward me.

"Tom, he's pointing a gun at your face, just do as he says."

"Two..."

"Tom, I mean it, don't make me lose you. Give him the fucking ring."

I stood firm, sure that he would back down, but everything fell into slow motion as I looked down the barrel and watched his finger move for the trigger. He was red with rage at being defied and his eyes looked wild. I took a sharp inhale of breath and clenched my eyes closed as I realised I'd gotten it wrong.

"One!"

A shot rang out and I waited to hit the ground, to feel the bullet rip through my skin, but neither came. I opened my left eye first, then my right. In a crumpled heap on the floor in front of me lay Arthur's body, his blood already washing towards the quarry and over the edge.

I turned to Gwyn to make sure he was alright and in the distance behind him, shotgun in hand and quivering in shock stood Mair. She was as white as a sheet.

"What did you do?" Gwyn's voice was filled with concern as he ran to his sister and pulled her into an embrace. She dropped the gun to the floor and reached up to grab hold of his arm, her mouth wide but no sound coming out. "Mair, are you ok?"

She nodded her head, her eyes never leaving Arthur's body. "I had to do it."

"Does anyone know you came up here?" he asked, his tone turning to panic.

"You didn't come home." Her voice trembled as she spoke, her eyes vacant. "I came to find you. I heard the gunshot from the field and when I got here he was pointing the gun. I had to do it, Gwyn. I had to."

"Mair!" he asked again, shaking her at the shoulders. "Does anyone know you're here?"

She shook her head and suddenly became frantic, speaking quickly and pulling on her brother's arm. "We can go home; pretend we knew nothing about it." She rushed over to me and grabbed my arm. "Come on, Tom, we need to get you out of here."

"I can't," I said, and I rushed to the edge of the quarry to look over. Graham was already more than halfway up the track and showed no sign of slowing down. "He's already seen me. Whether I run or not, he'll say I killed his cousin. I have to stay. Running will only make it worse. You two go. He doesn't know either of you are here."

"I'm not leaving you."

"You have to, Gwyn. Go."

He reached for my arm but I moved away and put some distance between us.

"Tom, your pocket!" Mair said, pointing at me.

The rain had turned my white shirt see-through and as I glanced down at my chest the ring shone like a small beacon from my breast pocket.

"No," I said, shaking my head. I covered my chest with my hand trying to hide the light and I looked at Gwyn with panic. "No."

The realisation had set in and despite the rain that soaked his face I could see the tears form in the corners of his eyes as he began to step toward me. I shook my head again, my chin beginning to quiver, and he pulled me into his chest and sobbed as he rested his head on mine.

"You have to go," he whispered, and when he kissed me on the top of the head I felt like my world might fall apart if he ever let go of me. He took my chin in his hand and held my head up to look at him. He tried to force a smile through his tears and I clenched my hands tighter around his waist.

"I'm not leaving you!"

"You have to. If you stay, they'll hang you. I couldn't live with that, Tom. At least I know you'll be safe."

The tears flooding my eyes made it hard to see and my chest heaved as I sobbed. "But I chose you," I begged. "I chose you."

"And I'll always choose you," he replied, "but you have to put the ring on."

I leaned into him as closely as I could and brought my lips to his, feeling for one last time his face against mine, his touch on my skin, and I wished we could freeze like this forever.

"I'll come back to you," I cried, "I'll find a way and I'll come back to you. I promise."

He smiled through his tears and as he took a step back from me I let out a loud sob that made my shoulders shake.

I tried to be strong and force a smile. "You better wait for me, Gwyn Griffiths."

"Forever," he replied, taking his sister's hand for support.

"Tom, what're you doing, what's going on?" Mair asked, confused. She took a step toward me but Gwyn held her back.

"I'll see you soon," I said, raising my fingers to my lips and blowing her a kiss. "Look after him for me, ok? And tell the Hopkins… I dunno. Work something out."

With my hands trembling I reached into my pocket for the ring and held it in my palm. I stared at the glowing stone, wanting more than anything to stay and hating it for finally making me leave.

"Tom, wait!" Gwyn cried out, and I looked up as he ran to close the distance between us. He pulled me into him once more, his body against mine, and held my face in his hands. His eyes locked on mine and for the first ever time, he said, "I love you."

"I love you too," I said, then I pressed my lips against his as I slid the ring onto my finger.

Twenty-Six

"Where the fuck have you been?"

Lee looked like he might be sick at the mere sight of me, a ghost from the past standing before him on the doorstep, my clothes torn, face muddied, bruised and caked with blood. He brought a hand to his mouth and stared at me in disbelief as the colour drained from his face and I wondered whether I had the right to smile at him or if doing so might earn me another bruise to my jaw.

As I slipped the ring onto my finger and my lips brushed against Gwyn's, I'd been overwhelmed by an immediate feeling of sickness. My head buzzed and the sky grew dark and everything around me spun into chaos. I don't know if I'd closed my eyes or just become enveloped in darkness, but I had an instant feeling that I was falling, only without the sensation of ever hitting the ground.

Immediately my every sense came to life. I could hear the patter of every raindrop, smell the dust kicked up beneath me and feel the air as it danced along every inch of my skin. I remembered Gwyn, his handsome face watching me as I fell through the ether, his voice calling out my name, following me across decades as I slipped through the darkness and fell into nothingness.

And then, quiet.

I awoke some time later, though I wasn't sure just how long, soaking wet and lying on my back. For a moment as I lay in the rain I wondered if perhaps I had only fainted and hadn't actually moved but a cursory glance at my surroundings reassured me that I was indeed somewhere different. I didn't know where I was, or even *when* I was, but I knew that I'd at least moved.

I sat upright, wiping the drizzle from my face, and took another look around. I wasn't back at my office, that was for sure. It was another field, surrounded on all sides by a hedgerow that didn't allow me to see beyond. When the power came back to my legs I stood and made my way towards a small gate on the far side, hoping I'd find some civilization or sign of where I was.

As I neared it, a man climbed over the gate and began to walk towards me. Instinctively I clenched my fists, ready to fight.

"Are you alright?" he asked. He edged forward cautiously, noting the state of my clothes. My shirt and trousers, filthy and torn, were hanging from my body in shreds, flapping in the wind as I made my way towards him. He held his arms out, as one might do with an animal they were unsure of, and took another step forward. "Is everything ok, lad?"

I relaxed my fists a little. "Where am I?"

"Maybe we should get you to a doctor?" he said, pointing up at my face. I raised a hand to my cheek and brought my fingers into view. A wound had reopened beneath my eye and blood ran from it into my stubble.

"Where am I? I said again, this time firmer.

"Grantchester," he replied. He took a handkerchief from his pocket and leaned forward, keeping some distance between us as he waved it at me.

"Grantchester?" I repeated, and began to laugh. "That's close enough." I knew the area well. Five, maybe six miles from home. I looked around the field again and then back at the man. "What year is it?"

"You what?"

"The year. What year is it?"

"Look, I think yo-"

I rushed towards him and grabbed him by the arms and gave him a little shake. He looked startled, but not frightened, and I pleaded with him again.

"Please. Tell me what year it is."

"It's 1999, lad."

His eyes were flicking left to right as if trying to work out my thoughts, and I burst into laughter and threw my hands around him in a hug, letting out a loud yell of excitement as I clung to him.

"I need a lift," I said, stepping back from him. "Can you take me into town? I've lost my wallet and I need to get home."

He studied me for a moment, probably wondering if he was about to get murdered by some lunatic in his car, but he nodded anyway and led me to his vehicle to take me home.

"I said, where the hell have you been?"

I'd become frozen as I stared at my brother. He was the person I felt safest going to but the metre of space that separated us on that doorstep suddenly felt like a gulf and I lost all ability to speak or move. "And what the hell are you wearing?"

I looked down at myself, and then back up at him. I could have asked him the same question. I hadn't immediately realised it but he was wearing a shirt and tie, ironed, and his hair was neatly combed. Even his shoes were polished. His face had filled out a bit too and he looked healthier than I'd seen him in years.

"Can I come in?" I finally said, breaking my silence.

He stepped aside, his back against the door, and I had to squeeze past him to get inside. I walked down the hallway and into the open-plan kitchen and living area. It seemed so big now, and clean. No old magazines lying around the floor or empty food cartons, no dishes piled in the sink or overflowing bin bags. Everything was in order.

He followed me into the room and stood at arm's length, studying me as though he couldn't quite believe I was real. He sighed, then shook his head, then sighed again and brought his hands up to his face, dragging his cheeks downward as he contemplated my presence. On the counter behind me an alarm sounded, breaking through the silence and causing me to jolt and retreat backwards against the unit.

"It's just the food timer, what's wrong with you?" He rushed past me to turn it off then moved towards me, closing the gap that had been between us just moments before and putting his hands on my arms. "Tom, speak to me. We've been worried sick."

"I need clothes," I said, lifting up my left arm with the sleeve hanging off. He nodded softly then disappeared into the hallway towards his bedroom to fetch me something fresh to wear.

While he was out of the room I moved to the window that looked down over the street and opened it slightly. The dreadful racket of the city filled my ears and I slammed it again, flicking the lock to keep it out. The street was filled with people, heads down and ignoring each other or speaking on their mobile phones. No friendly greetings or nods, just the rush to get to wherever they were going. They weaved between the cars that whizzed by in both directions and lined both sides of the pavement. They navigated the litter-lined streets in their expensive work shoes, coming and going from jobs they despised in high -rise office blocks. Everything looked wrong. I hated it.

"Here, these should fit," Lee said as he came back into the room. I pulled the curtains closed, shutting out the world, and turned as he held out a pile of clothes to me. "I'm going to call Mum," he said as I began to remove my shirt.

"No!" I said abruptly. "Not yet. I'm not ready."

"Then get ready," he snapped back. "Do you have any idea what we've been through? Every day worried sick that we'd never see you again or that the next knock on the door would be to tell us they'd found a body. Tom, you were on the news. This is serious, where have you been?"

"You wouldn't believe me even if I tried to explain."

"Did somebody hurt you?" he said, his voice softening. He brought a hand to my chin and held my head up, inspecting my face. "How did you get into this mess?"

We stared at each other for a moment and I studied his face, so like my own, and wished that Gwyn could have met him. They'd have liked each other very much, I was sure.

I pulled on the shorts he'd brought me and moved to the sofa, sinking down into it. The thoughts of Gwyn and seeing my brother again overwhelmed me and as he came to sit beside me, I finally began to sob. He reached out, pulling me into his shoulder and we sat there silent for what felt like an hour until I was finally ready to talk.

I told him everything. From finding the ring to it glowing in the alley, waking up in Cwm Newydd and meeting Mair. I spoke about the mining disaster and meeting Gwyn, being taken in by the Hopkin family and how I'd learned to work the farm. I told him about Arthur Morgan and Elinor, who our father really was and what happened at the quarry, and for the duration of my story he sat in stunned silence.

"...and then when I woke up again, I was in Grantchester, and the man who found me brought me here. That's pretty much everything."

Hours had passed and night had set in but everything was off my chest. Lee reached for a packet of cigarettes on the table and lit one up, taking a big drag and filling the room with smoke. He'd smoked another two before he finally said anything.

"I don't know what to say."

"Say you believe me," I said, sitting up and leaning close to him. "I haven't gone mad. I know you're thinking it, but I haven't. I'm telling the truth, Lee."

"I know when you're lying, brother, and this ain't it." He took another drag on his cigarette and I felt an element of relief at his words, until he spoke again. "But maybe you just *really* believe that this happened. A bang on the head can do weird things to you."

"Don't give me that bullshit, Lee, I didn't just wake up from a concussion. It happened. Where do you think I've been all these months?"

"I don't know, Tom. I don't know. I'm just having a hard time with this. I mean, have you any proof?"

"Proof? Like what? It's not like I ran for mayor. I was just a nobody. There won't be any record of me."

"But you were arrested."

"What, so you want me to just pop in the car to Aberystwyth for a 400-mile round trip in the hope that they might have kept a drunk and disorderly record on file at the police station for the last hundred years?"

I was getting angry with him for not just accepting what I was saying. I knew deep down that if I was in his position, I'd probably face him with the same scepticism, more even, but I needed him to believe me. I needed him to be on my side with this. Why couldn't he just know that I was telling the truth?

"Even if I did believe it all, Tom, what then? Is this the story you're going to tell Mum? Is this what you're going to tell the police? Or the press? Even if what you're saying is the truth, nobody is going to believe it. They'll cart you off, Tom."

"I need money," I said, standing up from the couch and slamming my cup down on the table.

"What for? Where are you going?"

"I've lost all my bank cards. I need cash, what have you got?"

"Not much. Why? Where are you going?" He stood up and put himself between me and the door.

"Get out of my way, Lee."

He put his arm on the doorframe to stop me from leaving. "Not until you tell me where you're going."

"Back to Wales," I said, trying again to push past him.

"Wait." He put his hands on my chest and held me in place. "Why Wales? Even if what you're saying is real, there'll be nobody left. They'll all have died years ago. What's there for you now?"

"Answers," I said. "I want answers."

"Fine, let's go," he said, moving from the doorway and grabbing his coat off the back of the chair. "I'm coming with you. You're not running off again."

"What?" I looked at him puzzled, unsure if this was some sort of joke or test. Was he about to get in the car and drive me straight to my mother, or the hospital or some sort of psychiatric unit? Or would he actually come with me?

"If you're going, I'm coming too. If you want me to believe you then show me. He grabbed his car keys from a bowl near the front door then opened it and pointed outside. "After you."

Even with hardly any traffic on the road the midnight drive to West Wales took nearly five hours and was painfully silent. I was angry with my brother for not believing me, and I was angry at the stupid road map that I'd found wedged under the passenger seat that got us lost three times along the way.

In his defence, he'd at least tried to make conversation with me as we drove, but I remained sceptical of his intentions. Every question he asked about my time away felt like a trap to find holes and inconsistencies, or he'd tell me about how our mother had struggled to cope with my disappearance, which only filled me with guilt. I preferred the silence.

The sun had long since risen by the time we found our way to somewhere that I recognised. I sat forward in my seat, a sudden wave of excitement coming over me as we passed some old farm buildings that I recognised on the road that led towards Cwm Newydd.

"It's down there," I said, pointing to a turning that Lee had just driven past.

"You're supposed to mention that before we pass the junction."

He slammed his foot on the break and spun the wheel, pulling onto a verge at the side of the road in an effort to turn. The roads were no wider now than they had been in the past and the village still sat in the middle of nowhere, modern life having not encroached on the rolling hills and fields like it had in so many other places. The only hints of change along the whole stretch of road were the modern signs and the addition of road markings.

After several tight manoeuvres we were finally facing back the way we came. Lee edged the car forward and took a left in the road, beginning the descent down the hill into the village.

"I promise, you'll see. Everything I've said is real." I grabbed his arm excitedly and flashed him a smile. My anger had dissipated, replaced with an excitement and a warm feeling of returning home, even though I knew my friends would no longer be there.

"It's going to take some convincing," he said, putting his hand on my shoulder. "Tom, it's not that I think you're lying. It's just…" he paused, slowing the car down to a near stop. "I just don't know how to believe it. You understand that, yeah? What you're saying is just…"

"You'll see," I said.

We came to the junction at the bottom of the lane next to the pub. It had been painted white and a new modern sign hung over the door, but it was unmistakably the same place. Whoever owned it now had put picnic benches outside and every window had a flower pot on it, giving it a far more welcoming look than the brown stone and dark windows that I was used to.

I stared back at it through the passenger window as Lee pulled along the street and parked outside the church. I bolted from the car and stepped into the middle of the road, circling on the spot to take it all in.

"That was the post office shop," I said, pointing to the building that Mrs Hopkin would send me to for the week's supplies. It was gone now, converted to a house, and the second door had been bricked up and replaced by a window.

"And down here is the school," I said, motioning to the far side of the church. The building remained exactly the same but the playground had been fenced off and the ground was adorned with paintings of hopscotch and other children's games. It had a new roof, too. Probably several since I last saw it, but the main building was unaltered.

Only two other cars were parked in the street and they sat outside the row of cottages that faced the church. The whole row of houses looked exactly how I'd left them. Some had new doors and one had been painted pink, but otherwise little had changed.

I ran up to one of the small buildings along the row. "This was where Mrs Wilkes lived. The Jones' lived there. And up here," I said, rounding the corner near the pub, "is the lane up to Mair's house."

I stood at the edge of the road waiting for Lee to catch up to me. He'd been slowly walking around, taking in the village and listening to me excitedly pointing out all the different buildings. I felt like a kid dragging my parents through a theme park pointing out all the attractions while he pondered what was so exciting about a couple of houses and a pub.

When he caught up to me, we walked up the lane towards Mair's cottage. A bungalow had been built where some old pens used to be, though it looked like it had been there for many years and fit well amongst the older buildings.

"This is it," I said, as we rounded a small bend and the cottage came into view. I ran to the door but it was boarded up with a padlock on it. I pulled at it but it wouldn't budge, so I moved to the window, brushed away some dust, and put my face up to the glass to see inside. It was bare except for a few planks of wood thrown on the floor. A hole in the roof let some light in, shining against the fireplace that looked like it hadn't been used in years. The door to Gwyn's room was shut, but the one to Mair's room was missing entirely. There was still a bed in there, but it had no mattress on it and there was nothing else in the room that I could see. It was completely abandoned.

"Can I help you?" a voice called out, pulling my attention from the window. A woman was heading towards us from down the lane wearing overalls and wellies and her curly red hair hung loosely around her shoulders.

"What happened to this place?" I asked, sad to see it in such disrepair.

"Condemned," she said. "They're tearing it down soon once all the planning comes through."

"Who owns it?"

"I do. Who's asking?"

She looked at me curiously, an obvious stranger to her, probably wondering why I was hanging around her property peering through windows.

"We've been researching the family tree," I said, thinking on the spot. "We found out we had some distant family who lived in this village. The records pointed us here, to a woman named Mair Griffiths."

"Aye, that was my great-grandmother," the woman said, and my face beamed with excitement. "So how are you related exactly?"

I kept staring at her, grinning like a fool as she waited for her reply. She was older than I'd ever known Mair to be, maybe forty or so, but she looked like her. The same wild eyes and unmanageable looking red hair, the same impatient look as she waited for an explanation. It was uncanny.

"A cousin of her parents, I think," Lee stepped in, covering my silence. "But we're going to be on our way now. Lots to see. It was nice to meet you."

He grabbed my arm and pulled me back down the lane. I turned and flashed the woman a smile, wishing I had asked her name, then fell back into step with my brother.

"What did you do that for?"

"She probably thinks we were casing the joint," he said.

"But did you hear her? Mair is her grandmother. That proves what I'm saying, no?"

"Not exactly," he said, "but I'll admit I'm curious how you know so much."

"It's because I was here, I'm telling you. Why won't you just listen?"

He stopped in front of the church and leaned against the wall. He was looking at me as though he thought I was mad and that hurt my feelings more than him not believing me.

"Tom. Please, I don't want to argue with you, but you don't seem to be seeing it from my point of view here."

"What happened to you?" I asked, pushing through the gate of the church. He followed behind me and we walked slowly down the path that circled around the building. Just 48 hours ago, in 1890, I walked to this church for the wedding of Nellie and Gethin. Now, two days later in 1999, it looked exactly as it did then. The only evidence that any time had passed was the addition of a notice board near the door filled with modern printed leaflets. Even the broken wall at the back of the graveyard had never been repaired, with sheep from the field beyond still wandering in to graze.

"What do you mean?" Lee asked as we circled off to the left of the main building.

"This. Being so sceptical. Looking so smart. Your house looked like you've hired a cleaner and you're dressed like, well, like me."

"*Now* you wanna ask about me?" he said, and I felt an immediate pang of guilt.

I put a hand on his shoulder and apologised. He'd filled the last half a day with questions about what I'd been doing. He'd listened to my stories and brought me across the country and I'd paid nearly no mind to him or what he'd been through since I left.

"I've been completely sober for four months. Someone had to step in. You were gone, Dad was gone, Mum was in bits and the business needed someone. I stepped up."

"I'm really proud of you," I said, and I meant it. "I couldn't help not being there, Lee, but I hope you know how sorry I am that you and Mum had to go through that. I've missed you so much."

He pulled me into a hug and for the first time since I'd been back it felt like we fully reconnected, and I knew he felt it too.

"But now you're back," he said, pulling away but keeping his hands on my shoulders. "We can do it together, like we were always supposed to."

I let his comment linger, not wanting to answer. The truth was that I had no intention of picking up where I'd left off. Too much had changed.

I brought us to a stop near the back of the church. In amongst some weeds, where a small slate plaque once sat, stood a large headstone shaped like a Celtic cross. At the bottom, chiselled into the granite and partly covered with moss, it read;

Sophia Ann Hopkin
1879 - 1890

"Excuse me. Hello. Boys?" A voice from the gate caught our attention and we turned from the gravestone to see the woman from the lane making her way towards us. "Can you come here for a minute?"

"I knew she'd think we were robbing the place," Lee whispered through a gritted smile as we walked to meet her halfway down the path.

"I'm glad I didn't miss you. I knew you looked familiar," she said, taking a sheet of paper from her pocket and handing it to us. "I had to run and dig that out. Thought you'd like to see it."

Lee took the paper and unfolded it, then looked at me, back to the paper and then at me again.

"What is it?" I asked. He held it out to me and when I took it from his grasp, he began to rub his temples.

It was a photocopy of an old black and white portrait, much like the one that used to sit on the side table in the cottage, except this one featured Mair in a beautiful flowing dress. Gwyn stood to her right, a hand on her shoulder looking handsome and proud, and on her left, staring back off the page, was me.

"Must be some strong genes in your family," the woman said as I stared down at the paper in disbelief. "You can keep that. I've got the original at home."

I was aware that she had turned to leave but I couldn't tear my eyes away from the page and barely managed to whisper goodbye. It wasn't until Lee grabbed my arm and shook me that I finally looked up again.

"I can't believe it," he said, and he began to pace around. "Tom, you were actually fucking there."

"No," I said, furrowing my brow and shaking my head at him. "This isn't right."

"What do you mean?" He stopped pacing and stood in front of me and I held the sheet out to him, pointing at it.

"That's Mair," I said, roughly tapping on the paper. "And that's Gwyn."

"And that's you," he said, interrupting me.

"No," I replied, shaking my head again. "I never had this picture taken."

"You must have."

"Lee, I'm telling you, I didn't!"

He scratched his head and stared back at the image I was holding out to him. "So, what does this mean?"

I contemplated for a second, staring at the picture in front of me, then looked at my brother and smiled.

"It means I'm going back."

Printed in Great Britain
by Amazon